WHEN DREAMS

TREMBLE

What Reviewers Say About Radclyffe's Books

"…well-plotted…lovely romance…I couldn't turn the pages fast enough!"—**Ann Bannon**, author of *The Beebo Brinker Chronicles*

"The author's brisk mix of political intrigue, fast-paced action, and frequent interludes of lesbian sex and love…in *Honor Reclaimed*… sure does make for great escapist reading."—**Richard Labonte**, Q Syndicate

"If you're looking for a well-written police procedural make sure you get a copy of *Shield of Justice*. Most assuredly worth it."—**Lynne Jamneck**, author of *Down the Rabbit Hole* and reviewer for *The L Life*

"Radclyffe has once again pulled together all the ingredients of a genuine page-turner, this time adding some new spices into the mix. Whatever one's personal take on the subject matter, *shadowland* is sure to please—in part because Radclyffe never loses sight of the fact that she is telling a love story, and a compelling one at that."—**Cameron Abbott**, author of *To The Edge* and *An Inexpressible State of Grace*

"*Stolen Moments*…edited by Radclyffe & Stacia Seaman…is a collection of steamy stories about women who just couldn't wait. It's sex when desire overrides reason, and it's incredibly hot!"—**Suzanne Corson**, *On Our Backs*

"With ample angst, realistic and exciting medical emergencies, winsome secondary characters, and a sprinkling of humor, *Fated Love* turns out to be a terrific romance. It's one of the best I have read in the last three years. Run—do not walk—right out and get this one. You'll be hooked by yet another of Radclyffe's wonderful stories. Highly recommended."—Author **Lori L. Lake**, *Midwest Book Review*

"Radclyffe, through her moving text…in *Innocent Hearts*…illustrates that our struggles for acceptance of women loving women is as old as time—only the setting changes. The romance is sweet, sensual, and touching."—**Kathi Isserman**, reviewer for *Just About Write*

Visit us at www.boldstrokesbooks.com

WHEN DREAMS TREMBLE

by

RADCLYffE

2007

CREDITS
EDITORS: RUTH STERNGLANTZ AND STACIA SEAMAN
PRODUCTION DESIGN: STACIA SEAMAN
COVER PHOTOS: LEE LIGON
COVER DESIGN BY SHERI (GRAPHICARTIST2020@HOTMAIL.COM)

By the Author

Romances

Safe Harbor

Beyond the Breakwater

Innocent Hearts

Love's Melody Lost

Love's Tender Warriors

Tomorrow's Promise

Passion's Bright Fury

Love's Masquerade

shadowland

Fated Love

Distant Shores, Silent Thunder

Turn Back Time

Promising Hearts

Storms of Change

When Dreams Tremble

Honor Series

Above All, Honor

Honor Bound

Love & Honor

Honor Guards

Honor Reclaimed

Justice Series

A Matter of Trust (prequel)

Shield of Justice

In Pursuit of Justice

Justice in the Shadows

Justice Served

Change Of Pace: *Erotic Interludes*
(A Short Story Collection)

Stolen Moments: *Erotic Interludes 2*
Stacia Seaman and Radclyffe, eds.

Lessons in Love: *Erotic Interludes 3*
Stacia Seaman and Radclyffe, eds.

Extreme Passions: *Erotic Interludes 4*
Stacia Seaman and Radclyffe, eds.

Author's Note

Wolfe is quoted as saying, "You can't go home again." I don't disagree with that fundamental truth, because "home" is more than a place or even the people. It is a particular series of moments, defined by the unique interactions of individuals at a particular point in their lives. Life is ever changing and we can't go back, because the very act of living, day to day, changes us. I am not who I was at eighteen when I left.

But having recently moved "home," or within miles of where I grew up, I can say that the sense of recognition, and dare I say, belonging, is more than fond recollection made rosy with the passage of time. I know these roads—I learned to drive on them. I know the mountains and the lakes—I camped there with my parents. I took my partner to the very same roadside hot dog stand I frequented forty years ago with my best friends in high school. But despite the familiarity, the best part of being here now is that I am finally who I am in the place I had to leave to find myself. I am a lesbian, and I have the life I always dreamed of.

This story is set "just up the road" from the place I spent my last summer before leaving home for college. I did not know then exactly why I didn't fit, or what it was I sought. Fortunately, I discovered the answers not long after with a girl as innocent as I. We didn't know the words, but we recognized love.

My thanks go to my first readers, Connie, Diane, Eva, Jane, Paula, and RB, as well as my editors, Ruth Sternglantz and Stacia Seaman, and the generous proofreaders at Bold Strokes Books for making this a better book.

Lee and I spent a weekend at "the Lake" taking photos for the cover. Thanks to Sheri for capturing so eloquently the beauty I tried so inadequately to describe.

To Lee, who has never questioned the dream—*Amo te.*

Radclyffe 2007

Dedication

For Lee
And Dreams That Come True

CHAPTER ONE

A ll set to add another notch to your belt, LJ?"
Leslie Harris glanced up from the deposition transcript, hidling her annoyance at the interruption and the uninvited familiarity. She'd made the mistake of leaving her office door partly open when she'd arrived at 4:30 a.m., and now she discovered with a quick glance at her Piaget it was close to seven, and the troops were arriving. It wasn't like her to lose track of the time.

Absently tucking a strand of her shoulder-length, ash blond hair behind her ear, she smiled automatically at the junior associate who leaned into her office. Mentally, she ran his stats. Tom Smith. Eager, just like every other ambitious young attorney, and smart enough to recognize the important players in the firm. Points for that. Just the slightest bit obvious with his flirtatious attention. Minor demerit. She crossed her silk-stocking-clad legs beneath the skirt of her custom-tailored Armani suit and shrugged. "Just another day at the office, Tom."

"Oh yeah. Like it's every day we take on the Feds with a couple of million at stake."

"Uh-huh." Actually, for her it *was* a near-daily occurrence, because defending corporations in big-ticket, high-profile lawsuits was her specialty. And she liked to win. Every time. Her ferocious drive had shaped her career from the start, as had her unfailing ability to read a jury and emphasize just the right aspects of the case to garner their sympathy. She'd fast-tracked to partner seven years out of law school, and her pace, if anything, had picked up in the last year since she'd moved into a corner office.

But she had neither the time nor the inclination to point all this out to Tom. She'd barely squeezed in her daily workout at the gym before coming to the office to prepare for a big morning in court. She was also juggling six other cases that were every bit as important as the one she was due to defend in two hours before the United States District Court for the Eastern District of New York. She reached for her fourth cup of coffee of the morning and went back to reading.

"Get you something from the coffee shop, LJ? Bagel?"

"What?" Leslie glanced up again, surprised to see Tom still standing there. Didn't he have any work to do? "No. Thanks. I'm fine."

Breakfast wasn't on her schedule. She'd be lucky if she remembered to grab a yogurt at lunch, because the midday recess was a critical time to recap the case with her client and revamp strategy. *Working lunch* was just a euphemism for *more work*, and rarely included food. Fortunately, as far as tough battles went, today's case was middle-of-the-road.

United States v. Harlan Vehicles, LLC, et al. She knew the facts verbatim of course, but her defense wouldn't center on the facts. It was true that her client, Harlan Vehicles, had imported 11,000 pieces of gasoline- and diesel-powered equipment over the past nine months that didn't meet the federal Clean Air Act emission requirements. Arguing that point would be folly, because the measured levels of smog-forming volatile organic compounds and nitrous oxides in the exhaust was irrefutable. She never based a case on discrediting the science, because Americans were programmed to believe facts and figures. No, her ammunition had to be more personal, something that Joe Juror could relate to. And when the federal government assessed the company millions of dollars in penalties and fines after the special agents from the Justice Department and U.S. Customs seized the equipment, she had just the weapon she needed.

She couldn't make the charges go away, but she didn't need to. After all, what average citizen couldn't be made to appreciate that levying crippling costs on Harlan meant a higher price tag for *them* the next time they went to buy a snowmobile for their kids for Christmas? In this kind of case, reducing the monetary damages to tens of thousands rather than millions of dollars—what amounted to a slap on the wrist for a corporation the size of Harlan—was a major win.

Still mentally reviewing the order of her witness list, Leslie drained her coffee cup and rose to get a refill. As a sudden wave of dizziness rolled through her, she dropped her coffee cup onto the thick Persian rug. Reflexively, she braced both arms on the desk, lowered her head, and took several long, slow breaths. It was frighteningly difficult to catch her breath, and her heart felt as if it might dance its way up her throat and right out of her body. She blinked and forced herself to focus on the pens and papers covering her desk until the room stopped spinning and the black curtain obscuring her vision lifted. Then, when she was sure she wasn't going to faint, she carefully lowered herself into her chair. Worried that someone might have witnessed her *spell* or whatever the hell it was, she checked the door to be sure no one was nearby.

Thankfully, the hall was empty. The last thing she needed was for her colleagues to get the impression that she wasn't up to form. Her adversaries in the courtroom weren't the only ones who killed the weak. She got along well with her partners, but she wouldn't exactly call them her friends. Nevertheless, the thin veneer covering aggressive competitiveness didn't bother her. This was the battlefield she had chosen, or perhaps the one that had chosen her, and she intended to triumph.

"Ready to head over, LJ?" Stephanie Ackerman called from the doorway.

Leslie's paralegal, a voluptuous redhead four inches shorter than Leslie's five foot six, pulled a rolling cart with two enormous briefcases strapped to it. In the other hand, she carried a venti cappuccino.

"Just about." Leslie smiled brightly and hoped she didn't look as pale as she felt. Even though her breathing was more comfortable, she still felt an odd fluttering sensation in her chest. Maybe no breakfast after three hours' sleep wasn't such a good idea after all. "Do me a favor and grab a Danish along with another coffee for me, will you?"

"Sure. I'll meet you by the elevators."

Leslie waited until Stephanie disappeared to fill her own briefcase with the notes and files she'd need. By the time she joined Stephanie, she felt fine. While the elevator descended, she nibbled on the Danish and scanned the messages on her BlackBerry. When the doors slid open, she dropped the remaining half of the pastry into a nearby wastebasket. She didn't need food; the upcoming mental combat was all the fuel she needed to energize her.

❖

By three in the afternoon the next day, Leslie knew she'd have another win in her column. The trial was still a long way from over, but she'd sensed the subtle change of mood in the members of the jury, from wary and perplexed—as they'd listened to the assistant U.S. attorney recite dry statistics and a litany of rules and regulations—to sympathetic, when she'd pointed out the massive expense and time required for her client to comply with those same rules and regulations. Her subtle point, time and time again, had been that Harlan Vehicles wished to be in compliance with the law despite the heavy financial burden placed upon them by government regulation, and that levying huge penalties would only make it more difficult for them. Oh yes, any taxpayer would understand that.

As she listened to the testimony of another of the government's scientific experts, she ran numbers in her head, calculating how much she might be able to rein in the penalties. A very great deal, she wagered.

"Your witness, Counselor," the judge said.

"Thank you, Your Honor." Leslie rose quickly and strode briskly from behind the defense table. She had only a second to register the violent racing of her heart before she fainted.

LJ!

My God, Leslie! Someone get some water!

"I'm fine. Fine," Leslie said weakly. Vaguely aware of the fact that she was lying on the floor in the middle of the courtroom, she struggled to sit up. Someone held her down with the slightest touch to her shoulder, and she didn't have the strength to protest. Her vision wavered and she felt as if she were trying to breathe underwater. "No, please. Really. I…just need…a little air."

She heard the judge hastily adjourning for the day and flushed with embarrassment. She was used to being the center of attention, but not like this. Stephanie's face swam into view, and Leslie fixed on the bright blue eyes a shade lighter than her own. When her head cleared enough that she thought she could stand without falling, she said, "Help me up, Steph. I'm okay."

Stephanie and Bill Mallory, Leslie's second chair, guided her to her feet. Stephanie kept her arm around Leslie's waist. "You're white as a sheet, LJ."

"I feel like…" Leslie couldn't get enough air to finish the sentence and the room went dim. "I think I need…hospital."

❖

Almost 275 miles due north of the courthouse, Dr. Devon Weber waded into Lake George up to her waist. Her waterproof boots and waders kept her dry, but not warm, and the familiar ache in her right hip appeared before she'd gone ten feet. It might be almost mid-June, but the lake was still frigid, its temperature lagging far behind that of the air, which was only in the high sixties despite the bright sunshine. Still, she was used to being wet and cold and sore; it came with the job.

"Can't you do that from the boat?" Park Ranger Sergeant Natalie Evans called from shore.

"I can feel the bottom better when I walk on it!" Dev yelled back, thinking a little enviously that the petite brunette shuffling her boots on the packed brown earth at the water's edge looked warm and comfortable in her khaki uniform and spring-weight flak jacket.

"Mud's mud," Natalie said.

Dev smiled to herself. She was used to people finding her work and her interests strange, even professionals like Natalie who had a better understanding than most of what she was doing. Dev kept going until the water was an inch below the top of her waders and she felt the accumulation of soil, plant detritus, and decomposing organic matter change consistency beneath her feet.

"I can bring the launch out and at least hand you sample bottles," Natalie offered.

"Thanks, but you'll rile the waters with the boat. I'll just be a minute." Dev opened her canvas shoulder bag and slid out a plastic collection bottle the size of a maraschino cherry jar. With her other hand, she slowly inserted a long metal rod with a suction chamber on the far end straight down through the water and several inches into the lake bottom next to her foot. By depressing a button with her thumb, she was able to extract a small sample. She secured the specimen in the collection jar and dropped it into her bag. "That's number one."

On the shore, Natalie noted the date, time, ambient temperature, water temperature, and exact location on a lined sheet of paper affixed to a clipboard.

"I appreciate you playing secretary," Dev said as she waded back to shore. "I'm sure you've got better things to do than follow me around."

"Not a problem." Actually, Natalie did have *other* things to do, but none that she would have found quite as pleasant. She was a park ranger stationed on the western shore of Lake George in Bolton Landing, New York. She patrolled a portion of the three hundred square miles of parkland that surrounded the lake, which was thirty-two miles long and three miles wide at some points. Despite the fact that the enormous body of water, nestled in the heart of the Adirondack Mountains, was one of the most popular tourist attractions on the East Coast, much of the surrounding mountains was still as wild and untamed as it had been for centuries. It was her job to keep both nature and those who came to enjoy it safe.

"I'm supposed to have a summer intern starting next week." Dev's leg had progressed from sore to stiff, and she climbed awkwardly up the slippery slope in her heavy gear. When Natalie extended a hand to steady her, she grabbed it. Natalie's fingers closed on hers, warm and strong. "Thanks."

"Hey, it's kind of interesting." Natalie tried to keep her expression from revealing the precise nature of her interest as she observed the woman who had arrived the previous afternoon at the regional park headquarters. Everything about Devon Weber—from her collar-length, almost-but-not-quite-messy light chestnut hair to her tight athletic build and the casual self-confidence in her hazel eyes—said she was a lesbian, but Natalie never relied on impressions to make that call. Since they were going to be working together in close proximity for the next few months, she didn't want to create any kind of awkwardness between them. She was interested, but she could be patient. "Besides, I've got the radio, and if something comes up, I'll just leave you to fend for yourself."

"That's nice of you." Dev grinned. "I think."

Natalie smiled back. "Just how many samples do you plan on taking?"

"Well," Dev said, flicking the hair back off her forehead as they headed up the narrow path that had been cut through the thick pines on either side by animals making their way to the water, "between soil, water, vegetation, and fish specimens? Couple thousand."

"You're kidding."

When Natalie stopped abruptly, Dev bumped into her and Natalie's shoulder brushed across Dev's breasts. Natalie's long, dark hair was caught back with a soft tie at the base of her neck and the wind blew a silky strand smelling of mountain laurel into Dev's face. Dev's lips tingled and she stepped back.

"Nope. I'm serious. It's been eight months since the last multitiered biologic survey was done on the lake. With the increase in commercial and recreational boat traffic and the prevalence of industry in the adjoining areas, we need to revamp all our statistics."

"I always thought people at your level just sat in the lab while grunts slogged around out here collecting samples," Natalie teased as they reached the green and white truck with the emblem of the New York State Department of Environmental Conservation on the side.

"I'm old-fashioned, I guess," Dev said as she stripped off her outer gear and stowed it in the back of Natalie's SUV. Beneath it she wore jeans, a short-sleeved denim shirt, and a light zip-up navy vest. She climbed into the truck and shifted to find a good position for her sore hip as Natalie slid behind the wheel. "Sometimes the only way to know there's a problem is to see for yourself. If I just send out someone who isn't an expert on the water life to randomly collect specimens, we could miss the early signs of pollutant effects on the fish population."

"That's your thing, right? You're a fish guy?" Natalie backed out of the parking lot and headed north on Route 9, which wended its way along the shore and through the small villages that dotted the lakeside.

"Yeah, close enough." Dev unfolded her regional survey map to check the next sample site. "I'm a freshwater biologist. I started out studying fish populations and got interested in the effects of environmental alterations on breeding and population dynamics."

"So that's how you ended up with the DEC."

"Technically, I'm an independent consultant, but I'm heading up a joint survey this summer with the Derrin Freshwater Institute and the state."

"Fish, huh?" Natalie shook her head and laughed. "If you don't mind my asking, how the hell did you ever get interested in *fish*?"

Dev wondered if it would make any sense if she told her the truth. If she explained that she'd grown up a stone's throw from where they had collected the first sample. That the lake had been her first and, in the end, her best friend. That for as long as she could remember, she'd never fit in anywhere. Not at home, not at school. She'd spent hours on the water, in the water, from the time she'd been old enough to walk. She'd found peace in those quiet alone times as she'd lain on the dock in the hot summer sun watching the small schools of fish circle in the shallows. She had wondered then what it would be like to be part of a group like that, moving so easily together, effortlessly attuned. To be accepted, to belong. She didn't know then. She still didn't, but she didn't wonder any longer.

She didn't know Natalie well enough to share those secrets, and even if she had, she wouldn't have answered any differently. Those times were long past. "I spent so much time in the water when I was a kid, I guess I thought I was part fish."

"Well," Natalie said, deciding to fire the first shot as she gave Devon a slow, appreciative once-over, "you look to be all woman now."

Dev took a quick read and added up the findings. The answer was pretty clear. Natalie was very attractive, she wasn't wearing a wedding ring, and it was forecast to be a long, hot summer. Dev leaned back with a smile. "Nice to know you noticed."

CHAPTER TWO

B y the time the EMTs arrived, Leslie felt almost normal again. Certainly no worse than she had on quite a few occasions in recent weeks. She'd been working hard and sleeping even less than usual. It was nothing more than that.

"Look, really," she protested as a husky young blond with shaggy hair and a deep tan, who might have been called a surfer dude in another time and place, lifted her into a wheelchair with the help of his intensely serious female partner, "I feel perfectly fine now. Obviously I had a little dizzy spell, which has passed. Please let me up."

"Just try to relax, ma'am," the brunette said mechanically as she slipped a sticky EKG pad inside Leslie's blouse and affixed it gently to her upper breast.

Ma'am, Leslie thought with irrational temper. *She has her hand inside my blouse and she's calling me ma'am.* There was something terribly wrong with this picture. This was not her. In a move that startled even herself, she slapped the EMT's hand away. With the practiced voice that was calculated to make jurors sit up straight in their seats, she snapped, "I'm not going to the hospital."

The one who'd ma'am'd her leaned down with a hand wrapped around either arm of the wheelchair. She spoke quietly so no one else could hear. "It sucks to have everyone all over you like this, I know. But your blood pressure's still a little bit low and your heart rate's a tiny bit elevated. If you try to walk out of here, I think you're going to go down again. That will buy you a trip to the ICU. Just let us take you to the emergency room where you can be checked out."

Leslie studied the dark, deep eyes inches from her own. She

hadn't seen anyone look at her like that, with such compassion and understanding, for…so long, she couldn't remember. How was it that a stranger could touch her so deeply and those who supposedly knew her intimately never touched her at all? Truth be told, she *did* feel terrible.

"Just get me out of here quickly, please," she whispered.

"You got it. I'm Amy, by the way."

"You have beautiful eyes, Amy," Leslie murmured as she suddenly drifted away.

The next time Leslie opened her eyes she was propped up into a semisitting position on a narrow bed with a thin, hard mattress and covered by a stiff white sheet that smelled of strong detergent. A sickly-green curtain, a shade darker than the equally nauseating tiles on the walls, covered the doorway. The overhead light was so bright she was forced to squint. She was fleetingly very happy she didn't have a migraine. What she did have was a plethora of intravenous lines and leads and other things she didn't recognize connecting her to an assortment of monitoring devices that ringed the bed. Surely whatever was wrong with her didn't warrant this much attention. She felt a frisson of anxiety that she quickly squelched and fumbled around on the bed for a call button. Annoyed when she found none, she considered shouting, but decided that would only win her even more unwanted interest.

In search of the handle to lower the bed rail, she slid her hand along the outside of the stretcher. She'd just located it when the curtain was twitched aside and a smiling man in a white lab coat entered. The words Emergency Physician were embroidered in red, slanting letters over his left breast pocket. Beneath that was his name. Peter Erhart, M.D.

"I'm Dr. Erhart." He stated the obvious and pressed Leslie's hand by way of greeting. "How are you feeling?"

"Other than a little tired, fine. I hope you're here to discharge me."

The doctor pulled a stainless steel stool to the side of the stretcher and sat down. When he crossed his arms on the top of the bed rail, he and Leslie were nearly eye to eye. "We'd like to keep you overnight for observation."

Leslie's stomach tightened, but she knew from experience that nothing would show on her face. Calmly, she asked, "Why is that?"

"Your EKG shows frequent runs of supraventricular tachycardia and occasional short bursts of atrial flutter accompanied by a precipitous drop in your blood pressure."

"Which is why I fainted."

Dr. Erhart looked surprised. "I understand you're an attorney. Do you handle medical cases?"

"No, but my…an associate does. I understand what you're saying." She'd discussed enough malpractice cases with Rachel to understand the terminology. She wondered idly if anyone had called Rachel, and then realized no one would have had any reason to. A few people in the office, including Stephanie, were probably aware of her relationship with Rachel Hawthorne, but it wasn't as if they presented themselves as a couple. Which they weren't. Not technically. She realized her mind was wandering, something else that never happened to her, and she forced herself to focus. "What's causing it and what needs to be done about it?"

Dr. Erhart smiled. "I wish I could answer both questions right now, but I can't. Any number of things could be causing the accelerated heart rate, including fluctuations in hormone levels, medications, drugs."

When he let the last word linger in the air, Leslie narrowed her eyes. "I'm not on any medication and I don't take drugs of any kind. I don't smoke and I drink in moderation."

"Your baseline blood pressure is also off the charts for someone your age. So it might be something as simple as stress…perhaps something at work? Or at home?"

"No. Neither." Leslie made an impatient gesture, which was cut short by the taut intravenous line tethering her to a nearby pole. "Look. I understand the need to be thorough and—"

The fluttering in her chest started at the same time as the monitor next to the bed began to screech. She struggled to catch her breath and found she couldn't. She was aware of Dr. Erhart speaking into the intercom next to the door, and after what seemed like an eternity, a woman in scrubs appeared and injected something into Leslie's IV line. A minute later the monitor fell silent, and the wild churning in her chest subsided.

"Jesus," Leslie whispered, still short of breath. "What was that?"

"That was another run of very rapid tachycardia," Dr. Erhart said solemnly. He turned to the nurse. "Call admissions and tell them we'll need a telemetry bed for Ms. Harris."

This time, Leslie didn't argue. "I need to make some calls. Could someone see if Stephanie Ackerman is here?"

As Leslie suspected, Stephanie had come to the hospital directly from the courthouse. When she appeared, Leslie felt ridiculously comforted. "Thanks for sticking around, Steph."

"Hey," Stephanie said softly. "Of course I would." She glanced at the monitors on either side of the bed and then back at Leslie. "What's going on?"

"Oh, they're just being careful. CYA." Leslie trusted Stephanie, but she had no intention of sharing the details. After all, it was all going to be straightened out in a matter of a few hours. "By the time they finish with all their tests, I'm probably not going to get out of here until the morning. I'll need you to check with Bill and find out how the judge is going to rule on continuing the trial."

Stephanie made notes on the rest of Leslie's requests and promised to call her that evening with any follow-up.

"I think that does it." Leslie leaned back and closed her eyes, more tired than she'd realized. "Thanks. I'll call you when I get home in the morning."

"Sure." Stephanie hesitated. "Uh…anyone else you'd like me to call?"

Frowning, Leslie opened her eyes. "Did I forget something?"

"I meant personally."

Leslie blushed. "Oh. I don't know that that's necessary. But thanks."

"Sure."

Feeling as if she should explain, Leslie added, "I'll take care of those calls when I get upstairs."

"I understand. If you need anything, you know my number."

"'Preciate it." Leslie smiled goodbye, glad for the quiet and the chance to close her eyes again.

When a cheerful middle-aged Asian man arrived to transport her to her room, Leslie was surprised to discover that she'd slept for almost two hours. When she was finally settled and alone after repeating her medical history yet again to the nurses and resident staff, she used the bedside phone and asked the operator for an outside line. She wasn't surprised when the number she called rang to voicemail. "Rach, it's me. I know this is ridiculous, but I'm actually in…oh, I don't know why I'm even bothering you with this." She contemplated hanging up and then finished in a rush. "I'm in the hospital. It's nothing serious. Some little glitch in my hormones or something. I'll be released in the morning. I know you're wrapping up that big trial, so I'll call you when I get home. Don't worry."

As the sounds outside her room gradually quieted, Leslie lay awake staring at the ceiling while reviewing her upcoming cases, prioritizing her work, and rehearsing how she would explain away this event to her partners. Several times she was aware of the fluttering in her chest, which she now recognized as the irregular heartbeat. She determined to ignore it, until just after midnight when the frantic racing started and wouldn't stop.

"My God, Leslie," Rachel Hawthorne said, looking more aggravated than concerned when she strode into Leslie's room just after noon the next day. "Why did you wait so damn long to tell me there was a problem with your going home?"

"You didn't need to rush over here," Leslie said. "I just wanted you to know that I hadn't been released yet."

Rachel had obviously come directly from court. Her immaculately cut slate gray jacket and skirt hinted at her statuesque figure without being suggestive. Her lustrous copper hair flamed around her shoulders, and her green eyes that could look so warm and seductive during sex snapped with impatience now. Despite Rachel's annoyance, Leslie was glad to see her. Something as normal as Rachel's quicksilver temper made the situation feel normal, and the fear that had been niggling at her all morning dissipated.

"Why are you still here?" Rachel glanced at her watch and leaned down to kiss Leslie all in the same motion. "I've got twenty minutes, and then I need to be back in court."

"I seem to have this sensitive heart rate all of a sudden," Leslie said lightly. "And apparently my blood pressure problem is a little out of order."

"Let's cut to the chase, darling," Rachel said, folding her arms and canting one hip in a strikingly feminine yet unmistakably aggressive pose. "Details."

Leslie sighed. "I had an episode of atrial flutter in the middle of the night that they weren't able to control with medication. Finally at seven a.m. they cardioverted me."

For the first time, Rachel looked worried. "God. Why the hell didn't you call me?"

"Because I knew that you were in court this morning, and there was nothing you could have done here. They sedated me, and it was over in a second. I didn't feel anything at all." She smiled. "And I feel much better now. I'm just waiting for another cardiogram to confirm that the rhythm has been corrected, and then I'm getting out of here."

"I'm not going to be able to wait." Rachel closed her eyes and rubbed the bridge of her nose, sorting through alternatives. "Is it safe for you to take a cab?"

"I'll call a limo service." Leslie took a deep breath. "That's not what I needed to talk to you about, Rach. I know this is a bad time, but there just didn't seem to be a *good* time."

"What?" Rachel said sharply. "What else?"

"I'm going to take a few weeks off." Leslie looked away, then into Rachel's eyes. "The doctors pretty much told me I have to. This stupid rhythm problem can be controlled by medication, but I don't seem to be one of the ones where it's easy. The episodes might recur for a while. It's sort of unpredictable."

"So it could happen again," Rachel said with understanding.

Leslie winced. "Yes."

"Christ, Leslie. What a mess."

"Believe me, I know."

"Well, at least you've got plenty of vacation time stored up. I can't remember the last time either of us went anywhere."

Neither could Leslie. In the nearly two years they'd been dating, or whatever it was they'd been doing, they'd never gone anywhere together for more than a long weekend. Even then, they both brought work and frequently spent hours in phone consultation.

"What are you going to do?" Rachel asked curiously. The concept of days with nothing to do was not only foreign to her, it was vaguely discomforting.

"It's not exactly going to be a vacation. I talked to Rex Myers this morning," Leslie said, referring to the managing partner at the firm.

At Rachel's look of astonishment, Leslie held up a hand. "I had to tell him something. I explained that I needed to cut back on my hours for a short time because I just started a new medication that wasn't agreeing with me. Which is definitely true." Leslie laughed shakily. "We've got a regional office in Albany, which isn't that far from my parents' house in Bolton Landing. I'm going to stay at the lake while this gets sorted out and work out of that office as much as I can."

"You're going *home* home?" Rachel shook her head. "I thought you didn't get along with your parents. You haven't been up there for one holiday since I've known you."

"It's not that we don't get along. We just don't…always see eye to eye on things."

"I don't get it. Why don't you just stay here and work part time out of the main office?"

It made sense. It made perfect sense. Leslie didn't have words to explain how frightened she'd been in the middle of the night when she couldn't breathe, when she'd felt as if her heart would pound its way out of her chest or simply stop beating altogether. She wasn't superstitious. She didn't believe in omens. But that morning, as they'd been injecting the drug into her arm to put her to sleep while they administered an electric current strong enough to completely inactivate her heart, her last thought had been that she wanted to go home. She just wanted a few days to breathe free again. She looked at Rachel and knew there was no way her totally focused, driven lover would ever understand that. Rachel lived to work. So did Leslie. It was the strongest bond they shared.

She couldn't very well explain to Rachel what she didn't understand herself.

"I don't want to go into the office every day and have people look at me as if there's something wrong with me," Leslie said, which was partially true. So many half-truths. "I'll get this straightened out while I'm up there and be done with it."

"I don't know that I can get away, darling. You know what my calendar—"

"I don't expect you to." Leslie reached through the aluminum bars of the railing for Rachel's hand. Her skin was smooth and soft. "I'll miss you if you can't find a way to come up, but I'll understand."

Rachel leaned over the railing and kissed Leslie quickly. "Good. Call me when you get settled up there. I'll see what I can do."

"Okay. You should go before you're late." Leslie watched Rachel walk out the door, wondering when she would see her again. Rachel likely wouldn't even miss her, not when she was this tied up in a big case. With an increasing surge of melancholy, Leslie admitted that she didn't really mind.

CHAPTER THREE

S hortly after 6 a.m., Dev opened her eyes to sunshine and the unmistakable sounds of morning in the mountains. Birdsong. Wind rustling in the trees. A far-distant hum of an outboard motor. Her rented cabin was the last in a row of ten similar rustic log cabins that were situated at fifty-yard intervals within small clearings in the woods. A meandering dirt path connected them to one another and to the main lodge at Lakeview Cottages. Similar wooded trails led from each small front porch down to the water and a sliver of sandy beach. She couldn't see the other cabins, most of which were still empty so early in the season, or the lodge where the owners also lived, nearly a quarter of a mile away. The solitude was welcome, and although meals were included in her weekly rent, she had yet to avail herself of that amenity in the three days she'd been at Lakeview. She hadn't quite gotten over her uneasiness at finding herself at the Harrises'.

When she'd called the park ranger headquarters a month before to explain who she was and the work she'd be doing in the lake area that summer, Natalie had extended the professional courtesy of arranging local accommodations for her. Dev had been happy to have one fewer thing to do, her only stipulation being that she wanted a private cabin that was as far from the popular tourist haunts as possible. She hadn't even considered that Natalie might reserve a place for her at the Harrises' secluded resort just north of Bolton Landing, and when she'd found out, there hadn't really been a good reason to refuse it. It was close to the Institute's labs, and she doubted that anyone would recognize her. No one had.

Even so, when she'd arrived to check in, she couldn't shake the disorienting effect that seeing the place again produced. She hadn't expected to be bothered—it had all been over so long ago. Dead and buried and gone.

At the moment, though, lying naked beneath a soft floral print sheet that smelled of wind and water, she was very glad to be there. Turning on her side, she just enjoyed the beauty outside her windows. She also reflected on the question of why she was enjoying it *alone*. When Natalie had casually asked her to dinner at the end of the workday the night before, it had seemed natural to say yes. They'd worked well together all day, collecting samples, planning when and where to take others, and conversation had come easily.

Dinner hadn't had the feel of a date, not quite. It had the feel of two women who liked one another at first meeting, getting to know each other better. And when they'd returned to the park office so that Dev could pick up her truck for the drive back to her summer quarters and Natalie had casually kissed her good night as they'd stood in the dark parking lot, that had felt natural too.

Recalling the kiss, Dev knew if she'd done any more than return it lightly and then step away, they might be waking up together right now. She suspected that would have been pleasant. It had been a long time since she'd met someone like Natalie, someone who might offer uncomplicated but satisfying intimacy. It was an unusual combination, and hard to find. Which was probably why she hadn't had sex in over a year. But there was no rush, and she might be wrong. Not worth the risk.

Still, thinking about it would give her something to enjoy in the shower. Smiling, she stood and stretched and headed to the small, neat bathroom to start her day.

At 1:00 that afternoon, Dev pulled her black Chevy Colorado into the parking lot at Lakeview, planning on a fifteen-minute stop to change clothes before driving to a meeting in Troy. As she climbed down from the cab, she nodded to Eileen Harris, who looked over from where she was leaning beneath the hood of her dusty green Jeep Cherokee. Dev recognized it and figured it had to be twenty years old.

"Hey," Dev said. "Problem?"

Eileen Harris, in her early fifties and still looking youthfully blond and fit in her baggy jeans and well-worn blue cable-knit sweater, gave an exasperated sigh. "The damn thing won't start. Again." She wiped sweat from her forehead with the back of her hand and left a streak of grease behind. She looked even younger then. "Paul has been promising to look at it, but you know how that goes. He's ferrying a group of campers out to the islands right now."

Lake George Islands campsites, accessible only by boat, offered some of the best recreational fishing, hiking, bird watching, sailing, and camping in upstate New York. Not for the fainthearted, however, since everything had to be packed in by water, and private arrangements needed to be made for trips back to the mainland. If her husband had gone out with a group, he might not be back for a while.

"I'd lend a hand," Dev said, "but I don't know as I'd be much help. Can I offer you a lift somewhere instead?"

"Ordinarily it wouldn't be such a problem," Eileen said. "But I have to be at the train station in Rensselaer this afternoon, and even if I reach Paul and get him back here, *and* he can fix it, I don't think I'll make it in time."

"I'm about to drive down to Troy for a short meeting. If you've got guests coming in by train, I can pick them up and bring them back." The Rensselaer train station stop on the Amtrak line that ran from New York City to Montréal was ten minutes from where she was going to be.

"I hate to ask you to do that. I imagine you must be busy."

Dev sensed her hesitation and was embarrassed that Eileen Harris felt uncomfortable accepting a simple favor from her. Eileen's reserve was probably due to the fact that Dev had avoided Eileen and her husband since her arrival. Dev hoped she could make up for the rudeness now. "It's right on my way. Really."

"Well," Eileen said, clearly still torn. She glanced once at the truck, then smiled gratefully at Dev. "That would be great. My daughter's coming in from New York City, and I hate for her to wait there or find some other way up."

"Your daughter." Dev heard her voice and it sounded normal, but she felt like she was hearing it underwater.

"Yes. Leslie. She's an attorney in Manhattan, and she called unexpectedly. Just this morning. It's been a while since she's been here, and I…"

Dev was trying to follow the slightly disjointed conversation but she didn't seem to be catching all the words. Leslie. Coming here.

She looked past Eileen down the grassy slope to the lake and the boathouse. It looked exactly the same as it had fifteen years before. She could actually hear the music.

The party at the Harrises' boathouse was in full swing when Dev arrived close to midnight. The parking lot was jammed with dusty pickup trucks, old sedans, and even a few shiny new graduation cars here and there. She rode her motorcycle onto the grass under some trees and sauntered down the slope toward the music and the swell of voices. Every teenager in the area would be there, including those who were only living at the lake for the summer while they worked at the area restaurants and resorts. It was the last big bash of the summer before half of the kids there left for college.

Dev wouldn't be leaving just yet. She'd missed the age cutoff for starting kindergarten with most of the kids close to her age by a month, so she still had a year before she graduated. She looked eighteen, although she had six months to go, but she never got carded when she bought beer or tried to get into the Painted Pony, a local drinking hangout. The fake ID she'd gotten mail order from a place in New York City didn't hurt, either. Fortunately, there were so many kids in Lake George during the summer, it was all the cops could do to keep the really young ones under control. She never got stopped on her motorcycle, and no one bothered about what went on at private parties.

Dev strode through the crowd that had spilled out onto the grass in front of the boathouse, looking straight ahead and ignoring the few people who stared in her direction. She knew she looked nothing like the pretty girls in their shorts and pastel blouses or even the boys who stood with their arms around those same girls, nuzzling their necks and casually brushing their fingers under the curve of their breasts, arrogant with their male privilege. Knowing she didn't fit and knowing why, Dev wore her tight jeans smeared with engine grease, her heavy motorcycle boots, and her frayed white T-shirt with angry pride. Her hair was shaggy and dark with sweat. She ignored even the few who greeted her; she had only one thing on her mind.

The boathouse, extending out over the water on three sides, was as big as a basketball court and sweltering, the air thick with sweat and smoke and the sexual energy of a hundred teenagers in the last throes of innocence. Huge speakers in the back corners blasted Aerosmith, and writhing bodies filled every inch of the room. Most of the lights were off and the cavernous space was so dim she could barely make out anyone's features until she was almost in their face, but she knew she'd find her. She always did. It was like they were connected. Except only she felt it.

She grabbed a beer from a row of coolers below one of the open windows, popped the top, and guzzled half of it. It was her fourth in two hours, but she didn't feel it. The adrenaline rush of riding her bike at high speeds along the curving roads bordering the lake had burned off a lot of the alcohol. She loved the way the wind felt blasting against her face at sixty miles an hour, like another body molded to hers. The rush of speed and the engine throbbing and the pulse pulse pulse of the pressure against her body was enough to make her come sometimes. The pleasure was enough to make her forget for a little while that she was alone.

She drank the beer and tossed the can into the corner. Leslie was perched in one of the open windows, her face turned toward the water, her hair blowing ever so lightly in the breeze. Moonlight highlighted her slim form, the curve of her breasts and the arch of her bent legs so beautiful it was like a pain in Dev's heart. On the far side of the room, Leslie's boyfriend Mike was standing with a group of boys shooting pool, his legs spread wide, posturing with the cue stick angled against his crotch like a phallic extension.

Dev snagged two more beers and eased her way along the wall in the near dark until she was next to Leslie at the window. She placed a cold, sweating beer can against the outside of Leslie's thigh and laughed softly when Leslie jumped with a small sound of surprise.

"Want another beer?"

"Dev!" Leslie smiled and took the beer. "I thought you said you weren't coming."

Dev shrugged and leaned her shoulder against the window frame. The big rectangular window swung out on hinges and canted over the water, the glass reflecting the shine of moonlight on the black surface of the lake. "Changed my mind."

"Yeah?" Leslie sipped the Budweiser, trying not to grimace. It was the guys' favorite, so that was what they had at the parties. "How come?"

"Just thought I'd hang out here for a while."

"I'm glad you came by."

"You leaving this weekend?" Dev knew she was, but somehow she kept hoping to hear Leslie say, *No, Dev. I changed my mind. I don't really want to go three hundred miles away from home. From you.*

But she wouldn't, because that was just Dev's dream. Not Leslie's.

"Uh-huh. Sunday. My folks are driving me down."

Dev thought she sounded just a little bit wistful, and that made the ache in her belly worse somehow. She dared to touch Leslie's bare knee ever so lightly. Leslie's skin, damp from the mist off the water, was cool against Dev's hot fingertips. "You'll be okay."

"Oh, I know." Leslie smiled brightly. "It'll be great. I can't wait."

"So you're still gonna be a landscape architect, huh?"

"Someday. You know, after college and everything."

Dev nodded, although she really didn't know much about how college worked. She wasn't really too interested, since she figured she'd end up working in her parents' convenience store after high school. They expected her to help out, save them the cost of hiring someone. Her older brother had left home as soon as he could, refusing to be tied to the drudgery that seemed to be their parents' lives. So Dev worked, in his place, after school and on weekends.

She didn't care. She didn't think about it much. When she looked into the future, she could never see anything except more of the same. Her. Alone.

"So when will you be back? You know, vacation or whatever," Dev asked.

Even in the moonlight, Leslie's face was shadowed. "Thanksgiving, I guess. Not that long."

"No, I guess n—"

"Hey, Leslie!" One of Leslie's girlfriends shouted above the din. "Come on, come outside. We're gonna smoke a joint."

Dev knew the invitation didn't include her. Her friendship with Leslie was something that Leslie's crowd just ignored, clearly unable to understand why Leslie would give Dev the time of day. After all, Dev was a year behind them, and if that weren't enough to make her company less than desirable, she was strange. Different. But for some reason, Leslie and she were always able to talk. It had started by accident the year before when they'd shared a table during study hall. Leslie was having trouble with a math problem, and since it was the one subject that Dev could pick up just by sitting in class without doing any work at all, she'd shown Leslie how to set up the solution. The next day she helped her again, and somehow they'd started talking about other things. Everything, really.

Dev had never met anyone she could talk to so easily. Leslie always listened. Always made her feel like what she had to say was important and interesting. They never met outside of school, never visited each other's homes. Never did anything social together except sit for an hour every few days on the lawn outside school or walk down to the lake, and talk. Except once. Just once, Leslie had ridden on the back of Dev's motorcycle, laughing and pressed up against her with her arms around Dev's waist. Dev had been nearly light-headed from the sensation of Leslie's breasts against her back. She cherished the memory, revisiting it nearly nightly before she went to sleep, coming sometimes while imagining Leslie's arms around her.

"Go. That's cool," Dev said, sensing Leslie's friend waiting impatiently. "I just wanted to…" *See you again. Tell you how hard it's going to be when you leave. How much I'm going to miss you. How empty I feel inside.*

Maybe something showed in her face, because Leslie said, "You go ahead, Sue. I'll catch you in a little while."

When Sue made an exasperated sound and melted into the crowd, Leslie took Dev's hand and jumped down from the windowsill. "Come on. Let's go for a walk."

Leslie only touched her fingers for a second, but Dev's legs felt shaky. Mutely, she followed, tied to Leslie by that invisible string she could always feel, tugging her back to her even when she knew she should stay away.

"God, I feel so much better out here," Leslie said as they walked along the water's edge, leaving the boathouse and the noise and the smoke behind. She sat down on one of the park benches her parents had placed around the lake for the guests and tilted her head back. "I wonder if the stars will look like this in the city."

Dev didn't know. She'd never been to a big city. Her parents never took a vacation, they never left the store in anyone else's hands. "Probably. I think they're everywhere."

Leslie turned her head on the bench and smiled at Dev. "Yeah, probably."

Dev didn't mean to kiss her. She didn't even know she'd moved until her lips touched Leslie's. She'd never imagined Leslie's lips would be so warm and soft. Dev slid trembling fingers over Leslie's throat, felt Leslie's heart racing just beneath her skin. Then Dev was suddenly aware of Leslie's hand stroking the back of her neck, of Leslie kissing her back, pushing against her so that their breasts touched through the whisper-thin layers of their cotton T-shirts. Leslie moaned softly and the dam inside Dev's heart broke and everything she'd been holding back forever spilled out.

"Oh, Les," Dev whispered. She framed Leslie's face with her hands, kissed her again, angling her body onto Leslie so that their legs entwined. Leslie grasped her waist, holding her close. Dev groaned. "Les, I lo—"

"Jesus! Fuck!"

Someone grabbed Dev's shoulder from behind and yanked her off Leslie, throwing her to the ground hard enough to knock the wind from her. Stunned, Dev gasped and fought to catch her breath. A foot drove into her side, and she groaned and curled into a ball.

"What the fuck do you think you're doing?" Leslie's boyfriend Mike shouted.

Distantly, Dev heard Leslie screaming for Mike to stop. She didn't care about the pain in her side or the next blow that landed on her hip, or the next. Or the next. Nothing that ever happened to her again could hurt as much as what she heard Leslie shout.

Mike, it was just a joke! I was just fooling with her. She doesn't mean anything to me. She's nobody!

Dev blinked in the bright sunlight and stared at Leslie's mother.

"…can't thank you enough," Eileen said. "As long as you're sure it's no trouble."

"No," Dev said, forcing a smile though her face felt numb. "No trouble at all."

CHAPTER FOUR

Ten minutes before the Amtrak Adirondack was expected to arrive in Rensselaer, Dev pulled into a parking slot opposite the metal stairs leading down from the train tracks. She sat watching the platform, fingers curled around the steering wheel as if to ground herself firmly in the present, wondering if she would recognize the girl who had filled her heart and dreams for so long, grown into a woman now. Had she known it was Leslie arriving in need of a ride when she'd talked with Eileen Harris, she wouldn't have volunteered to pick her up. She doubted it would be a comfortable ride back for either of them.

Even though her first thought had been of Leslie when she'd received the memo outlining the details and location of her new assignment, she hadn't seriously expected to run into her over the summer. The last time she'd been in the area—on a one-night stopover six years before to wish her parents well in their move to a retirement community in Florida—she'd made careful inquiries about Leslie Harris with some of the locals. The story had always been the same. Leslie was one of the young, ambitious up-and-comers who had left the provincial village never to return, and no one could recall seeing her in years. Like Dev, she had moved on.

Leslie's mother had said she was an attorney in Manhattan. Dev remembered all the hours Leslie had spent explaining to her about landscape architecture and how she wanted to create outdoor environments where people could live in harmony with nature. She was going to come back to the lake area and open a practice. Maybe work with the park services. It sounded inspiring and meaningful, and Dev had fallen a little bit more in love with her every time they talked about it. She had had no such grand designs for her own life, but Leslie hadn't seemed to think less of her for it. When Dev had mumbled that she didn't have any plans, Leslie had just smiled and said 'there was plenty of time to decide.

Leslie had apparently made different choices after she'd left Bolton Landing for Yale. Dev doubted she would recognize the idealistic young girl now. At any rate, she would soon know, because a series of whistle blows alerted Dev to the train arriving. A sudden case of nerves set her stomach jittering as she watched the passengers exit the station.

She'd been wrong about not recognizing her. Leslie had changed, just as Dev had, but Dev knew her the instant she started down the stairs, an expensive-looking leather briefcase swinging from a strap over one shoulder and a suitcase in the other hand. She was far thinner than Dev ever remembered her being, her face and body sculpted by maturity. An atmosphere of tension surrounded her. Even at a distance her body seemed tightly coiled, wary and alert—predatory. Up close, her blue eyes were cool and appraising. She was beautiful in a way she hadn't been as a teenager, the innocence having given way to razor-sharp elegance. But for just a second Dev saw the air shimmering around her and imagined she felt the tug of the invisible string that had once connected them.

As Dev stepped from the truck, she reminded herself that that tie had only been in her mind and that it had been irrevocably severed long ago.

Leslie stopped at the curb and scanned the parking lot for her mother's ancient Jeep. Rensselaer was not a busy stop on the train route, and there were only a handful of cars waiting. Her mother's wasn't among them.

"Damn," she muttered, sliding her hand into her briefcase and unerringly closing her fingers around her BlackBerry. She'd just pulled up the lodge number, since her mother didn't have a cell phone, when someone spoke her name.

Startled, Leslie looked up into hazel eyes that she knew better than her own and tumbled back in time fifteen years.

Leslie wasn't all that surprised that the party was turning into a drag. Mike was drinking too much as usual and generally being an asshole. Fortunately, he was off playing pool and at least leaving her alone for the time being. She hated it when he put on a big show of making out with her in public. As if she was going to let him feel her up in front of all his buddies. Yeah right.

Restless, not knowing why, she left him to his game and drifted away from the crowd. It was so hot and stuffy in the room and the beer was already too warm and she knew she should be having a good time, but she wasn't. She was sad. She shouldn't be sad, and that just made it worse. She'd just graduated from high school at the top of her class and she was going to a great college. Everything was turning out just the way she'd hoped. Well, Mike wasn't going to the same school. His grades weren't good enough. But he wouldn't be that far away and she didn't really mind if she didn't see him all that often anyhow. Sometimes, she was glad that she'd be with new people who didn't know her. It felt almost as if she'd be starting her life all over again, and that part was exciting.

So why was she so sad?

She unlatched the huge wooden-paned window, swung it out over the water, and climbed up onto the broad sill. She leaned her head back as the breeze washed over her and watched the moon flit in and out between the clouds. It was amazing how bright the night sky could be. It wasn't really black at all, more like a dark, dark blue. It was beautiful. She'd miss the lake and the woods and the way the air smelled like it had never been breathed before. And there was something more important that she would miss. Something she knew she should understand, but she couldn't find the words. Every time she tried, all she felt was frustration and, oddly, fear. That was just crazy and, besides, she could always come back, so there was no reason to feel sad about anything.

Leslie jumped at the sudden cold on her leg and heard the voice she been waiting for all night but hadn't expected to hear.

"Dev! I thought you said you weren't coming."

Even in the moonlight, the smile in Dev's eyes was clear. As Leslie reached for the beer, her fingers glanced over Dev's, and although she gave it no more than an instant's thought, *she felt her sadness wash away.*

Leslie Harris saw no sign of a smile in those eyes now, not that she would have expected one. Annoyed at the uncharacteristic slip in her concentration and where her thoughts had taken her, she kept her expression neutral as she rapidly regrouped. The fragments of a past that felt as if it belonged to someone else melted away like frost on a windowpane, leaving nothing behind but an unnoticed trail of tears. Then she was herself again, calculating and in control. "Hello, Dev."

"Hi, Les," Dev said.

"My guess is this isn't a coincidence." Leslie suspected her displeasure showed in her voice, because Dev shrugged apologetically.

"Your mother's Jeep is on the fritz, and since I'm staying at the lodge, I offered to pick you up. Sorry."

"No, I appreciate it. Thanks." Unconsciously, Leslie studied her the way she would a prospective witness, searching for the whole truth, the real story. It disturbed her when she couldn't read anything in Dev's face. "I hope you didn't go out of your way."

"No. I was in the area." Dev lifted Leslie's suitcase. "My truck's over here."

"Would you mind waiting just a minute while I get a cup of coffee in the station? Whatever they were trying to pass off as coffee on the train was undrinkable."

"Sure. That black Chevy is mine."

"Can I get you anything?"

"A Coke would be great. Thanks."

God, this is going to be an interminable ride home, Leslie thought as she stood in line at the coffee bar. *Maybe I should rethink my plans for this visit if we might run into each other again.*

"Large black coffee and a Coke, please," Leslie said automatically while checking her BlackBerry for messages. She didn't give a second thought to the fact that she was supposed to limit her coffee consumption. Upon her release from the hospital the previous afternoon, part of the discharge instructions had been no caffeine—along with an admonition to avoid chocolate, get plenty of rest, reduce her stress level, and schedule the follow-up tests as soon as possible. She'd also been given a prescription for a blood pressure med and verapamil, which was supposed to keep her heart rate from rising too rapidly. Thus far, her only form of compliance had been to limit her morning coffee to three cups instead of five.

The fact was, she felt perfectly fine.

By the time she'd gotten home the night before, she'd decided that the severity of the entire episode had been vastly exaggerated. Whatever had happened could easily be chalked up to a few days of excessive stress and poor eating habits. Since she'd already cleared her calendar, and she'd still be able to work while upstate, she decided to go through with her plans to spend a week or two with her parents. Other than that, as far as she was concerned it was back to business as usual.

As she carried the drinks to the truck, she observed Dev through the window. If they had passed in the parking lot, Leslie wasn't sure she would have recognized her, although she certainly would have given her an appreciative glance. Her hair was still on the shaggy side, but Dev had filled out and grown another inch or two, and she'd been taller than Leslie even in high school. Back then Dev had been wiry and wild, and now she was broad shouldered and muscular looking in her white button-down-collar shirt and black jeans. It wasn't just Dev's body that had changed. They had once shared effortless communication, but now all she felt was a distant reserve. That was good, because the last thing she wanted was a trip down memory lane.

"Here you go." Leslie passed the Coke across the passenger compartment before grasping the handle above the door and climbing into the truck. Her skirt rode up to mid-thigh before she had a chance to pull it down, but she noticed out of the corner of her eye that Dev stared straight ahead out the windshield. Leslie was slightly and quite irrationally annoyed at being pointedly ignored, not that she wanted Dev to pay *that* kind of attention to her.

"Thanks." Dev slotted the Coke into the cup holder on the dash and started the truck. She pulled out of the parking lot, rapidly maneuvered the bypasses around Albany and Troy, and headed north on Interstate 87.

Fifteen minutes passed in silence before Dev said, "Your mother tells me you're a lawyer."

"Yes. I'm a partner in a law firm in Manhattan."

"Partner already. You must've worked your ass off," Dev said, duly impressed.

"Not really," Leslie said, unbuttoning her blazer as the cab warmed up in the late afternoon sun. She wore an off-white silk shell beneath it, conscious of the fact that a hint of her lace bra showed through when her blazer was open. Whereas Dev felt like a stranger—*was* a stranger—Leslie was acutely conscious of her presence. Even if she had known nothing about her, Leslie would have assumed she was a lesbian. Dev was undeniably attractive in a rough, earthy kind of way. But the last thing in the world she wanted was for Dev Weber to have the slightest indication that she found her attractive.

Dev looked in Leslie's direction for the first time, her expression one of mild disbelief at Leslie's easy dismissal of her accomplishments. Dev's glance drifted down, taking in Leslie's long legs, sleek beneath her sheer silk stockings, and the swell of her breasts beneath silk and lace. Leslie had turned into the beautiful woman that the lovely teenager had foreshadowed. Maybe it was the unexpected juxtaposition of the woman upon her memory of the girl, because Dev ventured into territory she had never meant to revisit. "What happened to landscape architecture?"

Taken by surprise at the question very few people in her life knew her well enough to ask, Leslie laughed harshly. "I haven't thought of that in ages. It was just one of those things that kids think they want before they know anything about life. Once I got to college, everything changed."

No, Dev wanted to say, *it changed long before that.* But then she realized that was just her truth, not Leslie's.

"So you like what you're doing?" Dev asked, hoping to fill the time with safe conversation until they reached the lake and could politely go their separate ways once more.

"I don't know that I'd say I *like* it," Leslie said, "but it's satisfying." She grinned. "I like winning cases. So what about you? Are you running the store for your parents now?"

"No, they finally sold the place and moved to Florida about six years ago." Leslie's question brought home to Dev how little they knew of one another now. There might have been a time when they'd understood each other without words, but now there was nothing between them. "I'm working up at the lake this summer, though. I'm a biologist."

"You're kidding," Leslie said before she could catch herself. "Jesus, I'm sorry. That was rude."

Not insulted, Dev laughed as she exited onto Route 9 North, the twisting two-lane lake road that she once could have driven from memory. "No. I don't blame you. I'm sure it's nothing anyone who knew me in high school would've guessed I'd be doing."

"I just never remember you being interested in that kind of thing."

"I wasn't."

"So what caused the big switch?"

Dev swung into the driveway to Lakeview and parked in the lot beside Eileen Harris's Jeep. She shifted on the seat and met Leslie's curious gaze. "After the accident I couldn't do much more than read, and studying kept my mind occupied."

Leslie paled at the unexpected reference to a time she assiduously avoided thinking about. Ambushed by guilt and regret, she felt a sudden need for air. She yanked the door handle up and stepped out in front of her childhood home. The rambling, three-story white clapboard house with its wraparound porches and gabled upper windows looked just the same as it always had. Her mother, also seemingly unchanged in jeans and a sweater Leslie thought might once have been here, waved from the front porch. On the far side of the parking lot the grassy slope led down to the boathouse. The boathouse. There were some things she couldn't forget, no matter how much she wanted to.

Leslie looked back into the truck. "I'm sorry. So sorry. I'd undo it all if I could."

As Dev watched Leslie walk quickly away from her and the painful past that had suddenly resurfaced, she heard the words she'd never be able to forget. *She's nothing to me. She's nobody.*

And still, even knowing she'd been wrong about everything, she'd never wanted to change any of it. Dev climbed from the truck, pulled Leslie's luggage from behind the seat, and started toward the lodge. Leslie's parting words, in the past and the present, reminded her more powerfully than any blow that she and Leslie had never shared the same dream. It had all been in her mind. A fiction created from her own need and foolish hopes.

Thankfully, those long-ago dreams had been put to rest, but she was still going to need to find another place to stay. She had never expected that seeing Leslie again would hurt quite so much.

CHAPTER FIVE

L eslie stopped a step below her mother and tried to decipher the expression in her mother's eyes. Despite the fact that it was only a three about trip, Leslie hadn't been home in over three years, and the last visit had been only for a few hours one Christmas. She'd never had to lie about the reason for her absence. She always had work to do, even if that was only a convenient excuse. There was warmth in her mother's eyes, but wariness too. After Leslie left for college they'd lost the easy companionability they'd had when Leslie was a teenager.

No, Leslie reminded herself, *after you decided to go to law school.*

"Hi, Mom," Leslie said.

Eileen wrapped her arms around Leslie's shoulders and hugged her. "Hi, honey. I'm sorry I couldn't pick you up."

Leslie felt the stiffness in her mother's embrace and imagined that her own body felt much the same. "That's okay. I didn't give you any notice, after all."

"Well," Eileen said, looking past Leslie down the gravel walk, "I'm glad Dr. Weber was able to give you a ride."

Leslie turned just as Dev reached her, Leslie's briefcase under her arm and the suitcase in her hand. "*Dr.* Weber?"

Dev shrugged, coloring faintly. "Not the regular kind."

"You didn't need to bring my luggage up," Leslie said, reaching for the suitcase.

"No problem," Dev replied, climbing the stairs. "Where do you want them?"

"Your old room's available," Leslie's mother said, "if you want it.

I don't rent that one out unless I really need to, and the lodge isn't full now. You'd have plenty of privacy."

Not if Rachel manages to come up, Leslie thought. There was no way she was going to subject Rachel to her mother's scrutiny or have sex in her childhood bedroom. That wasn't exactly the way she wanted to introduce her mother to the idea that she had a girlfriend. Plus, even if Rachel didn't visit, she didn't want to spend two weeks in the constant company of her parents and be faced with the subtle disappointment in their eyes. "I'd rather have one of the cabins. They're not all full, are they?"

"Not yet, but we've got reservations—"

"Actually," Dev said, wondering if the other two women had forgotten her presence, "she can have mine. I…uh…should probably get a place closer to the lab."

Eileen look startled, and Leslie scrutinized Dev intently before saying, "Mom, let's settle the room situation later."

"Of course. Let me double-check the registrations, and we can decide after dinner. I'm sure I can work something out." Eileen looked at Dev. "I hope you'll be able to join us tonight."

"Thank you, but—" Dev said, scrambling for a polite way to decline when the phone rang inside and Eileen turned away.

"Wonderful." Eileen hurried inside, leaving Dev to stare after her.

Leslie lifted the suitcase Dev had deposited on the porch. "I'll make your excuses, if you want to pass on dinner."

"I'm that easy to read, huh?"

"You might take a little bit of coaching before I'd put you on the witness stand." Leslie smiled softly. "Besides, your eyes always did give you away."

"No, they didn't," Dev said quietly. "You were just always able to tell what I was thinking. No one else could."

When Leslie's face lost all expression and she hastily glanced away, Dev knew she had no good reason to put off sitting down to dinner with the Harrises. Until now she'd avoided them because she didn't want the subject of Leslie and their shared past to come up. She hadn't wanted to be reminded, and she hadn't wanted to talk about it. But the past was standing right in front of her, and she couldn't have stopped thinking about Leslie now if she got into her truck and drove a thousand miles away. What she needed was to understand that this woman was not the girl she remembered, and whatever friendship they'd shared had ended the night when everything in her life had changed. Maybe a casual dinner where it would be apparent they had nothing in common any longer would do the trick.

"Sorry," Dev said.

"For what?" Leslie said, shifting her eyes away from the boathouse and back to Dev.

"For bringing up old history. I'm just surprised to see you."

"I won't be staying long," Leslie said abruptly, feeling inexplicably claustrophobic. She was standing outside in the June afternoon sun, looking out over a vista of forest and clear blue water that was still unspoiled by the trappings of modern life. She couldn't imagine a place where she might feel more free, but instead she found herself trapped in memories she had no desire to relive. "There's no need for you to move out of your cabin. We're not likely to see each other. I'll be working most of the time, and I imagine you'll be off doing whatever you do."

Dr. Weber, her mother had said. Leslie could barely believe that this woman was the angry, often sullen, teenager she remembered. Dev had never studied in school, and her grades had shown it. Even though Dev had almost failed her junior year, Leslie always knew she was smart. She could tell from the things they talked about. Dev seemed to know something about almost everything, but she never cared about doing well in school or whether other people approved of her. That was one of the things Leslie always loved...

"I'll stay in the lodge," Leslie said.

"You ought to be able to stay wherever you want while you're here," Dev pointed out reasonably. "It's your home, after all."

"No it isn't." Leslie shouldered her briefcase and started to add that she didn't care where she slept when she felt the fluttering sensation well up in her chest. The surge of panic that followed only made her heart pound faster. With a gasp, she dropped her luggage and sat down quickly in the nearest porch chair.

"Les, are you okay?" Dev took the final two stairs to the porch in one long stride. Leslie was very pale, but even more disconcerting, she looked frightened. Dev knelt by her side. "Les?"

"Fine," Leslie said with a wave of her hand. She felt just a little bit breathless, but the fluttering sensation was already starting to subside. "Hot. I should have had something to drink on the train besides coffee."

"I'll get you something to drink from inside." Dev started to rise when Leslie caught her arm.

"No, don't. My mother…"

"I won't tell her." Dev, stiff with shock, stared at Leslie's fingers wrapped around her wrist. It was odd, they were exactly as she remembered them, incredibly soft and strong at the same time. Satin over steel. Her body remembered every place that Leslie had ever touched, even casually, and she shuddered at the explosion of sensation. Gently, she drew her arm away. "I'll tell your mother it's for me. Pepsi, not Coke, right?"

Leslie bit the inside of her lip. Two years together, and Rachel could never remember that, but somehow, Dev had, even after all this time. She felt dangerously close to tears, and barely recognized herself. Of course, she'd hardly slept in two nights and what little rest she'd managed had been uneasy. Part of her kept expecting to wake up breathless with that terrible pressure in her chest. She nodded, because she needed a minute to settle herself and she didn't want to have Dev see her so shaken. Dev always could see too much. "Thanks. Yes, Pepsi would be great."

"No problem." Dev put her hands in her pockets because she had the overwhelming desire to touch Leslie on her shoulder, or her hair. Somewhere, just to reassure her, or maybe herself, that everything was all right. For a second, she'd thought that Leslie was going to faint, and she still didn't look quite right. "Don't move. I'll be right back."

Relieved to be alone, Leslie rested her head against the back of the white wicker rocker and closed her eyes. She pressed her index finger over the pulse in her wrist. It seemed fast, but steady. She could breathe again. It *was* hot for June. And, she had to admit, seeing Dev had thrown her. She'd known that coming home was going to be difficult to begin with, and now she couldn't remember why she'd ever thought it was a good idea at all.

Since she'd changed her mind about doing something environmentally related as a career and gone into law instead, her relationship with her parents, especially her mother, had been awkward. Her parents were one step up from hippies—well, old hippies now—but she could remember riding on her father's shoulders during equal rights marches and carrying signs at supermarkets to protest the treatment of migrant farm workers. As a child she used to play on the rug in front of the huge stone fireplace, listening to her parents and their friends debate everything from abortion rights to global warming. Her parents still grew their own organic vegetables, and the only boats that put out from the boathouse at Lakeview other than the outboard her father used to ferry campers to the islands were sailboats or other non-motorized craft.

She was a disappointment to them, and she knew it.

"Here you go," Dev said, squatting down again beside Leslie and handing her a sweating glass of soda. "No ice and a straw."

Dev didn't say *just the way you like it*, but Leslie heard the words all the same. She took the glass and managed to smile, although she wasn't certain she could take any more kindness. "Thanks."

"How are you feeling?"

Leslie sipped the Pepsi, giving herself a few extra seconds to chase away the disturbing disorientation that came over her every time she looked at Dev. Forty-eight hours ago she had been immersed in another world, a world she had chosen and in which she knew exactly who she was. She'd been in charge, in control, sure of herself. She'd been…satisfied. She'd also been certain that was as close to happy as she could be.

"Les?" Dev stared at Leslie's left hand, then gently cradled it in her palm. There was no engagement ring, no wedding band, but that wasn't what held her attention now. She looked from the bruise surrounding the healing puncture site to Leslie's face. "What's wrong, Les?"

"Nothing." Leslie drew her hand back, closing her fingers into a fist and turning her hand away so that the IV site was no longer visible. She'd forgotten that was there. There was another one on her right forearm, but her jacket covered it.

Dev didn't repeat the question, but Leslie could see it still swirling in her eyes. When she'd first seen Dev at the train station, she hadn't thought she would recognize her if they'd passed on the street, but she realized now that she'd been wrong. It was true that Dev had grown into a woman even more attractive than she'd been as a teenager, but if Leslie had ever seen her eyes, she would have known her anywhere.

Her eyes were the same, and Leslie hadn't exaggerated when she'd said they always gave Dev away. When she was angry those tiny gold flecks that Leslie had always coveted disappeared and her irises darkened from hazel to gray. When she was happy, they sparkled with a hint of green as pure as new spring grass. When she was worried, like now, the colors swirled like shadowy eddies in the lake during a hard rain.

"Really. I'm just getting over a bug of some kind." Without thinking, Leslie rested a hand on Dev's shoulder, surprised at the hard muscles beneath the cotton shirt. They felt so different from Rachel's firmness or her own gym-toned body. She considered herself strong, but what she sensed in Dev's body was power.

"There's probably time for a nap before dinner," Dev said, not completely sure she believed Leslie's story. But she had no right to question her either. She eased back on her heels and breathed a little easier when Leslie removed her hand. The physical contact made her uncomfortable. "Your mother said to tell you she freed up cabin nine indefinitely. I'll take your luggage down."

Leslie set her glass aside and stood. "I'll get it. You've done enough this afternoon. You don't have to play bellboy as well."

Dev grinned. "I did that for a while in college. It paid pretty well."

"Where did you go?"

"Syracuse."

Leslie smiled wanly. She had always planned to go to the College of Forestry at Syracuse. She and Dev often talked about it when they sat together by the lake after school. But when she'd been accepted at Yale, where she'd only applied because her guidance counselors had insisted, she hadn't been able to resist the lure of attending an Ivy League school. And she admitted now, she'd been eager to experience something bigger than her small-town life. There'd been fewer than a hundred seniors in her graduating high school class. She'd known them all since kindergarten. Everyone she knew in school looked the same, thought the same, shared the same plans for the future. Except for Dev. Dev was the only one who was exciting and different, and their friendship…well, that was something that had always seemed apart from the rest of her life.

"Well, I'm sure you've got better things to do now than carry luggage."

Dev shrugged and picked up the suitcase. There was no way she was going to let Leslie carry it a quarter of a mile to the cabin. "You're wearing heels, Les."

Leslie made a face. "I'm used to dressing this way, Dev, and if I can handle a sprint through JFK airport with a loaded briefcase and two suitcases, I can handle a stroll through the woods."

"Fine." Dev handed her the briefcase but kept the suitcase herself. "Here you go."

"I don't remember you being this stubborn," Leslie complained, half annoyed and half amused.

"I guess I've changed," Dev said quietly.

Leslie sighed and slung the briefcase over her shoulder. "We both have."

Dev smiled softly. "Come on. I'll walk you home."

CHAPTER SIX

*C*ome on, let me walk you home. Standing outside the high school on a late spring evening, Leslie regarded the flat tire on her mountain bike with disgust. She looked over her shoulder at Dev, who slouched against the base of a tall maple with both their backpacks looped over one arm. She wore ripped jeans, her motorcycle boots, of course, and the barest hint of a smile.

"You'd just better not laugh." Leslie almost pouted but caught herself. Dev *would* laugh then. "I can't believe I don't have a patch kit."

"You don't have a pump, either," Dev pointed out. "So it wouldn't do any good to fix the leak." She raised her eyebrows as she scanned Leslie's pale green slacks and low-heeled shoes. "And you're not exactly dressed for doing bicycle repairs."

"Ha ha." Leslie tugged on the sleeve of Dev's faded blue T-shirt. "You are. Don't you have something in your motorcycle bag you can fix this with?"

Dev laughed. "They're not exactly the same kind of tires, Les."

"I know that, *Devon*," Leslie said with a huff, but she was smiling. She knew Dev would change the tire for her if she had the equipment, and Leslie would probably let her, even though she could do it perfectly well herself. Dev liked doing things for her. Carrying her backpack and schoolbooks when they walked down to the lake. Fixing the lock on her locker when it kept jamming and the maintenance man kept forgetting to replace it. Dev had even shoveled the snow away from around the Jeep in the school parking lot one day last winter when Leslie had driven her parents' car to school and got snowed under. Leslie could've done all those things, but she could tell that Dev wanted to do it. And she liked seeing how happy it made Dev. It was weird, but it was nice too.

"So you know I don't have anything that will work on a bicycle tire," Dev said. "We should get going. It's going to get dark pretty soon."

"You don't have to come with me. You'll just have to walk all the way back for your motorcycle if you do."

"I don't mind." Dev glanced across the deserted school parking lot. "It's over a mile to your house, Les. I'm not letting you push your bike all the way there in the dark. Besides, you can't carry your books and—"

"I know! Give me a ride home on your motorcycle." Leslie grabbed Dev's hand. "We'll leave the bike chained up here and tomorrow I'll bring a patch kit and a pump and you can fix it."

For a minute, Leslie thought Dev was going to refuse. She had an odd look on her face, almost as if she was afraid of something, and her hand shook. Dev never let anything bother her. Leslie quirked her head. "Dev?"

"Sure. That'll work. Come on."

Leslie relocked her bike and followed Dev to her motorcycle. After Dev secured their books in her saddlebags, Dev climbed on and held out her hand to Leslie.

"Climb up behind me. Have you ever been on the back of a motorcycle before?"

"No."

"Just hold on to me and lean when I lean. Just stay tight to me, okay?"

"Okay. But let's go for a ride around the lake before you take me home. Do you have time?"

Dev hesitated again, then nodded. "Sure."

Leslie straddled the motorcycle behind Dev. It was wider than she'd realized and she had to lean forward against Dev's back to keep her balance. When the big engine roared to life, she wrapped both arms around Dev's waist. Dev jerked as if Leslie had surprised her.

"Is this right?" Leslie asked, her mouth close to Dev's ear.

"Yeah. It's great." Dev glanced over her shoulder at Leslie, and her eyes seemed impossibly dark. "You ready?"

Leslie nodded, feeling a tingling in her stomach as she leaned against Dev. Nerves, she guessed. When Dev pulled out of the parking lot and onto the road, the wind rushed around her so hard that she felt exposed to the world in an exciting and unexpectedly scary way. She pressed even closer to Dev, amazed at how strong Dev felt. Her waist was narrow and firm, her back broader than Leslie had expected and hard with muscle. Leslie rested her cheek between Dev's shoulder blades, letting their bodies move together, *and felt completely safe.*

"Do you want me to take this suitcase inside?" Dev asked, stopping at the end of the path to Leslie's cabin.

"No, I can get it. Thanks." Leslie took the luggage. "Do you know if there's Internet access in the cabins?"

Dev laughed. "Uh, Les? There isn't even a phone."

"Great," Leslie sighed. "I thought by now they'd have done that, at least. I guess I should be glad there's electricity and flush toilets."

"You've been living in the city too long. You're getting soft."

Leslie regarded Dev with indignation. "You obviously don't know anything about Manhattan."

Dev grinned. "True."

"Where *are* you living?"

"I've got a place up near the Finger Lakes. But I move around a lot for the job, so half the year I'm practically itinerant."

Leslie was curious about just what had finally captured Dev's interest, but it was almost 6 p.m. and unless things had changed drastically, her mother would have dinner ready for the family at seven thirty, right after she set out the buffet for the guests. If she was going to shower and catch a few minutes' sleep, she needed to go inside. Plus, being around Dev seemed to bring up things she hadn't thought of in years. On top of her fatigue, the memories were starting to make her feel as if she'd tripped into an alternate reality. What she needed was to check her e-mail and call the office. Then she'd start feeling more like herself.

"Well," Leslie said. "Thanks again."

"No problem."

In a few seconds, Dev disappeared into the trees and Leslie was alone. She carried her bags into the small, plain pine cabin and looked around. It was just as she remembered from her days of cleaning the units on weekends and during summers. One big room with a kitchenette against the rear wall and a bedroom partitioned off to one side. The tiny bathroom adjoined the bedroom, also in the rear. There was a fireplace on the left wall as she entered and a sofa flanked by chunky end tables facing it. Two large front windows overlooked the porch and the clearing and the path that led down to the lake.

Leslie put her briefcase on the coffee table in front of the sofa and dragged her luggage into the bedroom. The bed was somewhere between a single and a double in size, neatly made up with a chenille bedspread, the likes of which she hadn't seen since she'd been a teenager. She kicked off her shoes, draped her blazer over the back of a chair, and slid off her silk shell. The skirt went next and then her stockings. She stretched out on the bed in her bra and panties and closed her eyes. As she drifted off, she was distantly aware of a tingling in her stomach and the sensation of her breasts pressed against a firm body, the muscles rippling against her nipples.

Dev settled into a wooden deck chair on the front porch of her cabin with her laptop, intending to enter data while she still had some daylight left. She and Natalie had collected a fair number of samples the previous day and that morning. She worked a few minutes, then glanced to her left, squinting to see through the trees to the neighboring cabin. It was still impossible to believe that Leslie was over there right now.

Dev hoped she was taking a nap. Up close, she'd realized that Leslie was unhealthily thin, with tension etched into the tight lines around her eyes and mouth, and an aura of fragility surrounded her that seemed totally foreign. Leslie had always been feminine, that was true. Dev laughed. She actually used to think of her as girlie, in a really nice kind of way, but she'd also been athletic and fit. Leslie was a terrific swimmer, far more fluid in the water than Dev, who tended to power through rather than work with the waves. When they'd run into each other at the public beach, Leslie would almost always beat her when they'd race for the dock that floated a hundred yards offshore. Leslie would pull herself up onto the wooden platform, laughing as she looked down at Dev, the sun and water gleaming on her smooth, tanned flesh.

"Jesus, let it go," Dev muttered when she felt the old familiar ache of longing. "You were kids."

"They say it's dangerous to live alone in the woods," Natalie said, standing at the end of the path to Dev's cabin with her hands on her hips and a big grin. "I guess they're right, because you've only been here a couple of days and already you're talking to yourself."

"Hey," Dev said, quickly closing her spreadsheet and powering down the computer. When she glanced at her watch she realized she'd been daydreaming for the better part of an hour. It was already after seven. Natalie wore low-cut jeans, a short-sleeved red blouse with several buttons open at the top, and sandals. Her dark hair, which she kept tied up when in uniform, was loose and longer than Dev had thought. She looked...pretty. Very pretty. "I hope you keep that a secret. I swear I'm harmless."

"I'm not sure I believe that," Natalie said with a flirtatious smile. "But I promise not to tell anyone about your private vices."

Dev grinned and gave a little bow. "Thank you."

"Look, I hope you don't mind, I stopped by to see if you wanted to get something to eat, and Mrs. Harris told me which cabin was yours. Am I interrupting your work?"

"No, I was just inputting some data. Hold on a minute." She stepped back inside and put her computer on the end table. When she returned to the porch, Natalie was waiting for her, her back against one of the posts, the soft evening sunlight slanting across her face. At this distance, Dev saw that she'd applied a light touch of makeup. And she smelled wonderful. "I appreciate the dinner invite, but I told Mrs. Harris I'd have dinner at the lodge tonight. I've been here almost a week and I haven't yet, so I hate to back out. I'm really sorry."

Natalie shook her head. "That's okay. I just took a chance that you might be free. Some other night?"

"Absolutely. Come on, I'll walk you back to the lodge." As they strolled down the path, Dev said, "I want to spend a few days out on the islands collecting samples at eight-hour intervals. Do you have camping gear I can borrow?"

"Sure. I'll take care of getting the permits."

"Can you try to keep a few campsites right next to me empty?"

Natalie nodded. "It's still early in the season, so that won't be a problem. In fact, depending on where you go, you may be the only one on the island."

"That's great."

"When are you going?"

"Actually, I'd like to go next week to collect the first set of samples and then again at least once later in the summer."

"I'll take care of it."

"Great, I'll give you a list—" Dev broke off as Leslie came down the path from her cabin. She saw Leslie's eyes go from her to Natalie and register surprise before Leslie's expression quickly became unreadable. "Hi, Les."

"Hello."

Natalie smiled and gave a half wave. "Evening."

"Leslie, this is Natalie Evans. She's a park ranger. Natalie, Leslie Harris."

Natalie extended her hand. "I'd guess you're Eileen's daughter. You look like her."

"So I've been told. Nice to meet you."

The three continued toward the lodge in silence, Leslie quickening her pace so that by the time they neared the lodge, she was well ahead, leaving Natalie and Dev alone.

"Was it something I said?" Natalie asked.

Dev stared after Leslie, trying to decipher her attitude. She seemed angry, but Dev had no idea why. "I don't think so. At any rate, I wouldn't worry about it."

"Well, I don't want to keep you from dinner, Dev," Natalie said when they stopped at the foot of the walkway to the house. "How about I swing by and pick you up in the morning. Say seven o'clock?"

"That sounds fine. Sorry about dinner."

Natalie rested her hand on Dev's shoulder and stood on tiptoe to kiss her cheek. Her voice was low, throaty, when she said, "I'll take a rain check."

"Deal."

Dev waved goodbye as Natalie crossed the parking lot and climbed into her SUV, then turned toward the house. She was surprised to see Leslie standing on the porch. She hadn't noticed her before and wondered if she'd been there the entire time.

"Your friend was welcome to stay," Leslie said. *More than just friend, it looks like.*

Dev joined Leslie. "Thanks, that's nice of you. Maybe some other time, then."

"My parents are big fans of all the park employees." Leslie turned abruptly and walked into the house, her words trailing behind her. "I'm sure they'd love her."

Leslie crossed through the entryway that opened into an L-shaped room with the great room off to the right and the dining room ahead. A buffet was set out on several tables along the far wall. She nodded to the guests sitting at the small square tables scattered through the room before pushing through the swinging doors at the rear into the kitchen. Beyond the cooking and prep area, an archway led to a combination sitting/dining room on the adjacent screened-in back porch. That was where she'd always taken her meals with her family. Her mother was at the stove now, stirring something that smelled wonderful.

"Hi, sweetie," Eileen said, glancing over her shoulder.

"Is Daddy home?" Leslie asked.

"Down at the boat dock. He'll be up in a few minutes."

"Is there any wine?"

"I just opened some. White okay?"

"Yes, thanks."

Eileen smiled as Dev entered the kitchen. "Hi. Just make yourself comfortable out on the porch. Something to drink?"

"Whatever everyone else is having. Can I do anything?"

"Yes," Eileen said as she handed Dev and Leslie each a glass of wine. "Keep Leslie company while I finish in here."

Leslie and Dev sat in two wicker porch chairs with floral print cushions and watched the sun go down over the lake. Dev brushed her hand over the fabric, thinking how some things never changed. Her parents had had the same chairs on their small back porch behind the store. They'd had a small bit of land running down to the lake too, and that was where she'd spent most of her time, reading or daydreaming on the rickety, narrow dock.

"What is it exactly that you do, Dev," Leslie asked, breaking the silence.

"My original focus was population dynamics among freshwater fish." She grinned when Leslie's eyebrows rose. "I know. Sounds sort of bizarre, doesn't it?"

"Just a little." Leslie laughed. "I take it that led to other things."

"Believe it or not, it has some practical application. I study the effects of environmental pollutants on freshwater marine life. Mostly the fish, but also the other water life as well."

Leslie felt herself slide into that place of perfect emotional control where nothing showed on the outside. She couldn't remember when she'd learned to do that, but it was one of the big reasons she'd advanced so quickly in the law. No matter what she was feeling, no matter how unexpected the turn of events, nothing in her expression or her tone of voice or her body posture ever gave her away. "So you work for the state? Is that how you know the park ranger?"

"No, I'm a private consultant." Dev stretched, enjoying the wine and the warmth and Leslie's company. "Right now, I'm at the Derrin Freshwater Institute in Bolton in a short-term research position. But I do a lot of work with the Department of Environmental Conservation when there are concerns about industrial contamination. That sort of thing."

"I see."

Dev heard the chill in Leslie's voice. "What?" Half joking, she said, "Are you opposed to protecting the environment?"

"No," Leslie said carefully, "I'm primarily opposed to the government forcing unnecessary regulations with unproven results on private industry."

"The government forcing…" Dev set her glass aside and regarded Leslie intently. "What kind of law do you practice, Les?"

"I defend corporate clients, mostly."

Dev was aware that Eileen had joined them, standing quietly off to one side of the room. The tension had ratcheted up until it was visible in the air. "Like the kind that violate EPA regulations."

"Yes," Leslie said, standing, "on occasion." She smiled thinly at her mother. "I'm going to walk down to the lake and tell Dad it's time for dinner."

Dev rose as well, watching Leslie go, her wine forgotten. She was trying to come to terms with the fact that the young woman she had loved had turned out to be someone she didn't know at all.

"Have you and Leslie met before?" Eileen asked. "Before today, I mean."

"No," Dev said, then caught herself. *This* woman was a stranger to her, despite their past. "We knew each other in high school. But things were different then."

So very very different.

CHAPTER SEVEN

Naked on top of the sheets, Dev turned onto her back and stared at the ceiling. Though the windows were open, there was very little breeze and the room was warm. She couldn't sleep, but it wasn't because of the heat. She kept replaying the events of the day. She'd picked up Leslie at the train station less than ten hours ago, and now she couldn't stop thinking about things she had assiduously avoided recalling for fifteen years. Memories were deceptive, she knew that. The sun always shone brighter, the water was always bluer, the pleasure always so much more poignant when viewed from afar. But even the ache of betrayal and abandonment had not tarnished the simple truth of what she'd felt, and what she'd tried so hard to forget.

The room was suddenly too small to contain the images that assaulted her. Leslie sitting on the bank of the lake beneath fresh spring pines, her cheek resting on the top of her bent knees, her face soft as she confided her dreams. Leslie curled up beside her on a bench in the park, listening intently as Dev told her about a book she'd read or how she planned to dress out her motorcycle as soon as she had the money. Leslie laughing and nudging her shoulder, trying to get Dev to crack a smile when she was pretending to be cool. Leslie that last night, reaching for her, moaning into her mouth, burning her alive with kisses.

"Christ," Dev muttered, jumping from bed. She couldn't believe that a kiss she'd shared with a teenager could arouse her now, but it did. She was wet and throbbing and seconds away from reaching down for relief. Somehow, the idea of climaxing to the image of a woman, no, a *girl*, who no longer existed seemed wrong.

She fumbled in the dark for jeans and a T-shirt and pulled them on without bothering to find underwear. She stepped into the boots she'd left by the door and started down the path to the lake with the moonlight as her guide. The water was black as it always was at night, an onyx surface that glistened beneath a sky gleaming with stars. The water lapped gently inches from her feet, a soothing sound like the murmur of lovers in the dark. Dev took a deep breath and smelled pine sap and rich earth.

The tension in her chest and groin began to ease. She remembered who she was, where she was, and she remembered, too, how that long-ago kiss had ended. The phantom passion, like the taunting memory of a lost limb, might refuse to die, but she did not need to breathe life into it.

She took another deep breath and turned to go back to the cabin. Out of the corner of her eye, she caught a flicker of light from a hundred feet away. The lake curved inward to form a tiny bay just below the lodge, and the boathouse, almost as large as the lodge itself, extended out into the water. Dev stared, wondering if the light she'd seen had just been moonlight glinting off the water, but then she saw it again, shining for an instant through one of the windows in the center of the building.

It was probably one of the guests, suffering from insomnia like herself, or a pair of lovers looking for a private place to share their passion. But as she watched the light glimmer in one window and then the next, she started walking toward it.

The air was still and quiet, unlike the last time she'd approached the boathouse, and when she stepped inside, the music played only in her memory. Still, the shadows undulated as if those long-ago dancers had left their energy and their desires behind. As on that last night, she had only one destination. When she reached the far end of the room, she wasn't surprised to see Leslie perched on the windowsill, her head tilted back and her eyes closed. The wash of moonlight erased the years from her face, and Dev gasped as the old familiar connection punched through her.

Leslie turned her head and regarded the dim figure standing by her side. "Hello, Dev."

"Hi, Les," Dev said, her throat raspy. "Couldn't sleep?"

"No. You?"

Dev shook her head.

"I'm sorry about dinner," Leslie said.

"What do you mean?" Dev leaned her shoulder against the window frame opposite Leslie. A few inches of hot summer air and a heart full of broken dreams separated them.

"It couldn't have been pleasant for you trying to eat with all that tension in the room." Leslie shrugged. "I'd forgotten why I don't visit very often. My parents don't approve of me."

"I got the impression they didn't approve of your *job*," Dev said, recalling just how carefully Leslie and her parents had tiptoed around anything that broached upon Leslie's life in Manhattan or her career. Instead, Eileen and Paul Harris, a tall, thin quiet man, had questioned Dev with enthusiasm about the Institute and her work for the Department of Environmental Conservation.

"Is there a difference?" Leslie couldn't quite keep the bitterness from her voice. "After all, we are what we do."

"Why do you do it?" Dev asked mildly.

"Because I'm good at it."

Dev laughed. "I bet. But, I mean…what made you decide to do it? What made you change your plans?"

Leslie hesitated, sorting through any number of answers that would suffice while revealing nothing personal. Personal revelation was not something she did lightly. If she was honest, it wasn't something she did at all. And she was very good at deflecting conversations that verged too close to the intimate. "You first."

"Me? All right." Dev paused, giving the issue serious thought. "I've always liked fish."

"That's not an answer," Leslie said, but she couldn't help smiling.

"Actually, it's the truth. When I finally started studying, I realized how much there was to learn about the things I saw every day. The lake is part of me, I guess." Dev sighed. "And the fish, well, besides creating interesting social orders, they're beautiful."

"You make it sound romantic," Leslie said seriously.

"I wouldn't go that far," Dev said, thinking that romance was something *she'd* changed her mind about since last they'd met. "Your turn."

"Remember how I used to hate math?"

Dev nearly gasped at the unexpected twist of pain. She wondered how Leslie imagined she could forget anything that had happened between them. "Yeah. I remember."

"I thought it was because I didn't have a logical mind. You know, back then I wanted to work outside, tend the land, that kind of thing. That was probably me channeling my parents' dreams." Leslie swiveled on the wide window ledge and swung her legs outside the building to dangle in the moonlight. "Once I got away, got exposed to other things, I discovered that I was actually very good at dissecting complex issues. I also have a knack for finding flaws in arguments."

"So you got interested in the law." Dev spoke carefully, recalling how defensive Leslie had seemed earlier when the subject of her work had come up. "So what about the rest of it? Why the kind of law that you practice?"

"I like competition." Leslie glanced at Dev. "It's just a big chess game."

"You *were* always good at that, but…defending big businesses that operate with no concern for what they might be doing to anyone else? Jesus, Les."

"The simple answer is that everyone is entitled to the best defense possible, including corporations." Leslie slid off the windowsill. "But it's not that simple, Dev. Sure, some of the regulations are reasonable, even if they are almost prohibitively costly to implement. But even my parents, if they just thought about it, would admit that government intrusion in the private sector isn't always the answer. In fact, sometimes it just creates more problems."

Dev caught Leslie's arm as she turned her back to walk away. "Look, I'm sorry."

"For what?" Leslie snapped. "Clearly, you and my parents are on the side of the angels. And I've sided with the devil."

"It's not my place to judge you. Or theirs either."

"Well, thank you very much for that."

Dev couldn't see Leslie's face in the shadows, but she could feel her shaking. Underneath the anger was pain, and Dev felt it as if it were her own. She slid her hand along Leslie's forearm until she reached her hand and squeezed Leslie's fingers before letting go. "I didn't mean to bring up a sensitive subject."

"Forget it." Leslie stepped close to the window again and curled her fingers around the sill. She leaned out and let the breeze cool the heat of anger from her face. "What are you doing out here anyway?"

"I saw the light. What are you doing down here?"

"Trying to figure out why the hell I came home."

A hint of Leslie's perfume drifted to Dev. She had no idea what it was, but it smelled like Leslie. Sharp and hot, with a hint of sadness just beneath the surface. "Your mother said your visit was sudden. Does it have something to do with that intravenous line and the *flu*?"

Leslie's head whipped around as she stared at Dev. "You haven't changed. You always did see everything."

"I've changed, Les. But it didn't take any great deductive skill to figure out something's wrong. You almost fainted on the porch this afternoon." Dev lifted Leslie's hand and unerringly brushed her thumb over the exact spot where the intravenous line had been. "You got this in a hospital."

Leslie was stunned by how much Dev had noticed. She was even more shocked to find herself telling Dev the whole story. "So," she said when she'd finished, "I didn't really think things through very well. I knew if I stayed in the city I'd end up going into the office, and then I'd have to make excuses about cutting back for a while. I suppose I just wanted to preserve my privacy."

"Thanks for telling me," Dev said.

"You could always get me to tell you everything."

"No, not everything." Dev realized she was still holding Leslie's hand and that she had the unbearable desire to brush her lips over the bruise. She wanted to make that visible sign of Leslie's frailty disappear. She wanted to erase the tension in Leslie's face, wipe out the strain in her voice. And because she wanted to touch her so badly, she gently released her hand. "Did you tell your parents?"

"No. They'd only worry. Besides, it's not a big deal."

"When are you going to get the tests?"

"I don't know, Dev," Leslie said impatiently. "I have to call and schedule them." The whole thing was becoming more absurd by the moment. Running home, as if there were something here she needed. Telling Dev, a stranger, the details of this ridiculous illness, when she hadn't even explained it all to her lover. Rachel. God, she hadn't even thought to call her and tell her she'd arrived. Her whole life was badly out of focus. "I need some air. I'm going for a walk."

"Les, it's one o'clock in the morning."

"We're out in the middle of nowhere, Devon. It's perfectly safe."

"You don't know that." Dev followed Leslie outside. "You have a flashlight, don't you? That's what I saw blinking through the window. You'll need it in the woods."

"Yes, but I don't want every moth and mosquito in five miles to hone in on me. I can see well enough to walk back to the cabin along the lake. That's the way I came."

Unasked, Dev fell into step beside her as Leslie started along the shore path. After a moment, she said, "Promise you'll call about the tests tomorrow."

"I'm going into our Albany office tomorrow. Once I work out my schedule, I'll call about the damn tests."

"I thought you were supposed to be taking it easy. Isn't that why you're here?"

Leslie laughed shortly. "Believe me, anything I might be doing up here *will* be a vacation."

"Why don't you come out with me instead," Dev said on impulse. "I can guarantee it will be relaxing."

"You want me to help you collect fish?" Leslie stopped dead and flicked her flashlight into Dev's face. At Dev's protest, she switched it off. "I just wanted to make sure you didn't look as completely crazy as you sound."

"Why not? You're supposed to cut down on stress, right? So come out on the lake and get some sun. That'll probably be just what you need to kick this thing."

Leslie had to agree that made some sense. And oddly enough, she didn't really want to go into the office the next day. Being home, seeing Dev again, had brought back vivid images of all the things she'd loved about the lake in the summer. The lush, wild beauty of the mountains and the clear, brisk promise of the lake under the summer sun had always called to her.

"Besides," Dev went on, "I'm not collecting fish. I'm collecting water, soil, and organic samples. Natalie's been helping with the records when she can get free, but she's got her own work to do. You can keep notes."

"Now I know you're nuts. My secretarial skills are somewhat lacking," Leslie said dryly.

"That's okay," Dev said, feeling unaccountably lighthearted as they jested like old times. "I'll help you get the hang of it."

"Oh, thanks." Leslie was tempted. One day off wouldn't seriously cut into her productivity. *Natalie's been helping out...*

"All right. Tomorrow?"

"I don't suppose early hours bother you, do they?"

Leslie snorted.

"How about seven, then? I'll call Natalie in the morning and tell her she's got a reprieve."

"Come to breakfast at six thirty," Leslie said, wondering if Natalie would consider not spending the day with Dev any kind of bonus.

"Okay."

They'd reached the juncture of the shore path and the wooded trail that led up to the cabins. Leslie switched on her flashlight, but the batteries she'd found in the kitchen drawer must have been old, because the cone of light was very faint. She reached out in the darkness and found Dev's hand. With their shoulders and arms lightly touching, they climbed up through the woods.

"Should I walk you down? It's pretty dark," Leslie said at the turnoff to her cabin.

"I'm okay. There's plenty of moon."

Leslie hesitated, reluctant to say good night. Dev's hand was warm in hers and the sound of her voice in the dark was like a soft caress. She tightened inside and heat flared for an instant before she ruthlessly forced it down. God, what was she thinking? But that was just it, she wasn't thinking at all, and her body was clearly in some kind of crazy rebellion. She spoke carefully, wanting to be certain that her voice was steady.

"I'll see you in the morning, then."

"Good night, Les." Dev released Leslie's hand and made herself step away. She didn't want to move. The palm of her hand where Leslie had just touched her felt naked, exposed, as if the skin were missing. She took another step and then another and when she reached the trees that separated the clearings around their cabins, she waited until she heard Leslie's footsteps on the porch and the sound of the door opening and closing quietly.

"Sweet dreams," she whispered into the night.

Then she slowly made her way back to her cabin, stripped off her clothes, and lay down on the bed. The room had cooled, but her body was too warm even for the light cotton sheet. She closed her eyes and prayed she wouldn't dream.

Fifty yards away, Leslie sat on the side of her bed, still fully dressed, and pressed Rachel's number on the speed dial. She wasn't surprised when her call was directed to voicemail. She closed her eyes and tried to conjure Rachel's face. It was difficult.

"Rach, hi, it's me. I'm here." She hesitated, trying to remember Rachel's schedule. Was it really just a day since they'd talked?

"I'm sure you nailed the closing. Have a drink for me to celebrate."

She paused again, aware of the silence stretching between them, far deeper than just the seconds ticking away. She took a breath. "I miss you."

She wanted that to be true and hoped that the reason it felt like a lie was just because she was so damn tired. Without even bothering to undress, she kicked off her shoes and curled up on the bed. When she closed her eyes, she heard the echo of long-ago laughter on the wind.

CHAPTER EIGHT

Y ou're up early," Eileen Harris said when Leslie poked her head into the kitchen a little after six the next morning.

"Not really," Leslie said. "I'm usually in the office by now. Do I smell coffee?"

Eileen pulled a tray of scones from the oven and inclined her head toward an insulated carafe on a nearby counter. "If you wouldn't mind, carry that out into the dining room for the guests. I'll put on another pot for us."

"Sure. Thanks."

When Leslie returned, her mother slid a plate with a steaming scone onto the scarred wooden kitchen table and handed her a mug of coffee. "Still like blueberry?"

"Yes," Leslie said, settling at the table with her coffee. She broke open the pastry and reached for the butter. "But they never taste the same from the bakery."

Eileen smiled. "I thought you might sleep in, seeing how you're on vacation. Going fishing? Your dad's down at the dock."

"I am, but not that kind. I'm going out with Dev while she collects some samples."

"Really," Eileen said carefully. "You two seem to have hit it off. I didn't realize you knew each other."

"She was a year behind me in school. Her parents ran the convenience store in Diamond Point."

"Weber's. Of course, I remember them, but for some reason, I don't remember her. I thought I knew all your friends."

"She wasn't part of that crowd," Leslie said.

"We're just going to hang out down at the boathouse," Leslie said, watching Dev stow her gear in her motorcycle bag. The sounds of car engines revving and friends shouting to one another surrounded them. "Just come for a while. It's just girls."

Dev shook her head. "I don't think so, Les. I should get home. My parents will probably need me in the store."

"It's still early. Just for an hour," Leslie wheedled. For some reason, she really wanted Dev to come to her house after school. It was hard to duck her other friends all the time, and sometimes days would go by before she could see Dev alone for a walk or for a few private minutes just to talk. In a couple of weeks, she'd be graduating and summer would start. Dev would be working in the store more and she'd be helping her parents at the lodge. It might be even harder to see her then. If Dev would only socialize with the rest of Leslie's friends, Leslie could see her more. She missed her when she didn't see her. "Please, Dev."

"Come on, Les. You'll probably all be sitting around talking about makeup or guys."

"I promise I won't mention Mike once within your hearing." When Dev's expression tightened and she looked away, Leslie felt a surge of alarm. Dev was so sensitive, and it was so hard to tell sometimes what she'd said wrong. She hurried on, wanting to make Dev smile again. "I promise. We'll play some pool or something."

Dev shot her a look. "Since when?"

"Hey!" Leslie grinned and slapped Dev's arm. "I can play. I'm damn good at it."

Laughing, Dev caught Leslie's wrist, and when Leslie took another playful swing at her with her free hand, she caught that one too. "And what will we do after I beat you in ten minutes?"

"Oh, you think?" Leslie gave Dev a teasing shove, and when Dev stumbled back in surprise, still holding Leslie's wrists, Leslie lost her balance too and fell into her. They ended up in a tangle, half sprawled over the wide tank of Dev's motorcycle, Dev on the bottom with Leslie's stomach and thighs pressed against her, Leslie's hands on Dev's shoulders. Their faces were inches apart. Leslie could feel Dev breathing hard under her, as if she'd been running for a long time. Dev was only an inch or so shorter than Mike, and her body felt nearly as hard, except where her small breasts just grazed Leslie's. Leslie felt the tingling again, like she had the week before when she'd ridden on the back of Dev's motorcycle, their bodies pressed close together. Except she wasn't nervous this time. This was Dev, and she had nothing to fear. So close like this, she could see that Dev's eyes were more green today, probably because the sunlight slanted into them, making them glow. Leslie watched, fascinated, as Dev's pupils widened and her lips parted soundlessly. She felt hands skim her waist.

"You ought to get up, Les," Dev said unsteadily, "before we tip the bike over."

Leslie didn't want to move. Her breathing had speeded up, and her heart seemed to race at the same pace as the pulse that hammered along Dev's tanned neck. The May sunshine warmed the backs of her bare legs, but she was warmer still inside. Lazy and liquid and warm, like sugar bubbling on the stove. Beneath her, Dev shivered. "Dev. What—?"

Her voice came out thick and she wondered if she'd be able to stand up. Her legs felt so heavy. She began to tremble.

Sounding almost panicked, Dev said more sharply, "Leslie. Get off." She grasped Leslie's hips and pushed her away as she levered herself into a standing position. "I gotta go."

Leslie stared in an unfamiliar daze as Dev straddled her bike, kicked the engine over, and roared away, leaving Leslie lonely *in a way she'd never experienced.*

"Leslie," Eileen Harris said, giving Leslie a concerned look. "Are you feeling all right?"

"What?" Leslie said, looking around the kitchen as if she'd never seen it before. She blinked and the past receded. "Sure. Just daydreaming."

Eileen rinsed her hands in the sink and dried them on a dish towel. "I guess Devon wasn't exactly the kind of girl who would have fit in very well back then."

Leslie's eyes narrowed. "What do you mean by that?"

"I didn't mean anything negative by it," Eileen said, clearly surprised by the heat in Leslie's voice. "She's obviously intelligent and very nice. She just seems…well, I can't picture her as a girl interested in the things you and your friends—"

"Thanks, Mom," Leslie said, rising quickly. She stalked to the sink and flung the dregs of her coffee into it before banging the cup down on the counter. "You make the rest of us sound like we were airheads who spent all our time fixing our hair and gossiping."

Eileen's eyebrows rose. "I wasn't judging you or your friends, I just meant that she seems different."

"Different?" Leslie folded her arms over her chest. "Different from who? Who you *think* we were or who we really were? Did you even have any idea who I was?"

"I thought so," Eileen said quietly. "At least as much as you let me know."

"Me?" Leslie wanted to pace. More than that, she wanted to scream. That was the moment she realized she was losing control, and she very deliberately shut the door on her anger and her hurt. It was as if a cold wind blew through her, obliterating the emotions that threatened to cloud her judgment and disturb the balance she prided herself on having. "This is a ridiculous conversation. Those things are long past, and whatever either of us did or didn't do doesn't matter anymore."

Eileen poured herself a cup of coffee. Quietly, she said, "Do you really believe that?"

"Believe what?" Leslie said, comfortable now that reason ruled. She and her mother had this kind of conversation every time they were in the same room together for more than an hour. Since the day she'd left for college, something critical in their relationship had changed. They couldn't agree on anything anymore.

"That things left undone, unresolved, don't haunt us. That we can just walk away from the past as if it never happened?" Eileen's voice was pensive, tinged with sadness. But there was no challenge, no accusation.

"I know that people change, everything changes. We are who we are now." What she didn't add was *strangers.*

"Well, it might be nice to get acquainted again."

Part of Leslie wanted to believe that, and part of her wondered how to begin. She wasn't even sure she wanted to try. "You should finish making breakfast. All the guests will be clamoring at the door in a minute. Why don't I help."

"You can get the eggs out of the refrigerator," Eileen said, turning back to the stove and sliding a large skillet over the gas burners. "Ever hear from Mike?"

Leslie froze with the door to the refrigerator half open. "No. Why?"

"He lives in the area and we see him from time to time. He always asks about you."

"I don't think we'd have anything in common any longer."

Eileen slit the plastic on a pound of bacon and lay strips in a cast-iron pan. "Are you seeing anyone special?"

There it was, the opening that Leslie needed to tell her mother just how little she actually knew of her. She realized that her mother was just making casual conversation, and not probing for private information. The decision was hers—reveal herself, or preserve the comfortable distance she had created between herself and her family, and by extension, all that had existed up until the day she'd left for college.

"I'm seeing someone," Leslie said, wondering how to characterize her relationship with Rachel. Not exactly serious? That wasn't quite true. It was exclusive and reasonably long term, so didn't that make it serious? On the surface it seemed that way, but that wasn't how it felt. In fact, the only word that came to mind was *casual*. Well, it wasn't necessary to examine all the details, when only one was truly relevant. "A woman."

The fork in her mother's hand stilled above the pan of sizzling bacon for just a second, then she resumed turning the meat. "Is that something recent?" She looked at Leslie over her shoulder. "I never realized you were interested in women that way."

You never told me. The accusation hung in the air and Leslie carefully edged around it. Trying to explain why she'd never mentioned it meant revisiting events and feelings that had no place in her life now. She slid the cardboard carton of eggs onto the counter next to her mother. "I've known for a few years. Since college."

"That's quite a long time now," Eileen said, the hurt evident in her tone.

"I guess it is." Leslie sighed, knowing she'd added another disappointment. "It just never seemed to come up."

"But this is what you want? You're happy?"

Happy. Why was that the word that everyone used to define what mattered? As if that were all that anyone should strive for, some fleeting, irrational, and often false emotion. "It's who I am." She refilled her coffee cup and started toward the door. "I'm going to skip breakfast. I'll see you later." She didn't wait for her mother's reply.

Dev carried a plate laden with scones, scrambled eggs, and bacon in one hand and a cup of coffee in the other. Watching the path from the cabins for Leslie, she settled into a wicker chair on the front porch and balanced the plate on her knee.

She jumped when a voice behind her said, "You eat like a lumberjack."

"It's the air. Whenever I'm in the mountains, my appetite triples." Dev grinned up at Leslie, who was backlit in the morning sunlight. All she could see was her silhouette and the halo of gold around her face. She was angled so that the dark, smooth curve of her breast arced above the plane of her body, reminding Dev of the mountains rising above the lake. She swallowed, her hunger suddenly shifting to something far more primal than breakfast. "You eat already?"

Leslie settled onto the substantial porch railing and wrapped one arm around the smooth column that rose to the roof. She sipped her second cup of coffee. "Yes."

Somehow, Dev had a suspicion that coffee was Leslie's main breakfast staple. She wore jeans, a short-sleeved boat-neck T-shirt, and sneakers. Although her dress was more relaxed than the day before, nothing else about her was. Her body still looked like an overly tight spring. Dev could nearly hear the tension humming in the air around her.

"Have you been waiting long?" Dev asked, since she'd arrived precisely at 6:30 a.m. She hadn't seen Leslie inside.

"I got here a half an hour ago or so. Then I went for a walk down to the lake."

Dev tried a scone, which was delicious, and sipped her coffee. "I'll be finished in a few minutes and we can get going."

"There's no hurry. We're on your schedule today."

"No schedule. What we don't get done today, we'll do tomorrow. Or the next day."

Leslie shook her head. "Interesting approach."

Dev grinned. "Probably not what you're used to."

"No." Leslie scanned the house, then followed a couple as they came out the front door and disappeared down the path with their arms around one another. She blocked out the image. "Not exactly."

"Something happen this morning?" Dev asked quietly.

"No. Why?"

"I just wondered if you were always this uptight, or if something special caused it."

"I'm not uptight." Leslie frowned, thinking of all the work she had left unfinished and the fact that she was essentially blowing it off to follow Dev around. "I'm just not used to inactivity."

"I don't suppose you have one of those do-it-yourself blood-pressure kits, do you?"

"What?" Leslie stared. "What are you talking about?"

Dev slid her plate onto the table next to her chair and stood. "I think you should get one. I bet your blood pressure is through the roof right now."

"I bet it will be if you keep being so irritating," Leslie snapped, sliding off the railing. "I didn't tell you about my little problem so you could badger me."

"I'm sorry." Dev resisted the urge to catch Leslie's wrist as she stalked to the steps. "It's not my business."

Leslie turned at the foot of the stairs and looked back up, shading her eyes in the glare. "You're right. It isn't. Are you ready to go?"

"Let me take my dishes inside and I will be."

When Dev rejoined Leslie a minute later, she said, "Your mother asked if we wanted lunch packed, but I told her we'd probably be back by then. She said to tell you to have a good time."

Leslie sighed as they started toward the parking lot. "I told her I was going out with you this morning. I hope you don't mind."

"Why would I?" Dev unlocked the passenger door to her truck for Leslie.

"Some people value their privacy. Besides, you didn't used to be this social."

Dev walked to the driver's side and got in as Leslie climbed in next to her. She slid the key into the ignition but didn't start it. Instead, she turned in the seat to face Leslie, who regarded her with faint suspicion. "That was a long time ago, Les. And I didn't have a lot in common with most of my peers."

"Makeup and boys," Leslie murmured.

"What?"

Leslie shook her head. "Never mind."

"Maybe this isn't such a good idea," Dev said quietly. "I thought spending a few hours out on the lake might be fun for you, but I just seem to be adding to your aggravation. I don't want to spoil your vacation."

"It isn't you."

"I'm the only one here."

"I had one of those mother-daughter moments this morning," Leslie said, the words pushing out as if they'd been under pressure to escape. "A few moments, actually. I told my mother I was a lesbian."

Dev stiffened and for an instant, she felt dizzy. She gripped the steering wheel and waited for the world to stop spinning. It was the last thing she'd expected to hear. It hurt her head, broke her heart all over again, just to hear the words. Leslie had turned from her, rejected her, wiped out everything they'd ever shared, because Leslie hadn't wanted her. Because Leslie hadn't felt what she felt. Because Dev had been wrong, different, queer. She'd lived with that eating away inside her until she'd buried it, all of it. And now the past rose up to mock her hard-won victory. How could it be that Leslie was a lesbian?

Dev reached down and turned the ignition, but her legs shook so badly she couldn't step on the gas. The engine idled.

The silence in the cab was stifling. Leslie saw the blood drain from Dev's face, and she wondered if Dev felt as her mother did, that the past was a ghost that haunted the present until the injustices were atoned for. Some of their ghosts, Dev's and hers—perhaps all of them—were shared, and she had no idea how to exorcise them. When Dev finally turned to stare at her, her eyes held more sorrow than Leslie could bear. Knowing she was the cause, she had to look away. "I didn't know, Dev."

"It's not your fault," Dev whispered.

Leslie shook her head and forced herself to face Dev. "It was. You know it was."

"Les—"

"You almost died, Dev. Because of me."

CHAPTER NINE

*T*he *fog had rolled in* off the water, as it often did in the mountains, and the combination of the haze and the pain and the beer made it so hard to focus on the narrow sliver of blacktop that flickered in and out of Dev's sight. Her side ached like a bad cramp from running too hard and too far, the beer rolled around in her stomach in search of a way out, and she hurt. God, how she hurt. The echo of Leslie's words shredded her heart. *She's nothing to me. She's nobody.*

Dev blinked back tears, but her vision was no clearer. She burned with hot shame and guilt for what she'd done. She hadn't meant to. She hadn't meant to kiss her. Not even to touch her. *No. Not true.* She could admit it now, couldn't she? After what she'd done. She'd wanted to touch her. For so long. She hadn't thought of anything else for months except seeing Leslie, being close to her, stealing accidental touches. She thought of nothing but her smile. *Not true. Stop lying.* She thought about her eyes, how soft they got when Leslie was telling her some special secret. She thought about the curve of her lips, the way they parted in surprise and grew moist when she laughed. She thought about her breasts, the way they rose beneath her T-shirt and swayed just a little in her bathing suit.

Dev choked back a groan and revved the engine harder. She knew the road by heart, she didn't need to see it. She leaned into the turns, so low her knee nearly dragged over the road surface. *Admit it. Tell the truth.* She'd thought about Leslie's breasts, and her hips, and what lay between her thighs. She'd thought about touching her there while she'd touched herself. At first she hadn't understood, had pretended not to recognize what she felt. But after a while, she couldn't pretend that the ache in the pit of her stomach and the hot hard longing between her legs wasn't because of Leslie.

Tears streamed from her eyes. *She's nothing to me.* Distantly, she heard the sound of an engine roaring. Bright lights slashed into the fog, blinding her. She torpedoed into the first curve of an S-turn hard and fast, fighting to keep the big machine upright. She hurt. She felt sick. The roaring sound was inside her.

Metal screamed over the pavement, showers of sparks flared like fireworks on the Fourth of July, and she was burning. Burning with shame. Burning with pain. *Burning with the unspeakable agony of loss.*

Dev bolted from the truck and made it as far as the trees at the edge of the parking lot before she vomited. Shivering, she leaned with one arm against the rough bark and fought down the next swell of nausea.

"Oh my God, Dev!" Leslie skidded to a stop a few feet away, afraid to touch her. "Dev, what—"

Not turning around, Dev waved her off. "Go away. I'm okay." She didn't feel okay. She felt like her legs might give out. She hadn't felt anything like this since she'd come to in the hospital three days after the accident. Even then, her body had been so wracked with pain, she hadn't felt the excruciating wrench of betrayal until weeks later. Then it had seemed unending.

"I'm sorry," Leslie said miserably. "God, I didn't mean— If I'd known, I wouldn't have told you."

"It's not because of what you said." Dev wiped her mouth on the back of her arm and slumped onto the grass a few feet away. She leaned against another tree and closed her eyes. "Bad memories. It's been a long, long time since it's been this bad."

Leslie caught her bottom lip between her teeth. She wanted to cry. Nothing, *nothing* ever made her want to cry. Not for years and years. Not like this, not from some place deep inside her where it felt as if wounds never healed and wrongs were never righted. She hurried down to the truck and pawed through the cooler Dev must have placed in the back earlier. She pulled out a soda, popped the top on her way back to Dev, and knelt down close to her. "Here. Coke."

"Thanks." Dev opened her eyes, took the soda, and drank half of it down. She caught a glimpse of Leslie's eyes, huge and filled with sorrow. Leslie was pale, and Dev wanted to stroke her cheek, wanted it as much as she had fifteen years before, and just as then, she knew she couldn't. "Don't go back there, Leslie. Don't hurt for the past."

"I let you ride off on that motorcycle," Leslie whispered. "I knew you shouldn't drive. I knew it was wrong. I let you go."

"I climbed onto that bike, Les." Dev finished her soda and crushed the empty can in her fist, resting it on top of her knee. "There's nobody responsible for that except me."

"I hurt you. I'm so sorry."

Dev shook her head. "You don't need to apologize for not feeling the way I felt. You didn't do anything wrong." Dev took a deep breath and hoisted herself up. "If you don't mind, I'm going back to the cabin and get cleaned up. Why don't we postpone our trip to the lake."

"Of course." Leslie stood, reminding herself they were adults now and what had been between them had ended on a dark night during the last moments of their innocence. "Are you all right? I can walk you back."

"No." Dev shook her head with a small smile. "I'm okay. I apologize for the little scene. That's not normal for me."

Leslie laughed humorlessly. "I don't quite know what's happening, but I haven't felt like myself since the moment I arrived."

"Well, don't let me add to your troubles. I never blamed you then. I certainly don't now."

Leslie watched her walk away, wondering if Dev realized that before she'd jumped from the truck she'd been crying. Tears that fell in silence, bridging the years as if they'd never passed. Leslie had wanted to brush them from her cheeks, but she'd been afraid to touch her, knowing instinctively that Dev was somewhere far away. Somewhere that Leslie could not join her, because she'd forfeited that right when she'd closed her eyes, closed her heart, and let Dev walk away alone, carrying the pain for both of them.

Dev was gone now, and Leslie was left wishing what she'd wished so many times since she'd finally admitted who she was. She wished she could take back the lies.

Her BlackBerry vibrated on her hip and she automatically scanned the readout. Rachel.

"Hi," Leslie said.

"I got your message. It's hell down here. The Dow Corning case finally got on the docket and I'm scrambling to get experts lined up. Of course, summer's coming and everyone is suddenly unavailable."

"Some people have a life," Leslie murmured as she walked down the long slope toward the water, scanning the shore for Dev's figure.

"What? Missed that. I'm in the parking garage."

"Nothing."

"You must be bored out of your mind by now."

Leslie laughed. "It's different."

"When are you coming home?"

Home. Leslie considered the word. She and Rachel didn't live together. They didn't share a home. Her condo, where she slept and ate and worked, felt like an extension of her office. If she had a home, it *was* her office. That's where she really lived. That's where she was the person she had become. She should leave. She should go back to being herself.

"I'm not sure yet."

"Well, keep me informed. Listen, darling, I have to run. Call me. Oh, how are you feeling?"

"I'm fine." Leslie wondered why lies so patently transparent were actually believed.

"Wonderful. Bye, darling."

"Yes. All right. Bye."

Leslie walked out onto the dock and sat on the edge in the sun. The water that lapped two feet beneath her was so clear she could see the sandy bottom. Schools of minnows darted just under the surface.

She heard Dev's voice. *I've always liked fish.*

"Oh, Dev. Why didn't I know?"

Dev looked up from where she knelt on the bank at the sound of footsteps behind her. She waved, feeling a bit of her melancholy lift when Natalie sauntered down the trail. She was in uniform, her cuffs buttoned neatly at the wrists, her name tag above her left breast pocket, various patches denoting department and rank sewn onto her sleeves. Her dark hair was twisted into a loose bun at the back of her neck and held with a plain gold clip. Her smile was radiant.

"Hey," Natalie said. "I thought that was your truck up there in the turnoff. Weren't you going out on the lake today?"

"Change in plans. I'm doing a little close-in work instead."

"Uh-huh." Natalie squatted down beside her. "You could've called me."

"Something tells me you have better things to do than babysit me. But thanks."

"Other things." Natalie skimmed her fingertips along Dev's jaw. "Definitely not better. How about I collect on that rain check tonight. Dinner?"

Dev hesitated. Natalie's message was clear. And honest. She owed her the same. "I think I'd be lousy company."

"You'd be surprised what a decent dinner and a good wine can do for your mood." Natalie stood, reaching for Dev's sample case as Dev collected the rest of her gear. "There's a nice little restaurant on the lake about ten miles north of here. Tables outside on a patio. Great view of the sunset."

Dev was tempted. She didn't look forward to an evening alone in her cabin with her thoughts because she couldn't be certain she could keep her mind off Leslie fifty yards away. She definitely did not want to have dinner at the lodge. "Dinner sounds good. There's one thing you need to know, though."

"Oh?"

"Besides the fact that I like you, it hasn't escaped my notice that you're very attractive."

"Good. I'm glad you noticed." Natalie smiled, and after a quick look over her shoulder, kissed Dev softly. "As I've mentioned, more or less, I happen to think you're very attractive too. As in keeping-me-awake-at-night attractive."

"I'm not sure going there's a good idea," Dev said.

"Dinner first," Natalie said easily. "After that we'll see."

"That okay with you?"

"Yes." Natalie nodded and ran her fingers up and down Dev's arm before stepping away. "It really is. I'll pick you up in an hour and a half."

"Okay," Dev said, taking her at her word. She waved goodbye as Natalie drove off, then loaded her gear and headed back to Lakeview. She circled around on the lake path so she could get to her cabin without passing in front of Leslie's. She didn't want to see her again for a while. Until she had time to get everything back where it belonged, safely locked away behind the walls she'd constructed.

❖

Six hours later, when she and Natalie walked hand in hand down the main path toward her cabin, Dev was pretty sure she'd succeeded in finding her balance again. The restaurant had been everything Natalie had promised. The food was excellent, the view breathtaking, and the weather had cooperated, remaining warm until well after sundown so that they were able to linger over dinner under the stars. The evening was still comfortable although cooling, and the moon nearly full, so she didn't need the flashlight she'd picked up from her truck when she and Natalie had returned.

As with every other time they'd spent together, it had been easy. Natalie was easy to talk to. Easy to laugh with. Very easy to look at.

Very easy to kiss, Dev thought as Natalie stopped her with a tug on her hand, then leaned into her and slid both arms around her neck. Natalie's mouth was soft and warm, her tongue a delicate tease along the edge of Dev's lips. Her breath was sweet, her body firm in the way of a well-toned athlete, yielding in the way of a woman. Natalie hummed an appreciative sound in the back of her throat and tightened her fingers in Dev's hair. The kiss ratcheted up a notch and Dev felt a trickle of warning. She eased her head back.

"We'll attract bears if we keep this up out here. Come up to the cabin and let me give you that nightcap I promised."

Natalie laughed. "We'll attract something, I suppose. Yes, let's get more comfortable."

Once inside, Dev went to the tiny kitchen and reached into the cabinet over the sink for the brandy she'd stored there. Natalie's arms came around her from behind and she felt the firm press of Natalie's breasts against her back. For just a second, she was back on the motorcycle with Leslie behind her. The memories were coming so hard and so fast in the last few days; she couldn't seem to stop them from streaming through her mind. Things she hadn't thought of in years felt as if they'd happened yesterday. She shivered.

"Dev?" Natalie stepped back and waited for Dev to turn. She regarded Dev quizzically. "You just went somewhere, didn't you?"

"How did you know?"

"I felt it."

"Sorry."

"Like I said. Dinner. And after that we'll see." Natalie held out her hand for the brandy. "Let's go outside and toast the moon."

"Yeah," Dev said. "Let's do that."

"I probably should've asked this before now," Natalie said as they sat side by side on the top step of Dev's porch, "but are you involved with someone?"

"No."

"On the serious rebound?"

Dev laughed. "Not that either. I don't get…seriously involved."

Natalie shifted sideways to look at Dev's face. "Never?"

"Nope. Just not my thing, I guess. I probably should've told you that before now."

"I don't see why," Natalie said, laughing. "We just had dinner. That's not exactly grounds for posting the banns."

"Still, you should know."

"What I *know*," Natalie said, setting her glass aside, "is that I like you and I like kissing you. That's quite a lot for a week."

"I suppose it is," Dev murmured as Natalie moved closer. Part of Dev's mind yielded to the pull of the moon, and the warm fragrant breeze, and Natalie's sweet, hot kisses. But deep inside, she remained remote and untouched. And it was that part of her that finally pulled away. "You're hard to resist."

"Do you want to?" Natalie's voice was breathy and low.

"Yeah. I think I better."

"I can think of a million arguments against that," Natalie said, caressing the back of Dev's neck. "Some of them, you might even buy. But"—she kissed Dev's cheek—"it's a long summer. Wanna walk me back to my car, or should I have another brandy and sleep on the couch?"

"Is that a trick question?"

Natalie laughed.

Leslie knew she should go inside. It was chilling fast, and even the blanket she'd pulled around herself when she curled up in the porch chair wasn't keeping her warm. After parting with Dev in the parking lot that morning, she'd used the wireless connection at the lodge to download work from the office, and she'd kept busy for the rest of the day and evening. She'd worked straight through dinner and finally relaxed with a bottle of wine out on her porch. Dev's cabin had been dark until after eleven, when the lights came on. A few minutes later she caught the murmur of conversation, although she couldn't hear any words. However, she could make out the unmistakable sound of feminine laughter.

She told herself that she was glad Dev had company and that she was feeling better. She meant it, too, at least part of it. When she heard the quiet thump of a door closing and the voices disappeared, she finally dragged herself inside in search of sleep. Lying alone in the dark, images that she'd thought long ago expunged returned to haunt her. Half dragging Mike back to the boathouse while he raged and accused and she denied and pleaded. The fleeting glimpse of Dev staggering to her bike and careening from the parking lot. The look of broken despair on Dev's face.

Leslie closed her eyes tightly as the frantic fluttering in her chest stole what remained of her breath. Grief and guilt felt so much the same, she could no longer tell them apart.

CHAPTER TEN

Natalie was a light sleeper and the quiet movements across the room woke her. She turned on her side beneath the cotton blanket and watched Dev making coffee. She could have told her she was awake, but she was enjoying the opportunity to observe her. Dev wore a T-shirt that had seen better days—hell, better years—and a pair of faded plaid boxers. She was barefoot, and muscles rippled in her arms and thighs as she stretched and reached into cabinets. Her hair was wet from the shower and a shade darker than usual, slicked back behind her ears and curling in small tendrils over the back of her neck. Those delicate strands gave Dev an unexpectedly vulnerable look, and Natalie felt a dangerous stirring in her heart. The stirring in her loins that the sight of Dev always elicited didn't bother her. Lust was a familiar and not unwelcome sensation. It assured her that her heart was beating and that all systems were functioning. If she'd looked at Devon Weber and felt nothing, she'd have been worried.

However, what she did not want was to look at Dev and feel that little twisty sensation in the pit of her stomach and the tightening in the center of her chest that spoke not of lust, but longing. Especially not with the signals that Dev had been sending, which were not so much mixed as cloudy. Natalie sensed Dev's attraction and her desire, but something held her back. Something that she was willing to bet Dev wanted very much but couldn't, or wouldn't, admit.

I don't get seriously involved, Dev had said.

Maybe not now, but once she had. Natalie was certain of that. Somewhere, sometime, there had been a woman who had mattered. And whoever she had been, she'd left indelible marks.

There were other marks too. Ones she hadn't expected. A series of scars crisscrossed Dev's right thigh below her boxers, twisting as far down as her knee. The pale white rivulets were faded reminders of some distant injury, and Natalie ached to think of what might have caused them. She caught back a murmur of sympathy.

Dev turned and smiled. "Hey. Good morning. Sorry, I didn't mean to wake you."

Smiling back, Natalie consigned whatever history lay beneath those scars to the past. Dev was here now and looking very sexy. Natalie extended her arms over her head, arched her back, and stretched beneath the blanket with a contented purr. She was naked, and she could tell from the flicker of Dev's eyes down the length of her body and quickly back up to her face that the thin covering didn't do a whole lot to camouflage her shape. "No problem. You're a nice sight to wake up to."

"Can I tempt you with coffee?"

"You can tempt me with just about anything."

Dev laughed. "I trust the couch and the brandy left no ill effects?"

"Not a one." Natalie swiveled around to sit up, holding one corner of the blanket between her breasts. "I feel great."

Dev thought she looked great too. Her eyes and mouth were soft in the early morning light, her dark hair framing her face like an invitation. She was beautiful and warm and Dev wondered why she didn't cross the room to her and lift the blanket away and accept what Natalie was offering. Tenderness and shared pleasure. Natalie had asked for no promises, made no demands.

Maybe it was because Dev liked her, really liked her in a way that she rarely experienced because she seldom made close friends, that she didn't. Shouldn't she have something to offer too? Shouldn't there be something more than desire?

As if reading her mind, Natalie said quietly, "Sometimes things are enough just as they are, Dev."

Dev poured coffee into two white ceramic mugs with *I* ♥ *Lake George* on the side. "Black, right?"

Natalie nodded.

"Just in case you thought otherwise," Dev said, setting Natalie's coffee on the maple Americana end table beside the couch, "it's not about you." She leaned down and softly kissed Natalie. "I'm a little turned around these days. Sorry."

"Thanks for the coffee." Natalie didn't reach for her because she had a feeling if she pushed just a little harder than she had been, Dev would relent. And it wasn't about having her. Not entirely. She wanted her, but not like that. Not when she knew something inside Dev would end up hurting more. "I understand, by the way. If you want a sounding board sometime, anytime, I'm available."

"Thanks, but it's something that talking won't change. Just some old stuff that needs to stay in the past, where it belongs." She retrieved her own coffee and sipped. "I know the minute you drive away, I'll feel like an idiot."

"Good. You should." Natalie wrapped the blanket around herself and stood. "I'm going to take a shower. Do you have time to wait?"

"Sure. They make a good breakfast at the lodge. How about it?"

"I'll be ready in five."

Leslie awakened just before six, relieved to see the morning. The night had been filled with fragmented dreams and disturbingly erotic half-formed images of making love with Rachel who became Dev who became Mike who became Leslie herself in an endless loop of increasingly frantic and unrequited desire. More distressing still, her body thrummed heavily with lingering arousal. Surprised, she traced her fingers between her legs and discovered that she was wet. The ER doctor had clearly been right when he'd said hormones might be at the root of her heart and blood pressure problems, because something was definitely amiss with her body.

While she enjoyed sex, it wasn't something she ordinarily paid much attention to. Certainly thoughts of making love never occupied her conscious mind or disturbed her concentration. She couldn't ever remember feeling as if she *needed* sex. When it occurred, it was a pleasurable interlude. Even on the infrequent occasions when she and Rachel spent the entire night together, she couldn't recall waking aroused, not even with Rachel's body against hers. Rachel particularly enjoyed sex in the morning, so they made love then, but Rachel always initiated it. Leslie apparently was a good partner, as Rachel always seemed satisfied. As for herself, Leslie found being intimate with Rachel pleasant, and she almost always achieved orgasm. And then it was over and she was free to focus on the things that *did* occupy her mind.

She never woke up with the urge to be touched. Not like she had right now.

"What I have," Leslie muttered as she abolished the remaining pieces of the dream and headed for the shower, "is way too much time on my hands."

No wonder she never took vacations. She was mentally and physically completely out of sync. As she twisted on the shower knobs, she spoke aloud as if that would ensure results. "All that's about to change. What I need is a trip to the office."

By 6:30 a.m., she was dressed in casual business attire—slacks and blouse and low heels. Briefcase in hand, she started along the path to the lodge, intent on regaining control of her life. When she ran into Dev and her overnight guest, she realized that her plan might turn out to be a bit more challenging than she anticipated. Dev's companion had her arm loosely around Dev's waist, and she looked relaxed and comfortable. Confident.

Leslie greeted them both politely, surprised when Dev blushed. Natalie reintroduced herself, although Leslie remembered her name quite well.

"Going to work?" Dev asked.

"Yes," Leslie said as they moved on as a group. She could have walked ahead, but why give the impression that anything about the situation bothered her? Dev had every right to entertain women in her cabin. Why should she care who Devon Weber slept with?

"A working vacation?" Natalie asked pleasantly.

"More like a working visit." Hoping to divert attention from herself, Leslie asked, "How is the season going for you?"

"It's gotten off to a better start than most," Natalie said, shooting a quick smile in Dev's direction. "With the economy the way it's been recently, we expect more people to opt for less expensive vacations. It's getting busy and should stay that way all summer."

"Do you have time to join us for breakfast, Les?" Dev asked, slowing as they climbed the steps to the lodge.

Leslie opened the door and held it while Natalie stepped inside. She glanced up at Dev, who hesitated in the doorway by her side. "No, thanks. I'm just going to grab some coffee and see if I can borrow my mother's car. Hopefully, my father's revived it."

"If not, you can take my truck."

"Thanks, I appreciate it, but I can always rent a car."

"The offer's open anytime." Dev glanced after Natalie, who had settled at a table on the far side of the room. "What about the other?"

"The other?" Leslie frowned, then realized Dev was asking about her health and the yet-to-be-scheduled tests. "Oh. That. Just as soon as I check in with the office up here. I'm not really sure how long I'll be staying, so if I don't see you again, have a good summer."

"I got the impression you were going to be here a few weeks."

"The peace and quiet are starting to get to me."

"Leslie, if it's me—"

"It's not you, Dev," Leslie said sharply. How many more times could she let Dev accept the responsibility for the pain they couldn't seem to stop causing one another? "Really. I need to get on the road before traffic gets heavy." She gestured toward Natalie with a slight tip of her chin. "Your friend is waiting."

Dev grabbed Leslie's hand before she could move away. "Your mother has my cell phone number. Call me if you need my truck. Or anything."

Leslie closed her eyes and sighed. "Dev. You always were way too nice."

"Don't worry. I've grown out of that."

"I don't think so." Gently, Leslie drew her hand away. "Take care, Dev."

Dev followed Leslie with her eyes as Leslie disappeared into the kitchen. After pouring a cup of coffee from the large urn on the sideboard, she joined Natalie. "Ready to hit the buffet?"

"Definitely." As they waited for the few people ahead of them to fill their plates, Natalie said, "Looks like you and Leslie have history."

"We went to high school together. How did you know?"

"You can always tell. The way you look at each other, the shorthand sentences. You know the sort of thing."

Actually, Dev didn't. She hadn't had any friends other than Leslie in high school, and since then, the people whose acquaintances she'd made were just that. Acquaintances. But she didn't comment. She was thinking that Leslie looked even more run down and pale than she had when she'd first arrived. And she was willing to bet money that Leslie wouldn't schedule the tests that she was supposed to get.

Just then, Leslie came out of the kitchen, travel mug in hand, and strode briskly through the dining room and out the front door. Dev wanted to go after her. Leslie had said she might be leaving soon. That thought left Dev feeling hollow, until she reminded herself she was being ridiculous. In fact, Leslie leaving was the best thing that could possibly happen. Then they could both get on with their lives without constantly reminding one another of something that had happened long ago, but that still apparently had the power to hurt them both. Leslie was doing the right thing. Making the correct choice. Dev took a deep breath, absorbing that simple realization and enjoying the peace that went with it.

"Do you happen to have my permits for camping on the island?" Dev asked.

Natalie looked startled at the abrupt change in subject, but nodded. "That and the gear you'll need to stay for four or five days. Everything should be set for you by tomorrow."

"Good. Then I'll head out the day after tomorrow." Getting away from Lakeview and the memories that had sprung to life around her was just what she needed, especially if Leslie was leaving. With any luck, she could get back to work without constantly seeing Leslie's face in her mind or hearing her voice or just…remembering.

"Thursday. Hell," Natalie said. "I have to be in meetings almost all day. But I can get someone else to run you out—"

"No problem. I'm pretty sure Paul Harris will be able to do it." Dev touched Natalie's shoulder. "Believe me, you've been a huge help already."

"It's no hardship." Natalie reached under the table and brushed her fingers along Dev's thigh. "I told you that the first day. Remember?"

"I do seem to recall something like that."

Natalie stopped her teasing caress just short of Dev's crotch. She wasn't usually so blatant in her seduction tactics, but Dev got to her in ways that other women didn't. As much as Dev held back physically, she didn't hide what she was feeling. Or maybe she couldn't. Natalie had seen the way Dev looked at Leslie Harris, and watching Dev's face when Leslie had disappeared out the front door, she'd finally understood the phrase *wearing your heart on your sleeve*. Dev probably didn't realize it, but when she looked at Leslie, her eyes were filled with helpless longing.

"Were you out in high school?" Natalie asked, suddenly getting the picture. But Dev couldn't possibly be carrying a torch all these years, could she?

"No," Dev said, her voice hoarse. "I didn't know anyone who was gay. I didn't really understand myself, what I was feeling, not for sure until…" *The night I kissed her.*

The pain in Dev's face was so naked, Natalie ached. Obviously she'd been wrong about the importance of whatever Dev had felt back then. Impulsively, she covered Dev's hand where it rested on the tablecloth. "Never mind. Water under the bridge, right?"

"Absolutely," Dev said, thinking that until a few days before, she'd believed that. She drained her coffee and pushed her uneaten plate of food away. "Thanks for last night. It was just what I needed."

Natalie held Dev's eyes and let Dev see what was in hers. Her interest. Her desire. Last night *had* been great. What she might as well admit was that she wanted more than kisses. She wanted more than a night or two of pleasure with Dev's great body. She wanted to be the one to erase the hurt in her eyes. And that was dangerous thinking. But then, anything worth having was worth the risk of a few bumps and bruises. "So let's do it again soon and see what else you might need. Tonight? Tomorrow?"

Shaking her head, Dev pushed her chair back, her legs stretched out in front of her. "I've got a couple of solid days' work at the lab before I head out to the islands. How about another rain check?"

Natalie let her eyes wander up and down Dev's body, taking her time and not bothering to hide exactly what she was thinking. "I'll pray for storms."

Laughing, Dev rose. "Don't let the tourists hear you say that."

On the way out, Dev waved to Eileen Harris, who stood in the doorway between the kitchen and the dining room, watching them with a pensive expression.

Chapter Eleven

At just after 6 p.m., Dev turned down the driveway to Lakeview. She'd had a good day at the lab. Arno Rodriguez, her summer intern from Oswego State College, had shown up and proved to be eager, if more likely to be of use analyzing data than collecting it. Arno's practical expertise left a bit to be desired, but his computer skills were excellent. Truthfully, she didn't mind. She had always preferred to be out in the field, but in the last few years more and more of her time had been consumed by preparing reports for one government agency or another and presenting recommendations at state and federal budgetary meetings. And lately, she'd had another, even less pleasant job added to her résumé—testifying for the state as an expert witness at trials involving EPA violations.

So this summer was almost like a sabbatical for her, and she welcomed the opportunity to do the fieldwork. She'd been so absorbed all day she hadn't thought of anything personal until she'd reached the Lakeshore Road. Then she couldn't help but think of Leslie and wonder if she had left to return to New York City. She told herself that was for the best, but it didn't feel that way in the pit of her stomach. The heavy throbbing there felt almost as bad as losing her the first time.

When she rounded a curve in the narrow road that wound through the trees and saw emergency vehicles with lights flashing parked haphazardly just below the lodge, her heart lurched. *Leslie!* She stomped down on the gas and rocketed into the parking lot, fishtailed to a stop, and jumped from the cab of the truck. As she ran toward a small crowd at the verge of the long slope leading down to the boathouse, she scanned the back porch where half a dozen guests were gathered. There was no one there she recognized. Everyone appeared to be staring in the direction of the lake and the docks below. She started down, and that was when she saw EMTs guiding a stretcher up the grassy incline. She recognized Eileen Harris hurrying along beside the clump of medical personnel, and her stomach tightened into a cold knot.

It had been so obvious that Leslie was ill. Why hadn't anyone said anything—why hadn't she? Because it wasn't her place. Because Leslie's prickly temper and aloof manner kept everyone at arm's length. Because she didn't want to risk Leslie shutting her out. When had she resorted to cowardice, or was that just the way she'd always been around Leslie?

Racing downhill, half skidding on the damp grass, she called to Leslie's mother. "What happened? Is it Leslie? Is she hurt?"

"What?" Eileen, who looked confused and distracted, nevertheless seemed relieved when she recognized Dev. "Oh. No, no. It's Paul." Breathless, she grasped Dev's arm and pulled her along. "One of the winches pulled loose and the boat slipped…and, oh God—"

Devon grasped her hand. "Take your time. It's okay. What did the EMTs say?"

"It looks like his leg is broken. They're not sure what else," Eileen said in a calmer voice. "I can't reach Leslie. I've called her, but I can't reach her."

"Cell reception is spotty up here," Dev said. "Where are they taking him?"

"Glens Falls."

They'd reached the ambulance, and Eileen bent down to murmur something to her husband, whose face was covered with an oxygen mask. Dev couldn't tell if he answered or not. As the EMTs loaded him into the van, Eileen wrapped her arms around her waist and shuddered.

"I need to go to the hospital, but the guests…" Eileen murmured. "I should stay until Leslie—"

"No, you go. I'll keep an eye on things," Dev said, extracting a card from her wallet. "Here's my cell number. As soon as you're settled, call me and tell me where you are. I'll give the message to Leslie so she can meet you there. You can fill me in on what to do here when you call."

Eileen shook her head. "You're a guest. You shouldn't be doing this."

"Hey, I used to be a neighbor. I'm not really a guest."

"You're very kind," Eileen said with a faint smile. She squeezed Dev's arm. "Thank you. I have to go. I'll call you. Leslie's number—"

"I've got it. Remember, you gave it to me the day I picked her up at the train station."

Dev watched as Eileen climbed into the back of the ambulance, immeasurably relieved that it wasn't Leslie strapped to the gurney as the doors closed with a resounding thud. When the emergency vehicles disappeared from sight, she hurried off toward her cabin. She needed to shower, change, and get back to the lodge. She needed to reach Leslie.

Twenty minutes later, after being routed directly to voicemail at least a dozen times, she reached her.

"Les? It's Dev."

"Dev? Hi, what's going on?"

"Where are you?"

"About fifteen minutes away on the Northway. Why?"

"Can you pull over for a minute so I don't lose you?"

"Hold on…okay, go ahead."

Leslie sounded composed, unrattled.

"Your dad's had an accident—it looks like a broken leg, at least. Your mother's with him, and they're on their way to Glens Falls Hospital right now."

"All right." Leslie took a deep breath. "Is he in any danger?"

"I don't know, Les. I don't think so, but I got here just as the EMTs were transporting him."

"I'm headed there now, then. Thanks, Dev."

"Call me if you need anything." Dev heard the crackle of static. "Les? Les?"

She disconnected, feeling impotent. Even though she knew Leslie didn't need her, she wished she could join her. She shook her head, wondering at the strength of the ties that she'd once thought were irrevocably broken.

❖

Most of the lights were out in the lodge when Leslie pulled into the parking lot shortly after 11 p.m. She was so tired she felt numb. She contemplated going directly to her cabin, but she needed to make sure everything was all right with the guests. Thankfully, it wasn't yet the height of the season and they weren't full. She tossed her briefcase in the backseat of the Jeep, locked the door, and made her way inside.

A single lamp burned on the walnut sideboard just inside the wide double doors. The great room and the dining room beyond were empty. Light shone beneath the swinging door from the kitchen and she headed that way. She stumbled to a stop as she shouldered the door open and stepped into the next room. Dev, in a navy T-shirt and blue jeans, stood at the long kitchen counter with a white butcher's apron tied around her waist, covering platters of food with plastic wrap.

"Dev?" Leslie said in surprise.

Dev set aside the carving knife that she'd been using to slice ham. "Hi. How's your dad?"

"He's sedated, but stable. What are you doing?"

"Cleaning up after dinner." Dev walked to the refrigerator and pulled out a bottle of Heineken. She held it up in Leslie's direction. "Want one?"

"God, yes." Leslie slumped onto a stool at the central island. "They're going to operate on him early tomorrow morning. My mother wanted to be close tonight and got a room at a motel across the street from the hospital."

Dev opened two bottles, handed one to Leslie, and pulled a chair around the table so she could sit facing her. "What did they say, exactly?"

Leslie shrugged. "What do they ever say? His leg is shattered and there's a hairline fracture of his pelvis. There might be some nerve damage." Leslie's voice cracked and she covered her eyes. Her fingers trembled.

"Hey," Dev said gently, resting her hand on Leslie's knee. "You look beat. Why don't I walk you down to your cabin so you can turn in."

"No. I need to get some things together for my mother. I promised her I'd bring them first thing tomorrow." She scanned the kitchen.

"Besides, you need some help in here. God. You shouldn't even be doing this."

"Why not?" Dev said, feigning affront. She pointed to a row of typed pages affixed to the refrigerator with multicolored magnets shaped like fish. "Your mother has the menu laid out for every meal, every day of the week, and she cooks ahead. It was easy enough to find everything and put it together." She grinned. "At least, no one complained. Yet."

"There's only, what, eight guests? In another week, there'll be thirty. Are you planning to give up your day job?" Hearing the sharp edge to her voice, Leslie covered Dev's hand and squeezed. "But thanks. If you hadn't been here, my mother would have had to stay, and she'd be out of her mind with worry."

"It was no problem," Dev said. "And I'm not volunteering for permanent K.P. I'm only good until we run out of the semi prepared stuff. But your mother's not going to be able to manage by herself."

"I know. I'm going to have to get some temporary help in here for her right away." Leslie set her beer aside and started to pace. "A cook, for sure. And someone to run the boats and look after maintenance, because my father's not going to be able to do much for the rest of the season. And that damn truck has to go. I had to stop twice to let the engine cool off."

Dev sipped her beer and watched Leslie slide effortlessly from exhaustion and distress into sharply focused control. It was impressive. It was probably costly too, she imagined, physically and emotionally. She wasn't surprised that Leslie had a blood pressure problem.

"All that's going to take more than a few days," Dev pointed out.

"I can stay another week or two," Leslie said, her expression distant as she calculated what needed to be done and how she would manage that and the work she wanted to do. "I was planning on being up here a few weeks anyhow. If I need a little longer, I can keep working out of the local office while I get things squared away here."

"Uh," Dev said carefully, "I sort of got the impression you were supposed to be taking it easy while you were here. Not taking on another job."

Leslie waved a hand impatiently. "I'm fine. I haven't had any problems since I've been here."

"You did the day you arrived."

"I'd just gotten out of the hospital and hadn't had any sleep at all." Leslie fixed Dev with a pointed stare. "Not that it's any of your business, Devon, but I arranged for the damn tests they wanted me to have."

Dev grinned. "Good."

"Of course," Leslie said, searching through the utility drawer for paper and a pen, "I'll have to reschedule those now."

"Why?"

Leslie started making a list. "Because I'm supposed to get most of them tomorrow afternoon, and that's impossible."

"Why?"

"You know, I don't remember you being such a pain in the ass," Leslie muttered.

"Neither were you."

Leslie gave her a sidelong glare, but she smiled. "My father's going to be operated on tomorrow and I'll need to stay with my mother in the morning. Then I have to deal with this place."

"My schedule's flexible. I can keep an eye on things here."

"You must have your own work to do."

"I was going out to the islands the day after tomorrow, but I can postpone that a few days. I've got plenty of work to do around here." Dev got up to finish slicing the leftover ham. "At least until things are more settled with your dad. I don't mind, really."

Leslie sighed. "It would help a lot."

"One stipulation."

"I don't usually make deals." Leslie folded her arms and regarded Dev appraisingly. "But I suppose you can try."

Dev leaned against the counter and met Leslie's gaze steadily. Seeing the calculation and unmistakable power in Leslie's eyes, Dev appreciated for the first time that this was not the woman of her memories. Like Dev, Leslie had changed. Every now and then Dev caught a glimpse of the girl she had known, when a little bit of humor broke through her steely control or when compassion softened her unyielding reserve. When they'd been young, Dev had been attracted to Leslie's softness and her gentle innocence. Now she found her strength every bit as appealing, if quite a bit more irritating.

"You get the tests tomorrow," Dev said.

"Dev—" Leslie started to protest, exasperated, then considered how much help Dev had been. And how much her concern touched her. "Okay, look. If I can, I will."

"Good enough." Dev opened the refrigerator and slid the tray of sliced meat onto the bottom shelf. "I was thinking of scrambled eggs and the rest of this ham for breakfast. What do you think?"

Leslie laughed. "I think you're crazy."

Dev grinned. "See? Some things don't change."

As Leslie undressed for bed, too tired even to shower, she remembered the conversation in the kitchen.

Some things don't change.

She marveled at just how much everything *had* changed. How much Dev, especially, had changed. Dev was so much less angry now, and sure of herself in ways she'd never been as a teenager. Physically, she moved with confidence, and she clearly owned her sexuality. It didn't take seeing her with Natalie to know that. The image of Dev standing in the kitchen just hours ago with that foolish apron slung around her muscular hips or sprawled in a chair on the porch with a cup of coffee in her hand gave Leslie a hungry feeling in the pit of her stomach. Dev was sexy without even trying.

But then, she'd always been sexy, although Leslie hadn't consciously acknowledged that. Looking back, she appreciated how intriguing Dev had been as a teenager, with her dark moods and rebellious dress and refusal to conform. She realized just how attracted she'd been to Dev and what she'd done when awareness had crashed in upon her in one hot, wild instant. She flushed with embarrassment.

Dev was far more forgiving of her actions back then than she was. There were times like tonight when the burden of guilt felt as if it might crush her. As she lay down, exhausted but too keyed up to close her eyes, she wondered who Dev saw when she looked at her.

CHAPTER TWELVE

At five thirty the next morning, Leslie made her way up the path to the lodge just as the sun broke over the horizon. She stopped before climbing the steps and turned to watch the morning dance across the glassy surface of the lake. Orange and magenta streaked the sky and reflected off the blue water so brightly she shielded her eyes with one hand. She'd seen it thousands of times growing up and hadn't thought of the silent beauty for years, but it hadn't lost its power to enchant her.

"It never gets old, does it?" Dev said quietly from the shadows of the porch. She walked forward to lean against the railing.

"I'm not sure why not," Leslie said almost to herself. "Maybe because I've never seen a painting or a photograph as beautiful."

"No, it's not something we can capture or re-create. I guess that makes it special." Dev watched as the emerging sun highlighted the angles and planes of Leslie's face that had not been there in the softness of youth. Her hair glinted with gold; her eyes mirrored the crystal blue waters. She was beautiful now, as she had been then, unique and familiar as the dawn.

Leslie hesitated on the top step, struck by the pensive note in Dev's voice. The expression on her face was hard to decipher. She looked a little sad, but her eyes were warm as they caressed—that was how it felt, caressed—her. Leslie shivered, unable to look away and not wanting Dev to, either. She hadn't expected to see Dev so early and wondered if Dev had gone back to her cabin at all the night before. Then she noticed that Dev had changed from her jeans and T-shirt into khaki pants, a dark shirt, and work boots. She looked solid and steady and Leslie felt oddly comforted.

"You always did make me feel safe."

When Dev jerked, Leslie realized she'd spoken aloud.

"Did I?" Dev asked quietly. "I always had the impression that everyone thought I was kind of scary. Or maybe just a little crazy."

"I never did. You know that." Leslie wanted to tell her how she always felt braver when she was with Dev. As if Dev's differentness allowed Leslie to be just a little bit different too. To be someone other than the girl all her friends and even her parents expected her to be. But she didn't say anything, because she couldn't go back there now. It made her sad. It made her wish for things she couldn't have and didn't have time for. And there were things she had to do. "I forgot some of the things I need to bring to my mother. I wasn't at my sharpest last night."

"There's coffee," Dev said, walking inside with Leslie. "That might help."

"Did you get any sleep at all?"

"Some. Enough. You?" The lights had been out in Leslie's cabin when Dev had passed it on the way to her own the night before. For one crazy instant she'd considered walking up the path and tapping on Leslie's door. What she would have said if Leslie had answered, she wasn't sure. Now, in the light of day, she was glad she hadn't. The pull of the past was powerful, but it was obvious that Leslie had no desire to revisit it. And neither should she.

"I slept on and off," Leslie said. She looked around the dining room and saw that Dev had already set out plates and utensils and that the big coffee urn was full. She grasped Dev's arm. "This is terrific. I can't thank you enough. I should've thought to come up and do this myself…"

She wasn't thinking clearly at all and wondered why not. It was true that her unexpected illness and this impromptu visit had totally disrupted her normal routine—she hadn't been to the gym, hadn't had a decent meal, hadn't had a full night's sleep in days, no, a week now. Still, when she'd been involved in a particularly difficult trial there had been long stretches when she hadn't slept or eaten or exercised, and she'd never lost her focus. Never forgot things. Never found her mind wandering into the past or musing about things she couldn't change or control.

"I just got here, Les. Besides, you need to get to the hospital. We've already discussed this, remember?"

"Why are you doing this, Dev?"

The question surprised Dev. Leslie so rarely revealed the slightest bit of vulnerability. Her armor was very effectively established by her elegantly understated blouse and slacks, her designer shoes, her expensive haircut and her subtle but perfect makeup. But Dev wasn't looking at any of those things. She was looking at the shadows beneath Leslie's blue eyes and remembering the way her hands had trembled the night before.

"The easy answer would be because I used to be in love with you."

Leslie's laughter was part shock and part embarrassed pleasure. "I'm afraid to hear the hard answer, then."

Dev shrugged and slid her hands into her back pockets, unconsciously canting her hips forward the way she used to when she was feeling insecure and wanted to act tough. "I know all that's in the past, but I can't help feeling that we're still friends. And that's what friends do, isn't it."

Leslie rested her palm against Dev's chest and leaned close to kiss her on the cheek. "I guess it is. Thank you."

Dev stood completely still as Leslie turned and disappeared up the wide curving staircase to the second floor, where her parents had their bedroom. If everything between them was in the past, why did being near Leslie still make her feel better and worse than anything she'd ever experienced, all at the same time?

Since she didn't know the answer, and doubted she ever would, she settled for doing something that did make sense. She went to the kitchen to make breakfast for ten.

"You don't have to stay here all morning," Eileen said to Leslie when Leslie returned to the surgical waiting area for the fourth time after stepping outside to make a phone call.

"Sorry," Leslie muttered as she sat down beside her mother in the surprisingly comfortable chair. The waiting room was carpeted, with small seating areas arranged so that families could have some privacy. She and her mother sat alone in the far corner next to several windows that looked out over a small landscaped seating area with trees and stone benches. The smokers congregated there. "Just a couple of things I need to take care of at the office."

"I guess you can never really go on vacation."

"If I didn't take care of things," Leslie said, crossing her legs and resting her head against the back of the chair, "they'd just be there waiting for me. The problems don't go away just because I'm not there."

"No." Eileen sighed. "The ostrich approach is tempting, but I've never known it to work."

Leslie laughed. "True on both counts."

"I mean it, though. I can call you when the doctors come out. It's likely to be at least another hour."

"I'd rather stay." Leslie looked at her watch. Her tests were scheduled for three that afternoon, across the street at the outpatient medical building. Unfortunately, she would probably be able to get there in plenty of time. She felt ridiculous wasting several hours when she felt perfectly healthy. Other than the embarrassing episode she'd had in front of Dev the day she'd arrived, she'd only had one other very brief period of the irregular fluttering sensation in her chest—just after she got out of bed that morning. It couldn't have lasted more than twenty seconds. In fact, it was over so quickly she wasn't certain it'd been anything at all. "Are you planning to stay here tonight too?"

"It depends on how your father's doing. I thought I might, especially with the truck acting up."

"*That* problem is going to be solved very quickly. If I have time this afternoon I'm going to put it out of its misery. Do you think Daddy wants another Jeep?"

"I think we should probably wait to ask him. I'm not certain we've budgeted for a new truck this year."

"Don't worry about that," Leslie said.

"Leslie," Eileen said, "it's a generous offer. I appreciate it. I really do, and so will your father. But it's not your responsibility."

Responsibility. Was that what it was called when you did something for someone you loved? What was it called when you didn't? Leslie knew the answer. It was called cowardice.

The sun coming through her bedroom window was so bright, it hurt Leslie's eyes. It hurt her head. It made her queasy. She rolled onto her side and closed her eyes tightly, wishing the morning away. Maybe she could go back to sleep and the next time she woke up, it would be Sunday and she would be ready to leave for college. She could leave and pretend that last night had never happened. She wanted to cry, but her eyes were swollen and her throat raw from too many tears already. Tears and, she remembered now, being so sick somewhere around two in the morning that she'd wanted to die.

Sometime after Dev had left the party, she'd had too much to drink. Way too much. The beer and wine—she remembered sharing a bottle or maybe two with Shelley—had made her sick, but it hadn't made her forget the sound of Mike's foot thudding into Dev's body, or Dev's soft moans, or her own screams. Shelley kept asking her what was wrong, and Leslie hadn't been able to answer.

What could she say? *Mike hurt Dev and it's all my fault? Dev kissed me and I let her. I didn't mean to let her. I didn't mean to kiss her back. It was a mistake.* Wasn't it?

Leslie tried to go back to sleep but she could hear the guests getting up and the sounds of activity outside her open window. The boathouse was probably a mess, and she really ought to clean up down there before her parents saw it. Groaning, she dragged herself from bed and wobbled on shaky legs into her bathroom. She was afraid she might vomit again, but she was sure there was nothing left to throw up. She was never going to drink that much again. She was never going to let anything like last night happen again. She was never going to let anyone kiss her like that again.

She'd never let anyone close enough to get hurt by her mistakes.

She kept the shower on cold and stood shivering with her arms wrapped around herself, hoping to drive out the sickness and the feel of Dev's body and the heat of her mouth and the terrible sound of someone's heart breaking. When she finally felt like she could face her parents without them being suspicious of the way she looked, she dried her hair and dressed and went downstairs.

"Hi, honey," Eileen Harris said. "I've still got plenty of breakfast left. There's OJ in the refrigerator. You want pancakes?"

Wanting to clamp her hand over her mouth at the sudden surge of nausea, Leslie turned quickly away and pretended to be looking out the window. "No thanks, not yet. I think I'll just have a Pepsi and go down to the boathouse. I want to make sure all the trash got bagged."

"Pepsi in the morning? You should eat something."

"I will. Later." Leslie started toward the back door, wanting to get away before her mother looked at her more closely.

"I'm so glad you had the party here," Eileen said, carrying a stack of dishes to the counter. She opened the dishwasher and began loading it. "And I'm glad that your friends are all responsible. Thank God they're all too sensible to ride motorcycles."

"What?" Leslie said, only half listening.

"Some local teenager had a terrible accident on a motorcycle last night."

Leslie stopped, her hand on the doorknob. Her heart pounded furiously and the queasy feeling in her stomach coalesced into a hard knot of dread. "Accident?"

"Mmm. Someone crashed their motorcycle on Lakeshore Road last night. Up north from here a bit." Eileen lifted two cast-iron skillets from the stove and propped them up in the sink. "Your father heard something about it on the news."

Leslie managed to walk out the door and across the porch before she vomited over the railing into the bushes. When she was done, she collapsed into one of the chairs. She knew it was Dev. She just knew it. Dev had been drinking, but not a lot. Dev was a good rider, but she was hurt. And she must've been angry too. Angry with her, and with Mike.

Mike. Mike had left right after Dev. He'd been gone almost an hour. He wasn't angry when he came back. He would hardly talk to her, not that she wanted to talk to him. And he was drinking a lot, even more than usual, off in a corner with some of his friends.

She knew it last night, and she knew it now. Something bad had happened. She should say something. She should tell her mother. She should tell someone *that it was all her fault.*

"I'm sorry I haven't been home for a while," Leslie said.

After a moment's silence, Eileen said, "I wish things were different now. What with your father—"

"No, it's okay. I'm glad I'm here." Leslie took her mother's hand. "Now, about that truck."

Eileen laughed weakly. "Your father will always be a Jeep man. If it's anything other than black or green, he won't drive it."

Leslie smiled. "God forbid we get him a yellow Hummer."

"If you do end up getting one, we'll pay you back. I'm just not sure when."

"Mom, come on. I can afford it. It's not a big deal."

"All right," Eileen said carefully. "Then if I can't get you to agree to take money, why don't you tell me why you're really here?"

"That's blackmail."

"Not when it's your mother doing it."

Leslie wanted to pace. She wanted to abort the conversation. She didn't have an answer, not one she was ready to share, especially not when her mother already had her father to worry about. Not one she could even verbalize completely to herself. She forced herself to sit still.

"I haven't taken any real time off in years, and I was due for a vacation. When I thought about getting away, the only place I thought about going was here." Leslie knew it was true. Maybe not all of the truth, but some of it. She met her mother's eyes, surprised by the uncritical welcome in them.

"It's funny," Eileen said quietly. "I had the feeling when you left for college that you couldn't wait to get away, and I've never understood why."

"I guess it must have seemed that way. I'm sorry."

That was as much of an answer as Leslie could give, because anything else would demand far too much confession. She couldn't explain about Dev and Mike. She couldn't say she'd needed to be somewhere else, be *someone* else. That she'd needed to leave behind the person she couldn't look at in the mirror, to reinvent herself.

She'd done a good job of it. She was successful. She was respected by her colleagues. She had a lover who was beautiful and smart. And yet here she was. Leslie wondered why.

What came to mind was the way the lake gleamed in the dawn light, and the crisp pine-scented air that blew through the windows of her cabin at night, and the way Dev had gazed at her that morning— as if she'd really seen her. She remembered asking Dev why she was being so kind.

Because I used to be in love with you.

Leslie shook her head. Past tense. Past dreams. Past mistakes. All behind her now. And that was where she was determined it all would stay.

"I'm going down the street to the Starbucks for coffee. Want one?"

"Tea, I think. Thanks."

"Be right back." As soon as Leslie exited the hospital, she pressed Rachel's cell number on the speed dial. To her surprise, Rachel answered. "Hi, Rach, it's me."

"Hello, darling. I've just got a minute, but I saw it was you and I was going to call you anyhow. Can you get down to the city this weekend? There's a fundraiser Saturday night we should go to."

"I can't. My father's had an accident—a broken leg. He's in surgery right now."

"Damn. I really need to put in an appearance at this thing." There was silence for a few seconds. "Maybe I can come up for a few hours on Sunday."

"Thanks, but you don't need to. I just can't get away right now."

"I'm so sorry, darling. Are you sure?"

"Yes. Really. There's nothing to be done, but I can't leave my mother with everything at the lodge right now."

Rachel's tone was cautious. "I suppose that means you'll be staying a bit longer?"

"At least another week or so." Leslie hesitated. "Maybe you can come up over the Fourth of July recess."

"I suppose that's a possibility. Look, we'll talk more later."

"All right. Call me."

"I will. Love you, darling. Bye."

"Goodbye," Leslie said, and slipped her BlackBerry into her purse. As she stepped into line at the coffee counter, she tried to bring Rachel's face into focus. When she couldn't, she told herself that was completely normal and meant nothing. Then, for just a second, she had a crystal-clear image of Dev, and the intensity in Dev's eyes was so sharp she gasped.

"Help you, ma'am?"

Leslie jerked and stared at the young man behind the counter, thankful for the diversion. "Yes. Large coffee. And a tea."

"Sure. Anything else?"

A little dose of reality would be good, Leslie thought. She smiled faintly. "No. Thanks. I'm fine."

She seemed to be saying that a lot lately, but she was starting to wonder. She glanced at her watch. Unfortunately, she'd still have time for the tests she'd scheduled. At least if she had them, she'd be one step closer to getting back to Manhattan and getting her life back. That was reason enough to keep the appointment.

Chapter Thirteen

D r. Weber?"
Dev glanced up from the microscope toward the young
redhead who stood in the doorway of her lab. "Hi, Susan. What's up?"

"There's a visitor downstairs for you. A Ms. Evans. Do you want
me to bring her up?"

"No, that's okay. I'll go down. Thanks."

Dev stored the specimens she'd been examining in the refrigerator,
tossed her lab coat over a swivel chair behind her desk, and walked
down the wide, brightly lit hallway to the stairwell. Her summer office
at the Marine Life Institute was on the fourth floor, and it only took her
a moment to reach the atrium lobby. Floor-to-ceiling windows offered
a picturesque view of the lake. Natalie, looking fresh and relaxed in
civilian clothes, stood gazing out. Her pale yellow blouse and coffee-
colored shorts complemented her subtle tan. She turned and smiled at
Dev's approach.

"Am I interrupting?" Natalie asked.

"Nothing that won't keep. Day off?"

Natalie nodded. "With the Fourth coming up in a little over a
week, the holiday visitors will arrive in force starting tomorrow. I can't
count on time off again for a while. Besides, I wanted to see you before
you head out to the islands."

"I have to postpone that for a couple of days," Dev said. "How
about we grab lunch and I'll explain."

"How about we pick up sandwiches and take my boat out for a
few hours. I keep it moored at the station. One of the perks of the
job."

Dev checked her watch. "I have to be back in by six."

Natalie threaded her arm through Dev's. "Don't worry. I'll get you home by curfew."

Laughing, Dev let Natalie lead her from the building into the bright sunshine. On the way to the ranger station, she explained about Paul Harris.

"So you're filling in at the lodge?" Natalie asked, eyeing Dev curiously. She pulled into the station lot and parked close to the boat docks.

"A bit."

"Nice of you." Natalie climbed out and pointed to a cooler on the backseat of her car. "Can you grab that?"

"Sure."

Dev wondered at Natalie's sudden silence while they checked gear and cast off, but once they were underway, Natalie seemed herself again—chatting casually about events at the station and pointing out her favorite spots on the lake. Twenty minutes later, they dropped anchor in a small cove on the far side of a smaller island in the Glen Island Group. Other than boats passing by within sight—but not shouting distance—they were alone.

"This is some boat," Dev said. Natalie's twenty-three-foot fiberglass SeaCraft had a cuddy cabin, an enclosed area in the front of the boat with sleeping and lavatory facilities, and a spacious rear deck for fishing or recreational activities. "Do you sleep out on her much?"

"Now and then." Natalie grinned. "It comes in handy for impromptu getaways."

"I'll bet." Dev spread her arms out along the back of the built-in bench and tilted her face up to the sky. She couldn't remember the last time she'd actually relaxed.

"You're going to roast in jeans and a T-shirt out here. I can probably find a suit for you in the locker," Natalie said as she pulled two St. Pauli Girls from the cooler. "Beer?"

Dev turned her head and smiled lazily. "Sure. Do you have any objection to underwear?"

Natalie froze with her arm extended, the beer in her hand. "I guess it depends. Are we talking on or off? And just what kind of underwear?"

"The utilitarian kind, I'm afraid." Dev stood, unzipped her jeans, and pushed them down. She wore navy stretch boxers underneath that reached to mid-thigh. She unlaced her boots, shucked her pants, and stripped off her T-shirt to reveal a black sports bra.

"I guess you meant on," Natalie said, swallowing hard. Dev's body looked exactly as she'd anticipated from the glimpse she'd had in Dev's cabin a few days before. Her shoulders and chest were nicely muscled, her breasts neither small nor large, her abdomen smooth and strong looking. The scars on her leg were more prominent in the sunlight. She handed Dev her beer and sat down next to her, their thighs separated by a few inches of air that seemed to undulate with heat. "Good thing you're keeping your assets covered."

Dev raised a brow.

"Too much water traffic to risk going *au naturel.*"

"It's great out here," Dev said as she took the beer. "Thanks."

"Believe me, it's my pleasure."

Dev grinned. When she noticed Natalie glance at her leg for the second time, she said, "Motorcycle accident. Youthful misadventure."

Natalie regarded her seriously. "It must have been a hell of an accident. I'm sorry if it's a sensitive topic."

"That's okay." Dev rested the beer bottle on her hip and regarded the scars pensively. Sunlight filtered through the green glass and created slashes of color across her thigh. Until the last week, she'd rarely thought about those times. Now she seemed to be practically immersed in the memories. "I learned several very important lessons and fortunately lived to appreciate them."

"How old were you?"

"Seventeen."

Natalie caught her breath. "God, that's tough when you're that age."

"I was lucky. I shattered my femur and had a pretty serious concussion, but I didn't break my neck or my back. I didn't lose my leg." Dev shrugged and pulled on her beer. "Christ, it could've been a mess. I got off easy."

Somehow, Natalie didn't think so, but she wasn't sure how deeply to probe. She stroked Dev's forearm, feeling as if her comfort was woefully inadequate. "You make it sound like you were being punished."

"Do I? I guess so. I guess I was—being punished in a way. I was drinking."

"Ah, God. That's hard."

"I was a hothead and a bit of a fuck-off," Dev said, smiling ruefully. "Fortunately, I wasn't so thickheaded not to appreciate the fact that I didn't wake up in a wheelchair. Or worse."

"Sometimes I wonder how any of us survived adolescence."

"You too?" Dev asked.

Natalie shrugged. "I went through a period where I tried really hard to fit in, even though I knew I didn't. I slept my way through my senior year in high school and part of my first year in college with any guy that came along. Then I got pregnant. And I had an abortion. Then I decided it was time to stop lying to myself about how I felt about girls."

"Did that solve your problems?"

"Most of them." Natalie laughed. "Of course, then I had to deal with getting my heart broken by the first few girls I fell for."

Dev turned her palm up and Natalie slipped hers into it. "I wonder if it would have been any easier if someone had told us it was okay to be gay? It's always hard to be different."

"Well," Natalie said, sliding closer to Dev until she was nestled against her side, "I think if *you'd* been around in high school I might have risked it."

"Don't be so sure. I was so far outside the popular circle, just being seen with me invited talk."

Natalie rested her cheek against Dev's arm and drew her legs up onto the seat. "No friends?"

"Just Leslie," Dev said quietly, wondering now what it had cost Leslie to befriend her.

"Leslie Harris?" Natalie said, stiffening slightly.

Dev looked down into Natalie's eyes. "Yes."

"Were you an item?"

"Christ, no," Dev said, laughing with a tinge of bitterness. "Leslie was so different than me. Probably a lot like you—pretty, popular, the girl every other girl wanted to be best friends with, and the one every boy wanted to date."

"But not you." Natalie spoke gently, understanding.

"Not me what?"

"You didn't want to be best friends with her."

"No," Dev said roughly. "That's not what I wanted."

"Is it hard, seeing her now?"

"Not really." Dev sighed. "Not when I remind myself that we're adults now. Different people."

"I wonder how much any of us really changes," Natalie mused. "I'm not the crazy, mixed-up kid I was ten years ago, but I don't know how different I really am either."

"If you'd asked me a few weeks ago, I would've said I'd changed a lot." Dev drained her beer. "Now, I'm not so sure."

Natalie shifted until she straddled Dev's lap, her hands on Dev's shoulders and their foreheads nearly touching. "Oh yeah? You don't look like such a bad girl now," she whispered. "But I bet you could be, under the right circumstances. Wanna find out?"

Dev rested her hands lightly on Natalie's waist. Natalie looked good. She smelled good. She felt even better. Dev's body tightened and throbbed. Her breathing ratcheted up. "If we'd just met, I'd be all over you right now."

Natalie's eyes widened. "I wouldn't stop you. I'm *not* stopping you. God, Dev, I'm so crazy hot for you."

"Ditto," Dev gasped, willing her hips to stay nailed to the seat. What she wanted to do was pull Natalie down and grind against her. She wanted to press her face between Natalie's breasts and lick the sweat from every inch of her skin. She wanted to fuck her. And that was the problem. Gently, she guided Natalie off her lap and back to the bench. "Somehow things sort of slipped past the point where I can have a casual fuck with you, Nat. I'm sorry."

"You bastard," Natalie said, half angry, half laughing. "How am I supposed to complain when you say something like that?" She groaned and ran her hands through her hair. "What if I told you I just wanted a nice friendly affair?"

"I'd say I had to think about it." Dev got up and pulled two more beers from the cooler. She popped the caps and handed one to Natalie. "When you weren't sitting in my lap and I wasn't turned on so bad I couldn't put two sentences together."

"You really are a pain in the ass, Dev," Natalie chided, sipping her beer.

"So I've been told."

Natalie patted the bench. "Sit down. I'm not mad, just horny."

"Sorry." Dev sat.

With a sigh, Natalie turned on the seat so her back was against Dev's shoulder and her legs stretched out in front of her. "Do me a favor, okay?"

"Uh-huh."

"I'm a big girl, and I know what I'm doing. So just think about it."

"Okay," Dev said softly. "I can do that."

Dev pulled into the Lakeview parking lot right behind a big, shiny black Jeep Cherokee. When she saw Leslie get out, she walked over to her.

"Nice ride."

Leslie grinned. "Wait'll my father sees it."

"How is he?"

"So far, things look really promising. They finished just after eleven this morning and the orthopedic surgeon thought the nerves were just traumatized—not permanently damaged."

"That's terrific."

"Yes. We'll know more in a few days." Leslie locked the truck and started toward the lodge with Dev. "I called you once he was in recovery, but I got voicemail. Did you get the message?"

"Sorry, I was out on the lake when you called and didn't get in until just a few minutes ago."

Leslie cocked her head. "You look like you got some sun. Working?"

Dev shook her head. "No. Natalie came by the lab and we took her boat out for a couple of hours."

"Oh," Leslie said. "That's nice." She stopped on the porch. "I can handle things here tonight, Dev. You've done enough already. Thank you." She turned her back and opened the door.

Dev caught the edge of the door with her hand and followed her inside. "I checked in four more guests this morning before I went to the lab. There's a pretty full house tonight."

"My mother has always been able to handle it. I should be able to." Leslie pushed through the swinging door into the kitchen and turned, exasperated, when Dev followed. "Let me see if I can be clearer. Go away."

"I won't help. I'll just watch." Dev folded her arms and leaned against the wall.

Leslie stared at her, resisting the urge to grind her teeth. Then she stalked to the refrigerator and pulled down the menu marked for that day. She groaned. She hated making salad. "Fine." She wrenched open the refrigerator door and reached inside. "Here."

Dev caught the first head of lettuce effortlessly. The second was a bit more of a challenge with one hand already full. The third and fourth left bits of green hanging from the collar of her shirt as she scooped them against her chest. "No," she shouted as Leslie drew back to pitch the fifth.

Laughing, Leslie stopped in mid-throw. "Oh my God. I can't believe I'm throwing lettuce in my mother's kitchen like I'm fifteen. What is it about this place?"

"Something in the air," Dev said, understanding perfectly.

"It must be." Leslie set the lettuce gently on the table, then went to Dev to relieve her of the others. "I'm sorry. Let me take those."

"I've got them. You go ahead and deal with the rest of dinner. I'll take care of these."

"You're sure?"

"Yeah." As Dev checked the cabinets for a colander, she said, "So tell me about the truck. When the hell did you have time to do that?"

"It's amazing how quickly things go when you walk onto the lot knowing what you want. Once you eliminate the barter, the process is surprisingly simple." Leslie shrugged. "When you don't entertain alternatives, it's easy to close a deal."

Dev recognized the tone of someone who was used to going up against opponents quite a bit more daunting than car salesmen and winning. "I think I feel sorry for them."

"Who?"

"The attorneys who square off against you."

Leslie laughed. "Most of the time they grossly overestimate the strength of their cases because they fall for their own rhetoric and believe their own frequently flawed statistics. It's not that difficult to challenge the majority of the regulations once you move beyond the emotion to facts."

"Doesn't it bother you that we're destroying the planet?"

Leslie slid the first of three tins of lasagna into the oven. "I think you just made my point."

Dev twisted a head of lettuce so hard it shredded in half in her hands. "I'm not being emotional. I'm a scientist. I can cite the facts. Better yet, I can take you down to the lake and show you the effects of thermal alteration and industrial contamination on the fish and floral growth."

"I'm sure you're an excellent scientist, Dev," Leslie said calmly. "But there's a big leap between documenting changes in fish populations and imposing sweeping governmental restrictions on the corporate sector. Businesses are run by people, you know. People who suffer because of these regulations."

A muscle in Dev's jaw twitched. She knew it wasn't the time or place for this kind of argument. Beyond that, she knew it wouldn't do any good. She doubted that Leslie would be doing any job she didn't believe in, as hard as it was to fathom that she'd chosen this side of the environmental debate. She tossed the lettuce into the strainer and reached for another head. "Fish are people too."

"Now there's an argument that just might win in court," Leslie said softly.

When Dev shot her a glance, Leslie smiled and some of the tension drained from the room. "Let's try for an easier subject," Dev said. "Did you get your tests today?"

Leslie shook her head. "I can see that you're every bit as hardheaded as you used to be."

"You're stalling."

"Yes, most of them. The big ones." Leslie turned her back and pulled two long loaves of Italian bread from a basket next to the stove.

"Which ones?"

"An echocardiogram and a stress test."

Dev felt a tightness in her chest just thinking that Leslie needed to have these kinds of examinations. As casually as she could, she said, "And?"

"There's nothing structurally wrong with my heart."

Dev slammed the lettuce down on the table, crossed to Leslie, and grabbed her by the shoulders. She pulled her around until they were facing one another. "Was that supposed to satisfy me?"

"I don't have to satisfy you. There's no reason I need to be telling you any of this," Leslie snapped, her eyes flashing. "And you can take your hands off me now."

"You're right." Dev lifted her hands and stepped back a pace. "Sorry."

"Dev—"

But Dev didn't hear the rest of Leslie's sentence. She was already out the back door and halfway down the steps. She hadn't meant to touch her. Not then. Not now. Leslie did things to her. Stirred places inside of her that she didn't even know were there until they bubbled up and exploded out of her. God, she'd thought that part of her, that crazy well of temper and helpless wanting, was gone. Wiped out on the highway with her blood, lost during the many months of pain while she'd struggled to find her way back to some kind of life.

It hurt to know she'd been lying to herself all this time.

CHAPTER FOURTEEN

S itting on one of the stone benches along the shore, Dev watched the sunset, trying to decide which was more beautiful, the beginning of the day or the ending. Sunrise always seemed to bring the promise of possibility, and with it, an undercurrent of joy. Nevertheless, she found this time of day to be her favorite, even though it always made her a little bit sad for something she couldn't name. Tonight, mist rose from the lake, and as the sun dropped behind the mountains, its last blue and purple rays were strewn across the water like angels cast out of heaven.

"It's almost too beautiful to look at, isn't it?" Leslie said quietly.

Dev continued to stare at the lake. She hadn't heard Leslie approach. "Sometimes I wonder why I live anywhere else. I think your parents might have the most beautiful spot on earth right here."

"Do you mind if I sit down?"

"No, go ahead."

After a few moments passed in silence and the colors leached from the sky, leaving behind a pewter gray that would soon become black, Dev glanced at Leslie. She'd changed into a V-neck sweater and jeans. Her hair was loose, and in the hazy light, she could have passed for twenty. Dev was stunned at an unexpected twist of longing and desire. "I'm sorry about what happened in the kitchen. I—"

"No," Leslie said quickly. "I'm sorry. That's what I came to tell you."

"How did you know where I was?"

"I didn't. But your cabin was dark and your truck is still in the lot." After the guests were taken care of, she'd gone looking for Dev. At first when she'd seen that Dev wasn't in her cabin, she'd thought Dev had probably gone somewhere with Natalie. It was pretty clear they were dating, and why that should bother her, she didn't know. But it seemed to put her in a foul mood. All the way home from the hospital, she'd been looking forward to seeing Dev and then when Dev had mentioned taking the afternoon off to spend with Natalie out on the lake, she'd felt foolish. The conversation about work and Dev's obvious disdain had frayed the last bit of her nerves, and she'd lost her temper. She never lost her temper. She never behaved like this at all. Constantly examining her every feeling. She didn't ruminate, she *acted.*

"You've been a great help in the last few days," Leslie said, determined to get back on sane footing. "And I want you to know I appreciate it."

"I didn't mean to get so personal tonight," Dev replied. "I shouldn't have badgered you about the tests."

"It's okay. It was…nice of you…to be concerned." Leslie meant it, and couldn't help but wonder why Rachel hadn't asked. To be fair, though, she *had* downplayed the entire thing with everyone.

Dev couldn't help herself. "Did everything else turn out okay? Besides the echocardiogram?"

Leslie sighed. "Not exactly. At the very end of the stress test I had a little bit of that irregular heartbeat thing happen. Nothing terrible, and I didn't really have any symptoms. I was a little short of breath, but I was running uphill at five miles an hour."

"So what did they say?"

"Oh, the usual. I should follow up with my physician. I should take my medication. I should avoid stimulants and stress—" Leslie snorted. "*That* should be simple enough."

"So you're going to do all that, right?"

It was almost dark, but Leslie could see Dev's eyes shining in the moonlight. Intense and penetrating. She'd know her eyes anywhere. She'd know her voice anywhere too. Husky and low.

"I suppose," Leslie said. She'd already decided to take the prescription medication she'd been provided, at least on a trial basis. Hopefully that would balance the coffee, because she had no intention of giving that up. As to the stress, she couldn't very well change her life.

"That's good." Dev's hand was only an inch away from Leslie's leg, but she resisted the urge to touch her. "Any news on your dad?"

"I talked to my mother right before I came down here. He's hungry and wants to come home." Leslie laughed. "Very positive signs."

"Great news."

"Yes. I'm sure he'll be a lot happier recuperating here than in the hospital."

"I can guarantee that."

Leslie caught her breath. Would they ever be able to talk without the past between them? Compelled by emotions that had lain buried since that night, she spoke almost without volition. "I'm sorry I didn't come to see you in the hospital."

"I wouldn't have known," Dev said quietly.

"That doesn't matter. I should have come." Leslie drew her legs up onto the bench and wrapped her arms around them. She rested her cheek on her knee, watching Dev's face, which was clearer now that the moon had risen. "I don't have any excuses, Dev."

Dev traced her fingertips lightly over the back of Leslie's hand, then pulled back. "You don't need any. You were young. We both were. It was all pretty confusing."

"You were my friend and I let Mike hurt you." Leslie ruthlessly quelled the tears that threatened to fill her eyes. "*I* hurt you. I don't expect you to forgive me, but I want you to know I regret it—have regretted it ever since that night."

"Leslie," Dev said softly. "You couldn't have stopped Mike. And I...I shouldn't have kissed you. It just happened."

"I wasn't expecting it. I didn't have any idea...I swear." Leslie gripped Dev's arm. "I didn't know what I was feeling back then. I didn't know what was happening between us."

Dev couldn't bear to hear the anguish in Leslie's voice. She cupped Leslie's cheek and traced her thumb along the edge of her jaw. "I know. It's okay. It wasn't your fault. It was mine."

"No! It wasn't your fault. There *was* no fault." Leslie caught Dev's hand, pressed her lips to Dev's palm. "How could there be, when we loved each other?"

Leslie's touch, Leslie's words—the nearness of her. It was more than Dev could take. She pushed her hand into Leslie's hair and kissed her. It was so like that first kiss, and so much more. She hadn't known then what lay beyond the soft warmth of Leslie's mouth, just as she hadn't fully recognized what her own body craved. She knew now with aching clarity. When Leslie's lips parted to allow her entrance, Dev kissed her more deeply. She wrapped an arm around Leslie's waist and pulled her tightly to her. Leslie's tongue met hers, not hesitantly, but every bit as questing. Every bit as demanding.

Leslie fisted Dev's shirt in both hands, pulling Dev closer still.

Dev reeled under an onslaught of sensation. Leslie's mouth was so hot, her body so firm and pliant as it cleaved to every curve of her own. When Leslie drew one thigh high over Dev's so their legs entwined, Dev groaned as heat rushed through her. She broke the kiss and crushed her mouth to Leslie's throat.

"God, Les," Dev moaned.

Leslie arched her neck and clasped the back of Dev's head, pressing her flesh against Dev's teeth, wanting to be devoured. She snaked her hand beneath Dev's waistband and yanked her shirt free, wild for the feel of Dev's skin. When Dev's hand skimmed beneath her sweater and closed over her breast, she cried out and raked her nails up Dev's abdomen.

Dev levered herself over Leslie's body and braced her hands on the back of the stone bench on either side of Leslie's shoulders. While her mouth roamed ravenously over Leslie's throat and jaw and mouth, she ground her hips between Leslie's legs. When she felt Leslie's fingers dig into her ass and Leslie's hips surge to meet her, the roaring in her head drowned out all thought. She was back in that other night, helpless with longing, drowning in emotions she couldn't even name. Leslie was her answer. Leslie was everything.

"Leslie," Dev groaned, dropping to her knees on the pine-needle-covered ground. She pushed up Leslie's sweater and kissed her stomach while she fumbled at the button on Leslie's jeans. She needed her. More than breath. More than the beat of her own heart. She needed her.

Dazed, Leslie thrust the fingers of both hands into Dev's hair, her back bowed off the bench, her head thrown back, her eyes nearly sightless as the inky sky and silver moon raced overhead. Leslie clutched Dev, afraid she might disintegrate and fly into pieces like so many bits of stardust.

Dev groaned. "Les, I love—"

Mike's voice roared out of the darkness. *Jesus, what the fuck—*

"Oh my God," Leslie gasped. "No!"

Dev jerked as if she'd been shot. She raised her head, her vision as wavy as if she'd been clubbed. It took her a second to realize where she was, what she was doing. Leslie's clothes were askew, her jeans unzipped, and *she* had her hand inside them. The expression on Leslie's face was something very close to fear.

"Oh, Jesus," Dev whispered.

Leslie shuddered, tears streaking her cheeks, staring at the shadows wavering around them, half expecting Mike to drag Dev away from her again. Then the dream trembled and broke and she knew where she was. What she'd done. "Dev," she murmured. "I can't."

"No, I know." Breathless, Dev forced herself upright. Her stomach was a hard ball of arousal, her legs shaking as if she'd run a marathon. She curled her hands into fists at her sides. "I'm so sorry. I don't know what happened." She took a step back, then another, then the darkness closed around her.

"Dev," Leslie called, but there was only the night.

Dev drove along Lakeshore Road for miles. This time, she was sober and careful, but her mind and body still echoed with memories of Leslie. Like the first time, but infinitely more intense. She smelled her, tasted her on her lips, felt her body along every inch of skin. Her stomach cramped with wanting. Her hands trembled on the wheel.

"Oh Christ," she groaned aloud. "Why can't I get free of her?"

She didn't expect an answer, because she knew there wasn't one. Because it wasn't Leslie, not the woman she'd practically accosted an hour ago, who haunted her. It was the girl she'd lost and never gotten over missing. It was the dreams that had died and that she couldn't let go of. It was something inside of her that kept the memories alive, even though she'd thought she'd put them to rest. She drove until fatigue replaced desire, at least for the moment.

By the time she pulled into the parking lot at Lakeview it was the middle of the night. The lodge was dark. She took a small flashlight from her glove box and used it to light her way through the woods to her cabin. She did not look toward Leslie's as she passed, although it took effort not to. When she turned onto the path to her own place, she felt a change in the air. She slowed.

"Les?"

"Can we talk?" Leslie said from the darkness.

She sounded as weary as Dev felt.

"Okay," Dev said as she climbed the steps to the porch. She sat next to her and switched off her light. "Have you been here the whole time?"

"Yes."

"You must be cold. I'll get you a jacket."

Leslie caught Dev's arm to stop her, then quickly let go. "No. That's okay, I have one. What about you?"

"I'll get one if I need it." Her voice was raspy, as if she hadn't used it in a long time. She dangled her arms over her knees, careful not to touch Leslie. She drew a breath to speak, but Leslie did first.

"There are some things I need to tell you," Leslie said.

"No, you don't. What happened—"

"Just wait. Just this once, don't be so sure you know what I'm going to say."

Dev stiffened, but nodded. "Okay."

"What happened by the lake that night was…innocent. You kissed me and I kissed you." She laughed flatly, thinking she'd heard that line somewhere before, but it meant so much more now. "That happens millions of times between teenagers everywhere, except it wasn't supposed to happen between us because we were both girls. Jesus."

"It wasn't all that innocent," Dev said quietly. "I knew—in my heart, I knew what I felt. What it meant."

"It was *still* innocent," Leslie said sharply. "How could it have been otherwise? We were in love."

The words tore through Dev's heart and she gripped her knees harder.

"What Mike did was horrible." Leslie paused, her breath shuddering from her. "And what I did was worse. What I said—" She turned, trying to read Dev's face in the shadows. "I don't know why I said what I said. It wasn't true. I was scared, I guess. Whatever, it doesn't matter now. I just want you to know it wasn't true."

"Thank you," Dev whispered.

"There's something else you need to know," Leslie said, finding the present truths even more difficult than the past.

Dev shook her head. "It's time to let all that go, Les. For both of us."

"I know. But it's not about then. It's about now."

The hollow note in Leslie's voice struck a deeper sense of dread in Dev's heart than Leslie's shocked cry earlier. Suddenly, she felt cold. She waited.

"I'm not sure exactly what happened down by the lake tonight," Leslie said hesitantly. "I think part of me was back there, the night we kissed and then Mike…hurt you. I remember how good you felt to me that night. How right." Her voice dropped to a hush. "How much I wanted you to touch me."

Dev's nails dug into her palms, and she bit her lip so hard holding back a groan that she drew blood.

"When you kissed me tonight, it was like before. All the old feelings came back and it was like I knew you. I wanted you."

"Except it wasn't really us anymore." Dev's chest ached with the sadness that welled within her.

"No," Leslie started to reach out, but thought better of it. Nothing she could do would change the truth. "Devon, you're seeing Natalie and I'm involved with someone too. We're neither of us free."

Free. The word mocked Dev, because she wondered if she would ever be free, or if she would merely move on while leaving parts of herself behind. Trying to explain that Natalie was a friend seemed pointless, because Leslie was with someone else.

"I might not know you now," Dev said, rising, "but you strike me as a one-woman woman."

"Well, one at a time anyways," Leslie said, trying to lighten the moment. She stood, noticing for the first time that Dev was shivering. "You should go inside. I just want you to know that it wasn't anything you did that upset me. Ever."

Dev put her hands in her pockets, because she knew Leslie was about to walk away. And God help her, she didn't want her to go. Even though every word Leslie spoke hurt her in a way she hadn't thought possible, she didn't want her to go. And that was exactly why one of them had to. And soon.

"Thanks, Leslie," Dev said quietly.

"For what?"

"For being the one to say no."

Leslie trembled as a flood of longing washed through her. Strangers or not, what she'd felt earlier in Dev's arms had made her feel alive in every cell. She was afraid to even think what that might mean.

"I'm glad you understand," was all Leslie could think to say. "Good night."

"Good night," Dev whispered. She waited until she heard the soft slide of Leslie's cabin door opening and the quiet snick of it closing. Then she sat back down on the steps and rested her face in her hands and wept for the love they'd once shared.

Chapter Fifteen

Leslie got up early the next morning after another night filled with fractured dreams and an impending sense of danger, although when she opened her eyes, the elusive feelings fled like bits of sand in the wind. She showered quickly, threw on jeans and a white boat-neck tee, and hurried to the lodge. Even though she knew it was foolish, she was inordinately relieved to see Dev's truck in the lot next to her parents' new Jeep. She had half expected Dev to be gone. The thought of Dev just disappearing left her feeling frighteningly hollow.

She pushed the disquieting sensation aside, reminded herself that the truck was still there and so was Dev, and went inside to take care of the work that needed to be done. She was in the midst of removing a second tray of biscuits from the oven when a sound behind her startled her into nearly dropping the entire thing.

"Ahh!" Leslie yelped. She managed to get the tray onto the counter before spinning around to discover Dev in the doorway. "Can you please stop sneaking up on me like that?"

"Sorry," Dev said without the slightest hint of contrition. Leslie looked great, and even in casual clothes, she definitely did not look like a woman who should be slaving in the kitchen at six in the morning. "Need some help?"

"Of course I need help." Leslie waved an arm at the general chaos of the kitchen, where baking pans, mixing bowls, and the ingredients for breakfast lay scattered over the counters. "I need a chef and a busboy and a gardener and a mechanic and someone to tell me how in God's name my parents run this place by themselves."

Dev frowned. "Are things really getting away from you?"

Leslie blew a loose strand of hair away from the corner of her mouth. "Not really. I can probably manage another day, and my mother's coming home later this afternoon. But even then, she's going to need help down at the dock and taking care of all the other things my father does."

"What about finding new hires?"

"I've got several people coming by this evening for interviews. At this point, anyone who hasn't just escaped from Sing Sing will be perfect."

Dev opened the refrigerator and started passing cardboard cartons of eggs to Leslie. "Scrambled are easiest." She checked the menu on the door. "Sausage. Piece of cake." She rummaged in the refrigerator's meat drawer and found the jumbo package of links, which she carried to the grill in the center of a cook island.

"What are you doing?" Leslie asked.

"Making my part of breakfast." Dev pointed a fork in the direction of the eggs. "You should start too, or else we won't be done at the same time."

Leslie opened a container of eggs, then closed it and carefully set it down on the counter. She watched the light blue denim shirt tighten across Dev's shoulders as Dev worked. Her hair curled over the collar, thick chestnut strands that were wavier than Leslie remembered. Dev wore her shirt tucked into an almost-tight pair of black jeans. It was an outfit Leslie had seen Dev wear many times when they were younger, but Dev no longer looked like the rangy teenager she had been. She looked like the strong, capable woman she was. They'd once been so close. They could be friends now, couldn't they?

After backing away from Dev last night and throwing up even more boundaries between them, Leslie knew that she would need to be the one to reach across the chasm. And since she'd been the one to walk away all those years before, that seemed more than fair.

"I thought you might have left," Leslie said softly.

Dev kept her back to Leslie and methodically arranged the sausages in two precisely even, side-by-side rows on the grill. She'd come close to piling her gear into the truck and driving away an hour earlier because she didn't think she could face Leslie and pretend she didn't feel anything. Not when she could still taste her. She might still have to go, but she wasn't ready yet. Leaving would be so final. "I thought about it."

"I'm glad you stayed," Leslie said, reaching for the eggs.

"Why?" Dev said quietly, her back still turned. She wasn't playing games. She really didn't understand what difference it would make to Leslie.

"You're handy in the kitchen." Leslie held her breath, and as the silence lengthened, she started to feel queasy.

Dev turned, a small smile curling the corners of her mouth. "You should see what I can do with a set of tools."

Leslie tried not to laugh, but the relief was so great she couldn't help herself. If she hadn't known better, she'd have thought that Dev was flirting. As it was, just this little bit of foolish conversation made her feel better than she had in days. "Well, you might be good with a wrench, but your sausage is burning."

"Shit!" Dev spun back to the grill and frantically began turning the small links.

Leslie took another second to enjoy watching Dev move, graceful even as she struggled to keep errant links from sliding off the grill onto the counter and floor, and then started cracking eggs into a bowl.

Dev dumped the sausages that were done onto a platter. When she'd finally gone to bed the night before, not expecting to sleep, she'd been ambushed by emotional and physical exhaustion. She'd fallen into a heavy dreamless sleep from which she'd awakened feeling fuzzyheaded and clumsy. When she thought about what had happened with Leslie by the lake, she'd been nearly as stunned as she had the first time they'd kissed. Except that back then, she'd known for a long time—although she hadn't been willing to admit it—that she'd wanted to kiss Leslie. Last night came out of nowhere.

"I appreciate you putting the brakes on last night," Dev said without turning around.

"Do you?" Leslie asked quietly. Although she was actually happy that Dev wasn't angry about her abrupt retreat, she wasn't entirely certain she was pleased that Dev didn't mind just a little.

"Seeing you has brought up a lot of old stuff for me," Dev said. "I've been a little off my game the last week or so."

"I'm sorry."

Dev shook her head and turned to meet Leslie's gaze. "It's okay.

It's probably all been a good thing." She grinned a little grimly. "I'm sure I'll think that, when I look back on it ten or twenty years from now."

Leslie smiled wryly.

"If I'd been thinking clearly, Les," Dev said, "I wouldn't have put you in a position of needing to say no."

"Oh, Dev." Leslie closed her eyes and shook her head. Then she opened them up on a long sigh. "At least at this point in our lives, let's agree that no more apologies are needed between us."

"Okay," Dev said softly. "Your eggs are done."

Natalie followed the scent of breakfast through the dining room, where one early riser sat sipping coffee and reading the newspaper. She stopped just inside the kitchen door to take in the sight of Dev and Leslie filling stainless steel warming pans with mountains of eggs, sausage, and biscuits. Both women looked pale and tired, but also oddly at ease as they moved around one another with ladles and skillets. Natalie couldn't put her finger on exactly what it was, but Dev and Leslie seemed in sync—connected. Now that was a thought she didn't want to dwell on.

"Boy, is my timing perfect," Natalie said, shrugging off the discomforting sensation.

Dev greeted her with a smile. "Hey! I thought you were tied up today."

"Good morning," Leslie said evenly.

"Hi, Leslie." Natalie turned to Dev. "I am. Meetings all damn day. I'll be brain dead by two. But I brought your gear and the permits over in case you decided to go out to the islands today on schedule."

"Thanks. I…" Dev glanced at Leslie, who seemed to be busy sliding the trays onto a cart. As much as she wanted to be available to help Leslie and her mother, she needed some distance from Leslie. She still felt shaky from the night before, and Leslie didn't look like she'd had a very good night either. Even thought they'd made a peace of sorts, Leslie had enough to deal with without the constant stress of having Dev around.

"I probably will head over if you can find someone to ferry me."

"I think Jimmy can do it. I'll call him," Natalie said, referring to one of the park rangers. "I know he's out on patrol and then he has to check on the campers who came in overnight, but—"

"I can take you over, Dev," Leslie said. "As long as you can wait until ten. I told my mother I'd pick her up around nine."

"You don't need to do that, Les," Dev said.

"No, really," Natalie interjected. "I'm sure I can—"

"You're a guest here, Dev," Leslie said, ignoring Natalie as she bumped the swinging door open with the front end of the cart. "Part of our service is taking campers to the islands. I'll call you as soon as I'm back from the hospital."

The door closed behind her with a resounding thump.

"Well," Natalie said, grinning at Dev. "I guess *that's* settled, then."

Dev frowned at the door, then muttered, "She's got enough to do without playing ferry master."

"How's her dad?" Natalie inquired. Leslie wasn't her type—a bit too polished and a bit too lethally beautiful, but she admired her spine. Under slightly different circumstances she could see them being friends.

"He's apparently doing really well. He might be home in a few days."

"That's great." Natalie liked both Eileen and Paul Harris, and she was pleased by the news. She was also happy because a quicker recovery for Leslie's father would mean Leslie's visit might be shorter. Natalie was sure there was more to the history between Leslie and Dev than Dev had told her, because Dev always looked a little unhappy when she was around Leslie. A little unhappy and a little hurt, both of which bothered Natalie a great deal. "Make sure you take one of the two-ways so you can contact the Harrises if you need to. They can get a message to me if there's anything you need or if there's a problem."

"It's pretty civilized out there," Dev said with a smile. "I don't expect I'll need to send an SOS."

"Maybe so," Natalie said seriously, "but you'll be a mile out in the middle of a whole hell of a lot of water on a little bitty piece of land. If there's trouble, you can't swim back and there's no phone."

Dev nodded. "I know. I'll make sure I've got everything." She tilted her head and grinned at Natalie. "Satisfied?"

Natalie slid a step closer and stroked Dev's upper arm. "Not yet. But I'm ever hopeful."

The door swung inward, and Leslie hurried through. She glanced at Dev and Natalie, honed in on the position of Natalie's hand and the way Natalie leaned into Dev, and quickly looked away. "I need more plates."

Natalie didn't move or take her gaze off Dev's face, but Dev eased back and lifted a stack of dishes.

"Got them right here."

Leslie turned on her heel and marched out. Dev followed in her wake as Natalie laughed softly.

Dev drove to the lab and made sure Arno had plenty of work to keep him busy for the next week. Then she took care of some correspondence, backed up her laptop to an external server, and finally loaded two plastic waterproof crates with the equipment she'd need for her work on the island. After carrying everything down to her truck, she made a stop for supplies, then drove back to the lodge. She pulled in just behind Leslie and her mother.

"Good morning," Dev said to Eileen as she climbed out of the truck. "Here, let me take your suitcase."

Eileen smiled, her face drawn and tired. "With pleasure. Thank you."

"How's your husband?"

"Doing very well." Eileen grasped Dev's arm. "Leslie tells me you've been helping out around here every day. I can't thank you enough."

Uncomfortable, Dev glanced at Leslie but got only a small shrug and a smile, as if to say, "Sorry, you're on your own."

"I really didn't do that much, Mrs. Harris."

"Well, you're not going to be paying any rent on that cabin this summer," Eileen said firmly.

Dev stopped abruptly. "Mrs. Harris, the Institute pays for my lodging, and I most certainly want you to charge. What I did, I did because… " *Because Leslie has always been more than just a friend.* Dev sensed Leslie watching her intently. "Because you and Leslie needed some help, and it was no imposition at all. Please."

"I'm not going to make you feel uncomfortable about it." Eileen squeezed Dev's arm and started across the lot toward the lodge. "Now, Leslie tells me you're going out to the islands today."

"Yes."

"We usually make just the two runs, delivery and pickup, but I'm sure we can arrange more frequent—"

"No," Dev said quickly, "that's fine. I won't need anything special."

They climbed onto the porch and Leslie reached for the suitcase Dev had carried. She said, "I'll be running the skiff for at least the next week or so. I don't have a problem swinging by your site to check on things."

Dev shook her head. "It's a good hour just to get out there, Les, and I know how much you have to do too."

Leslie answered lightly, "Multitasking is nothing new. Let me fill my mother in on what's going on here, and I'll meet you at the boat in a few minutes. Do you need help transferring your gear from the truck?"

"No, I've got it."

Thirty minutes later, Leslie piloted the twenty-foot Chris-Craft cruiser north toward the Glen Island chain. She handled the boat with confident efficiency. Despite the air temperature being in the mid-70s, the combination of wind and spray was cold. Dev's shirt was plastered to her chest, as was Leslie's, by the time they slowed on their approach to one of the undeveloped islands.

"Which side?" Leslie called, looking over her shoulder to where Dev sat. She stared for a second longer than was necessary, registering the unmistakable outline of Dev's breasts and remembering just how they had felt against hers the night before. Firm and tight-nippled and wonderful. She looked away.

"Northeast tip," Dev replied. As Leslie drew closer to shore, Dev pointed to a small sandy crescent rimming the thick woods at the water's edge. "What do you think about over there?"

"I think you're going to get the hell scratched out of you breaking trail through that underbrush."

Dev grinned. "I think you're right."

"I also think that's the only place to put up." Leslie looked back at Dev again. "This terrain is pretty rugged. Can't you do this work from a campsite on one of the other islands?"

"Too much water traffic." The engine noise had quieted enough for Dev to be heard without shouting. "Even with only a couple of boats coming in with campers every day, the turbulence from the prop wash stirs up the bottom. Can you drift in from here?"

Leslie cut the engine ten feet from shore. "I'm going to get out and pull her in."

"Forget it. You'll get soaked." Dev clambered up on the bow and before Leslie could protest, jumped into the knee-deep water to grab the towline. In a minute, she'd waded to shore and secured the boat with a line around a nearby tree.

"Does the wake really make that much difference to what you're studying?" Leslie asked, intrigued. She'd grown up on the lake, but she'd never really thought about it in such microcosmic terms.

"Yes. Here, start passing me the gear," Dev said. As Leslie handed down crates and Dev's tent, sleeping bag, and other supplies, Dev explained. "We've looked at water velocity at lake bottoms with Dopplers and measured the water turbidity with optical backscatter sensors—even motorboats running as slow as six miles an hour stir up the sediment and change the water clarity and nutrient composition."

"And?"

"Aquatic plant growth is altered, which affects the fish feeding patterns." Dev glanced out at the lake, then back at Leslie. "And the backwash makes it easier for contaminants in the water to be transported to other regions of the lake."

Leslie climbed down from the boat and hefted Dev's duffel. "What are you doing for food?"

"K rations. Dehydrated meals. I've got water-purifying tablets so I can use boiled lake water. I've done this before, Les. I'll be fine." Dev took the duffel from her. "There's no point you getting torn up too. I've got long sleeves. I'll be fine from here."

Leslie scanned the island. It was isolated from the others, densely forested and rocky, and not designated for normal camping. Dev would be here alone. The thought made her uneasy. "Do you have extra batteries for the two-way?"

"In my dry pack."

"I'll wear the radio. If you don't check in with me twice a day, I'll be out."

Dev frowned. "Besides the fact you'll contaminate my test waters, there's nothing for you to worry—"

"I'm really not interested in negotiating this, Devon. Either check in, or I'll be out here stirring up your sediment." Leslie gestured toward the woods. "Your other option is that I stay."

"To protect me?" Dev couldn't help herself. She grinned.

"You think I couldn't?"

Dev knew Leslie was capable of doing any number of things to her, and protection wasn't at the top of the list. Still, Leslie's concern made her feel good. Too good.

"I'll call in. Thanks."

Dev stared at Leslie across the pile of gear, aware of the sudden awkwardness. Leslie, in an uncharacteristic show of uncertainty, shuffled one foot in the sand as she scanned the woods behind Dev.

"You sure about this?" Leslie asked softly.

No. I'm not sure about anything where you're concerned. Dev nodded, grateful for the barrier between them. Sunlight slanted across Leslie's face, and she was so beautiful. Because looking at her was sweetly painful, Dev knew it was time for them to part.

"Yeah. I'll be fine. You should take off."

Reluctantly, Leslie climbed back into the boat. Dev waded into the water and pushed her out from shore, then returned to the tiny beach.

"I'll pick you up in five days, right?" Leslie called.

"Right."

"Be careful."

Dev waved and Leslie started the motor, carefully backing away from the shallows before revving up the power. Dev followed the boat until it was just a tiny speck in the distance. She hoped that when Leslie returned, the ache of longing she felt every time she looked at her would finally be gone.

CHAPTER SIXTEEN

How are things going?" Leslie asked, four days after she'd dropped Dev off on the island. She leaned against the porch railing and breathed deeply of the cool morning air, picturing Dev in the woods in her jeans, boots, and T-shirt. The radio transmission was remarkably good, and it sounded as if Dev were right next to her. She looked forward to their twice-a-day communications, not only because she worried with Dev working alone, but also because she enjoyed their brief shared updates.

"On schedule. I'm working my way around the southern tip of the island today, and should finish up tomorrow. How about you?"

"My father's coming home today. We have a new cook. Life is good." Leslie heard Dev laugh and realized life *was* good. Once her mother had returned, the two of them had been able to handle things at the lodge with enough time left over for Leslie to look over the cases from the local office. She worked, she walked on the beach, and she'd started to sleep more than three hours a night.

"Sounds good," Dev said. "So I'll see you tomorrow morning."

"Will do. Take care."

"Always."

Leslie clicked off the radio, smiling as she envisioned Dev at work on the island. She never would have predicted Dev as a scientist, and a fish expert at that, but now it seemed so natural. So *Dev*, really. Dev had always been an observer, apart from things, so very private. It had always been special when Dev had shared her thoughts and feelings, because Leslie knew it was rare for her. Being Dev's friend had made her feel special.

"Was that Dev?" Eileen asked.

Leslie jumped. She hadn't heard her mother come out onto the porch.

"Yes," Leslie replied, aware that her mother was studying her intently. "She's fine."

"Good. I'm glad you're checking in with her," Eileen said casually. She crossed the porch, carrying a cup of coffee. "How come I never met her when the two of you were teenagers? You're obviously very good friends."

Leslie contemplated some neutral explanation and then thought perhaps it was time to bridge another rift in her life. "We weren't friends like I was friends with the other girls. We didn't do social things together. We just…talked."

"But you were close, weren't you? I can tell from the way you talk to her. And the way she looks at you."

"What do you mean—the way she looks at me?" Despite herself, Leslie felt herself blushing.

Eileen sipped her coffee and smiled softly. "I think even if you hadn't told me you were a lesbian, I would have noticed that she follows you with her eyes the way I'm used to seeing men watch women."

Leslie snorted, thinking of Mike and the few men after him she'd dated. "I doubt it. Dev is nothing like a man."

"There are some men who truly do appreciate women," Eileen said gently. "Your father is one."

"I know," Leslie admitted. "You're right. Still, Daddy is special." She braced her hands on the railing and leaned out, letting the sunlight strike her face, enjoying the warmth and the smell of summer. "Dev always treated me as if I were precious," she said softly, almost to herself, because it was the first time she'd ever given a name to what Dev had made her feel. She looked at her mother. "I guess I wanted to keep that all to myself. Maybe that's why I never brought her home."

"Maybe it was because you didn't think I'd understand," Eileen said sadly. "I'm sorry if I made you feel that way."

Leslie shook her head. "No. It wasn't about you. I didn't understand myself what I felt."

"And you didn't…understand…until you were in college?"

"Not exactly," Leslie said with a sigh. She curled an arm around the porch post and sat on top of the railing, her legs dangling free. She leaned her head against the column and thought about how long she'd denied her feelings. "I never considered that what was happening between Dev and me was anything except a wonderful friendship. I was clueless." She shook her head. "God. Worse than clueless. And then one night she kissed me...no, *we* kissed...and I didn't handle it very well."

Eileen said nothing, but she briefly stroked Leslie's arm.

"Some bad things happened. Dev had an accident." Leslie closed her eyes. "Part of that was my fault." When her mother murmured with concern, Leslie waved her away. "It's a long story, and Dev and I have already talked it out. But it took me years to admit that what she and I had was what I really wanted."

"And you have someone now?"

Leslie hesitated. "Yes."

"Did you find it again?" Eileen asked softly. "What you had with Dev?"

"No." Leslie met her mother's eyes, her expression flat.

"Perhaps you will yet."

"There's no going back. Besides, everyone knows that first love is too sweet to ever last."

"Not everyone agrees," her mother pointed out gently.

Leslie shrugged. She wasn't in the mood to argue, not when they'd had their first real conversation in over a decade. "I can drive you to the hospital to pick up Daddy, if you want." She scanned the sky, where a few fluffy clouds floated by. Far to the north a darker cloud bank was just visible beyond the mountains. "We might get some of that rain after all."

"Didn't you say you wanted to spend some time at your office today?"

"Dev left me her keys so I could use her truck. I can go in this afternoon."

"Go ahead. I can handle things at the hospital."

"It will be good to have him home." Leslie slid off the banister and walked with her mother toward the front door.

"It certainly will."

"Are we still going to have the Fourth of July party Saturday night?"

"Of course. The guests always enjoy it, and so do the locals. I *am* going to have some of the food catered this year, though, so all we have to do is make sure the boathouse is in good shape."

"I'll take care of overseeing that."

Eileen squeezed Leslie's hand. "I'm glad you came home. I'm sorry there's been so much for you to do here, but it still feels wonderful."

"Every now and then, I actually forget I have another life." Leslie laughed. "A completely different life."

"You seem very much yourself to me," Eileen remarked, opening the door.

I never thought I'd say this, but I feel like myself here. Leslie looked over her shoulder down the grassy slope to the boathouse and the lake beyond. A few boats were out on the lake already. A few of the guests were walking along the shore, some holding hands. The sun was impossibly bright, the sky incredibly blue, the silvery surface of the lake hopelessly beautiful. In the back of her mind, she heard Dev's laughter. "Well, it is home, after all."

Leslie sipped her coffee and opened another file. It was amazing how quickly she'd slipped into work mode as soon as she'd reached the office. This was comfortable too—reviewing, analyzing, teasing out the critical facts from a miasma of information. She felt as if she were hunting, pitting her skills against a wily prey. To the strongest, or perhaps the smartest, went the victory, and she liked being the victor. She made some notes, scratched a memo to have her paralegal check several rulings, and rose to get another cup of coffee.

"Excuse me, Ms. Harris," the office receptionist said, "but Mr. Carpenter said we're going to close early today because of the storm. He wants to go secure his boat." The pretty blonde laughed. "He's totally weird about that new boat." Then as if just realizing that Leslie, although a visiting attorney, was technically her boss, she blushed. "I mean, he's—"

Leslie frowned. "Storm? What are you talking about?"

The blonde pointed to the window behind Leslie. "There's some kind of freak storm blowing in from the north. Like a summer Alberta Clipper, without the snow. They're predicting really high winds and—"

"Since when?" Leslie snapped, quickly pushing the files she'd been working on into her briefcase.

"Oh, you know these weathermen. In the winter, they forecast snow for a week and then we don't get anything. Then, when something important happens, like this, it's a big surprise. Anyhow, it's supposed to be a big one and—"

Leslie didn't hear the rest as she hurried from the room. She glanced at her watch on her way out of the building. It was almost four in the afternoon. Her mother and father would be home by now. She hoped. Outside, she faltered, staring at the sky with a rising sense of dread. Overhead, the crystal blue of the morning had given way to an ominous purple, and to the north, the sky was nearly black with roiling storm clouds. It felt as if the temperature had dropped twenty degrees since earlier in the day, and the air was oppressively heavy. Her skin clammy, Leslie shivered and sprinted toward Dev's truck. Flinging her briefcase into the backseat, she slid behind the wheel and speed-dialed the lodge at the same time. She was forty minutes from home if she pushed all the way.

"Mom? What's it like up there?"

"The wind is up and the lake looks nasty. It's going to be a good blow. Where are you?"

"On my way home."

"They're talking about trees down and power out. We aren't expected to get hit for another couple of hours yet, so you should be fine. Drive carefully."

"What about Dev? Have you talked to her?" Leslie asked urgently. Because she was out of radio range at the office, she'd left the two-way in the lodge for her mother to monitor.

"I was just about to call her."

"Tell her I'll be out to get her as soon as I get home."

"Leslie, you can't go out on the lake. The waves are two feet high already and there's a small craft warning."

"She can't stay out there in this!"

"I'll call the forest rangers, then. You're not going after her."

"Fine. Call Natalie Evans in the Bolton Landing office. Tell her she needs to go get Devon. Call her right now."

Leslie switched on the windshield wipers, although the rain, which had just started, was still light. "Mom?"

"You just worry about driving. I'll take care of things here."

"Call me back as soon as you know what's happening." Leslie tossed the BlackBerry onto the seat beside her. Thankfully, the Northway was relatively clear of traffic as everyone was trying to reach shelter, and she pushed Dev's truck to eighty. Then she switched on the radio, watching the road as she punched buttons in search of a local station. Finally, she found the all-news station.

"…winds to fifty miles an hour, small craft warnings on all regional waterways, and heavy flooding expected on many of the secondary roadways. The governor has declared—"

Leslie tuned out the rest of the weather report. Summer storms often brought high winds and torrential rain, but they usually weren't sustained for more than an hour or two. But an off-season variant of a clipper could last twenty-four hours or more and might dump a foot of rain. She thought about Dev in a tent on an island that was likely to be buffeted by gale-force winds and flooded by high waves. She stared at the phone, and as if she had willed it, it vibrated. She snatched it up.

"Hello?"

"Dev says she's fine. Not to worry."

"Bullshit. Of course she isn't fine!" Leslie flicked on the turn signal so vehemently the lever nearly snapped off. "I'm exiting now and I'll be home in twenty minutes. What did Natalie say?"

"I could only reach the officer on the desk. They're all out evacuating campers from the islands."

"Tell him you want to speak to Natalie Evans. Tell him it's an emergency. Tell him if you don't speak to her, I'm going to have someone's ass." Leslie gunned the truck onto Route 9 and fought with the wheel as it skidded on the wet pavement. "Son of a bitch."

"What?"

"Nothing. Just call them back." Leslie clutched the phone and switched the wipers to high as rain battered the windshield. Her chest tightened and out of the blue, the fluttering started. She blinked as a wave of dizziness swept through her and she shook her head angrily to dispel it. "I don't have time for this."

To her relief, the brief episode passed and her vision cleared. She concentrated on what needed to be done. If her mother didn't reach Natalie, her choices were few. In fact, there was only one choice.

The parking lot was empty, as were the grounds, as Leslie roared into the lot. She jumped out and sprinted through the steady rain to the lodge. The wind had picked up, and she noticed that most of the leaves had turned over, their bottoms to the sky. It was a sure sign that the barometric pressure was falling and a big storm was on its way. Eileen met her at the door.

"Did you reach Natalie?" Leslie gasped.

Eileen shook her head. "The ranger in the office promised to get a message to her. She knows Dev is out there, Leslie. She'll get her."

"Natalie's going to be lucky to get all the campers out of the campsites. And she has to do that first. She has to. Besides, she knows that Dev is better equipped than anyone else to ride out the storm, so she'll leave her till last." Leslie hurried to the small office beyond the dining room and snatched up the two-way. "Dev? Dev, do you read me?"

"Leslie...hear you."

Even through the static, the sound of Dev's voice instantly quieted her racing heart. "Hey you. I'll be there in an hour. Everything okay?"

"Don't ...co...ere. D...you read...on't... Les..."

"An hour, Devon. See you then." Leslie switched off and turned to find her father watching from his wheelchair in the doorway. Hastily, she bent down and kissed his cheek. "Hi, Daddy. Welcome home. I'm sorry, I have to go right back out."

"Your mother told me about your friend." Paul Harris backed his wheelchair up to allow Leslie room to pass. "It'll be rough out there on the water, sweetheart."

"Good thing you taught me how to handle the boat, then," Leslie called on the run.

"Check your gear before you head out," he shouted after her.

"I will. Don't worry." Leslie pulled her mother's rain slicker off a coat tree just inside the back door and slammed out. Pulling it on, she hurried down to the docks. There wasn't much of a margin before the storm really broke, but she calculated there would be just enough time to get there and back. She jumped into the boat and did a quick check in the storage lockers for the critical items—battery-powered searchlights, the GPS transmitter, an inflatable life raft, and PFDs. She shrugged into a life vest and zipped it up, then released the tie lines and pushed the boat away from the dock. As she turned the key in the ignition and revved the motor, she thought grimly of backwash and the effect of the propellers on the sediment in the shallows. Right now, that seemed far less important than reaching Devon. In fact, she couldn't think of a single thing that felt more critical.

She hunched her shoulders against the driving wind, narrowed her eyes in the pelting rain, and thrust the throttle to the max. The boat leapt forward, the big motor whining as the bow crashed heavily in the troughs between the waves. Her teeth knocked together painfully, and she clenched her jaws and spread her legs to steady herself, keeping a death grip on the wheel. She didn't think about the impending storm or the rising chop. She thought about Dev. This time, she had no intention of leaving Dev to face danger alone.

CHAPTER SEVENTEEN

L eslie! Leslie, do you read?" Dev held the two-way close to her ear with one hand and dragged her tarp over the equipment cases she had piled in a rocky cul-de-sac near her campsite with the other. She waited a full minute for a response, then jammed the radio into the front pocket of her anorak. "God damn it."

Rain drummed steadily against the leaves overhead, but the canopy was not yet saturated and only a slow drizzle was getting through to her. The wind had picked up, though, and it wouldn't be long before the rain penetrated the last remaining barrier between her and the angry sky. She piled rocks around the edges of the tarp and hastily trenched it as well as she could with the small folding shovel she'd packed with her camping gear. Then she trenched her tent and pounded extra stakes with additional guidelines into the firmest ground she could find. Thunder rolled and a sheet of rain sliced through the trees, hitting her in the back of the neck, immediately soaking her shirt. She couldn't even be bothered to swear, but just pulled her hood over her head.

After checking one more time to see that everything was as secure as she could make it, she skidded down the narrow path to the shore, following the trail through the trees she'd created by her daily trek to the lake. By the time Dev reached the shore, the wind buffeted her body and she needed to lean forward to maintain her balance. The thin rim of sandy beach was gone, washed away by the pounding waves. Clinging to the slippery bank with an arm around a tree, she pulled out the radio. "Leslie? Leslie, this is Dev. Where the hell are you?"

She hoped someone had had the good sense to keep Leslie off

the lake. The surface of the water was so churned up it looked like the ocean rather than an inland lake. The sky had darkened to the point where she needed to use her flashlight to check her watch. It'd been a little over an hour since her last communication with Leslie. Dev squinted into the rain and scanned the lake, but the visibility was less than fifty yards. She jammed her hands into her pockets, hunched her shoulders against the wind, and ignored the cold as icy rain soaked through her jeans below her anorak.

Five minutes later, she heard it—the sound of an engine laboring somewhere in the inky mist. She switched on her flashlight and waved it in a wide, slow arc above her head, squinting so hard into the rain that her eyes ached. The air howled like a creature in pain, and for a moment, Dev thought she'd imagined the sound of a motor. Then a flicker of light caught her eye, went out, and flickered on again. A rhythmic on and off that she recognized as a bow light, cresting and disappearing into the troughs between the waves as a boat fought its way to shore. She couldn't make out the figure in the boat as the craft wallowed, spun sideways, and threatened to go over. Miraculously, the pilot maneuvered the bow around until it pointed toward shore again, but the water was so rough the boat couldn't land. Holding the flashlight above her head with one hand, Dev waded into the water up to her thighs and stretched out an arm.

"Throw the line!" she shouted against the wind, knowing it was hopeless. She could feel the words being forced down her throat before they'd even cleared her lips. Nevertheless, a line snaked through the air and whipped across her chest. Reflexively, she caught it and wrapped it around her forearm. Fortunately, her jacket protected her arm, because the rope immediately tightened like a noose. She could feel it biting into her skin even with the protection of the nylon. Gritting her teeth against the pain, she leaned backward toward shore, using her body as an anchor to keep the front of the boat directed toward land. Each time the rope loosened she stepped backward, keeping the guideline tight. She could see Leslie's face now, screaming something to her.

One step. Two. Three. Dev stumbled, fell backward into the lake, and lost her flashlight. The rope around her arm loosened as she swallowed water and flailed in the shallows just offshore. Coughing and sputtering, struggling in her boots and wet jeans, she tried unsuccessfully to regain her feet. Then an arm circled around her waist and steadied her. She broke the surface spewing water and gasping for air.

"Are you crazy?" Leslie shouted. "You could've gone under the boat and gotten tangled up in the propeller. I could have killed you!"

"Look who's talking," Dev shouted back. "What the hell are you doing out here? You're lucky you didn't capsize in the middle of the lake and drown."

"The storm's coming in faster than they predicted," Leslie said, ignoring Dev's chastisement. "The lake's too rough to make the return trip now."

"Let's secure the boat and get to high ground!"

Even as they shouted, Dev and Leslie both grabbed the towrope and dragged the boat as far up onto what remained of the shoreline as they could. Then Leslie staggered up the muddy bank and began wrapping the line around a rocky outcropping. Dev joined her, and between them, they secured the boat as well as they could.

"We'll be lucky if it doesn't wash away," Dev said, her mouth close to Leslie's ear.

"We'll be lucky if *we* don't wash away!"

"Come on," Dev said, taking Leslie's hand. "Follow me."

Just as they cleared the underbrush and reached the relative sanctuary of the forest, a tremendous crash sounded overhead and a giant pine toppled and fell almost directly on top of them. Dev yanked Leslie with her as she dove off the trail and against the base of another evergreen. The trunk of the falling pine ended up canted against the tree that protected them, about four feet above their heads.

"Are you okay?" Dev yelled.

"Scratched up a bit, but in one piece," Leslie called back.

"We need to crawl out from under here and head uphill. I'll go first. Hold on to my jeans so you can follow me."

"Be careful."

Dev pushed at the branches with one arm and forced a tunnel through them with her head and shoulders. Now and then she registered discomfort, but her whole body felt bruised and battered and a little more pain barely mattered. Once she cleared the maze of branches, she turned on her back and reached down for Leslie's arms to pull her free of the debris. Leslie crawled out and collapsed on top of Dev. The rain was so heavy it felt as if they were at the bottom of a waterfall and, once again, Dev was breathing water. She coughed.

Leslie sheltered Dev's upturned face with her body. "You're bleeding!"

Dev pressed her cheek to Leslie's chest and managed to draw air into her lungs instead of rain. "I'm okay. The…campsite's…a hundred yards from here. Let's…go."

"Are you sure you're not hurt?"

"I'm good."

Reluctantly, Leslie slid to the side so Dev could get to her knees. Then Leslie wrapped her arm around Dev's waist and helped her up. When Dev tried to pull away, she tightened her grip. "Don't be stubborn. Just get us there."

Traversing the slope was like walking through a sluice jammed with logs. The rain was a solid wall of water, and branches skimmed by out of nowhere, bouncing off their bodies and scraping their faces and hands. After what felt like an interminable struggle, Dev stumbled to a halt next to a nylon tent. With hands numb from cold and swollen from batting away projectiles, she fumbled with the zipper and finally got it open. Together, she and Leslie pushed through the flap, Dev zippered it behind them, and they both collapsed onto Dev's sleeping bag.

For five minutes the only sound in the small tent was the rasp of their arduous breathing. Then Dev sat up, fumbled in the dark, and finally turned on a battery-powered lantern. The tent roof and sides billowed in and out as if it were a living, breathing organism.

"Some storm," Dev muttered, setting the light on the metal lid of a cooking pot in one corner of the tent.

"Uh-huh," Leslie said.

Dev pulled off her anorak and spread it out in one corner. "You shouldn't have come."

With a grunt of effort, Leslie rolled onto her side to face Dev. Although generously called a four-person tent, the tent was designed for two people to sleep with just enough space on either side for a little bit of gear. Dev had obviously brought all of her critical equipment inside, because there was barely room for the two of them on the sleeping bag. And that was taking into account the fact that the steel toe of one of Dev's spare boots was pressed into Leslie's backside.

"In case you hadn't noticed, all hell is breaking loose out there," Leslie said.

Dev glared. "My point precisely. That was a crazy stunt. Here, let me have your jacket."

Leslie handed Dev her wet rain gear. "If the weathermen had been even close to accurate, we should've had enough time to get back to the mainland."

"And when have you ever known that to happen?" Dev leaned down on one elbow, the length of her body stretched out beside Leslie.

Leslie hesitated. "Point taken." When Dev smiled, she said more softly, "I really thought we had another hour or two."

"I should say thanks for coming," Dev said quietly, "but I'm still too terrified to be gracious."

"Terrified?" Leslie arched a brow.

"I was worried about you." Dev touched a bruise on Leslie's forehead. "Looks like you got clobbered with something."

"A branch, I think." Leslie traced a fingertip over Dev's cheek. "You're bleeding."

Dev snorted and rubbed the blood away on her sleeve. "We're a mess." She shivered violently. "And it's getting cold. We need to get out of these clothes."

"I don't have spares."

"You can wear some of mine."

Leslie sat up and wrapped her arms around her torso. "Do you have a first aid kit? We ought to clean that scrape on your face."

"The scratch won't kill me. Let's get dry first."

"Good idea." Leslie glanced around the interior of the tent while Dev pulled a duffel into her lap and unzipped it. There was absolutely no possibility of privacy. Well, that shouldn't matter. They were both adults and this was an emergency. Still, Leslie's throat was irrationally dry. She'd never seen Dev naked. They hadn't been in the same phys. ed. class in high school, and Dev hadn't played any organized sports. There'd never been any reason to undress in the locker room in front of one another.

"Here's a sweatshirt and jeans. They'll fit you." Dev handed over the clothes, piled similar items at her feet for herself, and began unlacing her boots. Without looking at Leslie, she continued, "I've got socks for you but no dry boots."

"Thanks." Leslie decided that speed was the best option and hurriedly pulled her top and bra off together in one quick motion. She was soaked to the skin. "God, this is miserable."

"Here's a towel for your hair. It's the only one, so we'll have to sha—" The words died in Dev's throat as she half turned to hand Leslie the towel. Leslie's arms were extended over her head with the dry sweatshirt partway down. Her breasts were full and pale, her nipples puckered from the cold. Even in the lamplight, Dev could see the bluish tint to her skin. "Jesus, Les. You're freezing."

"I'm just—" Leslie went still, staring at Dev between the triangle of her raised arms as Dev leaned toward her.

Rising to her knees, Dev rapidly wrapped the towel she still held in her hands around Leslie's chest and began to rub her vigorously. "Christ, you're shaking."

It wasn't from the cold. Even through the towel, Leslie could feel Dev's hands on her. Her brain told her that Dev was just drying her off, but her body translated the movements into something quite different. She felt Dev's palms cup her breasts and Dev's thumbs flick her nipples. Against her will she arched her back, lifting her breasts and hips, seeking more contact. Her thighs and pelvis nestled into Dev. Leslie caught back a gasp. "You're wet too. You need to get out of that shirt and your jeans."

"In a minute," Dev muttered, leaning closer to reach Leslie's back. "Almost done."

Leslie couldn't tolerate the contact any longer. She either needed more, much more, or she needed to get away from the heat of Dev's body and the fire that ignited everywhere that Dev touched her. She yanked the sweatshirt down over her head, and once her hands were free, pushed the towel and Dev away. "Get dry, Dev."

Startled by the irritation in Leslie's voice, Dev stared at the towel in her hands, then into Leslie's eyes. Leslie's pupils were wide and dark, as if she were very angry or very aroused. Dev wondered what secrets her own eyes revealed, because while she'd been preoccupied taking care of Leslie, she hadn't allowed herself to consider what she'd been touching. But now, even when there was no contact at all between them, she could feel the weight of Leslie's breasts in her hands. She wanted to touch them again. "Take off your pants and get into the sleeping bag."

Leslie waited until Dev had turned her back to remove her shirt before unzipping her own jeans, struggling out of them and her panties, and climbing into the sleeping bag. Much as she had when Dev had cooked in the kitchen the previous week, Leslie watched the muscles in Dev's back flex and ripple as she dried her hair and chest. But in the kitchen, Dev had worn a shirt. Now the smooth expanse of muscle and skin shimmered and called to her. Leslie closed her eyes and didn't open them again until she felt Dev shift around on the sleeping bag.

"I can't get my pants on in here unless you get off the bag and give me a little room," Leslie said, feeling ridiculously like a mummy.

Dev, in a dry shirt and jeans, grinned. "I can't go very far, but I'll try." She got to her knees and straddled the sleeping bag. "That's about it."

"Great," Leslie muttered, twisting around in the bag, rocking against the inside of Dev's thighs before finally managing to knee her soundly in the crotch.

"Omph," Dev grunted. "Glad you don't have much range of motion in there. Could be dangerous out here."

Leslie couldn't help it, she laughed. "Shut up, Devon, and get in here."

Dev stared. "What?"

"What was your plan?" Leslie inquired evenly. "That I should sleep in the sleeping bag, all nice and cozy, while you lie on the outside and freeze?"

"Well, I hadn't exactly intended the freezing part."

"Just get in here." Leslie pulled back the flap and turned on her side to give Dev as much room as possible. "Do you think the roof will hold up in this rain?"

The torrent outside continued and gave no indication of letting up.

"It's good gear. We ought to stay dry." Dev turned out the lantern and then inched her way down into the sleeping bag, trying not to slide her body along Leslie's. When she was all the way in, they faced one another awkwardly with nowhere to comfortably place their knees and elbows. Dev blew out a breath. "The only way this is going to work is if one of us lies on her back and the other sleeps half on top. So, top or bottom?"

Leslie couldn't see Dev's face in the dark, but she thought she heard amusement in her tone. Tightly, she said, "Top."

"Works for me." Dev curved one arm behind Leslie's neck and shoulders, settled onto her back, and pulled Leslie down into the curve of her body. Leslie's head nestled on her shoulder, with Leslie's torso and one leg partially on top of her body. Dev took a minute to adjust to the unfamiliar and yet completely natural feel of Leslie lying in her arms. Then she whispered, "Okay?"

"Perfect," Leslie said sarcastically. She was fairly certain that Dev didn't realize just how much she meant exactly what she said.

CHAPTER EIGHTEEN

A re you sleeping?" Leslie whispered.

"No." Dev shifted carefully and resettled Leslie's head against her shoulder. She didn't feel tired, and even if she were, she doubted she would sleep. Being cocooned with Leslie had ramped her every sense to high alert. The smell of Leslie's hair, the tickle of Leslie's breath against her neck, the soft weight of Leslie's breasts molded to her side—Dev felt as if she were underwater again, only this time she was immersed in Leslie, and drowning was a welcome pleasure. Her body was vibrating, and she wondered why Leslie couldn't feel it.

"Cold?" Leslie unconsciously pressed closer, wrapping an arm around Dev's middle.

"No. You?"

"Uh-uh. Toasty." Leslie lay angled onto Dev's left side, her cheek against Dev's chest, above her heart. Dev's heartbeat, slow and steady, was a soothing counterpoint to the flurry of rain on the tent. Leslie had never been this intimate with a friend, and rarely with a lover. She and Rachel barely had time to have sex. They weren't into lounging in bed. Dev's body was solid, heavier than Rachel's; her hand where it rested lightly on Leslie's back was larger, her legs thicker with muscle. Leslie flushed with a body memory of Dev kissing her on the bench by the lake, the weight of her pinning her down, Dev's mouth on her bare stomach, moving lower. *Oh, God, don't go there. Not with her so close.* Leslie focused on something safer—the storm. "It's still coming down out there."

"We're probably in for another twelve hou—"

Somewhere close, very close, a crack like a rifle shot was followed by a thud that shook the ground beneath them. Leslie flinched and, unconsciously trying to shield Dev, flung her arm over Dev's face at the same time as Dev pulled Leslie's head into the protective curve of her neck. After long tense seconds, Leslie started to breathe again.

"I guess if you hear it, it didn't fall on you," Leslie murmured. Her heart was pounding, but she sensed none of the rapid irregularity that usually preceded one of her light-headed episodes. She was just plain damn scared. "I should've gotten to you sooner. We're like sitting ducks out here."

Dev laughed. "The ducks are doing a lot better than we are right now. Besides, when we talked this morning everything was calm and clear." She rested her cheek against the top of Leslie's head. "You came as soon as you could, and you shouldn't have come at all."

Leslie poked Dev in the stomach. "Don't start that again. I didn't do anything you wouldn't have done."

"Actually, you did," Dev said. "I couldn't have gotten that boat this far. I'm not that good."

Pleased, Leslie traced her fingertips along the open collar of Dev's shirt, just skimming the warm skin beneath. "I practically grew up around boats. I've been piloting one since I was tall enough to see over the steering wheel. When I was younger, I loved the speed."

"Yeah, I seem to recall that while you were tearing up the water, I was tearing up the road on my bike."

Leslie heard a wistful note in her voice. "Do you ride anymore?"

"No, the road shock really plays hell with my hip."

"I didn't realize it was a problem now," Leslie said quietly. She knew Dev had been badly injured, but she didn't know the precise extent. How could she? She'd never tried to find out back then, and hadn't asked recently. Still blocking it out, still running. God, what a coward. "You don't limp. I never realized it still bothered you."

"It doesn't, most of the time. Sometimes when I'm cold or stiff, my leg aches but—"

"God, this must be killing you! Lying on the ground with me on top of you?" Immediately guilty, angry with herself for not thinking of Dev—again—Leslie tried to lift herself off Dev. "Why didn't you say something? *Damn it*, Dev—"

Dev tightened her grip on Leslie's shoulder, and since there was very little room to maneuver in the bag, it wasn't difficult to keep Leslie in place. "It's plenty warm in here and my leg feels fine. Stop fussing before one of us gets an elbow in the eye."

Still grumbling, Leslie settled back down, but their positions had altered just enough that her leg came to rest between Dev's. She heard Dev gasp and knew that her own breath had caught audibly.

"Sorry," Leslie said, trying unsuccessfully to disentangle her leg. She needed to get away from Dev, immediately. The place where her thigh rested high up between Dev's legs was hot, and she imagined the warmth of Dev's sex cupped in her palm. The ridge of Dev's hipbone snugged into her mons, and she barely resisted the urge to rub against her. She was full and throbbing and Dev's firm body felt so good. So terribly good. When she clenched inside, instantly wet, she pushed at Dev's chest. "I need to get out. Can you reach the zipper?"

"What's wrong? Where are you going?" Dev asked thickly. Somehow her hands had ended up nestled in the curve of Leslie's lower back. Another inch and Leslie would be completely on top of her, and Dev would be lost. Most of her wanted to be lost, because somehow she knew it would feel like being found. But the little part of her that was still able to stand apart and look down at them in the sleeping bag, with the world a screaming, swirling chaos outside, told her it was not the time. She groaned softly. "When will it ever be the time?"

"What?" Leslie whispered when Dev murmured something into her hair that she couldn't make out. When Dev merely shook her head, Leslie stroked her cheek. Dev's cheek was damp, and she was shaking. Leslie wasn't sure why, but Dev was hurting, and knowing that was breaking her heart. Could the truth be so terrible? "I want to make love with you."

"I want to too," Dev said, lying absolutely still, her hands barely making contact. She was afraid of losing it again, like she had the first time and then again last week. But the wanting was a huge void begging to be filled, a pain more profound than any broken bone or mangled muscle had ever been. "I've wanted you for so long."

The tent filled with silence louder than the storm.

Truth, Leslie thought. The one thing she still owed Dev, what she would always owe her, was truth. The words tore at Leslie's throat. "I want you so much, but I'm afraid it's a mistake."

"I know it is." Dev ran her fingers through Leslie's hair, then cupped the back of her neck. Leslie's breasts were cleaved to hers, their stomachs moving together as they breathed, their intertwined legs trembling. Leslie lifted her head as if to speak and Dev kissed her tenderly, just the barest touch of lips. An ache of wonder filled her chest and her words came out on a sob. "I know it's a mistake, Les, but I don't *feel* it. When I touch you, when I'm anywhere near you, places open up inside of me that are filled with sunlight. Places that have been dark for so long."

"Oh God, Dev," Leslie whispered, wanting to kiss her so badly. She hungered for Dev's passion to flood over her the way it had every time they'd kissed, and the force of her wanting terrified her. "I can't tell anymore what's real and what isn't. Up until a few weeks ago I knew exactly who I was, what I was doing, where I was going. Now I…I hardly recognize myself."

"Do you love her?"

The question pierced Leslie's heart, because she had never asked it herself. Of herself. Even though she couldn't see Dev clearly in the pitch-black tent, Leslie closed her eyes. She didn't need to see Dev's face to hear the pain, and knew what the asking had cost her. She kept her eyes closed while she searched for an answer, because she couldn't bear to see ever again what her words did to Dev. Truth. God, what was truth? Were there gradations of truth? Was something true only if she didn't know any other way to be, any other way to feel? When had truth become relative for her? When had love?

Did she love Rachel? Two years. She'd been a willing partner in making the relationship whatever it was or wasn't. Rachel was not at fault for never giving Leslie what she hadn't demanded, and Leslie would not negate her as she had once negated Dev. She took a deep breath and refused to qualify or excuse—as much as her heart screamed out for her to. "Yes."

With trembling fingers, Dev traced Leslie's face in the dark—her forehead, her cheeks, her mouth. Then she unzipped the bag. "I'm going to get out. Keep the bag closed so you don't lose all the heat."

"What are you going to do?" Leslie forced herself to release her hold on Dev and rolled over onto her side as the bag opened and Dev extricated herself.

Dev sat up and rummaged for the lantern and turned it on, then checked her watch. "It's midnight. If the rain doesn't let up enough for us to chance taking the boat out on the lake in the morning, we'll have to try starting a fire to dry out some of our gear. The tent's holding, but the floor's damp."

Leslie caught Dev's arm. "What are you going to do for the rest of the night, Dev?"

"I'm going to hunt out whatever dryish wood I can and get it under a tarp."

"You're not going anywhere." Leslie threw back the top of the sleeping bag, sat up next to Dev, and clamped a hand on her arm. "Besides the rain, it's not safe out there. In case you've forgotten, trees are falling like matchsticks. If one comes down on you, I'd never find you."

"Les, I'll be okay."

"No."

Dev looked away. On Leslie, anger looked a lot like arousal. And Dev was still very close to boiling, and the pressure of Leslie's fingers digging into her arm was as potent as a caress. If they struggled in the small space, she'd lose the last frayed rein on the desire that was choking her. She'd be all over Leslie, and there were only so many times she could stop. "Okay. We should both try to get some sleep, then. I'll put on some extra clothes and sleep on top of the bag. I'll be okay."

"That's absolutely ridiculous," Leslie barked. "We ought to be capable of sleeping next to one another fully clothed. We're not teenagers, for God's sake."

Dev laughed harshly. "No, we're not. That part, I *do* understand."

"Then get back into the sleeping bag." Leslie fisted the front of Dev's shirt and pulled her down. Her expression softened as she barely resisted caressing Dev's stony face. "Get in, zip it back up, and turn on your side with your back to me."

Since it made as much sense as both of them sitting up for the rest of the night, freezing, Dev complied. It took some doing, but finally she lay with Leslie curved along her back and Leslie's hand resting on her shoulder. As much as she knew it was crazy, she was grateful for whatever bit of contact she could have with Leslie for however short a time. She was too tired and wound too tight to think much beyond that.

Leslie rested her cheek lightly against Dev's back and closed her eyes. Truth.

Do you love her?

Yes, but never the way I loved you.

❖

Leslie awoke in hazy gray light, damp and stiff and aroused. She was in the same position she had been in the night before when she'd fallen asleep, her belly and breasts snugged against Dev's butt and back. Her borrowed jeans were a size too big for her, but she still felt an uncomfortable tightness in her groin, a deep throbbing pressure that had her longing for release. She'd never been so aware of her body, or another woman's, or of the relentless urgency to be touched. She inched away and felt Dev stir immediately. Dev must have been lying awake.

"What time is it?" Leslie whispered.

"About six."

"I don't know what I want first. We skipped dinner and I'm hungry. I want to brush my teeth. And I have to pee."

Dev laughed, found the zipper, and opened the bag. She crawled out, gritting her teeth as pain lanced down her leg, and slowly worked her way into a sitting position. Her right hip was on fire. "The first two I can help you with. You're on your own with the last one." She leaned over and pulled a dry bag from a pile. "How about a protein bar to stave off starvation?"

"Let me take a quick run outside and I'll take you up on it." Leslie lifted one of her ruined shoes and grimaced. "They're a wreck. Would you mind if I wore your boots?"

"Go ahead."

After Leslie left the tent, Dev tried her two-way radio. The batteries were still good, but she couldn't raise anyone back at Lakeview. From the sounds of the storm, the wind was still high. She dug out the rubber boots she wore for shallow water work and followed Leslie out to take care of her own call of nature. When she was done, she inspected the trench around the tent. Even though nearly obliterated by the driving downpour, it had nevertheless protected them from a great deal of runoff. With a sigh, she turned to get the shovel from the tent to re-dig it.

"Your leg's bothering you, isn't it?" Leslie said, stepping from the woods into the small clearing around the tent. "You're limping pretty badly this morning."

"Too much time in one position." As sore, tired, and emotionally exhausted as she was, Dev couldn't help but smile. Leslie had rolled up the sleeves and cuffs of Dev's sweatshirt and jeans, both of which were a size too big for her, and she looked as young and fresh as she had when they were kids.

"What?" Leslie asked grumpily.

"Nothing."

Leslie cocked her head and squinted appraisingly at Dev, impatiently brushing rain from her eyes with one hand. The torrent had subsided to a heavy, steady deluge. "What do we need to do?"

"For now, just freshen up these trenches to keep the floor as dry as we can. If we have to sleep another night out here, I don't want the sleeping bag getting wet."

"I'm not sleeping out here another night."

"Don't worry, we'll be okay. Once we have a fire going, we can get things reasonably dry."

"Where's the shovel?" Leslie walked to the tent and yanked down the zipper on the flap. It wasn't about sleeping wet. She didn't care if she had to sleep under the trees in a monsoon. She couldn't spend another night next to Dev, not without imploding or attacking her. She couldn't even look at her without starting to ache. Dev had circles under her eyes, her wet hair clung in disheveled strands to her neck, and her work shirt and jeans were mud streaked. And she was absolutely gorgeous.

"I'll take care of it," Dev said.

Leslie turned abruptly and found Dev inches from her. She balled her fists so she wouldn't slide her hands into Dev's hair. "You won't. You'll get in that tent and lie down. You can hardly walk."

Dev's jaw tightened. Even in the rain and shadowy light, Leslie's eyes blazed. Dev wanted to kiss her. She wanted more than that. She wanted Leslie under her, naked and open and wet.

"Get in the tent, Dev," Leslie said, watching the hunger rise in Dev's face. No one had ever looked at her like that before, and she craved it now like nothing she had ever known. Her voice dropped to a whisper. "Please."

"Leslie—"

"Glad to see you two are still in one piece!" Natalie called as she materialized out of the woods.

Dev jerked and stepped back a pace. Leslie took a long breath and settled herself before turning to face the ranger. Natalie stood with her hands on her hips observing them with a curious expression on her face. She looked tired but disgustingly dry in a rain poncho, nylon rain pants, and boots. Leslie tried not to snarl.

"Sorry I couldn't get here sooner," Natalie said. "How about I give you two a ride back to land?"

"I'll take my own boat back," Leslie said.

"I'm staying here with my equipment," Dev said.

Slowly shaking her head, Natalie slid her hands through the slits in the poncho and into her pants pockets. "Sorry, no to both of those ideas. We're evacuating all the campsites, so you need to pack up whatever critical items you have, Dev." She regarded Leslie pointedly. "You were lucky to make it here at all, Ms. Harris. The lake is still far too rough for your craft. You'll be riding with me."

Leslie didn't like being given an ultimatum, but she needed to get back to the mainland. She needed enough space from Dev to be able to draw a breath that wasn't filled with need. "I want to be sure my boat is secure."

"I'll help you with that while Dev gets her stuff together."

Natalie turned and walked back into the woods, leaving Leslie no choice but to follow. When Natalie stopped on the lake bank, Leslie came up beside her and studied her boat rocking hard in the churning water. Natalie's larger, heavier departmental craft was anchored nearby. One of them would have to climb down the bank into the water to get more lines on her boat or it was going to break free. "We're going to get wet doing this."

"I'll get extra lines from my boat."

"I couldn't get much wetter," Leslie said when Natalie returned with the ropes. "I'll go. You stay up here to secure them."

When Leslie started down the steep, muddy bank, Natalie wrapped an arm around a tree that canted out over the water, leaned out as far as she could, and held out her hand.

"Here, grab on so you don't fall."

"Thanks." When Leslie took Natalie's hand their eyes met. Natalie's were dark and considering.

"That was pretty risky, coming out here yesterday," Natalie said conversationally.

"She was out here alone," Leslie said. "You would have done the same."

"I wanted to."

"I can imagine."

Natalie smiled faintly. "Can you?"

"Yes," Leslie said softly, "I can."

Chapter Nineteen

While Natalie stood at the wheel in the cockpit, her legs braced wide apart for balance in the buffeting wind and rain, Leslie huddled on the bench across from Dev. The sky was a muddy brown, the water an angry gray, and both suited her mood. She hated being rescued, even though she knew it was the wisest course. The swells were higher than she'd ever seen them on the lake, and even in the larger, heavier park service craft, the ride was harrowing. In her boat it would have been impossible. Conversation was impossible, too, but even if she'd wanted to talk to Dev, Dev clearly didn't want to talk to her. Dev sat with her body angled forward toward Natalie, her face impassive.

Leslie wondered what she was thinking. They hadn't had any time to talk since Natalie showed up at the campsite, but then Leslie wasn't sure what she would say to her. What could she say? *I'm sorry?* That hardly seemed to cover how many wrong turns she'd taken with Dev, starting when they'd been seventeen. Last night, though, might just have been her crowning moment. They weren't impulsive kids anymore, but she hadn't been able to keep her hands to herself or her mouth shut. She'd been in the midst of seducing Dev—Leslie cringed inwardly but there was no other word for it—she'd *told* Dev she wanted to make love, for God's sake. And then in the next breath she'd said no. What had she been thinking? Nothing, obviously.

When she looked back on her relationship with Dev, it was littered with regret. The only good thing to come of the entire visit had been that she and Dev had finally talked about what had happened between them the night of the accident. Of course, that conversation had nearly ended with them mindlessly screwing on the shore. Maybe it was better if they didn't talk. Leslie stared at Dev and her heart raced. No, it was better if they weren't anywhere near one another.

With a sigh, Leslie closed her eyes. Her father was home from the hospital and headed toward recovery, her mother had hired a temporary cook and part-time handyman, and *she* had even gotten the medical tests she was supposed to have. God knew, she'd certainly had enough rest and relaxation. Any more, and she would lose her mind. She'd stay to help her mother with the July Fourth bash, and then she was going back to Manhattan. Back to the orderly, satisfying life she had chosen, the one that suited her.

"You okay?" Dev shouted over the wind.

Leslie opened her eyes, her pulse racing when her eyes met Dev's. "Yes! You?"

Dev grinned ruefully and shrugged.

Even though relieved at the imminent prospect of heading back toward sanity, Leslie couldn't ignore the pang at knowing she wouldn't see Dev again. And with the heat of Dev's body still alive in her mind, Leslie feared it would take more than distance to extinguish the memory. When the sound of the motor revving down caught Leslie's attention, she looked away from Dev with both sorrow and relief.

Natalie was guiding the boat up to the wide, rain-slicked dock alongside Lakeview's boathouse. It was deserted, as were the grounds. Many of the cars that had been in the parking lot were gone, and Leslie expected that a fair number of people had cut short their vacations when the weather turned bad. In a way, that wasn't such a bad thing, because it would give her mother a break before the influx of new guests for the long weekend.

Natalie throttled down, eased the boat against the side of the dock, and called over her shoulder, "Someone want to climb out and grab the lines?"

Leslie was closer to the dock side and hurriedly clambered out, dragging the stern line with her. She pulled the craft against the cushioned bumpers attached to the side of the dock and wrapped a line around a cleat while Natalie jumped from the bow and did the same.

"Thanks," Natalie called, hunching her shoulders in the wind.

"No problem." Out of the corner of her eye, Leslie saw Dev stumble as she climbed from the boat onto the dock, a grimace of pain on her face. "Dev!"

Leslie lunged for her, but Natalie was closer.

"Hey there," Natalie cried, grasping Dev around the waist and steadying her so she didn't fall. Her face concerned, she smoothed her free hand over Dev's chest. "Your leg's taking a pretty good hit in this weather, isn't it?"

"Some," Dev said tightly, wrapping her arm around Natalie's shoulders for balance.

Leslie pulled up short, recognizing that her help wasn't needed and also aware that although smaller, Natalie was holding Dev up. It was also obvious that Natalie knew about the old injury to Dev's leg. Clearly, Dev had told her about the accident, and Leslie wondered how much else Natalie knew about that night. Not that it mattered.

"Come on, let's get the both of you up to the lodge and dried out." Natalie kept her arm around Dev as the three of them negotiated the wet slope up to the lodge. Once on the porch, Natalie said, "I'll let you know when you can go back out to the island for your gear, Dev. I don't imagine you'll be taking any more samples for a while."

"Not until the effects of the storm settle down. Probably a week or so." Dev eased out of Natalie's grasp and carefully put weight on her leg. "Thanks."

"My pleasure." Natalie smiled softly at Dev. "I may be busy all day, but I'll talk to you later." She turned to Leslie. "I'll give you a ride out to your boat tomorrow if the weather breaks."

"I appreciate it," Leslie said, trying to inject some warmth into her voice.

"Okay then. Take care. Get dry," Natalie said.

When Natalie turned to go back down the stairs to the path, Leslie stopped her with a hand on her arm. The woman had just motored over two hours in ugly weather to bring them home. "Come inside for coffee. I imagine you're going to have a long day."

Natalie's eyes flickered with surprise, then she nodded. "Thanks. Maybe your mother made some of those biscuits again."

Leslie smiled, finding it hard not to like her. And after all, there was no reason not to. So Natalie was involved with Dev and didn't bother to hide it. Why should she? Dev was...well, Dev was Dev, and what woman wouldn't be attracted to her? Leslie clenched her jaws, angry at herself for even thinking about whatever was going on between Dev and Natalie. She turned and walked resolutely inside.

They took their rain gear off and hung it on hooks by the door.

A few guests clustered around the fireplace in the great room, reading newspapers or books, or watching the Weather Channel on TV. Leslie led Natalie and Dev back toward the kitchen.

"Mom? Dad?" she called as she pushed through the swinging doors.

"Leslie?" her mother answered eagerly, appearing in the doorway of the adjoining family room. Beyond her, Leslie's father was stretched out on the couch with a newspaper on his lap, his casted leg propped on pillows. "Thank God you're back."

Leslie gave her mother a quick hug, then leaned down to kiss her father. "Hi, Daddy. How are you feeling?"

"A damn sight better now that you're home. Rough trip?"

"Sort of. The boat's okay, but we left it at the island. Sorry."

He shook his head. "Better that than you trying to get back in this stuff."

Eileen smiled at Natalie and Dev. "The three of you look like you could use hot showers, dry clothes, and something to eat."

"I need to get back out there, so I'll have to pass on the first two," Natalie said, "but I'll take you up on the food."

Eileen hooked her arm through Natalie's. "Come on in the kitchen. And thank you for bringing my daughter home."

"Don't mention it," Natalie said, disappearing through the doorway with Eileen.

"You doing okay?" Leslie said quietly as she and Dev followed at a slower pace. Dev's face was white and her eyes smudged with fatigue.

"Yeah. Just beat." Dev made a conscious effort not to limp, but with each passing hour her lower back and hip had gotten tighter to the point that every step sent a jolt of fire down her leg. The last time it had been this bad, she'd been sampling intestinal parasites from fish in the Finger Lakes in November. There'd been an early snow, and it had been twenty degrees on the dock where she'd knelt for three hours gutting the fish and opening their GI tracts. She'd managed to finish collecting the specimens, but she'd paid for it with two days in bed.

"You look like you can barely move." Dev's hurting was so apparent that Leslie ached just watching her walk. Knowing she was helpless to ease Dev's pain was so frustrating that she almost felt physically ill herself.

"I'll be okay once I get warmed up and take a couple ibuprofen," Dev said, trying to sound upbeat.

Leslie doubted that a few hundred milligrams of Motrin was going to touch Dev's pain, but she said nothing. She pulled a tall stool from against the wall toward the center island so Dev could sit on it. Her mother and Natalie were discussing the storm while her mother poured coffee into big white ceramic mugs. "Get some weight off your leg at least." She grabbed two mugs and carried them back to the island. "Here."

"Thanks. What about you," Dev asked quietly, sipping the hot coffee gratefully. "You've barely slept in two days. Are you feeling okay?"

Leslie's first reaction was to protest that she was fine, but she stopped herself from making the stock reply. Dev had asked, and she deserved an answer. "I feel like crap, but mostly because I'm wet and cold and hungry." She grinned weakly and decided she should leave out the part about being indescribably horny, which was even more distressing than all the other things put together. It was bad enough she'd woken up aroused. Even the biting wind and drenching rain and Natalie's possessive attitude toward Dev hadn't been able to put a damper on it. And every time she looked at Dev, she remembered how good it had been with Dev's body against hers all night. She tried not to look at Dev's mouth because whenever she did, the fluttering sensation inside started up, and it had nothing to do with her heart problems.

"Things have been pretty stressful." Dev watched Leslie's eyes darken from blue to indigo. She was beautiful, even sleepless and bedraggled.

"Stressful. Jesus, what an understatement." Leslie wanted to laugh, but she didn't want to draw attention to them. She knew they only had a few more minutes of privacy. "I had one tiny episode yesterday, but it was so short it doesn't even count." She glanced at her mother to make sure she wasn't listening. "The doctors who did the tests said that the medication should be enough. I intend to take it, because I don't have time for any more of this nonsense."

"Good." Dev squeezed Leslie's hand, and gently released it. "Aren't you supposed to quit coffee too?"

Leslie's face went cold. "Don't push it, Devon."

Dev laughed quietly, and Leslie finally smiled.

"Is this storm going to ruin the work you were doing on the island?" Leslie asked, because she wanted to change the subject and also because she cared. She knew how important Dev's work was to her.

"I got just about everything I need."

"I'm glad."

"Here you go," Eileen said, setting a plate of buttermilk biscuits in the center of the island.

Natalie grabbed one and leaned against the counter next to Dev. "How are you doing?"

"Better," Dev said.

"You three help yourselves to anything else you need," Eileen said. "I'm going to check on Paul and make sure the guests are taken care of." She rested her hand on Leslie's shoulder. "I almost forgot. Your friend Rachel from New York called here when she didn't get an answer on your cell."

Leslie grew still. Dev stiffened beside her, and Natalie's face took on an interested expression. "Okay. Thanks."

"She sounded worried when I told her about the storm, so you should probably call her pretty soon."

"I will, Mom," Leslie said tightly.

"Do you need her number? She left her cell and her—"

"I have them."

Eileen hesitated, then dropped her hand from Leslie's shoulder. "Natalie, you be careful out there today."

"I will. Thanks." Natalie waited until Eileen left the room, then asked nonchalantly, "Girlfriend?"

Leslie gave Natalie a long, appraising look. The question could be passed off as casual conversation, but she knew it wasn't. "Something like that." She rose, walked to the sink, and poured the last of her coffee down the drain. Then she looked at Dev. "Are you going to be okay getting down to your cabin?"

"I'll walk her down," Natalie said, "when she's done with her coffee."

"Fine. Thanks for the ride home," Leslie said tersely. She left them there, grabbed her rain jacket, and strode out into the downpour, oblivious to the discomfort as she stalked through the woods. Four more days and this entire surreal interlude would all be behind her.

When she reached her cabin she headed directly to her bathroom, pulling off her rain jacket and dropping it over the back of a wooden chair as she went. She closed the door, turned on the hot water in the shower, and began to remove her clothes. *Dev's clothes*, she thought as she bent to unlace Dev's boots. Dev's shirt, Dev's pants, Dev's hands—her kisses, her mouth, God, oh God, her mouth. How good Dev's mouth had felt skimming down her stomach. Closing her eyes, Leslie leaned back against the counter, slipping her hand inside Dev's jeans. Her skin was cold, but she was hot between her legs. And wet. And oh so hard and aching. With a soft moan she stroked the ache, but it only grew more fierce. She pressed harder, willing the wanting away, and groaned at the pleasure. Her legs shook and she gripped the counter with her free arm, her hand circling faster beneath the soaked denim. Oh God, it felt so good and she wanted it to stop. She didn't want this, this terrible longing.

"Oh please," she gasped, her head falling back, orgasm shimmering through her. She couldn't want this. She *couldn't*. Her will snapped as her climax surged and she cried out softly, bending nearly double with the pleasure. "Yes. Oh yes."

When the wracking tremors subsided enough for her to straighten, Leslie turned unsteadily and braced her arms on the counter, panting. While the last tendrils of orgasm washed through her, she stared at her reflection in the mirror, shocked by the sated expression in her bruised eyes and flushed face. *Oh God, who are you?*

After her shower, Leslie fell naked into bed and slept for nine hours. When she woke a little before seven in the evening, she felt hollowed out, far emptier than mere hunger could account for. She ignored the feeling as she reached for her phone and pressed the familiar number on speed dial without even looking.

"This is Rachel Hawthorne. I'm not available right now, so please leave—"

Leslie cut the connection and stared at the ceiling. She wondered how Dev was doing, if her leg was better, if she was going to be able to make it up to the lodge for dinner. Maybe she should go up, fix her a plate, and take it down to her cabin.

"What am I doing?" Leslie muttered, throwing back the sheets in disgust. She ran her hands through her hair. "Losing my mind. That's what I'm doing."

The phone vibrated and she snatched it up. "Hello?"

"Hello, darling. I'm in the car."

Leslie felt a quick rush of relief. This was normal. With Rachel, she knew exactly who she was. "Hi. I heard you called. Sorry I missed you. How are you?"

"Fine. Busy. Your mother said there was a storm."

Leslie laughed. "You could say that."

"Listen, darling, I'm on my way to a client dinner, but I've got good news."

"So do I. I'll be ho—"

"I freed up my schedule and I'm flying up for the Fourth. I'm afraid overnight is all I can manage."

Leslie's stomach clenched. "That's not necessary, Rach, really. I know how busy you are, and I'll—"

"Nonsense, darling. We'll have plenty of time to get reacquainted." She laughed throatily. "I'm pulling into the parking garage, so I'm going to sign off. I'll see you, darling."

"Rachel, wait! Rach?" Leslie was left staring at the silent phone in her hand, wondering why she didn't want Rachel there. Maybe it was just that this wasn't part of their life, and she had no way to explain to Rachel who she had been all those years ago. Or, she feared, it might be because she wasn't the woman Rachel was expecting to find when she arrived.

CHAPTER TWENTY

Leslie contemplated her choices in footwear as she pulled on jeans, a warm navy crew-neck sweater, and the thickest socks she'd packed. But all she had in the way of shoes were sneakers or dress shoes. Neither would hold up on the muddy path to the lodge. With a sigh, she pulled on Dev's boots. She could borrow a pair from her mother and return these to Dev later. She hoped that Dev had another pair of boots at her cabin and wouldn't need these tonight.

Flashlight in hand and a bundle of clothes under her other arm, Leslie set out toward the lodge. The rain had tapered off to a heavy downfall. Annoying, but not threatening. Nevertheless, Leslie felt as if she'd been slogging through water for days. Lights shone in one or two of the cabins she passed, but the cloud cover was too dense to allow any moonlight to filter through the trees. When a beam of light flashed from out of the woods and into Leslie's face, it was as bright as a car headlight, stinging her eyes.

Startled and annoyed, she complained, "Hey!"

"Oh, sorry," a woman called, and the light immediately cut down to the ground.

Leslie blinked away the water in her irritated eyes and cautiously approached. Then her uncertainty was replaced by something altogether different, a sinking sensation she didn't want to analyze. She raised her own flashlight until the edge of the beam illuminated Natalie's face. "Hi."

"Nice night," Natalie said lightly.

"Isn't it." Leslie took in Natalie's backpack and the plastic bag of what looked like groceries under her arm. She was clearly on her way to Dev's, probably bringing her dinner. Like Leslie had wanted to do. Like she had no right to do. And a backpack—overnight clothes? Her mood darkened. She sidestepped to make room for Natalie on the path. "Be careful. The trail's a mess."

"You too. By the way, I moored the department boat down at your dock. I can take you out to yours in the morning, if that works for you."

Leslie's jaw tightened. Natalie was staying the night. "That would be fine. Thank you."

"Right after breakfast?"

"Perfect," Leslie said flatly. "Good night."

"Night," Natalie called.

Leslie stood in the drizzle, watching Natalie disappear into the dark. To bring Dev supper. To keep her company on a cold, rainy night. To take care of her pain. Leslie suddenly had an image of Natalie curled into the bend of Dev's body, the way *she* had been the night before, and the ache was so huge it hurt to draw breath. She turned away and walked on in the rain, wishing she had never come home. Wishing she had never seen Dev again. Wishing she didn't want her and wondering when it would stop.

She trudged up to the lodge, grateful for a diversion, anything to keep her mind occupied until she could get back to Manhattan. A few people lingered in the great room, but the large dining room adjoining it was dark. Subdued light streaked beneath the kitchen door and Leslie made her way toward it. Her mother sat at the central counter on the same stool that Dev had occupied earlier, working a crossword puzzle.

"Hi, honey," Eileen said, swinging around as if to stand.

Leslie held up a hand. "Don't get up." She craned her neck toward the family room. "Is Daddy here?"

"No. He didn't sleep well last night and he went to bed early." She pointed to the bundle under Leslie's arm. "What have you got there?"

"Laundry. Do you mind if I do some?"

"Of course not. You haven't had dinner, have you?"

"No. I just woke up a little while ago."

Eileen rose. "I'll put the laundry in while you fix yourself something to eat."

"You don't have to do that."

"I know I don't. Give me the laundry."

Leslie wasn't really hungry, but she knew she should eat something. Maybe then the gnawing ache in the pit of her stomach would go away. Leslie sighed. "Thanks, Mom."

"Are these yours?" Eileen called from the small laundry room next to the kitchen.

"No," Leslie said as she opened the refrigerator and pulled out a pizza box and a bottle of Beck's. She peeked under the lid and saw with satisfaction that there were two slices remaining. "They're Dev's. Mine will have to go to the dry cleaners, and even then, I'm not sure they're salvageable."

"Put that in the microwave," Eileen said automatically as she rejoined Leslie and sat down at the counter again.

"It's fine." Leslie leaned an elbow on the counter, poured a glass of beer, and munched on the cold pizza.

Eileen shook her head, smiling faintly. "How's Dev doing? She looked pretty worn out this morning."

Leslie stiffened and took another swallow of beer. "I don't know. I haven't talked to her since we came back."

"I'll call her cell and see if she wants me to fix something. Maybe you can take it down to her."

"No," Leslie said abruptly. When her mother started in surprise, Leslie lowered her voice. "I'm sure she would have called if she needed anything. I saw Natalie on the way down toward her cabin. She looked like she had food with her."

"Oh. That's good."

Peachy. Leslie pushed the last half-eaten slice away and drained her glass. Then she went to the refrigerator and got another beer.

"Did you call your friend?" Eileen asked, absently filling in a word in the crossword puzzle.

"Yes." Leslie paused a beat. "She's coming up for the Fourth. She'll be staying overnight."

Eileen looked up. "We don't have any vacancies, but we can bring a day bed down to your cabin."

Leslie blushed, thinking of the not-quite-double bed in the small bedroom. "We won't need one."

"Oh," Eileen said with studied casualness. She crossed to the counter and poured coffee, then returned. "Rachel. That's her name, isn't it?"

"Yes, Rachel Hawthorne."

"And she's your….I'm sorry. Is girlfriend correct?"

"We're involved," Leslie said. "She's an attorney."

"At your firm?"

Leslie appreciated her mother's effort, but she didn't want to talk about Rachel or their life. Still, she answered impassively, "No. Another firm. She does malpractice litigation."

"I'm sure it's not easy going up against the medical establishment."

"Most of Rachel's work is defending hospitals and pharmaceutical companies." Seeing her mother's fleeting expression of displeasure, quickly hidden, Leslie said bitterly, "I guess neither one of us is on the side of the angels."

Eileen sighed. "I know some of the things I said when you decided to practice corporate law made it sound as if I don't approve of what you do—"

"Isn't that the truth?" Leslie snapped, her nerves uncharacteristically raw. God, why did they have to get into this again tonight, when everything else in her life was so out of control?

"I suppose I'd be happier if you were working for the ACLU or something—"

Leslie snorted and Eileen laughed quietly. "All right, never mind that. I think it's probably better that someone like you is doing what you do, rather than someone with no social conscience at all. And I've always trusted your judgment."

"My judgment is the last thing you should trust." Leslie was too tired and too heartsick to regret what she said, although she knew she would later.

Startled, Eileen leaned forward on the counter and gently touched Leslie's hand. "Why do you say that? What's wrong?"

Leslie shook her head and rubbed her hand over her forehead, closing her eyes against the headache that had sprung up out of nowhere. "Nothing. It's not important."

"Of course it's important. I've had a long time to think about what happened between us, Leslie," Eileen said intently. "Something happened when you went away to college. You shut down. Or shut me out. And I let you."

"Mom," Leslie said, "it's not—"

"Is it Dev?"

Shocked, Leslie could only stare. Finally she found her voice. "Why do you say that?"

"Because if I didn't know about Rachel, I'd think you and Dev were lovers."

Leslie's jaw dropped. "Why?"

Eileen laughed and lifted her hands as if it were obvious. "Because of the way you are together."

"We aren't any way at all together," Leslie said vehemently. "Of course we're not lovers! I haven't even seen Devon since two days before I left for college."

Eileen's eyes narrowed. "Why not? Why did you lose touch?"

"Because!" Leslie spun away and closed her eyes, appalled to feel tears slip from between her lashes. Her legs shook, and she reached blindly for a nearby stool. She slumped onto it and took several long deep breaths, centering herself, reclaiming her control. Then she brushed quickly at her face and turned back to face her mother. She spoke with no emotion, reciting facts. "I knew Dev in high school. I was a year ahead of her, and I went away to school and that was the last time I saw her."

"I knew that part, Leslie. What I don't know is the part you still don't want to tell me."

Leslie tugged at her lower lip with her teeth, biting down until the pain helped her focus. She could hold back her tears, but she couldn't hold back the truth anymore. "Mike found us kissing and he beat her up. He hurt her, and I let him."

"Oh my God. Leslie."

Leslie put her face in her hands and bowed her head. "I let him. God. I let him." She raised her head, her eyes filled with misery. "Then Dev had the accident on her bike and I went off to college and pretended it never happened."

"I am so sorry. I am so, so sorry you had to go through all that by yourself." Eileen rose and gave Leslie a quick hug. Then she rested her cheek against Leslie's hair, keeping her arm very lightly on Leslie's shoulders. "I'd like to murder Mike. I'm so sorry you and Dev were hurt."

"Dev was hurt. I just ran."

Eileen kissed the top of her head, then asked gently, "So you two were girlfriends, back then?"

"No," Leslie said with a sigh. "Well, we were but we didn't realize what was happening between us until that night. And then I kind of freaked out, and it took me years to figure it all out."

Eileen tilted Leslie's chin up and studied her face. "What about now that you and Dev are friends again?"

"I'm with Rachel. We've been seeing each other almost two years."

"Do you two live together in Manhattan?" Eileen settled back on her stool.

"No." Leslie shook her head, relieved not to be talking about Dev or the past anymore. "We both have our own condos. Our schedules are so crazy, we don't see each other that much anyhow, so there's really no point in living together."

"Well, making a life together isn't always about how much time you spend in the same place."

"We're not that kind of couple." Leslie frowned, realizing how that sounded, even though it was true. "We both have our own lives, Mom. We respect each other's work. We enjoy each other. Things are fine just the way they are."

"I see," Eileen said gently. "Well, it will be nice to meet her."

"Thanks," Leslie said, aware just how inadequate her summary of her relationship with Rachel must have sounded. But she'd been truthful. *What does that say about my life?*

"Soup's on!" Natalie called.

Tucking a faded blue-checked flannel shirt into her oldest pair of jeans, Dev made her way slowly out of the bedroom to find Natalie, barefoot in a white silk T-shirt and black slacks, spooning tomato soup into bowls. A fire crackled in the fireplace and a tray of cheese and French bread sat on the coffee table in front of the sofa. A bottle of white wine completed the picture.

"That looks great, thanks," Dev said, an uneasy feeling in the pit of her stomach. She hadn't been able to make it any farther than the sofa when she got home that morning, and she'd still been asleep when Natalie arrived, announcing her intentions to make dinner. Dev hadn't wanted company, but Natalie had come out in the pouring rain so she'd smiled and let her in. Now, showered and finally warm, she took in the room and realized that Natalie might be interested in more than dinner. Natalie's silk T was just sheer enough to reveal a hint of dusky nipples on her decidedly braless breasts. She wore her dark hair down, and Dev caught the hint of an earthy perfume. Natalie looked and smelled like walking sex.

"How's your leg?" Natalie carried the bowls to the coffee table, set one down in front of Dev, and curled up next to her with the other bowl balanced in her lap.

"Not bad," Dev said, sipping the soup. "This was nice of you."

"You looked like hell this morning. If I hadn't had to get the rest of our marooned campers off the islands, I wouldn't have left you here alone today."

"I would have been pretty lousy company. I crashed the minute I walked in and didn't move until you knocked on the front door."

Natalie shrugged, smiling softly. "I can think of worse things to do than watching you sleep."

Carefully, Dev set her bowl down. She liked Natalie a lot. Natalie was not only smart and capable, she was sexy as all get out. A month ago, Dev had seriously considered a night with her, maybe even a pleasant summer interlude. Now all she could think about was Leslie. All she'd been able to think about since the moment she'd seen her at the train station had been Leslie. She could still smell her hair, still feel her body stretched along hers, still feel her everywhere. She hurt so much inside she wanted to fall on her knees and beg for everything to be different. Christ, what a fool.

"Why does it bother you that I want to go to bed with you?" Natalie asked, putting her own bowl aside.

"That's direct." Dev grinned shakily. "I like that about you."

Natalie stretched one leg out and curled her toes into Dev's right calf. Then she slowly ran her foot up and down Dev's jean-clad leg. "I've wanted to get you into bed since the first time I saw you standing in the lake with water up to your waist. And unless I'm way off base, no one else is warming your bed."

Hitching her leg partway onto the couch, Dev turned sideways so she could meet Natalie's gaze. She caught her breath when Natalie slid her foot along the top of her thigh and between her legs. When Natalie's heel nudged the seam in her jeans, Dev stiffened.

"Tell me that doesn't feel good." Natalie's voice was throaty and low, her eyes soft and sultry.

Dev wrapped her fingers around Natalie's ankle and moved her foot away an inch. She was tired and weary at heart, but her body still screamed for release after the hours of arousal the night before, and Natalie was very good at seduction. "I'm not dead, Natalie. You're a beautiful woman and you're making me more than a little bit crazy."

Natalie drew her leg away, slid closer on the couch, and put her hand where her foot had been—high on the inside of Dev's thigh. She squeezed the tight muscle, released, then squeezed again. Dev gasped. "Let me make you feel good. I know what you need. Let me slide my fingers—"

"Natalie," Dev said, her voice rough, her stomach tight. "It wouldn't be right."

"Dev, for God's sake, I can tell you want me. What is it you think *I* want that you're so worried about?" Natalie moved her hand from Dev's thigh to her cheek, stroking her face. "All I want is to share what we both want to share. I'm not asking for anything else."

"I know, I believe you." Dev leaned her head back and stared at the ceiling, her breath coming in painful spurts. It had taken so long to feel anything for any other woman, and she didn't often give in to physical attraction. Too many times she'd been left feeling empty. She turned her head and met Natalie's troubled, questioning gaze. "I can't make love to you because I...I..."

"Because you're in love with Leslie Harris."

Dev closed her eyes as the pain washed through her. Natalie leaned forward and gently kissed her on the mouth. Natalie's lips were soft, moist, warm. Her full, firm breasts pressed against Dev's arm. She smelled like rain, she smelled like life. And Dev hurt so much. She wanted to keep her eyes closed and let Leslie open her shirt, unbutton her jeans, and stroke her sorrows into pleasure. She wanted Leslie to... Leslie. She wanted Leslie. She opened her eyes. "Yes. Because I love Leslie."

"She's not here, Dev," Natalie said, her gentleness softening the sting in her words. "I don't know why she isn't, but the reasons don't really matter. What matters is that you're here alone, hurting, and I want to be with you. We'll both feel better, I promise."

"I can't," Dev groaned. "I can't make love with you if I'm thinking about her. I'm sorry. I can't."

Natalie leaned back, her fingers slowly stroking Dev's arm. "Don't worry. You won't be thinking about her when you're with me." She smiled, a slow, lazy, confident smile. "I know it, and one of these days, you're going to know it too." She leaned close again and nipped at Dev's chin, then kissed the spot she'd bitten. "And when you do, Dev, I'll be waiting. And I promise you a night you'll never forget."

Dev laughed, but her eyes were serious. "It doesn't bother you? Knowing the way I feel about Les?"

"Of course it bothers me," Natalie said, her eyes blazing. "It bothers me a hell of a lot that you're so torn up. And it bothers me that I want you to distraction and can't have you. Yet." She blew out a breath. "But I can be patient. And I've got you for the whole summer."

Chapter Twenty-one

When Leslie walked into the lodge the next morning, Dev and Natalie were having breakfast in the dining room. Natalie wore her park uniform, and Leslie wondered if she had brought it with her the night before or had gone home sometime in the evening. The rain had finally stopped just before dawn, but it wouldn't have been an enjoyable walk back to the parking lot last night. Natalie probably stayed with Dev. In the tiny cabin. With only one bed. Leslie gritted her teeth, shook her head no when Dev gestured to the empty chair at their table, and pushed through into the kitchen.

The cook they'd hired was cleaning up after breakfast, and Leslie could hear her mother and father talking out on the screened-in porch. She poured a cup of coffee and joined them.

"Hi, Mom. Hi, Daddy. How are you feeling?"

"Like a turtle flipped over on its back in the middle of the Northway," her father grumped. His crutches were propped against the chair, where he sat with his casted leg supported on an embroidered footstool that looked barely capable of supporting the weight. "I can't get down to the dock on these crutches, especially not after all this rain."

"Is there anything you need me to do?" Leslie asked, leaning her hip against the end of the couch and sipping her coffee. "I'm going to bring the boat in this morning."

"That should be fine," her father said. "We'll make arrangements for someone to take guests out and back the rest of the summer." He glanced at Eileen, then at Leslie. "The doctors said eight weeks in this damn cast."

"Eight weeks, minimum," her mother interjected. "You can't rush these things, Paul."

"I was wondering, Les," he said hesitantly, "if you might be able to come up Labor Day weekend and give your mother a hand closing up."

"I can handle it, Paul," Eileen said, a hint of reproach in her voice. "Leslie's busy enough with her own work. I don't want her to think she's going to need to work *here* every time she comes home."

When Leslie thought of how much went into the end of the season closing, her first reaction was to beg off, pleading too full a schedule. The cabins and all the rooms would need to be inventoried and items marked for replacement or repair, the boathouse would have to be winterized, and the boat and equipment overhauled in preparation for dry-docking, just for starters. Supervising the process, let alone doing it, was an enormous load. Still, it was going to be a rough summer for her mother, and no matter how much extra help she hired, there were some things that couldn't be left to employees. She really should come home to help. And Dev had said she'd be here all summer. That fact made the decision easy.

"I'll come. It's no problem." Leslie knew it was crazy to come back while Dev was here, especially since she'd already decided to leave right after the Fourth of July celebration just so she *wouldn't* have to see Dev anymore. But she couldn't help herself. Whenever she thought of going back to Manhattan, back to her life, she felt both relief and sorrow. She was comfortable—more than comfortable, she was *satisfied* with the life she'd made for herself. It would be good to immerse herself in work again. Not to be constantly assaulted by conflicting desires. Not to be faced with the guilt of wanting Dev so desperately. But when she imagined actually leaving, of never seeing Dev again, she wanted to cry. By Labor Day, she'd have control of her life again. She'd be able to see Dev and put their relationship—their friendship—into perspective. Yes, it would be much better that way. "It'll be fun."

Eileen laughed. "Then you don't remember what it's like very well."

"It's funny, being home makes some things feel like yesterday." Leslie smiled and shook her head. "I'd better go see if Ranger Natalie is ready to ferry me out to the island."

"See you later, honey," her father said.

"I'm going to go into the office later this morning, Mom. I probably won't be home for dinner." In fact, Leslie thought, she intended to spend as little time as possible around the lodge until she was ready to leave. The less she saw of Dev the better.

"You really ought to try the pizza at Iannucci's," Natalie said, pushing her breakfast plate aside. "The crust is amazing. I'll pick one up for you tonight."

"I'm probably going to be at the lab pretty late," Dev said.

"So I'll bring it by."

"You don't need to do that."

"I want to." Natalie's eyes narrowed ever so slightly and Dev followed her gaze. Leslie, carrying an armload of laundry, was on her way over to their table.

"Thanks for the loan of the clothes, Dev," Leslie said, depositing the washed and folded sweatshirt and jeans on the empty chair next to Dev.

"You're welcome." Dev watched Leslie study Natalie with an inscrutable expression, and wondered if Leslie suspected that Natalie had spent the night. She felt foolish for wanting Leslie to know that Natalie had slept on the couch again. What could it possibly matter?

"Ready to hit the water?" Natalie said, smiling at Leslie.

"Sure. Can't wait."

Natalie laughed and rose. She brushed a hand over Dev's shoulders. "I'll be by with that pizza delivery."

"I'll walk you out," Dev said. She picked up her briefcase and clean clothes. "I'm heading into the lab now."

Once outside, Dev took the turn to the parking lot while Leslie and Natalie continued on down to the dock. Dev waited a minute before getting into the truck, watching the two women cast off. Natalie, dark and petite, Leslie lithe and blond. Both bright, both accomplished, both beautiful. She enjoyed Natalie's confidence, her laugh, her sudden flashes of authority. But looking at Natalie didn't make her burn the way seeing Leslie did. Leslie's smile had lit the path through some of her darkest nights, and she'd lain down to sleep countless times with the sound of Leslie's laughter ringing in her heart. Now she had the memory of Leslie in her arms, and for a while at least, whether she wanted it or not, there wasn't room for anyone else. Maybe when Leslie was gone, and the dreams finally died, there would be.

When Leslie turned in Dev's direction, one hand shading her eyes in the hazy glare of a fitful dawn, Dev gave a start. Although Leslie was too far away for their eyes to meet, Dev felt the tug of connection nevertheless. When the boat pulled away from the dock with Natalie at the wheel, Leslie settled onto one of the benches. She wrapped her arm around a cleat and faced forward, hair blowing in the wind. Even as the sound of the engine died and the boat disappeared like a candle winking out, Dev could still feel Leslie's presence.

Someday soon that link would be gone, and she wondered if she would rejoice or bleed.

Three days later Dev stood in almost exactly the same spot, watching Leslie's mother climb the hill from the boathouse toward her. It was Saturday afternoon on the Fourth of July and the weather had not disappointed. It was hot, and it was going to be hotter by nightfall in the boathouse. She could see from where she stood that all the windows had been opened. The large wooden frames swung out over the water on either side of the green rectangular building like rows of dominoes. The huge double doors that opened onto a concrete ramp leading from the water had been rolled back, probably in the hope of creating some cross-ventilation. Eileen was waving to her, so Dev, carrying her briefcase, walked to meet her at the top of the path.

"Hello, stranger," Eileen said, brushing a damp tendril of hair from her cheek. "I haven't seen you since the morning after the storm."

"I had a lot of catching up to do at the lab," Dev said, which was true. It was also a convenient way to avoid running into Leslie. She'd been leaving for the lab before six in the morning and returning well after ten every night. On her way, she grabbed coffee and a bagel at the roadside mini-mart that had once been her parents' store, and ordered take-out delivered to the lab for dinner. Natalie had shown up as promised with pizza one night, but she'd been busy too, with the holiday weekend looming, and Dev hadn't seen her since. All in all, Dev had managed to be at Lakeview only long enough to sleep. And for at least half of every day she managed not to think about Leslie.

"Leslie's been saying the same thing about work." Eileen fell into step with Dev up the gravel path toward the lodge. "She's been at her office every day from sunup until I don't know when. I've missed you two at mealtime."

"Sorry," Dev said.

"No need to apologize. I understand you've both got a lot to do." Eileen halted where the path branched off to the cabins. "I hope you're coming down to the party tonight. All of the guests will be there and quite a few of the locals too."

"Well, uh…" Dev gazed off over the trees toward the lake. She hadn't intended to come. "I might drop by for a few minutes. I'm not much of a party person."

Eileen laughed. "Well, I hope you do. Are you still planning on staying with us through Labor Day?"

"Yes," Dev said, frowning. "Is that a problem?"

"Oh no, not at all." Eileen smiled. "I'll see you tonight, Dev."

Dev waved goodbye and continued on toward her cabin. Somehow, she wasn't even surprised when she saw Leslie coming toward her. It didn't seem to be possible to avoid her, even when she tried. Not when they were anywhere near each other. In a flash, she took in Leslie's tailored tan slacks, her pale silk blouse, the sandals with just a bit of a heel. Her blond waves fell just to her collarbones, where gold glinted at her throat. Even from thirty feet away, Dev could tell she had dressed for someone special, and the realization struck her like a fist.

"Hello, Les," Dev said as they both slowed to face one another.

"Devon," Leslie said quietly. She had known today would be difficult; in fact, the next twenty-four hours were likely to be the hardest of any she'd experienced in years. Rachel was coming, and she wasn't certain she was prepared to see her. Dev was still here, and that would make it all the more difficult. But she'd had plenty of practice in difficult situations, where the slightest misstep or wrong word could be disastrous. So she'd showered and dressed and prepared herself as she always did before any kind of confrontation. Her shields were up, her emotions tucked away. When she'd left her cabin, she'd known she was ready. And still, the sight of Dev coming toward her in jeans and a blue button-down-collar cotton shirt had set her heart racing. She knew the rush of pleasure at seeing Dev didn't show, and she was glad. "Recovered from the storm?"

"Oh. Sure. I…" Dev ran a hand through her hair and gave a rueful smile. "I never was good at small talk."

Leslie smiled softly. "I know."

"How much longer will you be here?" Dev heard herself asking and knew it was dumb. As if any answer wouldn't hurt.

"I'm probably leaving tomorrow afternoon."

Dev couldn't hide her surprise. "So soon?"

"It's been almost three weeks, Dev."

"It doesn't seem that long." Dev moved closer to Leslie as a young man and woman, chatting animatedly, hurried along the path past them in the direction of the cabins. "But then again, sometimes a day here seems like forever."

Leslie took in the woods, the glint of blue water through the trees, the warmth of sunshine on her skin. "It hasn't changed at all, has it?"

"Not much. Being here with you this summer reminds me of what it was like when we were kids, and the future was so far away," Dev said, her words echoing with melancholy.

Leslie searched Dev's soulful hazel eyes, recognizing the loneliness Dev had never quite been able to hide, even behind her tough façade. They had always seen one another's truths. When they were together, the pieces of herself she revealed to no one else slid silently, seamlessly, into place. Even now, she felt it. But the feeling wouldn't last, how could it? The past was a place that existed only in wistful memories, softly colored by regrets and abandoned dreams. "But it really was another lifetime."

"I know," Dev said hoarsely. It was hard *not* to accept that, when the present was about to come crashing in. "Is Rachel coming today?"

Leslie was barely able to hide her surprise. "Yes." She glanced at her watch. "Her plane arrives around six."

"My truck's clean, if you need it."

"She's renting a car. Thanks."

"You never said what she did."

"She's an attorney."

Dev smiled. "I guess you have a lot in common. That's nice."

Leslie did not want to talk about Rachel with Dev. It was too much like all the times that she had avoided talking to her about Mike. Her relationship with Dev had always been private, intimate, something that was just theirs. Looking back, she saw that they had never let the outside world touch it. They had kept it safe. Right up until the end. Leslie rested her fingers lightly on Dev's arm. "You were so special to me, Dev."

Dev kissed Leslie softly on the cheek. "Thank you, Leslie." She stepped back and Leslie's hand fell away. Dev's eyes grew darker. "If I don't see you, have a safe trip back."

"Enjoy the rest of the summer. I hope the work goes well."

"Thanks. Goodbye."

"Goodbye, Devon." Leslie waited a second until Dev turned away, and then she resumed walking toward the lodge to wait for Rachel. Maybe she'd been wrong about the next twenty-four hours. Maybe the worst was already over. Leslie took a shuddering breath, unable to imagine anything worse than the pain of that goodbye.

CHAPTER TWENTY-TWO

L eslie selected a bottle of red wine from her parents' small but well-stocked cellar, found two glasses and a corkscrew, and carried everything out to the porch. She opened the bottle, poured a glass, and sipped it as she watched the afternoon slide toward twilight. Guests came and went, laughing together, strolling hand in hand, sharing the special freedom of vacation in the beautiful setting. She tried to imagine herself and Rachel spending a week in a place like this. She had difficulty creating the picture, and when her thoughts inadvertently strayed to all the hours she and Dev had spent sitting quietly talking by the lakeshore, she pulled herself back to the present. She refilled her glass and reviewed the details of the cases she'd been working on all week.

Just before eight, a gray Lincoln Town Car pulled into the lot. A second later, Rachel stepped out. Leslie hadn't seen her in three weeks, and her first glimpse stirred a slight shock of surprise at how striking she was. Rachel was Leslie's height but subtly fuller in the breasts and hips, and altogether arresting in tailored black slacks, low heels, and an open-collared, man-tailored white silk shirt. Many an adversary had been lulled into complacency by Rachel's ripe sensuality, but Leslie knew that those sensuous features masked a decisive, lethally predatory mind.

Leslie looked away to pour wine into the second glass and give herself a few seconds to settle her nerves. She looked up at the sound of footsteps on the stairs.

"Hello, darling," Rachel murmured, leaning down to kiss Leslie, her mouth lingering for a few seconds before she moved away. With a sigh, she settled into the chair on the opposite side of the small table that held the wine. "I certainly hope that glass is for me. I can use it."

"How was the trip?" Leslie said, automatically handing the glass to Rachel. They hadn't touched in three weeks and hadn't made love for several before that, and the kiss had felt strangely foreign. Uneasily, Leslie chalked it up to their long separation.

"Oh, the flight was all right," Rachel said. "But I barely made it to the airport on time, waiting for a courier to deliver files to the office for the deps next week." She grimaced. "Sometimes I think the world is filled with incompetents. No, actually I know it is."

"You really didn't have to come all the way up here, Rach. I've booked a flight back tomorrow afternoon."

Rachel sipped her wine, her expression contained. "I'm on a nine o'clock flight to Detroit tomorrow. I'll be gone most of the week."

"Oh," Leslie said, oddly relieved. "Still, squeezing this stop in wasn't necessary."

"Well, I think it was." Rachel's voice was throaty as her eyes dropped to Leslie's mouth, then back to her eyes. "It's been a hellacious month. I've been putting in eighty-hour weeks, dealing with idiots for the most part, and I've got a bit of a minefield ahead of me. Getting the asses of these CEOs at Pharmcore out of the fire is going to take a bit of work." She traced a finger along the edge of Leslie's jaw. "I've missed you."

Leslie forced a smile. She'd missed Rachel too. She'd missed discussing their respective cases, devising strategy, celebrating victories. She'd missed Rachel's acerbic humor and her ceaseless energy. They understood one another's need to win, and she missed not needing to defend herself. What she hadn't missed, as she read the unmistakable message in Rachel's eyes, were their intense, often frantic sexual encounters. Rachel had always needed sex more than she did. It was Rachel's outlet, the way she vented her frustration and settled her nerves. Leslie could always tell when Rachel was facing a difficult trial because Rachel wanted to see her more frequently. Then when they were together, Rachel was physically more demanding, more aggressive. Leslie never minded, because she often forgot about her own physical wants and having Rachel satisfy them, even when she hadn't realized she needed relief, was welcome.

"I'm sorry my visit turned out to be longer than I expected," Leslie said, growing more uncomfortable with her thoughts every second.

"It doesn't matter," Rachel said. "I probably wouldn't have been able to see you anyhow." She emptied her wineglass and set it aside, then leaned forward, her face shadowed as night closed in around them. "I've been thinking of all the things I want to do with you for the last two hours. Let's go somewhere so I can show you."

Leslie's stomach dropped, and she felt an altogether unfamiliar sense of panic. She wasn't ready. She hadn't made the transition from who she'd been the last three weeks back into the woman she was with Rachel. She didn't know Rachel. No, that was wrong. Rachel hadn't changed. Nothing had changed. She just needed a little more time for them to fall back into the old rhythm, then it would all make sense again. Her head pounded, and she had a fleeting thought that she was glad she had started the medication, because her heart was racing out of control. "Rachel, I'm sorry. I promised my mother I'd help her make sure everything was set down at the boathouse. The party is going to start in half an hour. I can't disappear."

Rachel gave a faint murmur of protest, but her voice was teasing. "You know when we haven't seen each other for this long, it never takes me half an hour."

Leslie flushed, not from arousal, but because of its absence. Something was wrong. Very wrong. She hadn't wanted to run away this badly since the night she'd realized that it wasn't Mike she wanted to make love to, but Dev. But she wasn't seventeen anymore, and she couldn't just run away from her life. She tried for a playful tone. "Can you stand waiting a few more hours?"

"I *might* be able to," Rachel said slowly, casting one quick look around as she moved. She leaned down over Leslie, bracing an arm on either side of her, fingers curled around the arms of the wicker chair. Her voice was barely a whisper. "But I can't promise I won't have to drag you off into some dark corner. I am terribly, *terribly* ready for you."

The heat of Rachel's body was like a furnace raging between them, and just as Leslie felt the first brush of Rachel's lips, the porch light came on and Rachel hurriedly straightened. Leslie rose quickly at the sound of a door opening and footsteps on the porch. When she turned, her mother stopped abruptly a few feet away, her expression uncertain.

"Mom," Leslie said in a rush. "This is Rachel. Rachel, my mother."

Eileen smiled and held out her hand. "I'm Eileen. It's nice to meet you."

"So nice to meet you too. Thank you for allowing me to barge in this way," Rachel said graciously. "It's very beautiful here."

"We think so too." Eileen turned to Leslie. "Honey, you don't need to he—"

"No, that's fine," Leslie said hastily. "Really. I'll just show Rachel the cabin so she can change, and I'll be right down to give you a hand." Leslie squeezed Rachel's hand. "Okay?"

Rachel nodded. "Of course. I just need to get my overnight bag from the car."

"You've been traveling all day. Stay here," Leslie said. "Let me have your keys, and I'll get it."

"Thank you, darling." Rachel handed her the keys. "I packed light—I might not have anything quite right for tonight."

Leslie laughed. "You're not required to wear jeans and hiking boots, I promise."

"I'm ever so relieved." Rachel smiled at Eileen, who appeared to be watching the exchange with interest. "I'd be happy to do whatever I can to help with the preparations too."

"Absolutely not," Eileen said with an emphatic shake of her head. "You're a guest. In fact, why don't you come inside and I'll introduce you to Leslie's father while I get a flashlight. Then I'll walk you two down to the cabin with the luggage."

"Thanks, Mom," Leslie said. "Rachel, I'll be right back."

Leslie hurried down the stairs, embarrassed to feel relieved that she and Rachel would not be alone for a few more hours. Surely by the end of the evening, by the time they were ready for bed, this disquieting sense of disorientation would be gone. Because if it wasn't, they were going to need to talk, and she wasn't even sure what she would say.

Dev sat on the front steps of her cabin listening to music and the sound of laughter flowing through the trees while she finished her second beer. It was eleven and she had put off going down to the boathouse for as long as she could. She'd told Eileen she would put in an appearance, but that wasn't the real reason she stood up and started walking, making her way down the wooded path by memory and moonlight. Leslie would be there, and she wanted to see her.

Knowing it was a fool's errand that would only end in pain, she asked herself for the tenth time why she didn't just call Natalie and spend the night with a woman who wanted her. The excuses she'd used to keep Natalie at arm's length were wearing thin, even to her own ears. Refusing to explore a relationship with Natalie wasn't about being fair or unfair to Natalie. Natalie hadn't asked for anything more than friendship and shared pleasure. No, refusing to become involved was about what it had *always* been about. It was about wanting the one woman she just couldn't have. Because Leslie was always with someone else.

Dev jammed her hands in the pockets of her jeans, resisting the path she had followed once to her own destruction. For the first time, she felt anger rather than resignation flare hot inside her.

She stopped on the ridge just above the boathouse, seeing it just as she had seen it fifteen years before—light spilling out the door, people crowded around the entrance, music floating from the open windows. People drank, flirted, loved, and she stood on the outside watching. She might have come full circle, but she had arrived back at the beginning not as a confused seventeen-year-old willing to give her heart away for a smile, but as a woman who wanted more. Leslie was with someone else, and all Dev needed to be free was to break the chain that held her to the past. There was one certain way to do that. She shouldered through the crowd into the boathouse in search of Leslie.

It only took her a minute to find her. Despite the dim light and the masses of people, Dev's gaze was drawn to her as if a beam of light, invisible to everyone else, emanated from Leslie's heart straight into her own. Rather than approach her, Dev moved deeper into the shadows along the wall where she could watch her without being seen. A woman partially illuminated in moonlight stood beside Leslie, an arm curved loosely around Leslie's waist. There was no doubt about their relationship. The woman held Leslie with an easy familiarity and subtle possessiveness.

Dev blinked as sweat ran into her eyes, but she couldn't look away. She'd never seen Leslie with a woman. She'd seen her with Mike, hundreds of times. At football games, at dances, on the beach. Mike had touched Leslie as if she were his too, but Dev had never believed it. Leslie had always held herself apart, always saved what was so essentially Leslie for the moments when she and Dev were alone together. Tonight was different. Tonight, a woman stood by Leslie's side and the truth was apparent. Leslie was with who she should be with, and Dev was not the one she had chosen. As Dev watched, the copper-haired woman inclined her head and kissed Leslie. The tie that had bound Dev to Leslie all her life snapped with the fragile grace of a simple kiss.

As if Leslie felt it too, she pulled her head away and half turned in Dev's direction. Dev knew Leslie couldn't see her across the crowded floor, in near darkness, but for just an instant, she felt their eyes meet. She whispered, *Goodbye, Leslie*, and this time, she meant it.

Dev strode from the boathouse, veering off at the end of the concrete ramp toward the shore. A faint breeze came off the lake and she tilted her head up to cool the sweat on her face.

"Dev!"

Dev looked over her shoulder and saw Leslie hurrying along the sand toward her.

"Go back inside, Les," Dev said, walking away.

"I can't."

Leslie's voice was barely a whisper carried on the wind, but the pain was so clear that Dev felt it in her heart. She stopped to face her.

"You don't belong out here with me, Les."

Leslie's anguished face was so vulnerable in the moonlight that Dev ached to hold her, but her anger was greater than her grief. Leslie stepped close to Dev and touched her fingertips ever so gently to Dev's cheek. "I'm sorry. I didn't mean for you to see that."

"Why not?" Dev caught Leslie's hand and jerked it away, more roughly than she intended. "She's your lover. Go back inside."

"I know things have been crazy this summer, but—"

"This summer?" Dev laughed harshly. "No, what's been crazy is everything up *until* this summer."

"I don't...I don't understand." Leslie didn't understand anything. She didn't understand why, when she'd looked up to see Dev watching Rachel kiss her, everything inside of her had grown cold. Why the entire room had disappeared until all she could see was Dev's face and the pain in her eyes. Why she'd made a feeble excuse about needing to check on her father and had run out into the night after Dev. But she couldn't just let her walk away. Could she?

"I've been in love with you all my life," Dev said, "and it wasn't until this summer that I realized I was just holding on to a dream that had died a long time ago." Dev shook with bitterness and anger. "You walked away, Leslie. You made a life, disappeared from mine, and I still couldn't let you go. Now *that's* crazy."

"Dev," Leslie said desperately. "It's not that I didn't care."

"I *loved* you," Dev said, her voice breaking. "Oh, God, I loved you with my whole soul." She turned her face away, refusing to let Leslie see the tears that streaked her cheeks, but her body trembled as the next words tore their way out from deep inside her. "And you left me."

"Oh my God," Leslie whispered, crying herself. "You don't know how it killed me to lose you."

Dev's head snapped around, her body rigid. "No. I *don't* know. Because you were *gone*." Her hands tightened into fists at her side. "And you're still gone. Go back to your lover."

"But I love y—"

"No! Don't say that. Don't!" Dev gripped Leslie's shoulders and shook her hard enough to make her gasp. "I'm done dreaming."

Leslie cried out and Dev realized her fingers had to be bruising Leslie's shoulders. She pulled her hands away as if they burned and stumbled back a step. "I'm sorry."

"No, I'm all right."

Dev shook her head. "I'm sorry for all of it." Then she escaped into the dark, leaving the dream to fade away on the hot summer air.

Leslie called her name, but Dev didn't stop. Running, her legs cramping and her breath little more than a sob by the time she reached her cabin, she still took the stairs two at a time. Inside, she quickly scooped up her keys. Then she was racing down the path to the parking lot. She wasn't spending the night in the cabin with Leslie and her lover next door. She didn't trust herself to see them together again. Right now she was numb, but she didn't know how long it would last. And her anger was even more frightening than the pain.

Chapter Twenty-three

As Leslie threaded her way through the waning crowd toward Rachel, she gave silent thanks for the dim lighting. She didn't want Rachel to know she'd been crying. How would she ever be able to explain what had just happened? She never talked about her past with Rachel. Rachel didn't know anything about Dev, or Mike, or what had happened. Rachel would think she'd had some kind of a breakdown if she told her she was crying over a teenage love affair that she hadn't even realized was happening at the time. Except her tears had been for more than the loss of that innocent love. She was losing Dev, and she couldn't think about that right now. Not with Rachel here, and her shoulders still burning where Dev had gripped her. She needed some space from both of them, to think her way through what had happened. Once she was home, back on familiar ground, she'd make sense of it all.

Taking a deep breath, Leslie edged up to Rachel. "I'm back. Did I miss anything?"

"Nothing that looked quite as entertaining as what I have planned for you," Rachel murmured, kissing Leslie lightly below the ear. "Have we made enough of an appearance that we can sneak out?"

"I'm sorry, you must be tired," Leslie said. "Of course, let's go."

"Thank you, darling."

Once outside, Leslie took Rachel's hand to lead her along the path. Rachel stopped her in a moonless spot and nuzzled her neck.

"Did I mention I've been desperate for you for days?"

"Do you know that bears can smell pheromones?" Leslie asked lightly, edging away.

Rachel laughed. "Then get me home, darling, or we'll be in real danger."

Leslie had left the porch light on in her cabin, and she had no difficulty leading them to it. She searched the trees around Dev's cabin for any sign of her, but there was only darkness and an eerie sense of emptiness. Leslie couldn't help but remember the last time Dev had left a party at the boathouse hurt and angry. That night she'd nearly died. But Dev was an adult now, and sober, and Leslie wanted desperately to believe that she hadn't hurt Dev that badly again. Leslie forced her attention back to Rachel as they climbed the stairs to the cabin.

"I can certainly see how staying here for any length of time would be relaxing," Rachel said wryly as she walked in.

"What do you mean?"

"It barely feels as if we're in the twenty-first century. I half expect to find you handing me a candle and directing me to the outhouse."

Leslie laughed and turned on a table lamp. "Voilà. All the modern conveniences."

Rachel turned in a small circle, eyebrows raised as she surveyed the living room. "Internet? Cable?"

"Ah, no cable. Wireless if the wind blows in the right direction."

"Well," Rachel's voice dropped as she took Leslie's hand and pulled her into her arms, "we'll have to find something else to occupy our time."

Rachel moved so quickly, Leslie had no time to anticipate the kiss. They'd made love countless times and the pressure of Rachel's mouth, the possessive sweep of her hands down Leslie's back to cup her hips, the demanding thrust of her tongue were all so familiar. Rachel was a skillful lover, and Leslie's body responded automatically, accustomed to the knowing touch. When her mind caught up to her body, she tensed, feeling unexpectedly uneasy.

"Wait a minute, Rach," Leslie said, pulling back from the embrace. "I don't want to get carried away out here. Let's go in the bedroom."

"Why," Rachel murmured, nipping her way down Leslie's neck to the base of her throat. She insinuated one hand between them and skimmed her fingertips over Leslie's breast. "There's no one to see."

Leslie gasped involuntarily as her nipple tightened instantly.

"Mmm, I love exciting you." Rachel flicked open the top button of Leslie's blouse and slid her hand beneath it, her fingertips gliding under the edge of Leslie's satin bra. "You have wonderful breasts, darling. So responsive."

Rachel tugged Leslie's nipple as she massaged her breast in firm, sensuous circles.

"Oh God," Leslie whispered, closing her eyes as tendrils of pleasure snaked downward, burying themselves deep inside. Somewhere in her rapidly blurring consciousness, she was aware that something felt wrong, but the sensations racing through her body screamed otherwise. Trembling, the intoxicating burn very close to claiming her, she steadied herself with a hand against Rachel's shoulder and pushed her gently away. "Please, Rach. Not out here."

Rachel's green eyes were hazy, her breath coming in short, quick pants. Grasping Leslie's hand, Rachel pulled her toward the bedroom. "Then hurry, darling. I'm ready to explode."

Aroused, confused, Leslie couldn't make sense of her jumbled emotions. This was Rachel, her lover, and they weren't doing anything they hadn't done dozens of times before. The strangeness, the frightening disconnection, was just because they'd been apart. She undressed methodically. Rachel threw off her clothes and then impatiently pushed aside the last of Leslie's. When Rachel pulled her down on the bed and immediately rolled on top of her, moaning Leslie's name and frantically grinding against her thigh, Leslie blocked the unsettling thoughts. Whatever was happening, whatever was wrong, was none of Rachel's doing. And Rachel needed her right now.

Leslie cupped the back of Rachel's neck in her palm, holding Rachel's head to her breasts, and arched to meet her thrusts. Rachel would come quickly this way, and then they could sleep, and tomorrow it would all make sense.

Rachel shuddered and cried out. After a few minutes, her breathing steadied and she slid off Leslie's body, laughing softly. "Sorry, darling. I've been wound up for days and I just couldn't last."

"I know, it's okay," Leslie said quietly, pulling the sheet over them. "You need to get some sleep. You've got that early flight tomorrow."

"You didn't come yet," Rachel whispered, caressing Leslie's stomach.

Leslie caught her hand. She was aroused. She could feel the wetness on her thighs and the tightness in the pit of her stomach. But she didn't want to come. Instead, she had the terrible feeling she was going to cry. She pulled Rachel's arm around her and turned on her side into the curve of Rachel's body. "I don't need to. I'm still not feeling all that great. Just hold me now."

"You sure?" Rachel asked drowsily, stroking Leslie's hair. "In the morning, then."

"Just go to sleep, Rachel." Leslie closed her eyes, but she lay awake long after Rachel's breathing had dropped into the slow rhythm of exhausted sleep. Rachel wasn't the stranger in her bed.

She was.

❖

Leslie braced her arm along the roof of the sedan and leaned down to the open window. "Be careful driving. You've got plenty of time."

"Sorry to leave so early," Rachel said, propping the travel cup filled with coffee that Eileen had just given her into the space in the console. "I just want to check my e-mail and take care of a few things at that Internet place in the airport before my flight."

"Good luck in Detroit. They won't know what hit them."

Rachel grinned, looking relaxed and confident, and Leslie knew it was only partly Rachel's exhilaration about the upcoming legal challenge. Rachel had awakened Leslie at first light, caressing her into awareness and fondling her to a shattering orgasm just as Leslie had come fully awake. While Leslie was still reeling with aftershocks, Rachel had urgently guided Leslie's fingers into her, coming hard before rising hurriedly to shower. Rachel made love like she did everything else, expertly and efficiently.

"It will be quick, but not necessarily painless." Rachel's eyes gleamed as she checked her watch. "I've got to run, but this little side trip was just what I needed. You were wonderful." She started the car and Leslie stepped back. "I'll call you later this week and let you know my schedule. Bye, darling."

"Goodbye," Leslie said softly.

Rachel wheeled rapidly out of the parking lot, and Leslie slowly climbed the path back to the lodge. Through the screen door, she heard her mother setting out the buffet in the dining room, but she didn't go inside. Eileen had offered her breakfast earlier when she and Rachel had stopped by the kitchen for coffee, but she wasn't hungry then. She still wasn't. Instead, she sat down in the same wicker chair where she'd waited for Rachel the evening before. It didn't seem possible that it had only been twelve hours ago. Her mind was on overload trying to process everything that had happened.

It didn't seem possible that it had taken her all this time to discover that sex and work were the only two things that connected her to Rachel. She searched her memory for the last time she and Rachel had talked about anything that wasn't a legal case, or an evening they'd spent together that had been more than a few hours of intense sex and exhausted sleep. She couldn't come up with one.

"I noticed you like quite a bit of cream in your coffee," Eileen said, sliding a mug onto the table next to Leslie before sitting down in the other chair. "Hope I got that right."

"Thanks." Leslie smiled wanly. "I've been trying to cut down on my caffeine. I'll probably get clogged arteries instead."

"Rachel's gone?"

Leslie nodded, her throat tight.

"I didn't see Dev last night at the party."

"She didn't stay long," Leslie said softly.

"I'm sure there's a better way to go about this, but I don't know what it is." Eileen sighed. "You look terribly unhappy. What's wrong?"

Leslie drew one leg up onto the chair and bent forward to rest her chin on her knee. The sun had crested the trees and bathed the porch in warm morning sunlight. "I think I've really screwed up my relationship with Rachel."

There was a beat of silence, then Eileen said, "How so?"

Leslie shook her head. She wasn't about to say that she'd had sex with Rachel when a big part of her hadn't really wanted to and that when she'd opened her eyes that morning in the middle of a screaming orgasm, she'd wanted it to be Dev who was making her come. "Never mind. God, I can't talk about it with you."

"Something you think a mother couldn't possibly understand?"

"Something like that."

"Maybe you should talk to Dev about it."

"Why?" Leslie said sharply.

Eileen rose and stroked Leslie's hair. "Because now I've seen you with both of them, and I haven't changed my mind about which one you're in love with."

Leslie said nothing, but she feared her mother was right.

❖

Dev turned into the parking lot and saw Leslie piling luggage into the Jeep. The sight made her feel as if she'd swallowed a ball of lead. Twenty minutes ago she'd had such an intense sense of foreboding surge up out of nowhere that she'd dropped everything at the lab and rushed back to the lodge. The entire trip back she'd been sick thinking that Leslie had already left. Now she wasn't sure it was such a good idea she'd come back.

Nevertheless, she climbed out of the truck and crossed the steaming blacktop to Leslie's side. Leslie looked fresh in an outfit similar to the one she'd worn the night before. Dev figured she must look like shit because she'd slept in her clothes. "When are you leaving?"

Leslie regarded her steadily, absurdly happy to see her, even if she had no idea what she was going to do about anything. "In about an hour."

"Can you take a walk with me?"

"All right."

Silently, Dev led the way down a narrow, pine-needle-strewn footpath that led to the lake on the opposite side of the lodge from the cabins. No one ever came down there. On the shore, she stopped at the foot of a huge outcropping of rocks as big as Volkswagens. She held out her hand. "The footing's going to be tricky in what you've got on."

Wordlessly, Leslie took Dev's hand and carefully climbed to the top. The rocks were pitted from years of weather and strewn with patches of moss. She'd sunbathed on these rocks when she'd been a child. She sat down next to Dev and watched a sailboat glide by on the lake.

After a moment, Dev shifted to look into Leslie's face. "I'm sorry about last night, Les."

"I was afraid it would be just like the last time," Leslie said, feeling so weary. So very nearly empty. "You were so angry. I was afraid you'd go off half-crazy and get careless and hurt yourself."

"I did." One corner of Dev's mouth lifted in a tired grin. "I slept on a couch that had the consistency of a slab of granite."

Leslie laughed softly. "You look terrible."

"I feel terrible." Dev lifted a hand to stroke Leslie's cheek, then stopped a breath away. "I…Jesus. I'm so sorry I lost my temper. Did I hurt you?"

"No." There were fingerprint bruises on the crest of both of Leslie's shoulders. She'd seen them in the mirror when she'd showered that morning. It was funny. Rachel never noticed.

"I don't want you to leave thinking I blame you for anything," Dev said, taking Leslie's hand before she realized she'd even done it. "What happened when we were kids—that's long over. Seeing you again just brought up a lot of old stuff. It kind of put me into a spin."

"I know what you mean."

"I need to tell you something." Dev had woken up feeling numb, but she was pretty sure that as soon as it hit her that Leslie was really gone, a lot of places inside were going to hurt for a long time. But she'd promised herself she wasn't going to talk about that now. She'd burned up the road to get back to the lodge because she didn't want to let anger and pain be their last memory. This time when they parted, she wanted the love and friendship that they'd shared to be what they remembered.

"Yesterday you said…" Dev's throat constricted unexpectedly and she looked quickly away, blinking rapidly. After a second, when she was certain she could hold it together, she met Leslie's gaze again. "You said I was special to you—back then."

"You were the bravest, the strongest, the most wonderful person in my life." Leslie's hands shook as she enfolded Dev's in both of hers. Raising Dev's fingers to her lips, she kissed them.

"Les," Dev murmured, rubbing her thumb gently below Leslie's eyes as tears fell like raindrops. "Don't do that. It's okay now."

Shaking her head, Leslie took a shuddering breath. "No one has ever known me the way you did."

"Loving you is the best thing I ever did. Being special to you is what made me strong." Dev got to her knees and cradled Leslie's face gently between her hands. She leaned down and kissed her softly, a gentle lingering kiss that spoke of all the things she'd feared to say when she'd been young, and had never wanted to say to anyone else. "I love you, and I'll never be sorry for that."

Leslie wrapped her arms around Dev's shoulders, one hand stroking her hair, the other her back. She knew this woman, this body, this heart in a place deep inside that no one else had ever touched.

"I love you too," Leslie whispered, brushing her mouth over Dev's neck to seal the taste of her in her heart.

Dev slid down off the rock and held out her arms. Leslie grasped her hands and climbed down beside her, then linked fingers as they stood together by the lake that had been the backdrop to all their precious moments.

After a minute, Dev said, "Whenever I see the lake at dawn, or walk in the woods in the moonlight, or wake up in the morning to birdsong, I'm going to think about you." She stroked Leslie's cheek, then kissed her one last time. "Look me up if you ever get tired of Manhattan."

"I will," Leslie whispered, backing away until their hands no longer touched. She left Dev standing by the lake and went back to her life.

CHAPTER TWENTY-FOUR

Leslie's BlackBerry vibrated just as she stepped off the elevator into the parking garage. She was tempted to ignore it because it was almost 8 p.m. and Rachel was due at her apartment in thirty minutes. She'd just left the office, and if it was anything important, whoever it was could e-mail her. Still, maybe it was Rachel calling to cancel. She pulled the BlackBerry from her briefcase and her heart gave a sudden lurch when she saw the number for the lodge on the readout. Maybe it was Dev.

"Hello?"

"Hi, honey," Eileen said. "Did I catch you at a bad time?"

"No, I was just leaving the office," Leslie said, feeling foolish and disappointed in equal measure. Why would Dev call her? They'd said everything there was to say when they'd said goodbye.

"Still working late, I see."

"This is pretty much the norm. Is everything okay?"

"Oh…yes. I hadn't heard from you, and I just…I should let you go if you're on your way home."

"No. It's fine. I meant to call, but it's just been crazy since I got back." Leslie unlocked her car, tossed her briefcase onto the passenger seat, and put the key in the ignition. It had taken her the better part of a week to catch up and another to get ahead of the game. If she was going to take time off at the end of the summer to go home again, she had to plan for it now. Besides, two weeks of nonstop work had helped take her mind off everything that happened at the lake, at least for a few hours at a time. As soon as she was alone and not working, though, she thought about Dev. Sadness washed through her and she focused on the call. "How's Daddy?"

"Grumpy."

Leslie laughed. "Can't you find something for him to do? He must be driving you nuts."

"He is, but he's finally able to get down to the boathouse, and that helps." There was a beat of silence, then Eileen said casually, "How's Rachel?"

"Fine, I think." Leslie started the car and switched to the hands-free mic. "She got back in town last week but we've both been too busy to get together. In fact, she should be on her way over to my place right now."

"Well then, I definitely don't want to keep you."

Leslie felt a quick clench of anxiety and just as quickly forced it away. Maybe she should talk it over with her mother. No, she'd thought things through, and she was sure. It wouldn't be easy, but she'd done harder things in her life. At least, she wanted to tell herself she had.

"How's Dev?" Leslie asked, slowing so she could run her ID card through the box at the security gate.

"I haven't seen her very much since you left. Every now and then I'll catch her at breakfast or dinner. She looks tired. I guess she's working hard too."

Leslie considered how she would phrase the next question. "How is the tourist business? Has Natalie said anything about the campsites being full?"

"I haven't had much chance to talk to her, either. I've seen her once or twice with Dev."

"At the lodge?" Leslie probed. For dinner? For breakfast?

"Mmm. Are you driving right now?"

"Uh-huh."

"Then I'm going to go. You need to pay attention to what you're doing, Leslie."

Leslie smiled. "I know, Mom. I'm trying."

"All right, then. Call sometime. I miss you."

"Me too," Leslie said softly.

❖

"Let me see if I understand this correctly," Rachel said, appraising Leslie steadily over the top of her wineglass. Sitting forward on Leslie's sofa, she took another sip of her Pinot Noir, then cradled the crystal goblet between her long, elegant fingers. "You're telling me you want to change the terms of our relationship, but you're not involved with anyone else?"

"That's right," Leslie said quietly.

Rachel tapped a finger on her glass. "You're not sleeping with anyone else, but you want to stop sleeping with me."

"Yes."

"Forgive me if I'm being dense," Rachel said, "because I was under the impression that we got along very well, in and out of the bedroom. But most definitely *in* the bedroom."

"We do." Leslie knew this was going to be difficult to explain. Not because she expected Rachel to lose her temper or create a scene, but because Leslie had never indicated that she wanted her relationship with Rachel to be more than what it was. And she hadn't, not until she'd felt what love was like. "I love thrashing out legal issues with you, and I enjoy being with you." She rubbed her forehead. "God, Rach, I'm really trying to avoid clichés here, but this isn't about anything you've done. It really is about me."

Rachel smiled wryly. "The next thing I know, you're going to tell me you want to be friends."

"I do want that. If we can." Leslie met Rachel's eyes and saw the confusion in them. This wasn't right. Rachel deserved more. She deserved the truth. "I'm not seeing anyone else. But there *is* someone else I...I'm in love with."

"A woman, I hope."

"God, yes," Leslie said, laughing briefly.

"You're in love with another woman, but you're not sleeping with her."

"I'm not doing anything with her. I told you, we don't have a relationship."

Rachel shook her head. "I'm not tracking here, darling. You're going to have to spell it out."

"When I was up at the lake, I rekindled a...a relationship with a woman I knew years ago. I was in love with her in high school, and I guess I've been a little bit in love with her all my life. Now I know it, and it doesn't feel right being with you."

"Does she know how you feel about her?" Rachel leaned back and crossed her legs, her charcoal pinstripe silk skirt sliding to mid-thigh. She stretched one arm out along the back of the sofa, her suit jacket falling open and her blouse tightening across her breasts.

It was a seductive pose, and Leslie knew Rachel knew it. She looked away. "Yes and no. About before, yes. About now, not exactly."

"So you're doing the honorable thing before you and she—"

"No," Leslie said quickly. "I don't...we don't have any plans for anything."

"You're going to stop seeing me because of a high school crush?" Rachel's tone was more incredulous than angry. "And you're not even pursuing her?"

"I'm pretty turned around right now, Rach. I just don't feel like I can be with anyone."

"Maybe you need to take some more time off. I've never seen you like this."

"You mean emotionally all over the place?" Leslie knew she always appeared to be in control because she always kept her emotions so tightly under wraps. But now she couldn't. She couldn't push the memory of Dev away, or what she felt for her, or what she didn't feel for Rachel. She couldn't go back to being completely focused on work and contenting herself with a casual sexual relationship. Part of her mind was always thinking about Dev. About where she was. What she was doing. If she was with Natalie. If she was happy. If she missed Leslie as much as Leslie missed her.

"A few weeks off won't change anything," Leslie said gently. "And it doesn't feel fair to keep seeing you when I feel this way."

"You can't be happy about this."

Leslie closed her eyes for an instant, then smiled weakly. "I'm not, but it's what I have to do."

"We have an excellent physical relationship, and we enjoy each other's company. You're not seeing anyone else, and neither am I." Rising, Rachel set her glass down and glided over to Leslie. She cupped her jaw and raised her head. "Why give this up?"

Leslie felt the familiar pull of Rachel's mouth moving over hers, those long fingers caressing her neck, a warm hand cupping her breast. Her nipple hardened in Rachel's palm and she heard Rachel's murmur of approval. Carefully, she eased back, breaking the kiss and the caress.

"My heart's not in it, Rachel. And I need it to be. I'm sorry."

Rachel straightened. "I'm not going to wait."

"I didn't think you would." Leslie stood. "I wouldn't ask you to."

"But," Rachel said, running her fingertip along Leslie's jaw, "I think it might take me quite some time to find anyone I enjoy as much as you, especially in the bedroom. So call me, if you decide you miss it."

"You can call me too," Leslie said softly, knowing Rachel wouldn't. Rachel didn't have friends, she didn't have time. She had colleagues to challenge her mind and a lover to satisfy her body. Leslie doubted Rachel would go long without finding someone else. She burned too fast and too brightly not to have her needs met. "I'm sorry. I hate hurting you."

"I know, darling." Rachel's eyes were cool, her expression remote. "I'll miss you, but I won't suffer. If I were the kind of person who did, you probably wouldn't be leaving."

Leslie said nothing. If she'd thought Rachel would be devastated, she still would have found a way to say goodbye. She wasn't doing either of them any favors pretending that what they had was enough for her. And no matter what they shared, it wouldn't be enough to keep her from wanting Dev.

"Take care, Rachel," Leslie said, walking with her to the door.

Rachel collected her briefcase and keys. "I've never known you to be a coward, Leslie. If you love the woman, for God's sake, do something about it."

"Thank you, Counselor," Leslie said, smiling fleetingly. "I'll take that under serious advisement."

"You should, because I'm never wrong. Goodbye, darling."

When the door closed behind Rachel, Leslie returned to the living room and picked up her wine. She sipped slowly, completely alone. It felt both liberating and terrifying.

❖

Dev slowed the park service truck at the mouth of a vacant campsite while Natalie jumped off the running board, trotted down the dirt path to the clearing, and checked that the fire was out in the fire pit. She jogged back, hooked her arm inside the open window, and steadied herself against the outside of the door. She grinned in at Dev.

"Only five more to go."

"You didn't tell me I was going to have to work for my dinner."

"I did say you could stay back at the office and wait for me."

"This saves time," Dev said, turning onto the last loop of road that snaked through the campsite. "Plus, if I waited there, I'd have to listen to Jimmy complain about the heat."

"Or the bugs."

"Or the tourists."

"Or—" Natalie laughed and hopped down as Dev slowed again. When she climbed back aboard and they moved on, she peered through the window again. "Hear anything from Leslie?"

Dev stared straight ahead. "No."

"You haven't called her?"

"No."

"Going to?"

Dev shook her head.

"Should I ask why not?"

"Among other things, she's got a girlfriend."

"Ah."

"This is your stop," Dev said, braking.

Natalie checked the last few sites on foot while Dev followed along the narrow dirt road. When she returned to the truck, she settled into the passenger seat and slipped her hand onto Dev's thigh. "I'm sorry."

Dev glanced at her. "About what?"

"For bringing it up. I waited two weeks. I thought that was a decent interval."

"It's okay." Dev pulled into the parking lot behind the ranger's office. Two weeks. It felt like two minutes. She could still feel the warmth of Leslie's hand in hers. She could still hear her voice, smell the subtle scent of her perfume. Leslie was everywhere around her, but never anywhere as much as in her thoughts. There was no time frame for missing Leslie. No beginning, and no end. It was simply part of her life and had been for as long as she could remember.

"Hey. Don't go drifting off, Dev. There's nothing back there but pain."

"I know," Dev said. "I'm okay."

"Not quite, but you will be."

"Your friendship means a lot to me. Thanks."

"Don't even go there," Natalie said. "We *are* friends. And that means you don't have to thank me."

Dev grinned and backed into a parking space. "Yeah yeah."

"And I'm still going to make a move on you." Natalie leaned across the gearshift and gently bit Dev's earlobe. "But I'm going to give you a little more time to get prepared. A day. Maybe two."

Dev laughed. "Thanks for letting me know."

Natalie patted Dev's thigh. "Anytime."

"I'm not in any shape to get involved, Nat," Dev said quietly as they locked up the park service vehicle.

"Can't shake her?"

Dev shook her head. Leslie was always in her thoughts, in her dreams. Leslie was in her blood.

"I could help." Natalie grasped Dev's hand as they walked toward her SUV.

"You do help."

Natalie laughed. "I meant in a bit more active way."

Dev laughed too. "I know."

"So when I make a serious offer," Natalie said, pausing before unlocking her vehicle, "you can tell me if it's what you want or not."

"Nat," Dev said gently. "I don't want to mislead you. I don't think—"

"Ah ah—you have to wait until I make my move to turn me down."

Lifting her hands in defeat, Dev nodded. "Okay. And just so you won't think I'm running scared, I'll tell you right now I'm going to be out of town for a couple of days at the end of the month."

"Oh yeah? What's up?" Natalie unlocked the doors and they slid in.

"I've been scheduled on and off for the last four months to testify in a case involving industrial contamination of a river upstate, and they keep rescheduling. I just heard it's finally going to go."

"So you're heading upstate?"

"No," Dev said quietly. "Actually, the trial is in New York City."

"Oh." Natalie glanced at Dev as she pulled out onto the highway. "And?"

Dev shook her head. "And nothing."

"Okay," Natalie said, reaching for Dev's hand. She squeezed it briefly, then let go. "My timetable still looks good, then."

Dev smiled, but she feared that time alone would not be enough for her to forget Leslie.

CHAPTER TWENTY-FIVE

I'll be out the rest of the afternoon, Steph," Leslie said to her paralegal. "I'll check messages later and get back to you on anything urgent."

"Finally taking a few hours off? You've been back a month and I think you've been in here every day." Stephanie fixed her with a reproachful frown and lowered her voice. "Weren't you supposed to be trying something new? Like taking it easy now and then?"

Leslie leaned both hands on Stephanie's desk and whispered back, "I *have* been taking it easy. I'm out by eight every night."

Stephanie shook her head. "That's not exactly cutting back."

"I feel fine. I'll be in court."

"Wait!" Stephanie quickly scanned her calendar. "I don't have you down for anything. Did I forget something?"

"No." Leslie shouldered her briefcase and started toward the door. "I want to check out the competition."

"What—"

Without looking back, Leslie waved a hand goodbye and disappeared down the hall. Forty minutes later she slipped quietly into the back row in a courtroom at the federal courthouse. She took a seat behind a fairly large gentleman and made notes on another case while listening to testimony with half an ear, absently noting that the state's attorney was knowledgeable and his questions sharp. She'd been up against him once, and that had not gone so well for him. She smiled at the memory. The young attorney representing the corporation accused of venting waste runoff into an unsecured drainage system and contaminating a nearby river also seemed on top of his game.

Twenty minutes after Leslie arrived, the door opened again and Dev walked in. Leslie shifted a little so that Dev would not see her as she strode down the center aisle. She didn't want to disturb Dev's concentration. Her own was shot to hell the second she saw Dev, so she quietly slid her notes into her briefcase and settled back to watch. Dev sat two rows behind the plaintiff's table, and Leslie had a good view of her in profile. Dev had dressed for court in a dark suit and pale shirt. Her chestnut hair had been trimmed to just above her collar, and it curled very subtly at the ends. She had that tanned, healthy gleam that women who worked outdoors often had, but beneath it, she seemed tired. And a little thinner. She was so damn beautiful, and Leslie drew a long slow breath to calm the butterflies in her stomach.

When the state's attorney called Dev to testify, Leslie positioned herself so that the gentleman in front of her shielded her enough that Dev was not likely to see her. Witnesses were usually instructed to look only at the jury or the questioning attorney during testimony. They rarely scanned the audience. Leslie could hear Dev, and she did not need to see her to know exactly how she looked as she answered. Hazel eyes intent, her handsome face honest and passionate.

The state's attorney had indeed gotten smarter with his questioning, but Dev was an ideal expert witness and made the attorney look better than he actually was. Dev reduced difficult science to understandable concepts and made human arguments that were guaranteed to sway the jury. Her personality alone was a significant added benefit to her value as an expert defending the river and its inhabitants. Knowing Dev, Leslie knew that none of her answers were calculated, but what she truly believed.

When the corporation's defense attorney began his cross-examination with a belligerent tone, Leslie shook her head, feeling sorry for him. She edged over slightly so she could see Dev's face as Dev countered every vehement challenge in a calm, reasoned fashion. Then, after a particularly sarcastically phrased question from the attorney, something in Dev's face changed. Her eyes glinted, and the bold planes of her face grew stronger. Leslie held her breath.

Dev leaned forward and regarded the attorney as if he had just made the most ridiculous statement she'd ever heard. Then she inclined her body toward the jury and moved the microphone a half inch closer to her face, even though her voice carried well without it. The jury clearly hung on her every word at this point, waiting for whatever critical statement she was about to make.

"What you have to understand," Dev said, her eyes seeming to meet those of every juror, "is that fish are people too."

Leslie bit her lip to stifle her exclamation, grateful that she wasn't the one going up against Dev. It was apparent that every single member of the jury believed every word Dev said. The corporation might as well have been dumping nuclear waste into their backyards, because that was how they now thought of those contaminated waters. Dev had made it personal for them with the elegant strength of her conviction. Leslie hated when the opposing team used her own strategy against her, and she'd never seen it done better. The questioning attorney appeared to share her assessment and hastily concluded his cross-examination.

When Dev finished her testimony and stepped down from the witness box, she hesitated for a second, her head tilted as if she were listening to someone speaking, although the room was quiet. Then she resumed walking, her gaze lasering to Leslie.

Leslie nodded hello, waiting anxiously for a response. Then Dev smiled, the same smile of welcome she had greeted Leslie with a thousand times before. It had always made Leslie feel beautiful and special, and it still did.

Dev checked her watch and tried not to fidget. It had already been late in the afternoon when she'd finished testifying, so she knew court would adjourn at any minute. She wanted to verify that she wouldn't be recalled to testify, and then she wanted to find Leslie. The first glimpse of her after a month of thinking about her had nearly stopped Dev in her tracks. At first she'd thought it was some kind of hallucination brought about by the fact that she'd done nothing on the three-hour train ride but replay every conversation with Leslie she'd ever had. Fortunately, she knew the details of the case thoroughly and hadn't needed to review them, because the closer she came to New York City, the more her concentration had waned. Just knowing she was going to be in the same city as Leslie made her blood hum. She knew it was crazy, but she couldn't stop it.

Then to actually *see* her, sitting in the courtroom so calm and composed with her perfectly styled hair and subtle makeup and fashionable suit, had pretty much thrown her off the tracks. She had to talk to her. Just talk to her. Friends could do that, right? That was normal. But the churning in her stomach that felt like hunger but wasn't—that wasn't normal. The way her skin tingled, shimmering like the air just before a huge bolt of lightning dispelled the pent-up electricity in the midst of a storm—that wasn't normal.

Dev studied her hands, clasped loosely in her lap. They were trembling.

None of this was normal. She was deluding herself, again. But it didn't matter, she still had to see her. Just—see her.

"Great job," the state's attorney murmured, jolting Dev back to the present. She looked around and saw that the jury box was empty and the crowd in the courtroom dispersing. Turning rapidly she searched the room behind her, but the aisle was already filled with people filing out. She couldn't see Leslie.

"Will you need me again?" Dev asked briskly.

"Shouldn't. If you can hang around until noon tomorrow, I'll call you to let you know for sure. I assume you'll be staying in the city?"

"Yes. I'm at the Hilton at Fifty-fourth and Sixth."

"What do you say we have some dinner. I think we can safely celebrate. You really nail—"

"Ah, thanks, no," Dev said, sidestepping into the central aisle. "I appreciate it, but I've got another appointment. Call me and let me know about tomorrow."

"All right. Thanks again!"

The aisle was clearer now, and Dev pushed hurriedly through the double doors into the hallway beyond. It was empty, and the pain of disappointment was so sharp she gasped. Dazed, uncertain now that she had even seen her, Dev mechanically pushed the down button on the elevator, stepped in, and rode to the lobby.

She was halfway to the front doors when she heard her name.

"Dev?"

Spinning around, Dev saw her standing off to the side beneath a marble archway. She stared for a heartbeat and then another, and when Leslie didn't disappear, she cautiously approached her.

"Les?"

"Hi," Leslie said, smiling almost shyly.

"What are you doing here?"

"My mother told me you were coming down to testify, so I thought I'd do a little reconnaissance and see what kind of ammunition the other side was using." Leslie brushed her hair away from her face, a nervous gesture that was totally unlike her. She'd never actually been alone with Dev when she'd been aware of what was between them. Not when there hadn't been insurmountable barriers keeping them apart. She hadn't been this keyed up around anyone ever, not Mike on their first date or Rachel the first time they'd made love. The only person who had ever made her feel anything like this buzzing excitement had been Dev, years ago, and she'd failed to recognize what it meant then. But she knew now. "You know, field research."

"Oh. Yeah." Dev couldn't hide her foolish grin. She felt just about as dizzy as she used to when she was sixteen and she'd leave school later than everyone else because she'd had detention for showing up late or smart-mouthing a teacher and Leslie would be waiting for her. All her anger and resentment would fade at the first sight of Leslie's smile. Dev leaned her shoulder against the marble pillar, a wisp of the cocky teenager she'd been in her stance. "So, Counselor. What do you think?"

Leslie edged closer, as if she were drawn by a magnet and helpless to resist the pull. She did just barely manage to resist slipping her hand beneath the edge of Dev's jacket and touching her. But her fingers quivered with the need for contact. Her voice came out breathy, but she couldn't control that either. "I thought you were fabulous. If I ever see your name on an expert list, I'm recommending we settle."

Dev laughed, knowing Leslie was playing with her. It felt so good. So good to tease with her again. She used to think it was the lake that created the magic around them, that made the rest of the world fade away so there was only the two of them. Maybe she'd been wrong, because they couldn't be farther from the lake than they were right now and she felt it still. The magic. Watching the happiness light Leslie's eyes, she felt the dream tremble and surge back to life.

"Let me take you to dinner," Leslie said quickly. "You're not going right back, are you?"

If she had intended to go home, Dev would have changed her plans immediately. She shook her head. "I'm here until tomorrow."

"Where are you staying?"

Dev told her, lifting her overnighter. "I should probably go check in now." She didn't move, loath to let Leslie out of her sight. "I could meet you somewhere?"

"Why don't I go with you?" Leslie said, having difficulty thinking clearly when every nerve in her body was jangling. Since her mother had told her a week before about Dev's upcoming trial and she'd tracked down the details, she'd anticipated seeing Dev. As the day had drawn closer, her anxiety—part excitement, part uncertainty—had climbed exponentially to the point where she could barely sleep. Now Dev was here, and she wasn't wasting a minute of their time together. "We can walk to dinner somewhere from your hotel."

"Sure. That sounds great." Dev thought anything sounded great as long as she could spend the evening with Leslie. Like an addict who knew she would wake up bathed in the clammy sweat of remorse and regret in the morning but who nevertheless downed the next drink or shot the next line or laid down the next bet, Dev reached for Leslie's hand. She didn't care how much it hurt tomorrow. Tonight the wounds that never completely healed would fade for a few merciful hours. "Let's go."

Still holding Dev's hand, Leslie hailed a cab and they climbed into the backseat. Their thighs brushed as the cabbie swerved through rush-hour traffic with the reckless abandon of a man with a death wish. At one point the cab jerked so violently that Leslie was thrown into Dev, and Dev automatically curved her arm around Leslie's shoulders. Leslie wrapped her arm around Dev's waist to steady herself. When the cab resumed a somewhat smoother course, Leslie didn't move away.

Dev stared straight ahead through the windshield, but she wasn't watching the traffic or the street signs. She wasn't aware of anything except Leslie leaning against her and the pressure of Leslie's arm wrapped around her middle. Her heart was pounding, or maybe that was Leslie's. Blood thundered through her chest, heat kindled in the depths of her abdomen, and she shivered as waves of arousal rolled through her. She stroked Leslie's arm and her fingertips burned.

"I can't do this, Les," Dev whispered, realizing that unlike the addict, she had no tolerance for her addiction. The pleasure would destroy her long before morning. "I thought I could. But I can't."

"Do what?" Leslie murmured, following the pulse rippling along Dev's neck through heavy lids. Her body felt tight, like ripe fruit ready to burst in the sun.

"I can't be this close to you." Dev shuddered as Leslie smoothed her palm in a gentle circle over the center of her stomach.

"You're shaking." Leslie drew away, searching Dev's face anxiously, her heart clenching at the agony in Dev's dark eyes. "Oh, God, Dev, what's wrong?"

"I thought I could be friends. Spend time with you, like friends." Dev's voice cracked, and she swallowed hard. "I can't. Not now." She edged away on the seat but it wasn't far enough. Two hundred miles hadn't been far enough to stop wanting her. Two thousand wouldn't be. "I'll need to pass on dinner."

"Hilton," the cabbie grunted as he rocketed the cab into the turnaround and slammed to a halt.

Leslie ignored him, her eyes on Dev. "I'm coming up with you. We'll just talk. Please, Dev."

Leslie was hurting, Dev could hear it. And she thought if she had to watch the cab drive away with Leslie inside, she'd end up howling like an animal with its leg caught in a trap. She couldn't let her go and she couldn't be near her without dying by inches. But given the choice between two miseries, she'd choose the one thing she'd always craved. Leslie.

Wordlessly, Dev nodded and got out of the cab. While Leslie paid the cabdriver, Dev walked around and opened Leslie's door, then extended her hand. Leslie's fingers closed around hers, and the charge of flesh on flesh almost rocked her back on her heels.

How could she say no? She could more easily stop her own heart from beating.

CHAPTER TWENTY-SIX

Dev glanced over her shoulder impatiently while the hotel receptionist ran her credit card and programmed her room key. Leslie was still there, waiting in the lounge area adjacent to the front desk. Leslie seemed perfectly composed, sitting with her shapely legs crossed, one arm resting along the curved edge of the upholstered armchair, upper body angled so that she faced in Dev's direction. Dev was anything but composed. She needed something to settle her down— a cigarette, a drink, something—but she didn't smoke and rarely drank more than a glass or two of wine and the something that she needed was Leslie. God, she needed her.

"Here you are," the receptionist said with a smile. "Enjoy your stay, Dr. Weber."

"Thanks," Dev said, waving off the bellman as she stuffed the paperwork into her jacket pocket. With the plastic key card in one hand and her overnighter in the other, she strode over to Leslie. "All set. I can take my things upstairs and be down in five minutes if you want to wait here. We can go out to dinner right away, if you're hungry."

Leslie stood, shaking her head. She slid the key card from Dev's hand and slipped her palm into its place. "Let's go upstairs."

"Okay."

It was a mistake, Dev knew it. But she couldn't imagine sitting across from Leslie in a restaurant, pretending she was hungry or trying to make casual conversation. At least in her hotel room she would be spared the social charade. They rode upstairs to the tenth floor in silence, their shoulders touching as they made room for other guests. Leslie kept her hand in Dev's the entire ride, their fingers loosely entwined.

Dev found the room, set her luggage down, and held out her hand for the key card Leslie still carried. "Okay?"

"Yes. Very," Leslie murmured, thinking that if Dev didn't open the door and get them inside soon, she wouldn't be responsible for what happened out in the hall. Dev looked so worried, so unsure, and Leslie hated to see her that way. It was her fault, she knew it. Dev had always been there for her, always clear about what she felt, always waiting for Leslie to understand. And now Dev didn't trust her.

Leslie was struck with a sudden stab of fear that maybe Dev had finally stopped waiting and moved on. Maybe her reluctance in the cab hadn't been because she didn't trust Leslie's feelings, but because she was no longer available. Leslie panicked, unable to imagine what she would do if she lost Dev now. "Hurry, Dev."

Surprised by the urgency in Leslie's voice, Dev sliced the card through the lock slot, cranked the handle, and shoved the door open with her shoulder. She kicked her overnighter into the room while holding the door for Leslie to enter. She flipped the wall switch just inside the door, lighting a small bedside lamp that suffused the room with muted light. The heavy floral drapes on the window were closed. Besides the king-size bed and entertainment console opposite it, there was a small sitting area with a sofa, coffee table, and desk.

Dev took it all in at a glance as the door swung closed behind her, leaving her to face Leslie, who waited a few feet away. Leslie took one step toward her, the expression on her face one that Dev had never seen before. Her lips, shining and moist with pale gloss, were slightly parted and curved tenderly at each corner. Her blue eyes, shimmering like lake water in the sunlight, were fixed intently on Dev's. A rush of heat swept through Dev so quickly she caught her breath and backed up a step, as if she could escape. Her back hit the door and she lifted her hands, palms up, helplessly.

"Don't, Les."

"Why not?" Leslie murmured, running a fingertip along the edge of Dev's jacket.

"I can't take it," Dev whispered. "I miss you so much, and I want you so badly."

Leslie slipped both hands beneath Dev's jacket and traced the ridges of Dev's collarbones, leaning her lower body lightly into Dev. Dev's body was rigid, but still Leslie sensed the barely restrained hunger, and she wanted it. God, how she wanted Dev to still want her in the delirious, boundless way she had before. She wanted it like nothing else in her life. "I miss you too. Terribly. Kiss me, Dev. Please."

"You'll break me," Dev warned hoarsely. "If I kiss you, I won't stop. Not this time. I can't."

"I don't want you to stop." Leslie caressed one hand up the side of Dev's neck and behind her head, curling her fingers into Dev's hair. She pulled slowly, easing Dev's head back as she pressed her lips to Dev's throat. "I don't want you to stop until you're inside of me where you belong."

Dev made a sound that was part groan, part sob, her hands flat against the door, fingers flexed against the metal. If she let go, if she touched her, she was afraid of what she might do. She wanted her, had wanted her since she was old enough to recognize her desire for a woman. And all the years of denial had honed her craving until it ran dangerously close to the wild part of her that functioned from primal memory, when mating dictated survival, not pleasure. She wanted Leslie beyond civilized reason, because without her, some essential part of her would die. She understood then why the great beasts tore and slashed their mates in the frenzy of joining. The same need scorched through her with unrelenting flame and fury. "I'm afraid I'll hurt you."

Laughing, eyes bright with exultation, Leslie pressed hard against her. Her full breasts tensed with arousal. Her hips rolled in a slow rhythm of invitation. She tightened her fingers in Dev's hair and slid her other hand around to Dev's back. She set her nails into flesh through the thin fabric of Dev's shirt, claiming her. "You won't. You can't. I love you. I *want* you to take what's yours."

Leslie punctuated each word with her teeth on Dev's neck, leaving marks, not caring. She hadn't known. All these years she hadn't known what passion was, what desire was, what belonging meant. She was liquid with desire, her need simmering like lava buried for millennia and finally streaking a path to freedom. "I need you so much, Dev, please, please. God, come to bed with me."

Dev couldn't breathe. Leslie was all over her, stroking her, exciting her, reaching inside and throwing open the bars on the passion she'd kept caged all her life. She hurt. Her body quivered. A terrible pressure filled her chest and belly, threatening to explode. "Rachel... what about—"

"Gone." Leslie wrapped both arms tightly around Dev, her hands raking Dev's back. "I left her. I had to." She tilted her head back, face suffused with need, eyes pleading. "I want you. Help me, Dev. Touch me."

Dev drew a breath, and another, each sweeter than the last. The painful pressure eased, replaced by pleasure. The beast was free, still fierce, but no longer hunted. No longer haunted. For the first time, she welcomed her passion.

"I love you," Dev whispered, cradling Leslie's face as gently as if she were holding a newborn bird. She brushed her mouth over Leslie's, soft as a feather. "I've always loved you."

Eyes closed, Leslie offered her throat. "Forgive me."

Dev kissed her throat, the hollow at the base of her neck, the V bared by the open collar of her blouse. "There's no need. Not now. Not then." She opened Leslie's blouse, one button at a time, her hands shaking. Carefully, she teased the bottom from beneath the waistband of Leslie's skirt until Leslie's abdomen was bare and the satin cups of her bra exposed. Dev splayed her hands over Leslie's breasts and Leslie sagged against her.

"I've dreamed of this," Dev murmured, teasing Leslie's nipples into erection. "I'm going to touch you everywhere."

"I've never been this excited," Leslie warned her breathlessly. "I feel like I'll come right away."

"It's okay if you have to. The first time." Dev skimmed her tongue over the surface of Leslie's lower lip, then sucked gently. "I'm going to make love to you all night."

"I need you to."

Dev kissed her again, tugging her nipples as she danced her tongue over the warm inner recesses of her mouth. Leslie's breasts seemed to swell and fill her hands, stretching the sheer fabric tightly over her tense nipples.

"Ready for bed?" Dev whispered, her mouth against Leslie's ear. Dev's thighs and abdomen ached from holding back, from going slow. The sounds Leslie made, the way she shivered as Dev plucked on her nipples, the insistent rocking of her hips against Dev's crotch were making Dev crazy. She wasn't sure she could hold out until Leslie touched her.

Leslie moaned and pressed her forehead to Dev's shoulder. "Yes. Please, now."

Hands linked, mouths searching for quick kisses, they stumbled to the foot of the bed. Arms entwined, they freed buttons and lowered zippers and shed shoes and clothes until they were nearly nude.

"Let me," Dev said as Leslie reached to unhook her own bra.

Leslie let her hands fall to her sides, clad only in her bra and pale silk bikinis. Her stomach was fluttering with arousal, her breasts almost painfully engorged. Her breath had fled at the first brush of Dev's hands on her skin, and she'd never recaptured it. "Oh, yes."

Dev, naked except for her briefs, slid her fingertips beneath the thin straps of Leslie's bra and eased them down over her shoulders. She dipped her head and kissed Leslie's breasts, first one, then the other, moving down the smooth curves as she lowered the bra, millimeter by millimeter, until Leslie's nipples were exposed. Rapidly opening the clasp, Dev freed Leslie's breasts completely and sucked a nipple into her mouth. Leslie cried out, her knees buckling.

"I'm so excited, Dev," Leslie moaned, clutching Dev's shoulders. "I feel like I might come."

"Let it happen," Dev whispered around the hard nub, refusing to release her. She pressed one hand flat against Leslie's stomach, sweeping her fingers in a slow steady arc, tightening inside as Leslie's hips thrust in the air. Keeping one arm firmly around Leslie's waist, she pushed lower, dipping her fingers beneath the edge of Leslie's panties, sucking harder. First one nipple, then the other.

Gasping, Leslie covered Dev's hand as it circled beneath the damp silk. "Oh, don't touch my clit. You'll make me come."

"I want to," Dev growled, her mind a red haze. Leslie was hers now. Maybe just for these few moments, but she was finally hers. "I want you to come. I want to hear you come."

"I will, I promise." Leslie didn't recognize her own voice. Her body was spinning out of control. It was wonderful. It was terrifying. "I'll come for you. I will. But I need to see your face, Dev. I need to see you when I come. Please."

Dev heard what sounded like fear and finally raised her head. Leslie's eyes were nearly closed, her lips trembling. Her face and neck were flushed, her breasts heaving. She was seconds from coming. The heat from Leslie's center beckoned and Dev ached to drive into her, drive her over. Take her hard and deep. She wouldn't hurt her, she knew she wouldn't. She would be inside her at last and Leslie would be coming for her. For her.

"Let's lie down," Dev said hoarsely, easing her fingers from beneath Leslie's panties. She guided Leslie to the side of the bed and yanked down the covers with one hand. She kicked out of her underwear as Leslie stretched out. Carefully, she slid Leslie's bikinis down her legs and settled beside her, one thigh over Leslie's. The touch of Leslie's hot skin against her tense clitoris made her want to come. She fought not to finish herself off against Leslie's leg, even though it would only have taken a second. Instead, she held very still until she mentally pushed back her body's demand to climax. Leslie's eyes were hazy, her legs twitching on the crisp white sheets, her hands restless and urgent on Dev's back. She whimpered, words beyond her.

"Take my hand, baby," Dev urged.

Leslie gripped Dev's wrist.

"Take me inside, Les," Dev pleaded. "Take me inside and come for me."

Barely breathing, eyes fixed on Leslie's, Dev kissed her. Dev moaned as Leslie guided her fingers between her legs. Leslie was wet, warm, open. At the first light touch of Dev's fingertips to the hard prominence of Leslie's clitoris, Leslie's head snapped back and she cried out.

Dev gritted her teeth at the surge of pressure in her groin. She wouldn't come, not yet. "More. Please, Les. Take me deeper."

"Oh, I am going to come," Leslie keened, thrusting onto Dev's fingers.

"Baby, you feel so good," Dev said.

Leslie caught her lower lip between her teeth, her eyes wide, the blue eclipsed by black as her pupils expanded wildly. She pushed Dev's hand lower, squeezing Dev's wrist hard enough to leave the crescent indentations of her nails in Dev's skin. Her back arched as Dev entered her completely. The sweet pleasure of Dev's palm caressing her, of her fingers stretching and filling her, was too much.

"I'm coming," Leslie groaned.

Dev held her breath, watching Leslie's face, feeling her spasm deep inside, listening to her cries of pleasure. She wanted to laugh. She wanted to cry. She wanted to shout with wonder. Leslie clung to her, sobbing quietly, and Dev buried her face in the curve of Leslie's neck.

"I love you," Dev whispered. "Oh God, Leslie, I love you."

Weakly, struggling to catch her breath, Leslie stroked Dev's back. Seconds passed, and Leslie slowly realized that Dev was shaking, her hips jerking against Leslie's thigh.

"Dev. Let me help you," Leslie murmured, sliding her hand between her thigh and Dev's body to cup Dev's swollen sex. She hissed in a breath when her fingers were instantly soaked. "Oh God, you're beautiful. Tell me what you need."

"Squeeze my clit," Dev gasped. "I need to come so bad."

Leslie stroked her firmly, squeezing and releasing, feeling her grow impossibly hard. "Is it good, love? Is it what you need?"

"Oh yeah," Dev sobbed, "oh yeah, God yeah, you're making me come."

Dev jerked in Leslie's arms and her fingers, still deep inside Leslie, thrust and flexed. Leslie cried out in surprise as another orgasm crashed through her, but she stayed with Dev, stroking her through her orgasm until she lay limp and panting in Leslie's arms.

"Can you come again?" Leslie whispered, smoothing the damp hair from Dev's forehead. She kissed her, pleased by the hazy bliss in Dev's eyes.

"Uh, maybe. In a year or two." Dev sighed. "Jesus, that was intense."

"Yeah?" Leslie smiled broadly. *She* had put that sated look in Dev's eyes, that lazy slur in her voice. She had done it, and she wanted to do it again. Now. Immediately. "That was just the warm-up, you know."

Dev quirked a brow. "You want more?"

"Oh yes," Leslie said, realizing just how much she wanted. "I want much, much more."

"I love you," Dev said quietly.

"I know." Leslie stroked her cheek. "I'm so sorry it took me so long, Dev."

"It's okay," Dev murmured, but she wasn't so sure. In the morning, they'd both return to their lives, and she wondered how she'd survive being without Leslie after this.

"You look sad." Leslie frowned with concern. "Dev?"

"No." Dev forced a grin. "Just gathering my strength."

With a laugh, Leslie pulled Dev on top of her and wrapped her legs around the backs of Dev's thighs. "You're plenty strong enough for what I have in mind. Now, shut up and kiss me."

Dev surrendered willingly to the siren call of Leslie's desire. The morning was at least a lifetime away.

CHAPTER TWENTY-SEVEN

When Leslie awoke, lying on her side with her breasts and abdomen pressed against Dev's back, the black plastic bedside clock read 3:20 a.m. in big white numerals. She wasn't entirely certain, but she thought she'd been asleep for at least a few hours. The last thing she could recall was coming endlessly in Dev's mouth. At the memory, she felt a trickle of arousal tease down her thighs. She couldn't believe she was still excited after coming...three times? Four? She couldn't remember. Each pinnacle of pleasure seemed to blend into the next, one sweeping crest of ever-mounting beauty and wonder after another. Smiling softly to herself, she kissed the curve of Dev's shoulder blade.

"Hey," Leslie whispered into Dev's ear as she slid her hand to the front of Dev's body and caressed her breasts. "You promised to make love to me all night long."

"Mmm?" Dev twitched and sighed, her nipples tightening beneath Leslie's insistent caresses.

"You," Leslie said, holding back a laugh. "Promised." She guided Dev onto her back and straddled her hips. "To make love to me." She swept her palms over Dev's breasts and down her abdomen, pressing her thumbs into firm muscle as she moved lower. "All. Night. Long."

Leslie slipped her hand between Dev's thighs and squeezed gently.

Dev's eyes popped open as her hips jerked. She groaned, her gaze moving from Leslie's nude body draped over her to the hand between her legs. "Jesus."

"Tired?" Leslie asked, her tone honey smooth.

"No," Dev said, reaching for Leslie's breasts.

Leslie caught Dev's wrists, one in each hand, and let her weight fall forward to pin Dev's arms to the bed. Her breasts brushed Dev's face before she arched her back just enough to keep her erect nipples a breath away from Dev's mouth. "Uh uh uh. No you don't."

"Come on, Les," Dev rasped, struggling to lift her shoulders from the bed. "Let me suck them."

"Oh, I don't think so," Leslie said lightly, even though her stomach quivered at the hungry look on Dev's face. It was raw, unvarnished lust, but she knew in her heart it was for her. Her. Not anyone, not any body. It was her, *her* body, *her* touch, that Dev craved, and she thrilled to the power. "You had your way all evening, and then"—she leaned down and kissed Dev until they were both panting—"you dropped the ball."

Dev made a sound halfway between a groan and a growl. "I was just letting you catch your breath."

Leslie's eyebrows rose. "Really." She inched her hips higher until her center rested on Dev's stomach. She rotated slowly, rubbing over Dev's skin until the friction and heat made her clitoris pound painfully. She rose and glanced down at the wet sheen on Dev's taut stomach. "Does that feel like I needed to rest?"

"No," Dev gasped, her face contorted with thwarted pleasure. "I was wrong. Jesus, let me touch you. I know you need me to."

"Oh, you think?" Leslie struggled not to let her arousal show. Seeing Dev's desire for her was enough to make her wet, and the heat pouring from Dev's body as she writhed between Leslie's thighs kept her so hard she feared she'd climax from an accidental brush of her clitoris over Dev's skin. Her thighs trembled from keeping herself poised just above Dev's body. "It looks to me like you're the one who needs to come. Do you?"

"Yes. No. Later." Dev tried to twist her arms from Leslie's grip, but besides the fact that Leslie's full weight held her down, her all-consuming arousal made her weak. Her arms and legs shook and the muscles in her stomach quivered. "Please."

Leslie dipped her head and swept her tongue over Dev's nipples. Ignoring her own screaming arousal, she rubbed her sex up and down the apex of Dev's thighs. Dev was wet. So wet. "Please what?"

"Oh, Jesus," Dev whimpered.

"Please what?" Leslie closed her teeth on Dev's nipple, biting down until Dev arched her back and cried out. "Hmm? What?"

Dev thrashed her head, fighting for breath. "I don't know. I don't know. God. I need you."

I need you. Dev's plea, so unguarded, so vulnerable, pierced Leslie's heart, and the heady sensation of control, of absolute power, was instantly replaced by aching tenderness. She kissed Dev's nipple, then her mouth. "Shh, love, I'm here."

Leslie released Dev's wrists and rapidly pushed herself down the bed until she lay between Dev's thighs. She spread her fingers over the soft, smooth skin, her breath catching as her fingertips glided through the hot, slick patina of Dev's desire. "Oh, you're so wet."

"For you," Dev gasped.

"Yes," Leslie breathed, skimming her lips through the fragrant perfume. "Mine." She rested her cheek between Dev's legs, feeling Dev's excitement beat against her face. She turned her head a fraction and kissed the pulse that throbbed in the center of Dev's sex.

"So good." Dev threaded her fingers into Leslie's hair. "That feels so good. Suck me?"

Gently, Leslie pulled her between her lips, feeling her own body grow tighter and tighter as Dev neared orgasm.

"Les," Dev whispered shakily, "be inside me when I come."

Leslie groaned, so aroused she feared she would fly off in a thousand directions before bringing Dev all the pleasure Dev had given her. Leslie eased into her and felt the quick tightening of muscles as Dev moaned.

"Okay, love?" Leslie murmured, her throat thick with tears. She'd never wanted to give so much yet felt so inadequate at the same time.

"Oh yes." Dev's fingers spasmed as she tried to stroke Leslie's face. Her voice thin with strain, she whispered, "I'm going to come if you don't...stop."

"Too late," Leslie laughed, taking Dev deep inside her mouth. At the same time she filled her and took her over, only stopping when Dev finally jerked away.

"Baby," Dev groaned, "baby, you gotta stop. I surrender."

Leslie leaned on an elbow and pushed her hair back from her

face with her other hand. She grinned with satisfaction, watching Dev fight for breath. Dev was covered in sweat, her body gleaming in the lamplight.

"You're so beautiful, Dev." Leslie stared at the scar that ran from Dev's hipbone down the outside of her thigh. She kissed the damaged skin. "I love you."

"Come up here." Dev struggled to sit up, extending one hand. "Let me hold you."

"Lie down. You're supposed to be basking."

"I'll bask when I can hold you."

Leslie settled against Dev's side, her head on Dev's shoulder. Languidly, she stroked Dev's chest and abdomen. "You make me feel sexy."

Dev laughed incredulously. "*I* make you feel sexy? After that little display? I didn't do anything except let you have your way with me."

"Mmm, that's what I mean." Leslie tilted her head and kissed Dev's neck. "I feel a hundred feet tall when I make you come."

"I know," Dev said, kissing Leslie's forehead. "It's the same for me when I touch you."

"It's addicting." Leslie propped her head in her hand, idly teasing Dev's nipple with a fingertip. "I want you again."

Dev hissed in her breath. "I might not survive the night."

"You better."

"Oh yeah?" Dev tapped Leslie's chin. "Are you a morning girl?"

Leslie grew still, thinking that she really had no idea. She'd never been this way with anyone. She'd never wanted so intensely, never hungered with an ache that felt as if it would never be filled. She'd never wanted to possess anyone this way. "I think with you I'm a 24-7 kind of girl. Is that going to be a problem?"

"Not in this lifetime."

Dev rolled onto her side until she faced Leslie. She kissed her, and what she'd meant to be a kiss of reassurance rapidly turned into one of desire. She kept kissing her as she slipped her fingers between Leslie's legs, knowing she hadn't come. Knowing she must still need to. When Leslie moaned, Dev guided her onto her back, stroking inside her mouth with the same sure, steady rhythm as between her legs. Leslie whimpered, her tongue probing, her fingers digging into Dev's shoulders.

Feeling Leslie tense, her pelvis thrusting against Dev's hand, Dev slid inside her. She stayed motionless, buried deep within, letting Leslie set the pace. As Leslie came, she jerked her head away, finally breaking the kiss and releasing a long, thin cry of pleasure.

"Oh God," Leslie finally gasped. "That's it. You're cut off until I have food." She nuzzled Dev's neck drowsily. "We didn't have dinner, remember?"

"So you're going to stand me up for food?" Dev grinned, kissed Leslie lightly on the tip of the nose, and jumped from bed.

"Where are you going?" Leslie sat up, pulling the sheets up to her waist. "Dev?"

Dev rummaged in the desk and returned with a leather folder in her hand. She pulled the phone closer to the bed as she climbed back in next to Leslie. "Room service."

"Sweetheart, it's four thirty in the morning."

"So?" Dev found the menu and flipped to the all-night section. "We're in New York City. The kitchens never close." She studied the page as Leslie curled up in her lap. "How about burgers and champagne? Will that do?"

"Dev," Leslie said quietly.

"Hmm?" Dev curled one arm around Leslie's shoulders and propped the menu on her raised knee. "And maybe some chocolate cake."

"Do you think it's possible for us never to leave this room?"

Dev laughed. "I can probably stay another night. I'll call in the morning about..." She trailed off and closed the menu. Her face lost all expression. "When do you have to leave?"

"I've got appointments scheduled midmorning," Leslie said. Her heart beat wildly, not from passion, but from fear. It had only been a few hours, a few hours of unexpected and indescribable happiness, and now she felt it slipping away. "I'm going to have to go in sometime today. Tomorrow. God, whenever it is. I'll call first thing and try to rearrange some of my meetings."

"Leslie," Dev said with a sigh. "You shouldn't do that."

Dev leaned her head back and stared at the ceiling. The heavy drapes were still closed, the bedside lamp turned down low. It was almost dawn, but it felt as if they were cocooned in a time capsule, and if they just stayed there, kept the door closed and the rest of the world outside, they could keep this precious connection safe. She knew it wasn't true. As much as her heart wanted to believe, she knew they couldn't hide from who they were or how vastly different their lives were. "We've got a few more hours. Let's just make the most of them."

Leslie sat up and swiveled on the bed until she faced Dev. "And that's it? You go back to Lake George and we write this off as a one-nighter that's just fifteen years overdue?"

"Hey," Dev said gently, cupping Leslie's cheek. "You know that's not what this is."

"No, Dev, I don't." Leslie shook her head. "I don't know what this is. I didn't expect to be here tonight. All I know is I had to see you because I couldn't stop thinking about you for the last four weeks."

"I haven't stopped thinking about you since I was seventeen years old, Les."

Leslie flinched, but she kept her voice steady. "All right. I deserved that."

"No, I'm sorry. I'm sorry." Dev pushed a hand through her hair. "Jesus, this isn't coming out right." She took Leslie's hand and rubbed her cheek against the back of Leslie's fingers. "I haven't wanted to care about anyone since the night I drove away from your house on my bike. I've been empty inside all this time. Except for how much I hurt missing you."

"Oh, God, Dev."

"It's okay." Dev grinned crookedly. "Well, after tonight, it's a hell of a lot better than it ever was. I've never felt anything like tonight. When we were kids and I was kissing you and Mike found us, I felt like I did tonight. Like you were all I needed to be whole. You were everything I needed, and then I lost you."

Tears streaked down Leslie's cheeks and Dev brushed them gently away.

"When we made love tonight," Dev said, her throat so tight she could hardly get the words out, "I felt that way again. You fill me up, you heal everything that ever hurt." Dev bowed her head over Leslie's hand, closing her eyes. "Tonight was worth any amount of pain, but I can't keep living day after day wanting you." She raised her eyes, unable to hide the agony of loss she knew was coming. "I'll never regret tonight, but I have to accept it was just one perfect night that ends in the morning, or I'm not going to make it. I can't keep living while I'm dying for you."

Leslie's hands were shaking as she caressed her fingers through Dev's hair, then cradled her face. She leaned close and kissed her. "For a long time, I tried to pretend that you and I were just really, really good friends. The best of friends." She laughed, the sound ending in a sob. "And oh God, we were, weren't we? Friends and so much more. I was so crazy in love with you back then."

"Yeah." Dev caressed Leslie's arm. "Yeah, me too."

"And after that horrible night with Mike, I couldn't face my own cowardice and I tried to hide it all away by pretending I didn't feel what I felt for you. And when I finally did admit I was a lesbian, I still wouldn't let anyone be important to me. Not the way you were."

"Rachel?"

Leslie shook her head. "I cared about her. But I didn't need her and I didn't want her to need me. There were a few others, always the same. I kept everyone a safe distance away."

"When I saw you at the train station, it was like those fifteen years didn't exist," Dev said. "When I kiss you, when we make love, I can almost believe it, almost. But I know it's not true. You have your life. We both do. Different lives."

"I just found you," Leslie whispered. "I'm not going to lose you again. I love you."

Dev swallowed hard, trying to hold everything inside, but she just couldn't. Her body, her soul, her heart were too open after hours of loving Leslie. She'd let her inside the places no one had ever touched before, and now she was defenseless. She pulled Leslie close and buried her face against Leslie's neck, her shoulders shaking as she sobbed. "I'm sorry. I can't. Fuck, I'm so scared."

"It's okay," Leslie soothed, stroking Dev's head. "It's okay, love. I promise." She wasn't sure how she would make it all right, but she knew she had to. "Will you just do one thing for me?"

Sitting up, Dev took a shuddering breath and rubbed her forearm across her face. "Anything."

"Let tonight be beautiful, because it is." She kissed Dev tenderly. "We both know what we had. Let's see what we can have. Don't give up, Dev. Please."

Dev closed her eyes and rested her forehead against Leslie's. "Will you call me?"

"Of course." Leslie knew then that Dev didn't trust her not to disappear. And why should she? She'd done it before. More than once. "I'm coming back up to the lake in a month. If I can get back sooner—"

"No, a month is good." Dev raised her head, a smile flickering valiantly. "I probably need a little time to get my heart rate back to normal. And tell me you're not busy here."

Leslie sighed. "I'm swamped. But I can handle it—"

"Oh, yeah. You can handle it. That's why you collapsed—what— six weeks ago, from stress and overwork?"

"I'm fine now," Leslie said firmly. "I am. Really. I'm taking the goddamn pills."

"No symptoms at all?"

"Dev, love, if I was going to have an episode, I would've had it sometime tonight." Leslie kissed Dev swiftly. "My heart's had quite a workout."

Dev couldn't hide a pleased grin. "All the same, you just got back. I'll see you in a few weeks and…we'll see."

"You'll be there when I come up, right?"

Dev nodded.

"Promise?"

Dev held Leslie tightly and tried not to think it might be one of the last times. "I promise."

CHAPTER TWENTY-EIGHT

M om?" Leslie called as she walked into the dining room at
Lakeview and dropped her suitcase on the floor. "Anybody
here?"

"Leslie?" Eileen called from the top of the second-floor staircase.

Leslie stopped and craned her neck, smiling when she saw her
mother. "Hi."

"You're early," Eileen said, her pleasure obvious as she descended
to the ground floor. "I didn't expect you until tomorrow."

"I got things wrapped up early this week and decided to come up
today." She tried to sound casual and not like she couldn't wait one
more day to see Dev, which was the real reason she'd left Manhattan
at noon on Thursday instead of waiting until Friday as planned. She
and Dev had talked on the phone a few times in the last month, but
their schedules rarely meshed and the conversations always seemed
rushed and superficial. At least, she hoped it was because they hadn't
had much time to connect. Dev had sounded distant, and there had been
no mention of the night they'd spent together. Or whether there would
be any more.

"Well, I hope you intend to actually rest this weekend. I'm not
going to let you work the whole time."

"I'm still going to help close up. But," Leslie hastened to add
when she saw her mother frown, "I promise to relax too."

After giving Leslie a hug, Eileen pointed to Leslie's luggage. "Do
you want a room upstairs since you're only going to be here a few
days?"

"Uh," Leslie said, feeling her face color, "I'd rather have the same cabin I had last time, if it's available."

"It's quiet this weekend—all the kids have gone back to school—so it's empty."

"Great."

"Hungry?"

Leslie laughed. "As a matter of fact, I'm starved. Let me get settled and I'll come back and get a sandwich or something. Where's Daddy?" She scanned the great room where a few guests were seated, but didn't see him.

"He's down at the dock with Dev."

"With Dev?" Leslie's breath caught in her throat and she knew her mother noticed. "I mean, I thought at this time of day, she'd be at the lab."

"Does she know you're coming?"

Leslie shook her head. "Not today."

"She happened to be around when they were pulling one of the boats out, and she and your father got talking about something to do with fishing." Eileen smiled. "Apparently Dev doesn't fish, but she appreciates that the fishermen know more about finding fish in the lake than anyone else. I think your father's been regaling her with stories for the last hour."

As her mother talked, Leslie drifted toward the front windows. She pushed the lace curtain aside and scanned the dock below the house. Her father sat in a deck chair in front of the boathouse talking to Dev, who leaned with a shoulder against the dark green clapboards, her legs casually crossed at the ankles and her hands in her pockets. She wore jeans and a red flannel shirt and even from this distance, she looked so sexy Leslie ached to get her hands on her.

"How's Natalie?" Leslie asked.

Eileen joined her at the window and answered as if the question hadn't come out of nowhere. "Well, she always seems to be in great spirits. It's been busy this summer, so I take it between supervising the campgrounds and keeping an eye on shenanigans out on the lake, she's been pretty busy."

"So I guess you don't see her too much."

"Sweetie," Eileen said gently, "why don't you just ask Dev if she's seeing Natalie?"

Leslie hesitated. "Because I'm afraid of what she might say."

"Would it be prying if I asked you about Rachel?"

"No," Leslie said softly, still watching Dev. "We're not seeing each other any longer. I broke it off right after the Fourth of July."

"Are you okay?"

"I think so. We ran into each other at a fundraiser a week ago and spoke for a few minutes. She seemed…like Rachel." The conversation had been what she would have expected—brief, pleasant, totally without intimacy. Rachel had been there with a date, although it probably wasn't obvious to most attendees that the leggy brunette who watched Rachel's every move was more than an acquaintance. But Leslie knew the signs. It hadn't bothered her, and she hadn't expected it to. "I know Natalie has a thing for Dev."

"Mmm, maybe." Eileen patted Leslie's shoulder. "What matters, though, is who Dev has a thing for."

Leslie sighed. "I wish it were that simple."

"Why isn't it? You're in love with her, aren't you?"

"Like crazy."

"And if she feels the same way?"

"We're completely incompatible," Leslie said. "Our jobs, our lifestyles, where we live. And Dev isn't interested in a casual relationship."

"Are you?"

Leslie leaned her head against the window frame, thinking that she'd only ever had casual relationships, no matter how long-term or monogamous. They had been convenient, simple, and satisfying in a limited way. She'd spent one night with Dev, whom she'd known far better as a teenager than as an adult, and realized immediately that that one night was more meaningful than all the other nights she'd spent with other women. "I think she's it for me."

"Then you'd best get around to telling her that. She's been jumpy and distracted all summer, and I'm willing to bet it's because of you." Eileen slipped her arm around Leslie's shoulders and gave her a quick hug. "Don't wonder how she feels, sweetie. Just ask her."

Leslie smiled. "Yes, Mom."

"If you want to find the big bass, you've got to go twenty miles farther north than ten years ago," Paul Harris complained. "And even then, you won't see the really big ones anymore."

Dev nodded, her eyes on the woman making her way down the grassy slope toward them. The late-afternoon sun had taken on the amber hue of approaching autumn, and Leslie, with her softly layered blond hair, pale silk blouse, and navy slacks, looked radiant.

Following Dev's gaze, Paul twisted in his chair, then grinned. "Hey, look who's here."

Leslie smiled as she leaned down to kiss him. "Hi, Daddy. How's your leg?"

"One more week," he said, thumping his walking cast. "Pretty good timing, huh? Just missed closing up."

"Very smart of you." Leslie squeezed her father's shoulder but her attention was on Dev. "Hi."

Dev pushed away from the wall, her heart thundering so loudly she felt as if she were in an echo chamber. "Hi. I thought tomorrow—"

"I know. I couldn't...I got a break."

"That's good." Dev knew she was barely making any sense, but she hadn't expected to see Leslie for another twenty-four hours. She wasn't ready. She wasn't ready for the body blow that just being near Leslie always produced. She felt shaky, a little light-headed, and hot. Her skin was hot. She was hot inside. She was burning, and Leslie was the cool, cool water she needed to soothe her, inside and out.

"Mom said you were talking about fish."

"Yes."

"How's the work going?"

"Pretty much done."

Paul looked from one to the other, his expression curious. He maneuvered himself out of his chair and into the nearby motorized cart Leslie had insisted on getting for him earlier in the summer. "I'm going to head on up to the house. See you for supper, Les?"

"Uh-huh. Probably."

"Well," he said, turning the key in the ignition. "I'll see you sometime this weekend, honey."

For a few minutes, the motor drowned out the possibility of conversation, and as the roar died off in the distance, Dev crossed the dock to Leslie's side.

"How have you been?"

"Fine, I'm fine. You?"

"Good." Dev grinned. "You look great."

"Thank you," Leslie said softly. "I've been watching you from the house for about half an hour."

"Yeah?" Dev leaned toward Leslie, her gaze skimming down her body.

"I want to tear your clothes off."

"Same here."

"Should we talk first?"

Dev watched Leslie's nipples tighten beneath the sheer blouse. "No. Not until I've heard you come at least once."

Leslie's lips parted in surprised pleasure. "You like that, do you?"

"Oh yeah. I've been putting myself to sleep for a month remembering how you sound when you come in my arms."

"Oh, that's not fair."

"I don't last very long, thinking about it," Dev murmured, watching Leslie's lids grow heavy.

"I'm not sure I can make it to the cabin."

"Boathouse?"

Leslie took Dev's hand and tugged her inside. The air was hazy with heat and dust and thick with the scent of old wood and water. She leaned against the wall in a dimly lit corner and dragged Dev against her, her hands sliding down to grip Dev's ass. "Do you have any idea what you just did to me?"

"I want to make you so hot you'll come if I just breathe on you."

"Keep it up and it won't take that much." Leslie straddled Dev's lean thigh. "I'm so wet already."

Dev tangled her fingers in Leslie's hair and kissed her roughly. Every day for the last month, she'd told herself that Leslie would be here, and while her mind had believed it, her heart had never been quite sure. Now that Leslie was this close, all she wanted was to feel that she was real. She sucked on the tip of Leslie's tongue and fondled her breasts, her hips pinning Leslie to the wall. Finally she pulled her mouth away. "I'm not going to fuck you out here. But God, I want to."

Leslie dug her fingers into Dev's tight butt. "You'll make me come just doing this."

"Les," Dev gasped, kissing her neck hungrily, unable to stop as Leslie rode her thigh harder. "Someone might walk in."

"No. There's no one…" Leslie turned her head and plunged her tongue into Dev's mouth.

Groaning, Dev pinched Leslie's nipple, twisting in time to her pumping hips.

"I'm going to come," Leslie moaned, her head falling back against the wall. "Oh Dev, God, I'm really coming."

Dev felt Leslie's knees buckle and grabbed her around the waist, holding her up as she trembled, her face buried against Dev's shoulder to stifle her cries. As Leslie's orgasm trailed off, Dev cradled Leslie, stroking her hair and her back.

"Okay, baby? You okay?"

"I'm totally humiliated." Leslie laughed softly. "Talk about no control."

"You're so sexy I thought my heart would stop." Dev nuzzled Leslie's neck. "You're beautiful when you're like that. When you want me."

"Oh, Dev." Leslie lifted her head and kissed Dev softly. "I want you so much I can't stand it." She caressed Dev's face. "And not just like this, either."

"We better try to get to the cabin."

"Are you in a bad way?" Leslie asked teasingly, recognizing the low, husky note in Dev's voice.

"I'm afraid something is about to explode."

"You got to hear me come." Leslie nipped at Dev's chin. "Let me watch you."

Dev sucked in a breath. "Here?"

Leslie stroked Dev's breasts, then reached down and popped the button on her fly. "Yes. It makes me crazy thinking about you making yourself come."

"You've got me so hot, it's going to take about two seconds," Dev whispered, bracing her arm against the wall next to Leslie's shoulder. She slid her hand into her jeans and groaned. "Touch me too. Just touch me somewhere."

"Whatever you need," Leslie murmured, caressing Dev's stomach and thighs as Dev tensed, her arm vibrating between her legs. "Feel good?"

"Uh-huh," Dev managed between gritted teeth. The muscles in her neck stood out and her thighs quivered as fire leapt in her belly. "Oh, Jesus, I'm close."

Leslie cupped the outside of Dev's crotch, spreading her fingers over Dev's where they circled beneath the denim. "Mmm, I can feel you getting ready to go. You're almost there, aren't you?"

"Close," Dev muttered, "soon, ah almost, Les."

"Need help, love?" Leslie crooned, licking Dev's neck.

"Push down on my fingers." Dev groaned as Leslie pressed rhythmically. "Harder, baby. Harder…har…oh, oh yeah."

Dev sagged against Leslie as her orgasm hit, and Leslie kissed her, swallowing her cries of release.

"Beautiful," Leslie sighed, cradling Dev's face against her shoulder, caressing her sweat-streaked cheek. "Thank you."

"Same here," Dev muttered, struggling to get her legs under her again. She braced her arms against the wall once more and pushed upright. Grinning, she kissed Leslie. "I think we've established we missed each other."

"It would seem that way." Leslie had never felt anything quite so perfect in her life, and she wasn't ready to examine what that meant. "And since I don't want to be tempted again until we're *really* alone…" She zipped Dev's fly and buttoned her jeans. "There. Can you walk?"

"Just about."

Leslie wrapped her arm around Dev's waist. "Let's go to your cabin."

"No fooling around on the way." Dev circled Leslie's shoulders with one arm, holding her close. "I have a short recovery phase, and I'll be ready again soon."

"I remember." Leslie rubbed her cheek against Dev's shoulder. "I have a few favorite memories for use at bedtime too."

Dev groaned. "See, you're starting already."

"Then we'd better hurry."

When they reached the cabin, Dev went to the refrigerator and extracted two India Pale Ales. She opened both and passed one bottle to Leslie, who leaned against the counter nearby. "I'm glad you're here."

"Me too." Leslie sipped the beer. "Can I ask you something personal?"

The corner of Dev's mouth rose. "I think we've reached that point."

Unexpectedly uncertain, Leslie studied her beer bottle. "Are you seeing anyone else?"

Immediately, Dev put her bottle on the counter and cupped

Leslie's chin. She lifted her face and looked directly into her eyes. "No. I haven't been with anyone except you for over a year." She waited, studying Leslie's face. "Natalie and I are friends."

"I had to ask," Leslie said quietly. "Because if I think about you with anyone else it makes me…pretty much insane."

"I like that." Dev kissed Leslie softly. "I like that a lot."

"And I…"

Dev stopped her with another kiss, then eased away and retrieved her beer. Still watching Leslie, she sipped. "When I was younger, I tortured myself thinking about you with Mike. Last month, when I thought about you with Rachel, it hurt so much I couldn't even let myself get that far. I guess that's some kind of progress."

"There's no one, Dev. No one I want to touch me except you."

"I love you, you know," Dev said softly.

"I love you too. Madly. Do you have any idea what we're going to do?"

"No," Dev replied, her expression suddenly unsure.

"Tell you what," Leslie said, grasping Dev's hand. "Let's have dinner with my parents, because they'll want to see me and we'll need to eat if we're going to do what I plan on doing for the rest of the night."

Dev grinned.

"And tomorrow, we'll talk."

"That means no touching, then."

Leslie sighed. "I hope it doesn't rain, because the only way I can promise that is if we're sitting outside in full view of my mother and everyone else in the lodge." And considering that just seeing Dev was enough to make her mind melt, she wasn't even sure an audience would be enough deterrent.

CHAPTER TWENTY-NINE

D o you think my mother will notice if I only show up for meals?" Leslie laced her fingers through Dev's as they walked through the woods toward the lodge for breakfast. "Considering that we disappeared right after dinner last night?"

Dev tugged her to a stop at the edge of the clearing. "If we walk in together again, and you still have that look on your face, your mother is going to know what we've been doing all night."

"What look?"

"That 'I've just been fu—'"

"I do not have that look," Leslie feigned indignation.

Dev dragged her off the trail and pinned her against a tree with the weight of her body, her forearms on either side of Leslie's shoulders. "You do. Your eyes are soft and dreamy," she kissed Leslie's eyelids, "and your lips are a little bit bruised," she skimmed her tongue over Leslie's lower lip, "and it takes you a lonnng time to make sentences." She cupped Leslie's breast and kissed her more seriously. "And you keep sending me signals that keep me hard all the time."

"Maybe I *want* you hard and hungry all the time," Leslie murmured. She returned the kiss vigorously, then abruptly pushed Dev away and snuck out from underneath her arm. She was breathing hard and she was wet again, and she was almost afraid to let Dev know how much she wanted her every single second. "But *I* happen to be hungry for pancakes."

"Then try to behave while we're in there," Dev threatened, seizing Leslie's hand once more. "Because you're driving me crazy."

"Oh good."

"Have a heart. I don't want your mother to see me whimpering and drooling."

"Why not? She knows we've got something going on."

"She does?" Dev asked in surprise.

"Well, she knows I've got the major hots for you."

"How?"

"Because I told her."

Dev stopped again. "You did? When?"

Leslie dipped her head, suddenly shy. "More or less all summer. I think she knew before I did how serious it was."

"Serious, huh?" Dev circled Leslie's waist and pulled her close. She brushed her cheek against Leslie's, then murmured in her ear, "How serious?"

"Very." Leslie wrapped her arms around Dev's shoulders and leaned her head on Dev's shoulder as she watched the mist rise off the lake and burn away in the early morning sunshine. "We're never going to make it to the lodge if you keep grabbing me."

"Can't help myself." Dev stroked Leslie's hair. "I've got a lot of time to make up for."

"Could take a while."

"I know."

"I'm hungry."

Dev laughed. "I love you."

"I love you. Give me a cup of coffee and something to eat and I'll show you just how much."

"Last night you promised to help your father down at the boathouse this morning."

Leslie frowned. "I did? That must have been when I was fantasizing about silk scarves and tying you—"

"Oh yeah. Sounds good." Dev kissed her quickly. "But we don't have to do it all today. We've got time."

"Do we?" Leslie asked softly.

"Remember our deal," Dev said softly. "Food first, then go help your father. We'll talk this afternoon *before* we go back to the cabin."

Leslie nodded seriously, wishing they could pretend just a little while longer that this magic time would never end. "All right."

"It will be okay, Les," Dev said, but her eyes were troubled.

"I know," Leslie said, wanting fervently to believe.

Dev leaned back on her elbows on the grassy slope, enjoying the sunshine, the breeze off the lake, and the view. The best part of the view was Leslie, cleaning and stowing gear under her father's direction down on the dock. She'd dressed for dirty work in cut-off blue jeans, a faded T-shirt, and old sneakers. Dev hadn't seen her look so casual, or so relaxed, since their last summer in high school. Leslie was all woman now, but her light laughter floating up the hill reminded Dev of when they were kids and the summer seemed endless. For the first time, the memories didn't hurt.

As Leslie walked up the hill, she studied Dev with a quizzical expression. "What are you thinking of?"

"You."

To her surprise, Leslie felt herself blushing. They'd spent nearly every minute since she'd arrived making love, and there hadn't been a place on her body Dev hadn't touched. But the tender way she spoke as she gazed at her—as if Leslie were the most beautiful woman in the world—struck a chord far deeper than even the intense physical passion they had shared. Leslie dropped down next to Dev and kissed her on the cheek. "What about me?"

"I was just thinking that being with you now has given me back some of the most important moments of my life." Dev covered Leslie's hand with hers. "I feel like I've spent my whole life loving you." She met Leslie's gaze. "And it's all good, now."

Leslie's lips parted as her eyes quickly misted over. "Oh, Dev. I don't think I can stand not to be with you."

With a sigh, Dev sat up and folded her arms on her bent knees. "I've been offered a research position at the Freshwater Institute."

"In Bolton?" Leslie said, picturing the lab only twenty minutes away from her parents' house. Three hours from Manhattan.

"Yes."

"Is that what you want, though?" Leslie asked, finding it hard to believe that Dev would be happy working inside in a lab all the time.

"I wouldn't take it unless they let me make my own schedule, including time away for fieldwork." Dev met Leslie's gaze. "I'd be a lot closer to you, then, most of the time."

"But is it what you want?"

"What I want, Leslie, is you."

"What about…what I do?" Leslie asked softly. "You must hate it."

Dev shrugged, smiling slightly. "I've spent enough time as an expert witness to know that the environmental protection laws aren't perfect. On some level, I understand what bothers you about them. And why you defend people accused of breaking them." She gazed out at the lake, thinking about the schools of fish that had been driven out by pollution and misuse of the waterways. "But they're the best we have, so I have to work with them. I have to do what I can while there's still time."

"And you don't think that would eventually come between—"

"Greetings!" Natalie called, striding across the lawn toward them. She was in uniform, and her hair was pulled back in a ponytail and tucked beneath a green cap with the forest service emblem on the front. "Hi, Leslie. Dev said you were coming up, but I thought it was tonight."

"I came up a day early, as it happens."

Natalie's eyes flickered to Dev, and Leslie saw her expression change to one of speculation. "Really. So how are you doing?"

"Fine. Great, actually," Leslie said, leaning back slightly to look up as Natalie stopped beside her. "How about you?"

Natalie squatted down with a shake of her head. "Ask me at the end of this crazy weekend. It's the last big rush until leaf season. Everybody's trying to catch the last little bit of summer."

"I feel the same way, even if the lake *is* already too cold to swim." Leslie realized she wasn't jealous, even though Natalie had probably expected to find Dev alone. Dev was by *her* side, had awakened in *her* bed, had called *her* name in the night. "I hope things stay quiet for you."

"They might," Natalie said with a sigh, her eyes narrowing as she stared down to the water. "If people would stop doing idiotic things like that."

Leslie followed her gaze. A tour boat, one of the broad, flat-bottomed sightseeing craft filled with rows of deck chairs for people to sit in while the boat made a slow circuit along the shoreline, lumbered into view. It was packed with people, standing and sitting. More people than Leslie could ever remember seeing in one of those boats.

"I can't imagine that's very much fun," Leslie said, "being crammed together like sard—oh my God!"

"Jesus Christ!" Dev shouted, jumping up.

The boat tilted to one side and, in a fraction of a second, capsized. Leslie, Dev, and Natalie raced toward the water as the panicked shouts of the people who had been thrown into the lake seventy feet from shore filled the air.

"We need rescue boats in Bolton Landing by the Lakeview," Natalie shouted into her radio. "And paramedics. We've got people in the water. At least two dozen."

While Natalie was organizing the rescue, Leslie and Dev kicked off their shoes and dove into the lake. Some people were already straggling to shore but others were clearly in trouble, flailing in the water and screaming. Leslie, her strokes hard and clean, swam past the people who were close enough to make it to safety on their own. She saw at least three people go under and not come up again. Dev was close by, slightly behind her. Dev had never been as fast as Leslie in the water.

Leslie reached the first floundering victim in less than a minute. "Stop struggling and let me help you," she shouted, treading water a few feet away to avoid being struck by the man's windmilling arms.

"I can't swim," he cried hoarsely, his eyes wild with panic. "My wife. My wife. I can't find my wife."

"I'll tow you to shore," Leslie called, cautiously approaching. "Let me grab your shirt. Don't hit me."

Her words seemed to penetrate his panic, because he relaxed enough for her to get her arm over his shoulder from behind and under his armpit. "Just relax and kick your feet. I'll do the rest of the work."

"My wife," he gasped. "Please find my wife."

When Leslie got him close enough to shore that he could stand on the bottom, she let him go. Natalie and her mother and some of the guests were helping people from the water. Leslie didn't stop, but turned and immediately swam back to the overturned boat. The white-painted bottom glinted unnaturally in the sunlight. She dove, powering down until she could peer around the side into what had been the open passenger compartment. She'd hoped that air, and possibly survivors, had been trapped beneath. There was nothing under the boat but a body floating lazily to and fro. Swallowing back her horrified gasp, she kicked away and pumped toward the surface, gulping air when she broke free. Then she grabbed the closest victim and started back toward shore.

"The boat's here," Natalie shouted, in water up to her waist, as Leslie wearily guided an elderly woman into Natalie's outstretched arms.

"How many…how many more can you see," Leslie gasped, her arms and legs leaden. She'd lost track of the passage of time or how many trips she'd made back out to the slowly sinking boat.

"Six or seven," Natalie said. "You're too tired, Leslie. Stay ashore."

But Leslie could still hear screaming. Ignoring Natalie, she turned and plunged back into the water. She thought she saw Dev dragging an unconscious man toward shore, but she wasn't sure. On her next trip back, she collapsed to her knees in the shallow water, struggling for breath.

"Leslie," her mother said urgently, "don't go back out. You're ready to collapse."

"Where's…Dev," Leslie rasped. "Is she…in?"

Eileen glanced anxiously around. The grass abutting the shoreline was covered with victims, some unconscious, others moaning or crying. The wail of sirens added to the chaos as paramedics raced down from the parking lot. "I don't see her. She must be here somewhere."

A surge of adrenaline spurred Leslie upright, and, heart pounding, she scanned the shore. Natalie was directing the paramedics toward the most seriously injured. A few guests from the lodge were handing out blankets, and her father was transporting the less injured up the hill in his cart. But she didn't see Dev. She spun toward the lake. Twenty yards offshore she saw Dev laboring slowly with another struggling victim in tow. As she watched, the woman flailed wildly and both she and Dev went under the surface. Leslie dove back into the icy water.

Leslie pulled underwater, stroke after stroke. She was faster underwater, and she didn't need to see. She knew these waters, this shoreline, this lake like she knew her own reflection in the mirror. She knew exactly where Dev was. Lungs screaming, she stayed under until she reached Dev's location. When she burst through the surface, she circled frantically. "Dev! Dev!"

The rescue boat was only yards away and Leslie thought she recognized the woman they pulled aboard. The one Dev had been towing. Dev wasn't there. Dev wasn't anywhere. *No. No no no.* She circled one more time, and suddenly Dev surfaced just beyond arm's reach. Her face was contorted with pain and even as Leslie's heart thrilled with elation, Dev slid beneath the water and did not come up. Jackknifing, Leslie plunged headfirst and reached her within seconds. She grabbed Dev's hand and dragged her up into the air.

Dev coughed and gagged as Leslie grabbed her shirt.

"You're okay, sweetheart. You're okay. I've got you," Leslie gasped.

"That…woman…lost her," Dev wheezed. "Need to…look."

"She's okay. She's in the boat. Can you swim? Dev! Can you swim?"

Dev shook her head. "Cramp in my…hip. Can't…"

"You hold on to me." Leslie gripped Dev's shirt so hard her fingers went numb. "You hear me? You hold on to me, and I'll get you to shore."

Dev didn't answer, but she did her best to help Leslie as Leslie swam them both toward safety. Natalie waded out into chest-high water to meet them and grabbed Dev around the waist.

"I've got her," Natalie said.

Leslie kept swimming, her hold on Dev never loosening. She didn't feel the cold or the pain in her arms and legs or the burning in her lungs. All she knew was that she would not lose Dev. Not ever again.

"Leslie," Natalie shouted. "Let go. I've got her."

Eileen joined Natalie and wrapped her arm around Leslie. "It's all right, sweetie. It's all right. Let Natalie help you. Let go now."

Natalie and Eileen dragged Dev and Leslie onto the bank. Slumping down, shivering violently, Leslie pulled Dev into her lap. She pressed Dev's face to her breasts and wrapped her as tightly as she could in her arms. Dev's lips were blue, her face terrifyingly white.

"Dev, love, are you all right?" Leslie cried. She brushed Dev's hair from her face, stroked her cheek, kissed her forehead. "Dev?"

"I'm okay," Dev gasped. "Les, I'm okay."

Natalie draped a rescue blanket around Leslie's shoulders and another over Dev.

"It'll be a while before we can get her to an ambulance," Natalie said. "They're overloaded and transporting victims as fast as they can."

"Don't need an ambulance," Dev said, her teeth chattering. "Just need to get warm."

"Go help the others, Natalie," Leslie said, rubbing Dev's back and arms. "I'll take care of her."

Natalie smiled and briefly touched Leslie's cheek. "I know you will. I'll be back. You stay warm too."

Leslie closed her eyes and cradled Dev, absolutely certain that there was nothing else in the world she wanted except Dev. She closed her eyes, fighting to stay awake. The sound of an engine approaching finally roused her. Her father guided his motorized cart up next to them.

"Can you get her up in here, honey? I'll take you both up to the lodge."

Dev opened her eyes and met Leslie's. "I can make it if you give me a hand."

"You bet," Leslie said, kissing Dev softly on the mouth. "Anytime."

CHAPTER THIRTY

As soon as her father dropped Leslie and Dev off in front of the lodge and hurried back down the hill to help transport other injured, Leslie took Dev upstairs, raided her parents' closet for dry clothes, and led her into one of the empty guestrooms.

"Let me help you get your clothes off," Leslie said, tugging Dev's shirt from her jeans.

"I got it," Dev rasped. "You get undressed too. You're shaking."

"At least I'm not blue," Leslie snapped, still remembering the terror of watching Dev slide beneath the surface of the lake. "Oh, God, I'm sorry." She brushed a trembling hand over her face. "I was just so scared." She pulled Dev, wet clothes and all, into her arms and hugged her close. "I was afraid I was going to lose you. I couldn't bear it, Dev. I just couldn't."

"It's okay." Dev wrapped her arms around Leslie's waist and rocked her. "We're both okay."

Still shaky, but immeasurably comforted by Dev's rapidly returning strength, Leslie leaned behind her to turn on the shower, keeping one hand on Dev's shoulder. "Let's get warm, and then I'll find something for us to wear."

Wordlessly, Dev stripped off the rest of her clothes and stumbled into the steaming water, leaving the door ajar for Leslie to follow. For long moments she leaned against the wall, not speaking, eyes closed, her hand linked with Leslie's. As the heat penetrated her body, her mind cleared. With clarity came disbelief. The events at the lake seemed like a surreal dream, a nightmare that had slid into her consciousness, leaving indelible images of horror behind.

"I still can't believe it," Leslie whispered, seeming to read Dev's mind.

"Neither can I." Dev flung her hair back out of her face and met Leslie's eyes. "You're amazing. I can't even guess how many people you just saved."

Tears brimmed in Leslie's eyes. "No more than you."

Dev shook her head. "I never could swim like you. I think you made two trips to my one. Jesus, Les. Are you okay?"

"I have no idea." Leslie's smile was brittle. "All I know is that you're here and that's all that matters."

"I love you," Dev said, gently drawing Leslie back into her arms. She rested her cheek against Leslie's hair. "And it feels so good."

"Better than anything in the world." Leslie kissed the base of Dev's throat, then her mouth.

A few minutes later, dressed in borrowed pants and sweatshirts, barefoot except for thick socks, Dev and Leslie went back downstairs. Leslie carried another sweatshirt under one arm.

"The sun is going down," Dev observed as she walked to the front window. "It's going to get cold pretty fast. Looks like they've got almost everyone into the ambulances now."

"Can you start a fire in the great room?" Leslie asked Dev. "I'm going to take this down to Natalie and see if I can get my mother and father to come inside. They've got to be freezing."

"Tell Natalie she needs to take a break. Get her to come inside and get warm too."

"I will," Leslie said, tugging on her mother's rubber mud boots. "I'll be right back."

By the time Leslie returned with Natalie, her parents, and a deputy sheriff, Dev had a roaring blaze going, the heat and flames chasing away the ghosts in her mind as well as the chill from her bones. While Natalie, Eileen, and Paul went to change into dry clothing, the sheriff— a short-haired blonde with the body of a rugby player who introduced herself as Jules Kipling—asked Leslie and Dev for their account of events. They were just starting the interview when Natalie, wearing khaki pants that were six inches too long and a faded blue cable-knit sweater, joined them.

"I'm Sergeant Natalie Evans, Park Service," Natalie said to the sheriff.

"Sergeant." The sheriff nodded a greeting as Natalie sat down on the couch next to Dev. "I suspect when things are all sorted out this will fall under Park jurisdiction because it happened on the lake. Just the same, I think we better consider it a joint investigation for now."

"Fine," Natalie said, studying the blonde. "I didn't get your name."

"It's Kipling." The sheriff smiled as her eyes held Natalie's just a beat longer than absolutely necessary. "But you can call me Kip."

Natalie flashed a weary grin. "Thanks. So shall we nail down the facts before we're too tired to remember the details?"

Jules Kipling took careful notes, as did Natalie, who wrote on a borrowed tablet of paper that Leslie provided her from Eileen Harris's office. All three witnesses' accounts were substantially similar. Forty minutes later everyone agreed that further statements could be taken the next day.

"How many didn't survive?" Leslie asked quietly. When Dev reached for her hand, she cradled it between hers, happy to feel the warmth in her fingers.

"Just one, thanks to all of you," Jules said, "and the medics think that might have been a heart attack."

Eileen brought a second carafe of coffee into the living room and set it down on the low table in front of the sofa and chairs where everyone sat. "I should have food ready in just a few minutes." She glanced from Natalie to Jules. "You're both welcome to stay. Something warm would be good for you right about now."

Natalie stood. "I appreciate it, but I need to get back to the office and follow up with the paramedics and the hospital. Try to get the identification started and...notification of families."

"Mind if I tag along?" Jules Kipling said. "If I give you a hand it will save us from duplicating efforts."

"No, that would be great." Natalie turned to Eileen. "Thanks for the clothes. I'll get them back as soon as I can."

"There's no rush. And don't be a stranger here just because the summer's over."

Natalie smiled. "Thanks. I'll remember."

As Natalie and Jules left, Leslie curled up next to Dev on the large sofa, pulling a nearby throw over their legs, even though the room was warm. "I'm still so cold. How are you?"

"Beat," Dev admitted. "What I really want is to get in bed and just hold you."

"Are you hungry?"

Dev shook her head. "We can come back later. Right now, I just need you."

Leslie pushed the blanket aside and stood, extending her hand to Dev. "Then that's what you shall have."

"Did I fall asleep in the middle of a sentence?" Dev asked when she awoke in Leslie's arms a few hours later. The bedroom in her cabin was aglow with orange shadows cast from the fire burning in the fireplace in the living room. She remembered reaching the cabin, Leslie starting a fire, the two of them crawling into bed after removing their borrowed clothes. She remembered Leslie holding her as if she were a precious treasure about to disappear and stroking Leslie's cheek in reassurance, telling her that nothing would come between them again. Or maybe she just thought she'd said that as she'd fallen into exhausted sleep.

"No, you finished the sentence," Leslie said, softly caressing Dev's shoulder. "You mumbled you loved me."

Dev smiled. "That would be the truth." She propped herself up until she could see Leslie's face. "And in case I didn't mention it, that would also be my long-term plan. I'm going to take the job at the Freshwater Institute."

"I've been thinking about things too," Leslie said. After Dev had dropped off, as tired as she was, Leslie hadn't been able to sleep. Maybe that was because she hadn't actually wanted to do anything except hold Dev. To be certain Dev was safe, and hers. "I want to be with you. Really with you. I could relocate to the office in Albany or just find another job up here."

"I kind of got the feeling that you're a high-power type of attorney," Dev said, her brows drawing together as she studied Leslie intently. "The big-city kind of attorney. Seems like things would be a little too tame for you up here."

Leslie laughed softly. "Well, there *are* people who refer to where I am now as a jungle, but—"

"I don't think you should do it."

"Dev," Leslie said, sitting up, "I love you, and I want us to be together. That matters more to me than where I work or what I do."

"And that's all *I* need to know." Dev took Leslie's hand in both of hers, running her thumbs over Leslie's fingers slowly as she spoke. "I don't want you to change your life because you love me."

"You're willing to," Leslie pointed out.

"I'm just changing my base of operations—I'm still doing the same work."

"You're splitting hairs."

Smiling, Dev shook her head. "No, I'm not. I probably won't be spending quite as much time in the field, but I'll still be away a fair amount. When I'm not, I'll be closer to you."

"We've already missed so much. I don't want to lose any more time with you."

"I'll buy a house here on the lake. You can come up when you're free, or I'll go down to Manhattan." Dev stroked Leslie's cheek as she frowned. "Lots of couples have jobs that require them to live separately part of the time. We'll manage."

"Say that's so. What about *what* I do, not where I do it?" Leslie leaned close and kissed the corner of Dev's mouth. "How are you going to feel about consorting with the enemy?"

"I've decided that you're a necessary evil. Figuratively speaking, of course."

Leslie straightened. "I beg your pardon?"

"Big corporations and even the government hire computer crackers to test their security systems, to look for flaws so they can build a tighter and more fail-safe system."

"And this relates to me how?"

"Well, you're like a cracker trying to break the system. If the laws are flawed or aren't properly designed to do what we need them to do, you're going to win cases. And that just tells us which laws to make better."

"There is a twisted sort of logic to that argument," Leslie said, struggling to hide a smile. "I think I ought to be insulted on some level, but I'm not sure I want to point out your errors in thinking." She kissed Dev again. "Not if you can live with things the way they are."

"What I *can't* live with," Dev said, framing Leslie's face, "is being without you. I've tried that for half my life. I don't want to anymore."

"It's a plan, for now. But," Leslie murmured, nuzzling Dev's neck as she caressed her, "if I can't stand being away from you so much, I reserve the right to change my mind."

Dev pulled Leslie down and slid on top of her. "I forgot to mention a few contingencies."

"What?" Leslie asked, distracted by the sudden pressure of Dev's leg between her thighs.

"You work more reasonable hours and take better care of yourself."

"Mmm-hmm." Leslie arched her back and settled more firmly into Dev's crotch, smiling when Dev gasped.

"I'm serious," Dev muttered, skimming her mouth up the column of Leslie's neck.

"That's good, because I am too." Leslie buried her fingers in Dev's hair, her body coming alive beneath Dev's in the way only Dev could excite her. "You're all the reason I need."

"I've dreamed of being with you all my life." Dev kissed her softly. "Now I want the real thing."

"Are you into long engagements?" Leslie whispered against Dev's ear.

"Isn't fifteen years long enough?"

Leslie laughed. "More than enough."

"Good thing."

And then she kissed her.

About the Author

Radclyffe is a retired surgeon and full-time author-publisher with over twenty-five lesbian novels and anthologies in print, including the 2005 Lambda Literary Award winners *Erotic Interludes 2: Stolen Moments* edited with Stacia Seaman and *Distant Shores, Silent Thunder*, a romance. She has selections in multiple anthologies including *Call of the Dark, The Perfect Valentine, Wild Nights, Best Lesbian Erotica 2006, After Midnight, Caught Looking: Erotic Tales of Voyeurs and Exhibitionists, First-Timers, Ultimate Undies: Erotic Stories About Lingerie and Underwear,* and *Naughty Spanking Stories 2*. She is the recipient of the 2003 and 2004 Alice B. Readers' award for her body of work and is also the president of Bold Strokes Books, a lesbian publishing company featuring lesbian-themed general and genre fiction.

Her forthcoming works include *Erotic Interludes 5: Road Games* edited with Stacia Seaman (May 2007), *Honor Under Siege* (June 2007), and *In Deep Waters: Volume 1*, an erotica collection written with Karin Kallmaker (2007).

Look for information about these works at www.boldstrokesbooks. com.

Books Available From Bold Strokes Books

Punk and Zen by JD Glass. Angst, sex, love, rock. Trace, Candace, Francesca...Samantha. Losing control—and finding the truth within. BSB Victory Editions. (1-933110-66-X)

Stellium in Scorpio by Andrews & Austin. The passionate reuniting of two powerful women on the glitzy Las Vegas Strip, where everything is an illusion and love is a gamble. (1-933110-65-1)

When Dreams Tremble by Radclyffe. Two women whose lives turned out far differently than they'd once imagined discover that sometimes the shape of the future can only be found in the past. (1-933110-64-3)

Fresh Tracks by Georgia Beers. Seven women, seven days. A lot can happen when old friends, lovers, and a new girl in town get together in the mountains. (1-933110-63-5)

Empress and the Acolyte by Jane Fletcher. Jemeryl and Tevi fight to protect the very fabric of their world...time. Lyremouth Chronicles Book Three (1-933110-60-0)

First Instinct by JLee Meyer. When high-stakes security fraud leads to murder, one woman flees for her life while another risks her heart to protect her. (1-933110-59-7)

Erotic Interludes 4: Extreme Passions. Thirty of today's hottest erotica writers set the pages aflame with love, lust, and steamy liaisons. (1-933110-58-9)

Storms of Change by Radclyffe. In the continuing saga of the Provincetown Tales, duty and love are at odds as Reese and Tory face their greatest challenge. (1-933110-57-0)

Unexpected Ties by Gina L. Dartt. With death before dessert, Kate Shannon and Nikki Harris are swept up in another tale of danger and romance. (1-933110-56-2)

Sleep of Reason by Rose Beecham. Nothing is as it seems when Detective Jude Devine finds herself caught up in a small-town soap opera. And her rocky relationship with forensic pathologist Dr. Mercy Westmoreland just got a lot harder. (1-933110-53-8)

Passion's Bright Fury by Radclyffe. When a trauma surgeon and a filmmaker become reluctant allies on the battleground between life and death, passion strikes without warning. (1-933110-54-6)

Broken Wings by L-J Baker. When Rye Woods, a fairy, meets the beautiful dryad Flora Withe, her libido, as squashed and hidden as her wings, reawakens along with her heart. (1-933110-55-4)

Combust the Sun by Andrews & Austin. A Richfield and Rivers mystery set in L.A. Murder among the stars. (1-933110-52-X)

Of Drag Kings and the Wheel of Fate by Susan Smith. A blind date in a drag club leads to an unlikely romance. (1-933110-51-1)

Tristaine Rises by Cate Culpepper. Brenna, Jesstin, and the Amazons of Tristaine face their greatest challenge for survival. (1-933110-50-3)

Too Close to Touch by Georgia Beers. Kylie O'Brien believes in true love and is willing to wait for it. It doesn't matter one damn bit that Gretchen, her new and off-limits boss, has a voice as rich and smooth as melted chocolate. It absolutely doesn't... (1-933110-47-3)

100th Generation by Justine Saracen. Ancient curses, modern-day villains, and a most intriguing woman who keeps appearing when least expected lead archeologist Valerie Foret on the adventure of her life. (1-933110-48-1)

Battle for Tristaine by Cate Culpepper. While Brenna struggles to find her place in the clan and the love between her and Jess grows, Tristaine is threatened with destruction. Second in the Tristaine series. (1-933110-49-X)

The Traitor and the Chalice by Jane Fletcher. Without allies to help them, Tevi and Jemeryl will have to risk all in the race to uncover the traitor and retrieve the chalice. The Lyremouth Chronicles Book Two. (1-933110-43-0)

Promising Hearts by Radclyffe. Dr. Vance Phelps lost everything in the War Between the States and arrives in New Hope, Montana, with no hope of happiness and no desire for anything except forgetting—until she meets Mae, a frontier madam. (1-933110-44-9)

Carly's Sound by Ali Vali. Poppy Valente and Julia Johnson form a bond of friendship that lays the foundation for something more, until Poppy's past comes back to haunt her—literally. A poignant romance about love and renewal. (1-933110-45-7)

Unexpected Sparks by Gina L. Dartt. Falling in love is challenging enough without adding murder to the mix. Kate Shannon's growing feelings for much younger Nikki Harris are complicated enough without the mystery of a fatal fire that Kate can't ignore. (1-933110-46-5)

Whitewater Rendezvous by Kim Baldwin. Two women on a wilderness kayak adventure—Chaz Herrick, a laid-back outdoorswoman, and Megan Maxwell, a workaholic news executive—discover that true love may be nothing at all like they imagined. (1-933110-38-4)

Erotic Interludes 3: Lessons in Love ed. by Radclyffe and Stacia Seaman. Sign on for a class in love…the best lesbian erotica writers take us to "school." (1-9331100-39-2)

Punk Like Me by JD Glass. Twenty-one-year-old Nina writes lyrics and plays guitar in the rock band Adam's Rib, and she doesn't always play by the rules. And oh yeah—she has a way with the girls. (1-933110-40-6)

Coffee Sonata by Gun Brooke. Four women whose lives unexpectedly intersect in a small town by the sea share one thing in common—they all have secrets. (1-933110-41-4)

The Clinic: Tristaine Book One by Cate Culpepper. Brenna, a prison medic, finds herself deeply conflicted by her growing feelings for her patient, Jesstin, a wild and rebellious warrior reputed to be descended from ancient Amazons. (1-933110-42-2)

Forever Found by JLee Meyer. Can time, tragedy, and shattered trust destroy a love that seemed destined? When chance reunites two childhood friends separated by tragedy, the past resurfaces to determine the shape of their future. (1-933110-37-6)

Sword of the Guardian by Merry Shannon. Princess Shasta's bold new bodyguard has a secret that could change both of their lives. *He* is actually a *she*. A passionate romance filled with courtly intrigue, chivalry, and devotion. (1-933110-36-8)

Wild Abandon by Ronica Black. From their first tumultuous meeting, Dr. Chandler Brogan and Officer Sarah Monroe are drawn together by their common obsessions—sex, speed, and danger. (1-933110-35-X)

Turn Back Time by Radclyffe. Pearce Rifkin and Wynter Thompson have nothing in common but a shared passion for surgery. They clash at every opportunity, especially when matters of the heart are suddenly at stake. (1-933110-34-1)

Chance by Grace Lennox. At twenty-six, Chance Delaney decides her life isn't working so she swaps it for a different one. What follows is the sexy, funny, touching story of two women who, in finding themselves, also find one another. (1-933110-31-7)

The Exile and the Sorcerer by Jane Fletcher. First in the Lyremouth Chronicles. Tevi, wounded and adrift, arrives in the courtyard of a shy young sorcerer. Together they face monsters, magic, and the challenge of loving despite their differences. (1-933110-32-5)

A Matter of Trust by Radclyffe. JT Sloan is a cybersleuth who doesn't like attachments. Michael Lassiter is leaving her husband, and she needs Sloan's expertise to safeguard her company. It should just be business—but it turns into much more. (1-933110-33-3)

Sweet Creek by Lee Lynch. A celebration of the enduring nature of love, friendship, and community in the quirky, heart-warming lesbian community of Waterfall Falls. (1-933110-29-5)

The Devil Inside by Ali Vali. Derby Cain Casey, head of a New Orleans crime organization, runs the family business with guts and grit, and no one crosses her. No one, that is, until Emma Verde claims her heart and turns her world upside down. (1-933110-30-9)

Grave Silence by Rose Beecham. Detective Jude Devine's investigation of a series of ritual murders is complicated by her torrid affair with the golden girl of Southwestern forensic pathology, Dr. Mercy Westmoreland. (1-933110-25-2)

Honor Reclaimed by Radclyffe. In the aftermath of 9/11, Secret Service Agent Cameron Roberts and Blair Powell close ranks with a trusted few to find the would-be assassins who nearly claimed Blair's life. (1-933110-18-X)

Honor Bound by Radclyffe. Secret Service Agent Cameron Roberts and Blair Powell face political intrigue, a clandestine threat to Blair's safety, and the seemingly irreconcilable personal differences that force them ever farther apart. (1-933110-20-1)

Innocent Hearts by Radclyffe. In a wild and unforgiving land, two women learn about love, passion, and the wonders of the heart. (1-933110-21-X)

The Temple at Landfall by Jane Fletcher. An imprinter, one of Celaeno's most revered servants of the Goddess, is also a prisoner to the faith—until a Ranger frees her by claiming her heart. The Celaeno series. (1-933110-27-9)

Protector of the Realm: Supreme Constellations Book One by Gun Brooke. A space adventure filled with suspense and a daring intergalactic romance featuring Commodore Rae Jacelon and the stunning, but decidedly lethal, Kellen O'Dal. (1-933110-26-0)

Force of Nature by Kim Baldwin. From tornados to forest fires, the forces of nature conspire to bring Gable McCoy and Erin Richards close to danger, and closer to each other. (1-933110-23-6)

In Too Deep by Ronica Black. Undercover homicide cop Erin McKenzie tracks a femme fatale who just might be a real killer…with love and danger hot on her heels. (1-933110-17-1)

Stolen Moments: Erotic Interludes 2 by Stacia Seaman and Radclyffe, eds. Love on the run, in the office, in the shadows…Fast, furious, and almost too hot to handle. (1-933110-16-3)

Course of Action by Gun Brooke. Actress Carolyn Black desperately wants the starring role in an upcoming film produced by Annelie Peterson. Just how far will she go for the dream part of a lifetime? (1-933110-22-8)

Rangers at Roadsend by Jane Fletcher. Sergeant Chip Coppelli has learned to spot trouble coming, and that is exactly what she sees in her new recruit, Katryn Nagata. The Celaeno series. (1-933110-28-7)

Justice Served by Radclyffe. Lieutenant Rebecca Frye and her lover, Dr. Catherine Rawlings, embark on a deadly game of hide-and-seek with an underworld kingpin who traffics in human souls. (1-933110-15-5)

Distant Shores, Silent Thunder by Radclyffe. Dr. Tory King—along with the women who love her—is forced to examine the boundaries of love, friendship, and the ties that transcend time. (1-933110-08-2)

Hunter's Pursuit by Kim Baldwin. A raging blizzard, a mountain hideaway, and a killer-for-hire set a scene for disaster—or desire—when Katarzyna Demetrious rescues a beautiful stranger. (1-933110-09-0)

The Walls of Westernfort by Jane Fletcher. All Temple Guard Natasha Ionadis wants is to serve the Goddess—until she falls in love with one of the rebels she is sworn to destroy. The Celaeno series. (1-933110-24-4)

Change Of Pace: *Erotic Interludes* by Radclyffe. Twenty-five hot-wired encounters guaranteed to spark more than just your imagination. Erotica as you've always dreamed of it. (1-933110-07-4)

Honor Guards by Radclyffe. In a wild flight for their lives, the president's daughter and those who are sworn to protect her wage a desperate struggle for survival. (1-933110-01-5)

Fated Love by Radclyffe. Amidst the chaos and drama of a busy emergency room, two women must contend not only with the fragile nature of life, but also with the irresistible forces of fate. (1-933110-05-8)

Justice in the Shadows by Radclyffe. In a shadow world of secrets and lies, Detective Sergeant Rebecca Frye and her lover, Dr. Catherine Rawlings, join forces in the elusive search for justice. (1-933110-03-1)

shadowland by Radclyffe. In a world on the far edge of desire, two women are drawn together by power, passion, and dark pleasures. An erotic romance. (1-933110-11-2)

Love's Masquerade by Radclyffe. Plunged into the indistinguishable realms of fiction, fantasy, and hidden desires, Auden Frost is forced to question all she believes about the nature of love. (1-933110-14-7)

Love & Honor by Radclyffe. The president's daughter and her lover are faced with difficult choices as they battle a tangled web of Washington intrigue for...love and honor. (1-933110-10-4)

Beyond the Breakwater by Radclyffe. One Provincetown summer, three women learn the true meaning of love, friendship, and family. (1-933110-06-6)

Tomorrow's Promise by Radclyffe. One timeless summer, two very different women discover the power of passion to heal and the promise of hope that only love can bestow. (1-933110-12-0)

Love's Tender Warriors by Radclyffe. Two women who have accepted loneliness as a way of life learn that love is worth fighting for and a battle they cannot afford to lose. (1-933110-02-3)

Love's Melody Lost by Radclyffe. A secretive artist with a haunted past and a young woman escaping a life that has proved to be a lie find their destinies entwined. (1-933110-00-7)

Safe Harbor by Radclyffe. A mysterious newcomer, a reclusive doctor, and a troubled gay teenager learn about love, friendship, and trust during one tumultuous summer in Provincetown. (1-933110-13-9)

Above All, Honor by Radclyffe. Secret Service Agent Cameron Roberts fights her desire for the one woman she can't have—Blair Powell, the daughter of the president of the United States. (1-933110-04-X)